Acclaim for *Jayne Anne Phillips's*

MOTHERKIND

"Luminous . . . an exploration of the incongruities, the paradoxes, the mystifying jigsaw pieces that make our existence on this planet unquenchably compelling."
—*Mirabella*

"Although many people before her have noticed the similarities between the beginning and the end of life, Phillips underscores the connection with a dreamy, precise, sorrowful longing that's genuinely touching."
—*Newsday*

"[*MotherKind*] is further proof of an extraordinary ability to reflect the texture of real life. . . . Phillips sets forth a mother-daughter relationship that is tender without ever bordering on precious. . . . You could use this novel as a textbook to teach beginning writers about the physical details that make a moment full."
—*The Washington Post Book World*

"The beauty and originality of *MotherKind* are undeniable. . . . Phillips illuminates, with precision and sensitivity, fundamental aspects of all mother-daughter relations."
—*The Times Literary Supplement*

"[*MotherKind*] achieves a finely rendered luminescence of grief. . . . [Phillips's] is a language-laden domain of both precision and nuance."
—*The Boston Sunday Globe*

"[Phillips] is the master of her craft and of a story and characters that reach far beyond mere sentimentality into a realm of profound reality. . . . Simple incandescent moments . . . provide the luminescent glow that transfuses the struggle with the soft light of resignation and love and lift the story out of sadness and sentimentality. . . . *MotherKind* is life at its most intimate and vulnerable, and also at its most real."
—*Rocky Mountain News*

"Richly layered. . . . An unstinting book about the true, terrible cost of motherhood, its enormous demands of self. . . . A book on understanding who you are when everything you knew has disappeared. . . . [*MotherKind*] captures the intensity and dislocation—the sheer self-erasure—of the first weeks of motherhood."   —*Detroit Free Press*

"*MotherKind* is a beautifully written, delightfully sensual and deeply moving novel which touches with enormous subtlety on big themes."
—*Scotsman On Sunday*

"*MotherKind* will resonate for mothers and daughters, for anyone who has lost a parent or stands to lose one, for anyone who has had a child or wondered what it would be like to give birth to a child—in short, for anyone who has marveled at the short dance of a family's life across the face of a vast and unpredictable universe."
—*Colorado Springs Independent*

"Affecting. . . . Linguistically beautiful. . . . Deeply felt."   —*People*

"Potent storytelling plucks apart the parent-child relationship and illuminates the complexities of loving and losing. . . . Wrought of pain and intimacy. . . . Imbued with intelligence and sensitivity. The writing purrs with a quiet, steady rhythm."   —*Time Out* (London)

"Present[s] precisely the right mood. . . . There is an ebb and flow, a sense of the life cycle in [*MotherKind*] that is very beautiful. . . . It is a work that could only have been written by a first-rate writer."
—*The Newark Star-Ledger*

Jayne Anne Phillips

MotherKind

Jayne Anne Phillips was born and raised in West Virginia. She is the author of two other novels, *Shelter* and *Machine Dreams*, and two collections of widely anthologized stories, *Fast Lanes* and *Black Tickets*. She has won the Sue Kaufman Prize and an Academy Award in Literature from the American Academy of Arts and Letters, a Bunting Institute fellowship, a Guggenheim Fellowship, and two National Endowment for the Arts fellowships in fiction. Her work has been translated into twelve languages.

MotherKind

A NOVEL BY

JAYNE ANNE PHILLIPS

VINTAGE CONTEMPORARIES
Vintage Books
A Division of Random House, Inc.
New York

FIRST VINTAGE CONTEMPORARIES EDITION, MARCH 2001

Portions of this work have appeared in *Granta* as "MotherCare" (#55, Autumn 1996) and "Big Boy Sports" (#66, Summer 1999), and in *DoubleTake* as "Age of Wonders" (Winter 1997).

The Library of Congress has cataloged the Knopf edition as follows:
Phillips, Jayne Anne, [date]
MotherKind : a novel / by Jayne Anne Phillips.—1st ed.
p. cm.
ISBN 0-375-40194-6
I. Title.
PS3566.H479 M68 2000
813'.54—dc21 99-049256
CIP

Vintage ISBN: 0-375-70192-3

Author photograph © Jerry Bauer
Book design by Robert C. Olsson

www.vintagebooks.com

Printed in the United States of America
10   9   8   7   6   5   4   3   2   1

Author's Note: I wish to express my thanks to the MacDowell Colony and to my Brandeis University colleagues for gifts of time and support during the writing of this work. I'm grateful to Pamela Rikkers, Jill McCorkle, Ivy Goodman and Gish Jen for thoughtful discussion and editing, and to Ann Close, my editor at Knopf, for her unerring instincts. Finally, I thank all my family for the spiritual generosity which allows a writer to write.

for my mother

MotherKind

There is no charming stewardess. The prop plane rumbles like an air-borne lawn mower, transporting twenty to the airport of a larger, neighboring town near Kate's own, which has no airport at all. She'd offered to rent a car in Pittsburgh and drive the two hours home, but her mother insisted on meeting her, and Kate insisted on flying closer. Katherine has struggled so with being sick; Kate wants to support her attempts to "live normally, do things." She took early retirement from her job as a reading specialist soon after being diagnosed; Kate declined a teaching job in Boston to help her recover after the initial operation. They'd held on to the phrase "50/50 chance," but Katherine's cancer returned in less than a year. She lives with her aging dog, encouraged and assisted by a circle of friends, by Kate's daily calls. Recently she's concluded a hospital stay for radiation therapy. "They say I've plateaued," she told Kate. "Fine with me. I'm trying to sit tight." Kate envisions her mother on a high, empty mesa, watching the sky for incoming weather while her tiny, failing poodle stands rigidly at attention.

The sky just now is azure. Kate touches her forehead to the window of the plane. The vibration is a tiny, felt hum, like a musical note, separate from the lumbering noise of the engines. Even the clumsy plane, with its nose propeller and hooded motors, seems invincible in such blue air, a day so clear and sharp that Kate sees the shadow of their passage move across fields below, over the dense summer canopies of the trees. Far down, the green foliage stirs as though in response. They're circling; Kate sees the airport and its block-size parking lot, the little city in the distance, the ribbon of highway leading home. Soon, then.

Her mother will be smaller, and very upright; no doubt she is looking up now at the plane, shielding her eyes. Kate sits still and feels, again, a tremor in the deep, wet dark of her body, so small, yet not imagined: the quickening of which women speak, barely discernible, distinctly other. Like a minnow in water, Kate thinks, the flutter of a soul. She will give birth before the turn of another summer; she's nearly four months along, though almost no one knows. She's come home to tell Katherine, because the decision is made, because her mother is ill, because her mother might not live to see the baby. Katherine and Kate; mother and daughter; mother and trial-by-fire, Katherine joked; mother and slightly successful expatriate, Kate responded. Ironically, she'd warned her mother years ago that she might well have children without benefit of marriage. She's thirty-one, certainly old enough to carry it off. But she'll raise this baby with Matthew, though she won't carry her mother far into that transformed life; Katherine's illness is terminal. The plane turns, banking sharply. Tilting in her seat, Kate feels her way into the word. Terminal. Terminus. Like a spiritual roundhouse, a circular station where all tracks meet, a center of travel, transfers, routes and sojourns. Words are so often maligned by their meanings; Kate conceives of words as implements of pure energy, washed, infused, shadowed or illumined by all they carry in endless combination with one another. She writes words and works with them, for pay and for succor; she believes words open in the intangible spheres of their construction, yet stay apart from the world of use, innocent of motive, of healing or harm.

Two years ago, before Matthew, before her mother began to die, she sat with Sumi at a rooftop cafe in Kathmandu. Sumi: thin, nearly wraith-like, nimble, ageless sidekick to Ram and Amrit. It wasn't clear what Sumi did, something in Ram's hotel, evidently; there was no family compound for him, no matriarch or shielded wife; probably he had come from the mountains. He described spheres with his hands as he tried to explain the word "namaste." He drew images on a scrap of paper: "namaste" was greeting and benediction, exclusion and inclusion, wholly Buddhist; "namaste" was thousands of years folded into syllables. Sumi sketched mandalas with a waiter's pencil: "namaste" was a sound. A pulse in the mouth, acceptance and surrender. Not an Ameri-

can specialty, Kate murmured. Americans did not accept anything, she explained; they were immigrants, travelers, eaters, users, owners; a country descended from Puritans who did not accept darkness and called it evil, set it apart, cut it from them. They could be floppy, armed children, Americans. Sumi listened; he said he was a simple man, he liked Americans, all of Kathmandu liked Americans, even those who still camped on Freak Street, but Americans could not understand namaste until they had lived as Nepalis for fifty years, and few of them would survive so long. How many Nepalis do, Kate asked. What was the infant death rate in Kathmandu, and farther up, into the Himalayas? Sumi smiled shyly. This did not matter. The Nepali people were born in namaste, and there was no death.

    Ah, death. Words in English were not life or death. They were only messengers, impulses traveling on a nerve, bearers of tidings. "Here," children said when the roll was called, as it was every morning, a ritual in the grade school Kate attended, the school her mother had attended before her, a two-story brick monolith with high ceilings and wide-board wooden floors, broad wooden staircases, each wide step worn in the middle. Generations of roll calls, as though the teachers couldn't make out who was absent without the recitation of names, the voices answering, "Here." Here, the doctor had said, indicating with his pointer the spots of shadow on the X-rays of her mother's lungs. And here, and here. Here. Katherine had sat wordless in her chair, in her hospital gown, as Kate stood behind her, gripping her shoulders. Then Kate moved to sit beside her and took her hand. Without chemotherapy, six months to a year. With chemotherapy, a few months more. No chemo, Katherine said quietly. Radiation will halt the spread in the spine, they were told, and it was true; within days, she was pain free. The disease encroaches, then sleeps, alive in its sleep like the sleeper in a coma whose hair and nails grow long. Kate closes her eyes and the plane's wheels bump reliably on tarmac. A smattering of polite applause runs through the cabin. And yes, here it is. Kate's landscape: no plateaus. Appalachian scrub hills wild with flower, the dense foothills and humped mountains, valleys, small skies, hay smell, cicada and locust, generations of farms and mining towns, the winding dirt roads and fields in dense shade or brilliant sun, silos and barn board, choke of sumac and bramble: all she sees in her mind's eye when she remembers what she fled.

1

Kate was expecting. Imminently. It was the last, frantic week in December, a Saturday, and they had Matt's sons to entertain. Christmas was in two days and frigid weather kept the boys inside. They ricocheted around the house, fighting and spatting. Kate's mother, too ill to live alone any longer, had arrived in October. For better or worse, she'd grown accustomed to boisterous Saturdays. Now Kate pushed open the door to her mother's room, then stepped in and shut it firmly behind her.

"Oh, no, you don't," her mother said. "Get out there and help him."

"What can I do?" Kate said. "Anyway, I'm sorry it's so loud. How are you feeling?"

"Every day, a little better. Tomorrow, no more meals on trays." She was sitting up in her chair. She always moved to the chair the minute she heard the boys arrive, as though to participate, even if she couldn't bring herself to leave her room. She smiled wanly. "Kids are all loud. Don't you remember how you used to fight with your brothers? Like cats in a sack some days."

Kate moved to her mother's bedside table to clear the lunch dishes. "I think it's because they're here, with us. Not in their own house. They get so fixated on each other."

"Well, of course, but I'd wager they do the same at home." She raised her brows in an expression that only emphasized her weariness. "You're only a small part of it, Kate."

Kate smiled ruefully. "I'm so gargantuan, I don't know how I could be a small part of anything."

"Oh, what do you care how big you are," her mother said, "as long as that baby is healthy." She struggled to sit more upright in her chair just as the boys crashed by in the hallway, lurching against the closed door. Kate saw her wince as something hard—perhaps the plastic Nerf gun they'd brought with them—cracked sharply against the wall.

Kate realized she would have to empty the house, at least for a few hours. She herself was as much a problem as the kids. If she weren't here, so aware of her mother's "recovery," Katherine would get into bed and rest. She'd agreed to chemo so that she could "live to see this baby." No one had promised a cure, but they hoped for what the doctors called a dramatic, temporary response. Kate grew larger as her mother grew smaller, buying time. Katherine had recently finished her second treatment. The X-rays already showed improvement, but the season had seemed endless. Through dank November and early snow, Katherine's chemotherapy had raged in the house like a banked fire, gobbling the air here, lighting up this or that corner. By its glow Kate opened boxes her mother's friends had packed—the christening dress Kate and her brothers had worn home from the hospital, the tiny hand-knit sweater with angora cuffs, still buttery and perfect in its tissue paper. "Newborns wore yellow then," her mother said. "There were no amnios, just that moment of truth. And so exhilarating!"

Now Kate stacked the plates and cups and turned with the tray. This room was far from where they'd started. Katherine had passed on her own name to her daughter, as though to stake a claim or hope. Meant to be her mother's daughter, Katherine's diminutive, Kate was now the taller, stronger one, the caretaker. She'd always been Kate, never Kathy or Katherine, in a version of her father's face, his light hair and eyes, straight nose and Scots chin, but it was her mother's voice she heard in her head like a counterpart, pervasive as atmosphere. "I think we're going out," she told Katherine. There were frantic cries from downstairs, a sign someone had suffered a major insult. Kate knew all their cries, though it wasn't usually she who rushed to aid or intervene. They wanted their father; of course they did. "Get some rest while it's quiet," she told her mother. "Promise me."

But her mother only smiled and waved her away.

In the hall, Kate balanced the tray on her round abdomen and pulled the door to. Somehow this deepest, darkest phase of New England winter brought out the beast in Sam and Jonah. The big Christmas tree had been up for weeks—too many—and stood twinkling like an outpost, vibrating as the boys veered to and fro. They ate breakfast, played board games, dominoes, badminton, I Spy and hide-and-seek, all of which degenerated until Matt and Kate bundled them into Matt's Volkswagen van in self-defense and looked for somewhere, anywhere, to take them.

They all needed to get out. Kate was so pregnant that walking over the ice seemed hazardous, and she'd stayed in the house for days. She'd brought home mounds of work from the publishing house where she edited nonfiction. Since Katherine's arrival, Kate had worked from home, an arrangement that would segue into maternity leave and, Kate hoped, ensuing freelance employment. As for her own writing, lines she'd nurtured floated in her head, but their means of connection seemed to elude her. She knew better than to stack the words, like bricks. Words could be walls enclosing her if she wrote too fast or too soon, yet the two slim volumes of poems she'd published seemed to her increasingly minimal and past tense—gestures made in another life. She'd finished only three poems in the months of her pregnancy, and all of them concerned her mother, as though, despite the resistance of her conscious mind, nothing else inhabited her heart.

Today she'd paced, rather laboriously, after the kids tired of Battleship and Operation, and done housework. Standing at the kitchen table, she wrapped a few last presents in flocked red foil. The baby's head had been engaged for almost a week, and Kate was too uncomfortable to sit in a chair. She had to stand, or tilt herself in a very particular fashion, and that worked better on beds or in cars. Riding around in the van was a relief, and Kate was a little nervous about staying at home without Matt for what would become an interminable wait. Matt was an internist and Kate could always reach him by phone at the HMO, but he tended to be gone for hours when he took off on weekends with the kids, as though he fell into them and got lost. Kate supposed the kids felt similarly about Matt's time with her—that he disappeared into a nameless maw on Mondays and Tuesdays and Thursdays, the days he didn't see them. Nameless because they weren't allowed to say Kate's name in front of their mother. "I know what her name is," she'd told the kids, "but I don't have to hear it in my own house." Kate thought her uncharitable, given that Matt had never acted that way about *her* boyfriend, in the months after she told him she had one, back when their marriage was breaking up. She'd moved into a friend's house in order to continue to explore her options, and at some point during that period Matt had met Kate. By the time Matt's wife realized he'd met someone, it was nearly Christmas (last Christmas), and the pull of hearth and home grew suddenly intense. She moved back in, and Matt moved out, into his own apartment. In a few weeks, he was living at Kate's. Matt and his wife, a legal aid lawyer, began something called divorce mediation; it seemed as though they might go on mediating for several years. Then Kate realized she was pregnant.

And now here they all were. It was December 23. Wreaths tied to the grilles of trucks shuddered, their plastic bows flapping. Snow blew across the highway in little swirls. Like puffs of spirit, Kate thought, wandering souls. Sam and Jonah were bouncing up and down in the big backseat, trying to see if they could touch the ceiling with their heads. "Guys," Kate said, "what about your seat belts? We've already blasted off, and you're not strapped in."

"Right," Matt added, "and here comes a shower of asteroids."

"What's asteroids?" Jonah asked.

"Space rocks, dummy," Sam answered. "They land and they make a big hole."

"Something sure made holes in this road. Where are we, anyway?" Matt glanced at Kate apologetically. "Sorry. I guess I should have headed downtown, toward civilization and smoother terrain."

"Well," Kate said, "it's pretty here. Look, there's the harbor. Downtown is across the water. Oh, I know where we are. That's the Kennedy Library. Let's go there."

"You've never been?" Matt slowed for the rotary, but didn't put his blinker on for a turn. "Here you've tramped all over India and Nepal, and you haven't taken in the hot tourist spots of your own adopted city."

"Hot tourist spot? Really? Should I bring Mom here when she's better?" Kate peered through the broad curved windshield of the van.

"Is she going to get better?" Jonah asked.

Kate turned and smiled at him. At least he'd asked. Maybe they did wonder. "She's actually better already. It's just that the medicine still makes her a little sick." But he was staring out the window as the hulking edifice by the water came into view. It glared white, lit in the winter sun, massive and lonely, and the surface of the water beside it rippled. One long wall formed a wavy curve between the building and the sea. "There's no one around," Kate said.

"There is so," Jonah protested. "I see cars parked in front."

"Dad," Sam said, "what is this place?"

"It's a kind of museum about President Kennedy. Do you know who he was?" Matt continued to circle the rotary.

"You missed the entrance," Kate said. "See the sign? You have to take that access road over to the—"

"I think I know," Sam said.

"You always think you know everything, Sam," Jonah said, "but you don't."

"I know a lot more than you," Sam said. "You're only in first grade. I'm two years ahead of you."

"So?"

"You both know a lot," Kate said. "Kids these days know so much, so much earlier than they used to. Jonah, you know a lot more than I did when I was six."

He looked at her pensively. Big brown eyes and blond curls. So much smaller than Sam, so much more comfortable. "Did you know about divorces?" he asked.

"I did know about them," Kate said. She willed herself not to break Jonah's gaze, not to look at Matt. "I didn't know very much, because my parents weren't divorced until I was a teenager. But you know about other things too, like the space program. When I was six, no American rocket ship had ever landed on the moon."

"Mom gave me a puzzle of the solar system," Sam said. "It has every planet. I know all about space."

"You do," Kate said, "and this museum tries to tell people all about the life of a man, John Kennedy. He was a president of the United States who was assassinated."

"What's that, Dad?" Jonah asked.

"Killed," Sam said.

"How, Dad?"

"He was shot," Matt said, "by a man with a gun who was far away."

"He was riding in a convertible," Kate said, "in a parade."

"Oh, yeah," Sam said, "I think I heard about it."

"Dad, Dad," Jonah shouted, "turn up the radio. That's my best song!"

They circled, blasted by phrases, until Matt drove onto the access road and into the parking lot. The museum rose into the air on its spit of land. One white rounded wall three stories high followed the contours of the cliff to a rocky bar of beach. The flat water of Boston Harbor existed there, unmoving; across its gulf lay the towers of the city, a few abstract shapes quite separate from each other, like a grouping of blocks. The far-flung runways of Logan Airport were discernible off to the right. Toy-size airplanes streaked toward home in straight lines, trying hard to stop, all silent as a game on a screen.

Where are we? Kate thought. We could be anywhere. But we're here.

"Everyone out," said Matt, and the boys bolted from the car.

Kate followed them with her eyes. Just as her mother had lived nowhere but home, Matt and his sons had lived nowhere but here—Matt in the nearby seaside town where he'd grown up before going to college near Boston, the children in their suburb. Sam and Jonah disappeared behind Matt before Kate could even hoist herself from her seat. They ran, these boys, as though their lives depended on triumph—one would get to the doors of the museum first, the other would know defeat. Exhausting, Kate thought, so many contests an hour, a day, a week. No wonder they seemed to turn to blows at the slightest provocation. They fought with an immediate violence that amazed her. On such occasions they had to be saved from themselves, but in general they felt entitled to any space they inhabited, and this amazed Kate as well. Her own mother had taught children to notice spaces held sacrosanct by others. Was she right or wrong?

Matt stood holding open the passenger door of the van, waiting for Kate. "Honey, ready to go?"

Kate smiled. "I guess I'd better be." She climbed out of the bus, cumbersome in boots and mittens, her big stomach hidden in the bulky coat. It occurred to her that Matt seldom called her by name. She wasn't herself anymore; she'd become a term of endearment. She was dear to him. What was dear to him, therefore, must grow dear to her.

"They'll wait for us," Matt said.

Matt and Kate walked the length of the parking lot. The air was pale blue, leaden with cold. The winter water spread along one side of the horizon like smooth slate. "Funny how we never thought of stopping by here before," Matt said softly, resigned. "I suppose it's educational. 1963. Let me think about it before I get inside."

Kate nodded. "I was in grade school. I had a male teacher for the first time, the only one in the school. Mr. Norris."

She'd looked up to him. His approval meant more to Kate than the approval of women, which was more readily obtained, more easily expressed. Mr. Norris was a big man with a quiet, definite presence and a slow drawl to his voice. He would be principal as soon as the older, balding Mr. Hanover, who was a diabetic, retired. Mr. Norris would sit on the bookshelf, leaning against the wall by the big schoolroom windows, while they read off the answers to their arithmetic homework. Arithmetic had been the curse of Kate's existence. That day, the trees beyond the old pocked glass of the windows were naked. The leaves had fallen and were nearly colorless now, dry, layered. The afternoon sky was blue. Mr. Hanover walked into the room unannounced and said loudly, over their heads, as though they were invisible, "The president's been shot." "What?" Mr. Norris stood suddenly, forcefully, and moved forward as though to perform some urgent action. But there was nothing to be done.

"I remember that arithmetic stopped," Kate said aloud. "I felt guilty because I was relieved—I hadn't finished my homework. They turned on the intercom throughout the school so the older kids could hear the radio. Listening, I was scared."

"I was so much older than you, then," Matt said. "A senior in high school."

"Practically a man," Kate joked. Then, worriedly, she looked for the kids. They were gone. "Where are the boys?"

Matt and Kate crossed the lot and were walking up the sidewalk to the doors of the building. "They couldn't have gone anywhere," Matt said. "There's nowhere to go."

There was only down, around the ocean curve of the building, and the boys were there, clambering up and down the rocky bank on the big-windowed sea side of the edifice. They looked so isolated, moving ceaselessly across the plaza, sharply angling between the sheer wall of granite and the edge of the gray, half-frozen water; they seemed to have been blown to this place by some errant wind.

Matt stood watching them. "I wonder who they'll see assassinated."

"Probably everyone," Kate answered.

Matt sighed and put his arm around her. "Gee, does pregnancy always make you so cheerful?"

Kate smiled and shrugged. "You're Jewish. I'm a Primitive Superstitionist. If I say it, maybe it won't happen. You know, appease the gods."

He nodded. "I hear you." He put his fingers to his lips and whistled, and the shrill music of his demand rent the air like a scream. The kids made a last foragers circle and drifted toward them.

"The museum is really still expanding," the attendant said. "Two dollars for children, six for adults. There's a photo and memento display and a film running continuously; we start every half hour."

One curved, chest-high wall of the lobby afforded a view into the deep, round room below. Jonah hung his arms over, peering down. "Dad, look," he said, pointing. "Can we climb that?" Architectural iron scaffolding rose the entire height of a massive, three-story glass panel on the far side of the building. Winter sunlight fell through flat and sharp as the edge of a knife; at the foot of the black scaffold, the vast stone floor nearly gleamed. "Dad," Jonah said, "we could climb those black pipes."

"Yikes," Kate said, "I think you'd have to be at least twelve before they'd let you." She moved closer to the wall. "Actually, that's quite a drop. Why isn't there a railing?"

No one answered. Matt shoved his money at the attendant and followed the boys along the curve of the lobby. The open space below was a continuation of the plaza outside, and the sweep of the harbor filled the vista of the towering glass window. Gray stripes of ice hunched in the still water. The theater must be beneath them, Kate realized, and they would exit up those broad stairs that curved seamlessly along the bowl of the wall. The empty space was a kind of church, meditative, full of sky, a place to emerge into out of the dark. The black scaffolding was skeletal and imposing, yet easy to ignore in all that light. Kate supposed people did climb it: those who cleaned that wall of glass, who'd hung the enormous American flag that fell in a straight drop from the ceiling.

"Excuse me." Kate lowered her voice and leaned toward the attendant. "I suppose everyone with young kids asks you this. What does the film show, exactly?"

The attendant looked up and their eyes met. "You'd be surprised how few ask. But there's no footage of the assassination. It ends as his plane is taking off for Dallas."

Kate nodded. "Right." Into the dazzling skies of Marilyn Monroe and Judith Exner and Castro and Jimmy Hoffa, and all the other mysteries.

"Some people complain," the attendant said.

"Pardon?" Kate looked past him at the boys, who were peering down over the wall at the empty plaza far below.

"They complain because that part is left out. The motorcade, and all of it."

"Oh," Kate said, pulling off her heavy coat. "Well. It tore everything apart so, didn't it, for people of a certain age. Maybe they can't help wanting to see it again."

"Then they should go to another museum," he said curtly.

Kate focused on his face. He was young and balding, and wore tortoiseshell glasses. She saw him notice her advanced pregnancy, which was what everyone noticed now, the minute her form came into view. Last week a stranger at the grocery store had queried, incredulous, "Shouldn't you have already *had* that baby?" The attendant's expression softened, as though he were privately amused that a person he'd taken for normal a moment ago could be so rotund, yet stand and offer opinions about the motivations of a generation. Kate continued to meet his eyes, and he glanced toward Sam and Jonah, who had dropped to their knees, wrestling near the wall as Matt approached them. "Guess you've got your hands full," he said. "Show begins in three minutes."

Kate moved toward the theater entrance and found herself in a square white room whose walls were hung with enlarged photographs. When she was out with Matt's boys, particularly as her pregnancy became obvious, people assumed she was their mother, rather than the villain of the piece. Did she qualify as the Other Woman, when Matt's wife had been somebody else's Other Woman first? Sometimes it did seem they were all involved in a graphic melodrama whose banal details were nearly as heartrending as pillbox hats and blood-smeared pink mohair, a melodrama Kate's mother had arrived just in time to witness personally. Real life had such enveloping dimension, Kate thought. Photographs, like the ones of the stained suit, were flat statements. That suit stayed its torturous color, even in black and white. Those photographs, Kate thought, all the ones not displayed here, were another reason American girls should never wear pink. "No pink" was one of many maxims Kate would have passed on to her daughter, were she carrying one. But she wasn't. Her baby was a boy. Her baby was Alexander, conqueror of the world, the world as it was.

Kate walked on, perusing photographs of the world as it was not: the Newport bride in white, surrounded by men in black. The ushers: black morning coats and cravats. Weddings were such pagan rituals, Kate reflected; everything about them was wishful superstition and bargaining. Long ago it was customary for bridesmaids to dress exactly like the bride, so that evil spirits couldn't tell which one hoped to be happy. Groomsmen stood in a line to flank their prince, confusing death, distracting the dark fates. As ever, the better safety was in numbers, money and power: the bigger the wedding, the more distraction. Her own wedding would be fifty or so people, but no bridesmaids. Kate felt she was already so firmly in the grip of fortune that it was pointless to try to bargain. Matt's divorce was final in a few weeks, but Kate refused to marry in the winter. Alexander would be sitting up by early summer, fat and happy: Kate wished him so. He could come to the wedding. What better reason to marry?

"Is this all there is?" Jonah stood looking up at her, his coat dragging behind him like a winding sheet, his fleece-lined cap on his shoe. His curls were tousled.

Kate leaned down and retrieved the cap. She smoothed his hair, only to touch him, really. His skin was soft and his hands so sturdy and small. She trailed her fingers gently through his hair, hair as cold and tangled as the coarse mane of a pony come in from a winter beach. "No," she told him, "this is a waiting room. There's a movie."

"A movie? A movie?" He turned and dashed through the gathering crowd, jostling everyone. "Sam! Sam! A movie! What movie is it?" Kate heard him shout.

But she didn't answer. She supposed he would find out. His father would tell him. Or Kate would, if she could ever catch up with any of them. Should she phone her mother, make sure she was all right? No. Better not to interrupt. Surely she was resting or sleeping, adrift in the interlude of their absence.

They all walked down into the amphitheater, a kind of vast, domed bunker. The long, descending aisles were carpeted; the screen was large and seemed to conform to the circular shape of the room. Plushly cushioned seats with padded armrests were arranged in semicircular rows to face the screen. Sam and Jonah walked in, stood looking for an instant, and began to run. They ran, hopped, skipped a careening descent to the bottom and started back up the long aisle on the other side. Twenty or thirty people scattered around the auditorium watched as the boys ascended, gaining the upper slopes at what seemed lightning speed. Kate sighed. It was impossible to rein them in without shouting. She gave Matt a frustrated look and took a seat. Matt stood waiting as the lights went down, signaling the boys as they aimed themselves in his general direction.

Later Kate and Matt would have a talk. Kate might list the offenses of the week. She would suggest that Sam and Jonah reconsider running like maniacs through enclosed spaces, including the living room of the house Kate had helped to purchase; that they be advised not to change places in movie theaters two or three times, crawling under the seats to pop up a row ahead or behind. She might mention the way they'd eaten pizza at a restaurant recently, clasping their hands behind their backs to prove they could eat like puppies. And she would admit she hated the way Jonah asked for more food at meals and then threw it all in the garbage. Food she'd cooked! And she hated herself for going on about their continuous infractions, which were infractions only to her. She felt like a dingy wren fluttering pathetically around an endangered nest, when the real dangers oppressing them all were too big to glimpse or imagine. This much was certain—the time drew near. Her mother would see the baby; she would hold Kate's baby.

As though on cue, music began; the blessing of darkness descended. Images of autumn, ducks flying above the funeral cortege moving up

Pennsylvania Avenue. Rain. The bleak air. Close-ups of faces in the crowd. A woman weeping. Catastrophe from afar: now everything would change, and what would happen? With a flicker, a flourish of color, the documentary focused on his past, Kennedy a boy in a suit.

Sam and Jonah didn't own suits. Kate's coming discussion with Matt would follow a prescribed pattern: Kate knew the scenario so well that she could make up dialogue for both of them. She heard it now against her will.

Matt might say, "They're kids," or "They're boys," or "Museums are places *you* like. They'd rather run in a field."

It was true. They were like ponies testing the dimensions of a paddock.

"Will they spend their whole lives in a field?" Kate would ask. "Do they need to learn behavior appropriate only to fields?" She imagined them running, running, running, the wind and the air, glorious.

"By the time they decide to go to a museum," Matt would reason, "they'll know not to run."

"How? How will they know?" Silence. "Aren't you counting on some vague peer pressure to teach them things you should teach them?"

"*I'll* decide what I want to teach them," Matt would say, in a tone of firm disengagement.

"Fine. But what am I supposed to do? Strike myself deaf, dumb and blind until such time as they embarrass *themselves* by running in public?"

"What *is* it?" Matt would demand at this point. "Why is this such a crusade with you?"

If Kate were honest, which she hadn't been in the past, because the truth was just now occurring to her, she would answer, in a crescendo of anger, "Because they get away with murder!"

The wild boys. No stalwart commandments engraved on the conscience. No unchanging boundaries, no sacred cows. It did make her angry, because they ignored her and everything she thought or felt, and because she was jealous. They moved happily this way and that, for miles of verdant plains and hills. They made it seem she and her brothers had grown up in a series of careful boxes. But had they? Her conception of metaphysical wild-boy fields was based on her own memories, on the acres of fields behind her childhood home, on the stream that flooded in spring, the wooded hills where dogwood bloomed early and stood out like bursts of popcorn. Kate and her brothers had played there through long afternoons in spring, summer, autumn, hiking and hiding and fishing in the creek. But they'd gone to church as small children too, sitting still for an interminable hour. Their mother always claimed she could take them anywhere and they'd behave, and it was true. Kate remembered now; she'd actually pretended to be a pony, swinging her dangling feet, watching the reflection of her black-patent shoes and white socks across the polished surface of the pew in front of them. Hard black hooves. Her brothers, dressed in sport coats, long pants, shined shoes, fidgeted but stayed in their seats, silent, miniature men. The sermons. Her mother reached out and held their hands if they poked or prodded each other. Long moments. Kate passed the time by pulling her mother's glove on and off, freeing each tightly fitted finger, covering it again. Under the glove, black kid in winter, white cotton in summer, her mother's diamond ring was a hard little rock.

Kate didn't like diamonds. She didn't like the way wives were expected to have one, the way women supposedly wanted them and showed them off. It was painful to see the things women did. Actually Kate didn't know anyone anymore who would display an engagement ring with pride, or even bother with an engagement. She thought of the girls in her small-town high school. Those unfortunate enough to marry at eighteen had stood by the battered green lockers, holding out their hands for everyone's approval. Most of them were pregnant and relieved. Kate didn't feel relieved. Pregnant, she felt magical and fierce, as though these were the qualities her son would require of her. Enormous, she was girded for battle. Now, in the documentary, Jack and Jackie weren't married yet; they moved toward each other on the porch of a summer house. The footage seemed a home movie clip, unrehearsed and jerky. It was the only footage Kate had ever seen in which Jacqueline Kennedy didn't seem an impossibly poised icon. Kennedy was bronzed, angular and thin; he squinted into the sun and Jackie stood behind his chair, looking directly into the camera. Quizzical, dreamy or nervous, she raised her hand to her mouth and sucked and bit at her fingernail. The gesture was so unexpected, so naked and vulnerable and adolescently sexual, that Kate felt something in her chest contract. She wanted to turn away, and tears came to her eyes. *My God, that's how we all start out, in thrall, slouching against someone's chair.* She heard a commotion in the shadows and felt a sharp kick to her shin. Jonah was crawling over the back of the seat in front of them, trying to get into Matt's lap. Kate exhaled slowly, always her response to pain. "I needed that," she murmured, but no one heard her.

Later, in the gift shop, she looked for something to buy Sam and Jonah. There were little presidential rocking chairs, coloring books, calendars.

Matt stood beside her, turning the postcard rack for Jonah. "Not a bad film," he said.

"I could have done without the pink suit," Kate said.

"They had to show them getting on the plane," Matt said.

"They could have just shown the plane. We would have assumed they were on it." She looked down at Sam, who'd picked out a plastic PT boat. "Right, Sam?"

"Dad," he said, "I got a boat."

"What did you think of the movie?" Matt asked.

"I liked the part where he was making the commercial, and he kept getting it wrong and then he said a curse word."

"He sort of said it," Jonah remarked. "You couldn't really hear."

"But you could tell," Sam said.

"Could not. They would have taken that out."

"That was actually an advertisement," Kate said, "to ask people to vote for him. And maybe the filmmakers left it in to show he made mistakes and got frustrated and had to do things over again, that he was an ordinary person."

"Oh, yeah. Ordinary," Matt said. "Dexter, Groton, Harvard, the Court of St. James's."

Kate smiled. "Not my point, Dad. Anyway, *you* went to Harvard."

"Yes, I did. And I got in even though my father was a businessman, not an ambassador."

"That's my point. Three generations ago the Kennedys were just immigrants, double-crossing their way to the top. And now we're standing here in the Kennedy Library."

"Are you guys fighting?" Jonah asked.

"We're not fighting, we're discussing." Kate touched her forefinger softly to the bridge of his nose and looked back at Matt. "I mean, land of opportunity. He did some good things."

"He wrote on the coconut," Sam said.

"Absolutely," Kate agreed. "And he might have done more. Everything might have been different."

"Isn't that a bit of a myth," Matt said gently, "about the war never happening if he'd lived?"

"What war?" Jonah said.

"He would have gotten into it," Kate said, "but he would have gotten out. He wouldn't even go through with the Bay of Pigs to fight Communists. Remember how he left those guys to get rounded up on the beach? No, he wasn't such a cowboy. He knew when to back down."

"Maybe," Matt said. "I notice there were no Cuban beach scenes included in the film."

"No," Kate said, "but still. They're all gone now, all the heroes. Thank God for Ted, no matter how much he drinks."

"Ted will stop drinking any day now." Matt looked over at Kate and arched his brows in mock flirtation. "He'll find a good woman."

"Dad, *I* want a drink," Jonah said, "and a boat like Sam's."

"You can't have one," Sam said. "I got the last one."

"Sam—" Matt began.

"Jonah, look at this." Kate picked up a blue plastic spyglass and looked toward Jonah through it. "There are pictures of PT boats inside, like the ones they used to look for Japanese boats in the Solomon Islands."

"Yeah, that's good." Jonah accepted the spyglass with a satisfied nod.

"Okay, okay," Matt said, "time to get going."

"I'm thirsty," Sam said. "I'm thirsty."

"We'll stop on the way home," Matt said. "Can we move toward the cash register, please? Kate, this way."

"I'm looking for the bathroom. I'll be fast—"

"Why do you always go to the bathroom?" Jonah asked.

Kate rested her hands on her drumlike abdomen. "Because I'm going to have a baby, and the baby has grown nice and round, and the baby presses on my bladder." She looked at Matt and shrugged. "I'd take them with me while you pay, but—"

"No way," Sam said, then he brightened. "Take Jonah."

Jonah tried to kick him and Sam grinned. "All right, all right," Matt said. "We'll see you in front."

Kate walked away. "I know about the baby," she heard Jonah say. "Of course you do," Matt was answering. "Then why do you ask dumb questions?" someone hissed. That would be Sam, peering at Jonah through wire-rim glasses. He broke Kate's heart. He would lie at home on the top bunk, trying to read without the glasses. "Dad," he would say, "my eyes are crossing." His hair was long and stringy and he had a space between his front teeth, an indication, in folk wisdom, of a lustful nature. "It means you'll travel far," Kate had told him, "and your heart is big." She didn't think she was lying; both travel and a capacity for strong feeling were ways of representing lust. And he did have such strong feelings, and so much difficulty expressing them. He seemed to deny himself until he exploded. Sports, Matt said, sports. Sports were invented for boys like Sam, boys who didn't talk.

Kate pushed through the heavy door to the rest room and closed herself into a stall. The tremendous effort of pulling layers up and down was worth the relief of sitting, her belly supported by her thighs. The baby moved. She flattened her hand against her lower left side and felt the heel of his foot or his elbow, something knobby and firm, roll against her palm. He was too crowded to turn now, he could only move his limbs. She was due on New Year's Day, but first babies were often late. She heard the clatter of her own urine falling into the bowl with a faraway sensation; her urine had no smell now, as though she'd turned pure and sweet, and she couldn't feel her muscles anymore. "Believe me, you'll feel them in labor," the obstetric nurse had said. Kate trained her gaze on the back of the stall door. The white metal looked new and untouched, but someone had scrawled, near the bottom in red ink, "Born to Die." Farther down, another scribe had written in script, "Bonnie loves." Lines begun and not completed were everywhere, Kate thought wryly. Loves what, she wondered, loves who?

She thought of her mother, floating in her sleep as they floated, all of them and the world itself, through various postures and traveling states, the boys tossed in the van against a soft drone of adult comment, this arching, inhabited monument on its spit of land, the coastline beyond, irregular and rocky, running on for hundreds, thousands of miles, into other weathers and zones of time. The turning of events might register across such distance as a ripple of liquid movement, a settling of limbs. Her father, during the years of her parents' marriage, would drive into town on Sundays to buy the newspapers. He'd called from the store. "Turn on the television," he'd said gravely. "Why?" Kate had asked, adolescent by then, eleven, twelve. "They shot Bobby Kennedy," he'd said, resigned.

The phrase floated still. Kate saw the words bobbing on water like a cast-off paper label, remnant of some drifting flotsam. She heard it in her father's voice as the baby moved, hard. Kate stood to give him room.

They'd all left the building by the time Kate got to the lobby, but she saw Matt standing just outside. He turned to hold the heavy door open for her. "I'm going to go get the van," Matt said, "so we won't have to slide you across the parking lot again."

"Great. Every little bit helps." Kate pulled the collar of her down coat up higher. "Everything's darker now," she said. "Is it so late?"

"No, but it's starting to snow. Listen, the kids are down there, on the plaza. Just keep an eye on them, okay? I'll pull up right here in the circle, then I'll give them a whistle."

He moved off into the spitting snow, and Kate walked up farther so she could see the boys. She stood at the top of the broad sweep of stairs to the plaza and watched them run back and forth in some sort of game. Sam seemed to be leading Jonah here and there, and Kate's eyes were drawn to the horizon above them. Who was Bonnie, lone despoiler of surfaces? Some high school girl bused in from Mattapan for a school trip, or maybe a resentful employee, a yearning purveyor of postcards who knew the score and belonged to no man. Or perhaps, writing, she'd hesitated, weighed down by her burdened heart. Whom to name, the wild boy who'd left her weeping, or the one who courted her now in his snaggled car? Truly, she loved them both, faces of the same unfurling need. But she'd written a sentence, with a period, like a philosophy: Bonnie loves. Would she, this employee, write her own name on the stall? Yes, Kate decided. Named for a song, she'd take chances. *My bonnie lies over the ocean:* a way of saying, my beauty, my smiling Joe or Jack, my lost one. All the little girls, boys too, sang it in primary music classes as a round, with hand motions. *Bring back, bring back, oh bring back my bonnie* . . . It was too late, though: he lay there, across the water, for always.

Kate's eyes stung in the raw air. But now she heard real crying, a plaintive alarm carried on the wind. She could see Jonah jumping at Sam, amok with frustration, as Sam held something above his head in a classic keepaway gesture. The spyglass, of course; Kate saw a sliver of blue in his hand. Sam must have decided he preferred it now that they were outside by the water and could peer over the harbor looking for attackers. The wild boys were like Siamese twins, bound for life. No wonder Matt often bought them the same souvenir, the same toy, which Kate thought was a cop-out. She saw Jonah slip—or had Sam pushed him? Hurriedly, she started down the steps, the wind whipping at her face, blinding her. Too late, she realized the concrete was sheeted with an invisible glaze. In slow, inevitable motion, she slipped and her right foot went out from under her; even as she grabbed for the handrail, panic engulfed her. But she had the railing; she slid two steps jarringly, then righted herself like an awkward, overloaded boat. A sharp pain throbbed in her back but she held to the railing and stepped down carefully, concentrating on each level of descent. She reached the plaza to see Jonah, prone on the ice, grab Sam's feet; Sam raised the spyglass like a weapon, taking aim. "Don't!" Kate called, but they were oblivious. They howled at one another, wholly betrayed.

Kate found she was breathless. She grabbed Sam's arm on the down-swing. "You don't want to hit him with that, Sam," she said. "You might really hurt him."

Sam looked directly at her, his glasses awry, his cheeks wet, as though he'd been crying for days. He struggled for the spyglass, grunting, and then he began to sob.

Kate bent over Jonah and tried to haul him up. "There, now," she said. "Never mind." He'd run so hard he was sweating in his winter clothes. His fleece cap had fallen off and his curls were plastered to his forehead. Damp with sweat and tears, he threw himself against Kate. "Sam!" he cried, as though shattered, and pressed his wet face to her neck. Kate knelt and bowed her head over him and turned them away from the wind. In the tent of their coats he grasped her ferociously, lying across her huge belly as though, desperate, he'd forgotten who she was. The moist, tearful smell of him was suddenly close to her, a small bouquet of warmth, salty and sweet. She breathed the smell in and felt something deep within her let go. One sharp cramp and then a rush, a suffusion of warmth and release of pressure. The water actually splattered out of her as though poured from a vessel, filling her boots and pooling on the concrete between her knees. A prickly, submerged heat radiated through her even as her wet legs grew cold. She wanted to lie down here in the wisping snow and give birth like a dog with her pups, but she raised her eyes and saw that Sam was already mounting the steps, walking away from them.

2

After the birth and the overnight in the hospital, she didn't go downstairs for a week. She'd lost some blood and she felt flattened, nearly dizzy, from the labor and then the general anesthetic. Alexander had been born at dawn on Christmas Day; since then she'd wept frequently, with incredible ease, and entertained the illusion that she now knew more than she'd ever questioned or known before. The illusion pursued her into sleep itself, into jagged pieces of sleep. New Year's came and went; Kate heard bells ring at midnight and revelers' horns blaring plaintively in the cold streets. She slept and woke, naked except for underpants, sanitary napkins, chemical ice packs. The ice packs, shaped to her crotch, were meant to reduce swelling and numb the stitches; the instructions directed her to bend the cotton to activate the solution; inside, the thick pads cracked like sticks. This bathroom looks like a MASH unit, Matt would say. But it's not your unit that's mashed, Kate would think. In fact, her vagina was an open wound. Her vagina was out of the picture. She couldn't believe she'd ever done anything with it, or felt anything through it.

She couldn't use tampons; there were boxes of big napkins, like bandages, piles of blue underliners—plastic on one side, gauze on the other—to protect the sheets, hemorrhoid suppositories, antibiotic salve, mentholated anesthetic gel, tubes of lanolin, plastic cups and plastic pitchers. She drank and drank, water, cider, juices. The baby slept in a bassinette right beside her bed, but her arms ached from picking him up, holding him, putting him down. On the third day her milk came in, and by then her nipples were already cracked and bleeding. The baby was nursing colostrum every hour but he was sucking for comfort, losing a few more ounces every day. His mouth was puckered and a large clear blister had formed on his upper lip; he was thirsty, so thirsty; finally, Kate gave him water, though the nurses had said not to. *He needs to nurse, to pull the milk in.* That night she woke in the dark, on her back, her engorged breasts sitting on her chest, warm to the touch, gravid, hard and swollen. She woke the baby to feed him. He began to cry but she held him away until she could sit and prop her arms with pillows, pour a glass of water for the thirst that would assail her. In the beginning, she'd moaned as he sucked, then, to move through the initial latching on, she did the same breathing she'd used throughout labor. She breathed evenly, silenced vocalizations cutting in like whispers at the end of each exhalation. The pain cracked through her like a thread of lightning and gradually eased, rippling like something that might wake up and get her.

She called LaLeche League every couple of days for new suggestions. Kate's favorite counselor was in Medford, a working-class part of Boston Kate didn't remember ever having seen. But the woman had no accent; she was someone else far from home. You'll battle through this, she would say, be stubborn and hang on. Women are made to nurse, she'd declare in each conversation, any woman can nurse; and then she'd say, in a softer tone, that people forgot how hard it was to get established the first time. "Don't let the pain defeat you," were her exact words. "The uterine pain actually helps you heal, and your nipples will toughen."

"What about stress?" Kate asked once. "Will I have enough milk—"

"Stress?" was the response. "Are you kidding? Any woman with a new baby is stressed to the max. She doesn't sleep, she's bleeding, she's sore, she might have other kids or a job she'll go back to. The baby is sucking for life. As long as you eat well and drink, drink constantly, your body responds. You don't need unbroken sleep. You don't need a perfect situation. Refugees nurse their babies, and war victims; theirs are the children more likely to survive, even in the worst of times."

I understand, Kate wanted to say. I understand all about you, and I understand everything.

"Have your husband buy you a Knorr manual breast pump at the hospital infirmary," the counselor had said, "and a roll of disposable plastic bottles. The pump is a clear plastic tube, marked in ounces. Use it each time your breasts aren't completely emptied by the baby. Increase production; you can't have too much milk. Freeze all you express. That's how some women work full-time and still nurse their babies. I'll send you some information in the mail. And if you feel discouraged, call back."

I just want to hear your voice, Kate wanted to say. We're in a tunnel flooded with light.

But she spoke an accepted language, words like "air-dry," "lanolin," "breast rotation," "demand schedule." And there was light all around her, great patches angling through the naked windows, glancing off snow piled and fallen and drifted, hard snow, frozen, crusted with ice, each radiant crystal reflecting light. Kate had brought her son home in the last week of December, and the temperature was sixty degrees, sun like spring. Her neighbor Camille had festooned the fence with blue balloons. Kate and Alexander posed for photographs, then she took him in the house, shutting the front door behind them. Immediately, the cold came back and the snows began. At night Kate was awake, nursing, burping the baby, changing odorless cloth diapers, changing his gown, nursing, nursing him to sleep; all the while, snow fell in swaths past the windows, certain and constant, drifting windblown through the streetlamp's bell of light. Each day Kate stayed upstairs and her mother padded back and forth along the hallway connecting their rooms. Just before Christmas she'd finished a full round of chemo, and the tumors in her lungs had shrunk. She had a few weeks of respite now before the next group of treatments, and she came to Kate's room to keep her company, to hold the baby while Kate slept, to pour the glasses of juice.

"Are you awake, Katie?" She sat in an upholstered chair that had once graced her own living room; Kate had moved that couch and chair to Boston and slipcovered them in a vibrant 1920s print, navy blue with blowzy, oversized ivory flowers.

"I'm always awake, more or less," Kate said. "How was your night?"

"No complaints," her mother said. "No nausea."

"Good." Kate smiled. "It's nice to see you sitting in that chair. I always see it in photographs, in one of its guises. In the old house."

"Yes," Kate's mother said. "By the time we moved into town, this chair was in the basement."

"Now you might admit I was right to drag it here. The cushions may be shot, but at least you have a comfortable place to sit." Watching her mother, Kate realized the print she'd chosen for the chair, dark blue with white, was nearly the reverse of her mother's choice. "Remember the fabric of *your* slipcovers, what you used on that chair? What did you always call that print?"

"It was a blue onion print, white with blue vines—"

"Thistlelike flowers," Kate interrupted, "like fans, with viny runners—"

"Yes," her mother continued patiently, "wild onions, hence the name."

"And you had those glass pots with lids, in the same print, on the coffee table. I remember. There they sit, in all the Easter pictures. When we're wearing our good clothes. You always matched things. But before, there was that dark living room."

"Dark?"

"The walls were dark green, and the drapes on the picture windows were dark green, with gold, and the furniture in its original upholstery, dark beige, with a raised texture—"

"Well, when kids are young you want things that are dark and tough. When you were older, we had the white fiberglass drapes and the lighter slipcovers. That first upholstery was chosen to last through climbing and sliding and whatever. Your brothers gave it a workout."

"It did last," Kate said. "It was what I covered up. It seems ageless."

"Yes," her mother agreed, "but it darkened. This was your father's chair, and the fabric darkened just in the shape of him."

"Really?" Kate asked. "You mean, as though his shadow sank into it?"

Her mother frowned, exasperated. "No, I mean it was worn. Worn from use. Am I speaking English?"

Kate laughed. "Your energy level is better, isn't it? You're your old feisty self, and I'm just lying here."

Her mother peered over at the bassinette. "I thought I might hold Alexander for you, but he's sleeping so beautifully. I've been downstairs already, to let that little girl in, the MotherKind worker. It's been wonderful to have her for a week. She came this morning with her arms full of groceries. She's just putting things away, and then she'll be up to see what you want her to do."

"It was so nice of you to buy help for me, Mom, such a great present."

"Well, I'd be doing all the cooking myself if I were able. But I must say, your requirements are pretty daunting."

Kate smiled. She'd asked for someone versed in preparing natural foods. No additives, no preservatives. No meat with hormones. "Your color is good today, Mom," she said. "You're sitting right there in the sun, and you look all lit up."

"I'm sure I do. It's so bright in this room. Why do you paint everything white? And not a thing on the windows, not even shades to pull down."

"The walls are linen white," Kate said, "and the trim is sail white. And I don't need shades; I'm not worried about snipers."

"Snipers?"

"My LaLeche League lady," Kate said. "She was telling me how war victims can go right on nursing their babies, even in foxholes."

Her mother frowned. "Some of these people are way out there. What do war victims have to do with you? You're not in a foxhole."

"Not yet," Kate said. "But really, if you want shades on your windows, I'll get some. You should have told me sooner."

Her mother waved away the suggestion. "I don't care. That big tree is in front of one of the windows, and the other faces Camille's house. I certainly don't care if she sees me, not that there's much to see at this point."

"But there's always Landon," Kate said slyly, referring to their neighbor's live-in boyfriend. "What about him?"

"Landon is occupied with greener pastures—I hope not too occupied. If he lives with Camille, I don't know why he has to have his own condo in the Back Bay. And his own crystal and china. And his own art collection."

Kate shrugged. "He's a big-time investment banker. Maybe he needs a place downtown. Anyway, he's cute. I remember how they charged over here the first day we moved in, on their way to some swank thing, and there's Camille, nearly six feet tall, in one of those long satin capes her daughter made her, and all her Navajo jewelry, with a huge tray of *assorted* handmade cookies *and* a raspberry pie."

"Camille is wonderful. Mark my words, though, *Lannie*"—she emphasized Camille's pet name for him—"is not in it for the long haul."

"Not everyone is into hauling," Kate said. "She's been divorced twice, he's been divorced once. Maybe they're better off just relaxing."

Katherine shook her head impatiently, signaling her annoyance with a click of the tongue. "She's certainly suggested he give up the apartment. Camille loves taking care of people; she'd like to be married. But *he* is not the right fellow."

"Gotcha," Kate said. She realized she often knew in advance her mother's response to a given topic, but she elicited the responses anyway, sometimes to her annoyance, more often for pleasure. She so valued her mother's sheer dependability, the slight cynicism of the old wives' tales she favored, her bedrock common sense, even the rigid provincial innocence with which she approached discussions of what Kate referred to as "modern life." There were so many topics on which Katherine held strong opinions based on scant experience. Like serial monogamy and live-in arrangements. Interracial relationships. Homosexuality. Literature. Film. When I go to a movie, she liked to say, I want to be *entertained,* not upset.

Kate leaned back on her pillows. She didn't want to be entertained; entertainment was far too demanding, and gave so little in return. Kate wanted someone to read stories to her, or speak intensely about a private matter. She wanted to be fed. The MotherKind worker brought her lunch on a tray, numerous plates of soft, warm tastes, samples of the various entrées she'd made to freeze, and sliced vegetables so cold and crisp they wore ice fragments. Her name was Moira, but Kate liked to think of her only as MotherKind; MotherKind put a flower on the tray, the head of a hothouse daisy or rose, never in a bud vase—too likely to topple during the journey upstairs, perhaps—but floating, the first day, in a cup. Then the flower always appeared in an antique shot glass taken from the good crystal. It was so pretty to see a flower, yet Kate felt the daisy and its lissome petals seemed sacrificial. The soft sphere of the scarlet rose sank inward, pulled from its stem. Kate touched the flowers, their surfaces, as though they were already gone. "It may be January in New England," Moira had said, "but it's still important to see something blooming. And don't worry, I work with unprocessed foods. I'm a vegetarian, though I don't mind cooking meat if that's what you want. My objections are strictly personal." Kate heard her now, her tread on the stairs and the subtle shifting of cutlery. The smell of food came closer and set up a dull fear in Kate, like a nervousness or excitement.

"Here we are," Moira said. "And I brought the mail up too." She placed the bed tray squarely before Kate and pulled her pillows back. "Might want to sit up a bit more. There's a tomato arugula salad and

French bread, and I made you a really hearty vegetable soup, with barley. I froze five pints."

"Great," Kate said. "We'll be thinking of you into next month, blessing the fact of your existence."

Moira nodded. She was so efficient, Kate thought, and she had a quiet, nonintrusive presence, but she seemed a bit humorless. Now she smiled her quick, disappearing smile. Perhaps she was only shy.

"This is my last day with you," she said, "so maybe we should come up with a plan. I know you want to do everything for the baby yourself, but the freezer is almost full of food. There's just room for a few pans of lasagna, which I'll make this afternoon. I'll do all the laundry again, but don't forget I could also give you a massage, or a manicure."

"Or you could read to me," said Kate.

"Don't waste the time you have left," her mother said. "*I* could read to you."

"How about a massage?" Moira asked.

Kate felt so sore, so weak, the thought of anyone touching her was alarming. But she thought Moira had a dreamy voice, soft, a bit insubstantial; Moira's voice would carry words and disappear in them. "A massage, maybe," Kate said, "and then a story."

"Sure." She nodded and took the mail from the tray. "There's a little package for you, and some cards. I left the bills downstairs. Now I'll go and get another lunch, so the two of you can have lunch together."

Kate's mother nodded in her direction. "No, I'll eat later, I'm coming down soon. You go ahead, Katie, before he wakes up and your arms are full."

"I'm coming down later too," Kate announced. "I hope you both realize that I'm dressed today. It's a nursing gown, but still—"

"You're right," Moira said. "I didn't even notice. There you sit, clothed to the elbows."

"Well, I've always been clothed below the waist, in my various bandages."

"Exactly." Moira busied herself straightening the covers of the bed. "And when you're nursing every hour and you're so sore, it hardly seems worth it to take clothes on and off, or lift them up and down."

"It's amazing how the two of you think alike," Kate's mother said wryly. "Anyway, I wasn't going to say anything. You've been mostly covered with sheets and blankets, and I figured you'd get your clothes on by spring."

"I have my gown on." Kate picked up her spoon. "That's all I'll commit to."

"And you do feel warm," Moira said, "when you're making milk. But I know you don't have a temperature, because I've taken it every day."

"You certainly have," Kate's mother said. "You've taken good care of her."

"Why don't we plan on the massage then?" Moira gathered used cups from the bedside table. "You eat all that, then he'll wake and you'll nurse, and by the time he goes down again, I'll be ready. I'll bring up my oils and a tape to play. All right?"

"You're in charge," Kate's mother said.

When Kate woke, the bed tray was gone. Her mother was gone, and the house was perfectly quiet. She remembered finishing the food and leaning back in bed, and then she'd fallen asleep, dreamlessly, as though she had only to close her eyes to move away, small and weightless, skimming the reflective surface of something deep.

She heard a small sound. Alexander lay in the bassinette, his eyes open, looking at her. His swaddling blankets had come loose. Propped on his side by pillows, he raised one arm and moved his delicate hand. Kate sat up to lean near him and touched her forefinger to his palm; immediately, he grasped her hard and his gaze widened. "They're your fingers," she told him. "You don't know them yet, but I do." Everyone had told her to leave him be when he was happy, she'd be holding him and caring for him so ceaselessly, but she took him in her arms, propped up the pillows, and put him in her lap. He kicked excitedly and frowned. She bent her knees to bring him closer and regarded him as he lay on her raised thighs; the frown disappeared. "You're like me," Kate said softly. "You frown when you think. By the time you're twenty-five, you'll have two little lines between your eyes. Such a serious guy." He raised his downy brows. He had a watchful, observing look and a more excited look—he would open his eyes wider, compress his lips, strain with his limbs as though he was concentrating on moving, on touching or grasping. He could feel his body but he couldn't command it to move or do; his focus was entirely in his eyes. And he did focus. Kate was sure he saw her. He wasn't a newborn any longer; today he was one week old. Perhaps his vision was still blurry, and that was why he peered at her so intently. His eyes were big and dark blue, like those of a baby seal. One eye was always moist and teary; his tear duct was blocked, they'd said at the hospital, it would clear up.

Now Kate wiped his cheek carefully with the edge of a cloth diaper, then drew her finger across his forehead, along his jaw, across his flattened, broad little nose. "Mister man," she whispered, "mighty mouse, here's your face. Here are your nose, your ears, your widow's peak. Old widower, here are your bones . . ." She touched his collarbone and the line along his shoulder, under his gown. His skin was like warm silk and his names were too big for him; she called him Tatie, for his middle name was Tateman, after her family, her divided parents. She cleaned him with warm water, not alcohol wipes, and used a powder that contained no talc. The powder was fine as rice flour and smelled as Kate thought rice fields might smell, in the sun, when the plants bloomed. Like clean food, pure as flowers. Across the world and in the South, those young shoots grew and moved in the breeze like grass. "Rice fields are like grass in water," she said to him. "We haven't seen them yet. Even in India, I didn't see them." Outside the wind moved along the house; Kate heard it circling and testing. Suddenly a gust slammed against the windows and Tatie startled, looked toward the sound. "You can't see the wind," Kate murmured, "just what it moves." The wind would bring snow again, Kate knew; already she heard snow approach like a whining in the air. Absently she traced the baby's lips, and he yawned and began to whimper. You're hungry, Kate thought, and he moved his arms as though to gather her closer. Her milk let down with a flush and surge, and she held a clean diaper to one breast as she put him to the other. Now she breathed, exhaling slowly. The intense pain began to ebb; he drank the cells of her blood, Kate knew, and the crust that formed on her nipples where the cuts were deepest. He was her blood. When she held him he was inside her; always, he was near her, like an atmosphere, in his sleep, in his being. She would not be alone again for many years, even if she wanted to, even if she tried. In her deepest thoughts, she would approach him, move around and through him, make room for him. In nursing there would be a still, spiral peace, an energy in which she felt herself, her needs and wants, slough away like useless debris. It seemed less important to talk or think; like a nesting animal, she took on camouflage, layers of protective awareness that were almost spatial in dimension. The awareness had dark edges, shadows that rose and fell. Kate imagined terrible things. That he might stop breathing. That she dropped him, or someone had. That someone or something took him from her. That she forgot about him or misplaced him. There were no words; the thoughts occurred to her in starkly precise images, like the unmistakable images of dreams, as though her waking and sleeping lives had met in him. Truly, she was sleeping; the days and nights were fluid, beautiful and discolored; everything in her was available to her, as though she'd become someone else, someone with a similar past history in whom that history was acknowledged rather than felt, someone who didn't need to make amends or understand, someone beyond language. She was shattered. Something new would come of her. Moments in which she crossed from consciousness to sleep, from sleep to awareness, there was a lag of an instant in which she couldn't remember her name, and she didn't care. She remembered him. Now his gaze met hers and his eyelids fluttered; she could see him falling away, back into his infant swoon. His sleep closed around him like an ocean shell and rocked him within it. In this they were alike, Kate thought, though he had no name known to him, no name to forget. He was pure need. She took him from the breast and held him to her shoulder, patting and rubbing him, softly, a caress and a heartbeat.

Moira came into the room so quietly that Kate was unaware of her until she reached the foot of the bed. She carried blankets, a tape recorder, plastic bottles of oils, a small cardboard box. Depositing her burdens on the floor, she mouthed, "Shall I take him?" and Kate gestured, no, not yet. She whispered, "I'll set up," and disappeared from view. Kate smelled the sulfur of lit matches and then citrus and gardenia, Moira's scented votives. Kate put Alexander carefully into the bassinette and looked through the books stacked beside her table. She chose one. Which passage? The beginning would do.

"I'm going to put the tape on very low. As he sleeps more deeply, I'll turn it up just a bit." Moira was beside her. "Is that the book you want?"

She smiled and took it, then indicated the rug at the foot of the bed. "I've made a space. It's better to have a firm surface."

"A space," Kate said. She stood and saw that Moira had made an alternate bed, blankets precisely folded, a pallet covered with terry towels. Sheets and more blankets were arranged over it, neatly turned down. Six votives were lit in a row of little flames at the head. "This looks ritualistic," Kate said. "Do I need a chaperone?"

"I don't believe so." Moira turned the tape on. "But I won't lie, it is a ritual. I'm sorry I can't lower the light. Evening is a better time, but I don't work nights."

"It doesn't need to be dark," Kate said. "Look how the sun falls across. I love the sun."

"Yes, you'll feel it. Can you lie on your front comfortably? I'll go out while you get ready."

"No need."

"No, I will. And take everything off. I'll bring the warm oils from the kitchen."

Kate watched her go, and sighed. What a lot of work this was. She walked past the pallet into the bathroom, pulling the door closed. There, the water running, getting warm. She took off her gown and pants, folded the pads and wrapped them in paper, threw them away. Slowly, she began to wash, water cooling on her legs in rivulets. They'd told her not to bathe yet; she stood like this, cloths and soap, carefully. At first, when she stood or walked, she'd felt as though she moved on the deck of a ship, as though some rhythm pulsed in the ground, the floor. Rooms subtly shifted. The effects of the anesthetic, Matt said, but Kate could see the movement even from her bed, from her window. The way the angles of the ceiling met the walls, how the floor slid to its four corners. How the earth turned. This is the way it's always been, Kate thought; she hadn't known. Now she did. She rocked the baby in the rocking chair and imagined sailing through the window, rocking, with no interruption, into the cold, the air billowing around them. You okay? Matt would ask. I'm fine, Kate would answer. As a child, an adolescent, an adult, she had almost never cried. Now she could. She didn't feel depressed, she felt amazed, and moved, and out of sync. Or she was in sync, but she couldn't explain how. She left her gown where it fell, dried herself and opened the door.

The music was a little more noticeable now, classical music, strings. A shaft of sunlight poured across the rug and motes of dust swam in the light. Moira knelt by the empty fireplace, waiting for her. "Sorry," Kate said. "I wanted to get clean." Moira nodded, and pulled back the sheets of the pallet for Kate to slip inside. Slowly, Kate was on her knees, and then prone. "We won't wake him?" she said, before turning over. "You wouldn't be comfortable away from him," Moira answered. "We won't disturb him."

Then the sheets and blankets were a silky covering. Moira moved her hands along Kate's form as though to gain some innate sense of her, pausing, exerting a gentle pressure. It's not New Age, Kate thought, it's from the oldest days, when floors were swept earth. Behind the music she heard Moira breathing, exhaling in time to the movement of her hands, as though she were draining Kate of fatigue or discomfort, releasing it through herself. Surely that was the idea. "So, Moira," Kate said softly, "what are your personal objections?"

The hands never slowed. "To what?"

"Meat. To meat."

"Oh. Health, basically, at first, theories about nutrition. But after I stopped eating meat, the smell of my body changed, and the taste in my mouth. I don't mind handling meat—I cook and do catering, and sometimes it's part of my job—but I don't want it inside me. And I didn't want my daughter growing up on a meat diet."

"You have a daughter?"

"Yes. She's three. I'm a single mom."

So she works days, Kate thought. Nights at home with her daughter. "You seem so content and organized," she said aloud. "Were you always single?"

"Yes, pretty much. It was a bit difficult at first, but for now, we're content. We do very well."

"Little women," Kate said. "But in those mother-daughter stories, there's always a virtuous hero offstage, the father off at war, or the rich neighbor."

"And so there may be," Moira said. "But I'll do whatever's best for my child. I don't need saved."

"What a relief," Kate said.

"Yes." Moira laughed softly.

"But we do have to save ourselves, don't we," Kate murmured. "Such a project."

"You're stronger each day," Moira said. "And you're doing exactly what you should be doing with this baby. It's so important to nurse, and to have him constantly with you."

Now the light of the sun had shifted; it seemed winter light again, flattened and diffuse, and the flames of the votives burned higher. Moira's hands were at Kate's hips, lifting her from behind, tilting heat into her abdomen. She moved up along Kate's spine with her fists, a hard and soft pressure, repetitive, patterned with heat that Kate felt in her forearms, in her thighs. She felt herself knit together, handled like something wounded; she realized how far she was from herself, and how she might begin to live here again, in her body. Slowly, it would happen. She might call and call now for her own return, but she only floated, inhabiting so many former selves with more conviction. Just now she saw the backs and jostling shoulders of her hometown girlfriends, all bundled in their coats and descending into snow down dormitory stairs; they still looked like high school blondes and brunettes in fur hats and boots, bright twine in their hair, but they were getting off on mescaline, falling into the first tinges of visuals, and someone was crooning, *Pleased as punch, pleased as punch.* In India, on the vast terrace of the Taj Mahal, boys approached Kate with open arms. *Sell blue jeans? Buy hashish? Extreme hashish. You sell blue jeans?* The young men, the slim ones, looked like boys, smooth-skinned and lithe. The middle-aged men on the train to Agra were toadish and portly in their tailored clothes; they seldom looked up from their newspapers. Mist rose from the steaming fields as though daybreak would go on for weeks and Kate saw silhouettes of movement, squatting forms, their morning toilette a slow, dark ballet. An old man, skeletal in white, hunkered by the tracks, brushing his teeth with a twig. On the tortuous mountain track to Chitwan, the Nepalese bus had stopped in a town; farmers disembarked with their caged chickens, and the women with their saronged babies; the Gurka soldiers piled out with their guns. The women merely lifted their layered, intricately sewn skirts to relieve themselves, standing to straddle the sewage ditch that ran along one side of the only road. Water rattled in it and the men walked farther up, discreetly, but Kate wandered behind the shacklike kiosks to pick her way down a rocky bank to the

river. Ropes of feces blackened among the stones. The riverbank flattened in a broad sweeping curve and the water was low; outcroppings
strewn with boulders rose in crescents from glistened sweeps too still
and silver to seem fluid. Kate dropped her loose cloth trousers to her
knees and crouched, urinating; to her left, two men appeared at the
curve of the river, balancing on their shoulders a long pole bent with the
weight of a body. The body, bound to the pole at wrists and ankles,
swung in delicate motion, the swathed, faceless head flung back.

Kate couldn't look away. Moira's voice came from above her. "It's
nearly time for me to go," she said.

"Yes, I know." Kate turned over and lay on her back. Behind her eyes
she saw a darkness reddened by light. "Good-bye, Moira."

Moira touched Kate's forehead with her fingertips. Her touch lingered deliberately, a firm little bruise specific as a kiss. Kate lay still. She
felt Moira close to her, just over her, her clove-scented breath, the oil of
her dark hair. Perhaps she always ended her massages this way. Perhaps
she thought Kate ridiculous, a privileged woman not yet alone with her
child. Kate raised her gaze to Moira's. "You look so grave," Kate said.
"But then, good-bye is a grave word."

"It's just a wish," Moira said, "like a blessing." She moved away. Her
hands pressed in a careful pattern above the tucked blankets, finishing
evenly. "He's sleeping," she said softly. "You sleep, too, if you like, but
here's your story." Kate heard a ruffling of pages. *Chapter one,* came a
voice. *"I am born . . . To begin my life with the beginning of my life, I
record that I was born (as I have been informed and believe) on a Friday
at midnight . . ."* Kate closed her eyes. The river was a high rattling murmur and the barefoot men moved ceaselessly forward in the islanded
riverbed. The men never looked at her. They were there still, Kate
thought, making progress down the Narayani to the mouth of the Bag-
mati, two days' trek. The cremation sites, in view of the blue-eyed stupas
and their gold spires, were raised earth bound by stones, and the flaming
pyres were set afloat, heaped with burning flowers. Kate smelled that
scent, like blackened oranges, sticky and boiled, so close she was
enveloped. *It was remarked that the clock began to strike . . . and I
began to cry, simultaneously. . . .* She knew she must stand up now and
walk, or the bus would ascend into the mountains without her.

. . .

Kate sat at the kitchen table, dressed in her clothes. MotherKind was finished; Kate herself was MotherKind. The downstairs of her own house looked strange to her, larger, more impersonal, as though she were a visitor with some dimly realized connection to this place. She lay other mail aside and opened only the little package from LaLeche League, postmarked Medford. Sealed into a white envelope were two small plastic objects and a handwritten instruction sheet: "How to Use Nursing Shields." The shields were gently conical and extremely simple. Kate considered regarding them as unpretentious S&M aids or punk rock falsies, but in fact they were objects seemingly more conducive to plastic food storage than to anything used for enhancement, protection or pleasure. Kate got the impression they'd been passed on to her from other women, other breasts. Circular plastic disks that snapped apart, they had a hole in the inner disk meant to keep the nipple erect and dry, and they had the added benefit of collecting the flow of milk that seeped into one's clothes before the baby could latch on. Milk seeped into Kate's clothes and sweetened and soured her chest and the cleft between her breasts every time she heard her baby cry, as soon as he cried. Milk wet her shirt when she sat down alone near her bedroom window and saw the exposed brown grass in the yard, rents in the snow, when she read some item in the newspaper about a child falling out a window, or saw a commercial for long-distance dialing on television. Sixty seconds of manipulative human-interest images and her eyes were wet, and she didn't bother wiping her face. Her breasts let down and her uterus cramped sharply, turning like a small animal inside her, contracting in its nest. When her eyes got wet, her breasts performed, as though she wept milk. She could cry and she could nurse, or when she nursed, she didn't have to cry. Or, nursing, she didn't need to cry; her body wept. She wept food and he grew on sorrow.

"What are those things?" Kate's mother stood behind her, peering over her shoulder.

"They're nursing shields. Look, they're like something out of *Barbarella*."

"What's *Barbarella*?"

"You know, that Jane Fonda movie where she's a blond space bimbo and she wears pointy warrior shields over her breasts, and silver gladiator boots and tights, and she gets picked up by an eagle—"

"An eagle?"

"Yes. She wakes up in this huge bird's nest looking—soporific. Anyway, the LaLeche woman sent these things to me for my breasts. They go inside a nursing bra, now that I'm wearing a bra, to keep the cloth from sticking and making everything worse."

"What else did she tell you to do?"

"Well, there's the wet method and the dry method. One school of thought is to feed through the pain and keep the cuts moist with lanolin, because otherwise the baby breaks them open anyway every time he nurses. But then nothing ever really heals. Or, you hope you heal, but it might take a long time. The other is to stop nursing, go naked and air-dry, express into a pump to feed the baby, but then the baby might refuse the breast when you start up again, or the nipples heal and crack repeatedly—"

"What do these things have to do with it all?"

"They keep you dry, and pull your nipples out if they're inverted so the baby latches on better. And I guess they beat going topless. I mean, suppose I want to answer the doorbell, or leave the house someday." Kate put one of the plastic shields inside her shirt, in her bra, over the more sensitive breast.

"Of course you'll leave the house again. My God, you had a general anesthetic, after that long labor. Think what you went through; you needed to stay in bed for a week. And then all this with the nursing." Kate's mother sighed and sat down in the chair opposite. "It's amazing how nature slaps women with everything at once—you take care of a new baby twenty-four hours a day, just when you're most exhausted."

Kate gazed at her mother's face and felt her wholly familiar presence. In this place, this house where they'd all lived less than four months, her mother was so real, so connected to all they'd come from, to everything Kate had taken with her, the burden and the weight, and the furious beauty she kept trying to turn around and see. She wondered if she would see anything of that first world, the world she'd come from, when her mother was gone. "Yes," she said aloud, her voice faltering, "it's so unrelieved. You never really wake up or sleep. Time stands still."

"And later," her mother went on, "you forget. You don't think you will, but you do. I must have gone through all this with nursing, but I don't remember. I do remember the time your brother bit me."

"Which brother?" Kate put her forefinger into the hole of the other nursing shield and began to spin it slowly on the tabletop directly in front of her. It made an unsatisfying, lopsided axis.

"I'll never forget *that*," her mother said. "He took a bite right out of me. He came away with blood all over his little face."

Kate looked up. "But I thought I was the only one you nursed."

Her mother frowned. "You're right. It must have been you."

"It had to be me." Kate laughed.

"What's so funny?"

"I'm thinking about the song. You look confused. Never mind."

"Oh," her mother said. "That song from the forties. That's 'It Had to Be *You*.' No, I'm just surprised. Aunt Raine, who was the closest I had to a mother-in-law, told me I'd never be able to nurse because I was a smoker, though I stopped each time I was pregnant. So I didn't try with your older brother, but I was determined to nurse you. I drank beer and milk shakes by the hour, and I had plenty of milk. You were so fat your boobs hung to your waist."

"That was fleeting," Kate said, "until now."

"You'll get back in shape. Actually, nursing takes the weight faster—it all goes to the baby. But with my third, I was too tired. I had three kids under four. Think about it."

"I can't," Kate said. "But bottle-feeding seems so much more trouble—all those bottles to wash and sterilize, and have you ever tasted formula? It's just chemicals and water. I think babies only drink it because they're starved to it."

"Maybe. Mine sure sucked it down." She paused. "But the boys were skinnier babies, much skinnier."

"No one would ever advise you to drink beer to nurse now. You must have been slightly looped all the time. Think of all the IQ points I lost. No wonder I bit you."

Kate's mother gave her an exasperated look. "I don't think it hurt you any."

Kate smiled. "By the way, how old was I when you gave me that IQ test? Fourth or fifth grade, I believe. Just think, if not for all that beer, I might have actually scored in the genius category."

"I didn't tell you what your score was," her mother said, abashed.

"No, but you told me *approximately* what it was, within precise parameters. I'm sure you remember. I lost out by a few points, and see, it was all your fault."

"Fine, fine," her mother said. "In any case, you're smart enough. If you were any smarter, you'd have been unbearable. I couldn't have coped."

"I'm not feeling smart," Kate said. "I feel as though half my brain is missing." She positioned the other nursing shield in her bra. The top of her breast felt hot. Under her palm, her fingers, she felt a hard spot, like a knot.

"You look a little flushed," her mother said. "Your cheeks are red. Maybe you'd better go lie down." She reached out to touch Kate's wrist. "Just rest. You'll soon be yourself again."

"No," Kate said, "I won't. And why should I?"

She had mastitis. Desperately, she wanted to walk outside into the cold, up and down the snowbound streets. Antibiotics, her doctor said. Hot compresses and bed rest, fluids, said her LaLeche League counselor. Give it a day. Antibiotics are a last resort, no one can really know how they'll affect the baby. Nurse even more frequently, and pump, and change compresses as soon as they begin to cool. If the fever reaches 102, take Tylenol. Is there someone to help you?

"Mom, please," Kate said, "open the window."

"Don't be ridiculous. You're feverish, and you have an infant here. Lie back and cover up. The water is good and hot. I just don't want to burn you." She came to Kate's bed with an aluminum basin in her arms, and Kate looked dully inside it at the steaming cloths. "Let me change the compress again," her mother said. "How long would you say the heat really lasts?"

"Oh, a hundred years or so."

"I know you're restless. Could you read?" her mother said. "Shall I turn on the TV?"

"No," Kate said, and threw off the coverlet. "You're terribly efficient,

Mom, but I don't see how we can go on like this all day. Weren't you just here three minutes ago?"

"Matt will take a shift when he comes home." She removed the cooling cloth and laid the hot one carefully across Kate's breast. "Should we see if Moira could come back?"

"That's not necessary." Kate held her hand above the steaming cloth and imagined the heat on her breast increased. "We can't afford another week of MotherKind. And this is not rocket science, it's hot washcloths."

"We have to keep them this hot," her mother said. "The more constant we keep the heat, the more likely you are to get results. You've worked so hard at this, I don't want you to have to stop nursing."

"I'm not stopping," Kate said, incredulous. "Who said anything about stopping?"

"Well, no one," her mother said worriedly. "You would only stop if your health were at stake." She put down the basin and took up the edge of the wrinkled duvet, smoothing the white flannel.

Kate sighed. "I see you've got the coverlet in your hand. Don't come at me with it. Unless someone has chills, you really don't bundle up a person with a fever. You only make them hotter. Where did you go to medical school, anyway? Mastitis is not serious; it's almost de rigueur. Nursing mothers who don't get it are really not even respectable veterans."

"I wouldn't be concerned about your status. With all you've got on your plate, you'll surely come out of this a veteran of something. Is that cloth cool yet?"

"Mom, you'll make yourself tired. Please, sit down. If you want to distract me, read to me from something panoramic. There, read from what Moira started. Not the first lines, I don't want to hear them again, but start anywhere on the first page."

Kate watched as her mother pulled the rocking chair close the bed and felt for the book behind her on the seat, where Moira had left it. "*I was born with a caul . . .*" she began uncertainly.

"No, no," Kate said. "Let's skip the whole beginning. I heard it earlier today and came down with a fever. Go near to the end, when it's all coming right. Didn't you ever read this book? Doesn't everyone have to read it in high school?"

"Good heavens, I don't remember what I read in high school. Do you want the very last pages?"

"No, a little earlier. Do the reunion scene; you'll like it." She took the book from her mother's outstretched hand and turned it to the right page. "Start with *Agnes, shall I tell you what about? I came to tell you.* Right here."

"This print is so small. I feel as though I need my glasses changed." Her mother leaned back slightly and peered at the page through her bifocals. *"Do you doubt my being true to you . . . what I have always been to you . . .* that part?"

"Right. *You have a secret, said I. Let me share it, Agnes.*"

"Now, if you know it from memory, why do you want me to read it to you?"

"Because I *love* it, of course. And who wouldn't? *Said I. Let me share it.* And the way he keeps repeating her name. My God, why don't people speak to one another that way every day, every hour?"

"People don't necessarily want to share secrets," her mother said. "And maybe I should read something else. The point of this was not for you to get upset."

"I'm not upset!" Kate leaned back on the pillows, took a breath, and lowered her voice to a near whisper. "Just read, please. I beg of you."

"Said I," her mother intoned. "All right. I'll start at the top of this next page."

She began to read, and Kate trained her eyes on a middle distance, a space informed by winter light. It was the space behind her mother's chair, a shape consisting of bare floor and air just in front of the window. When Kate peered into that space correctly, the snowy view of descending streets and drifted roofs lost specificity and interest. Her eyes rested in emptiness that held nothing but a particular light of day and time. The space seemed concave, difficult to hold or see if one tried, but effortlessly present within a certain focus. The mode of the listener was that focus and Kate let herself enter it, drifting and aware. Like active dreaming, infant dreams, dreams in which the body subtly flexes while the mind moves into other stories. Dickens's language was a story Kate knew, shadowed, burnished and detailed, even the descriptions of filth and ruin rendered in a language so controlled and rich, so confident that stories exist and listeners hear. Dickens's listeners were gone now; gone, all those living souls who'd paid to hear him speak in lecture halls, on stages, who'd stood within reach of his voice, all companions to a homeless boy, travelers to the death house, the poorhouse, all of them moving along streets made of stones, the horse-drawn wagons creaking, the clotted mud on flanks and boots. It was always winter in Dickens's London boyhood, always cold and foggy, and the bridges so long one couldn't see to the other side through wet, cloying mist. Everyone's hands looked chapped and old; so Northern European, Kate thought, that white, mottled skin, like the faintly mauve hands of kids from the coal towns, kids with old eyes. They knew how to say good-bye, those children, lined up in school hallways in their wrinkled coats, their chafed wrists delicate and dirty, the lines and whorls of their skin etched with old dirt. They were children from her mother's classrooms, children her mother had taught to read and write, children she'd clothed with whatever her own kids had outgrown. They boarded school buses at day's end and never waved, only looked, sideways glances through the rectangular windows. Kate had thought no one kissed them; she'd thought they'd be cold forever. Now in her mind's eye they cast their clear gaze through Dickens's unfurled words. *Toiling on, I saw a ragged way-worn boy, forsaken and neglected* . . .

In Sri Lanka, in India, babies burned with cholera or malaria. Moist skin, dark, lustrous hair; and the ripe gardens, fertile riots fecund with color and smell. Those babies could drown in dense scent, even through the membranes of their mother's bodies, through the protective caul of Dickens's story, any story. Kate watched her mother's mouth, a mouth not so generous as Kate's, a rosebud mouth perfectly suited to the bright red lipstick she'd worn all the years Kate had stood near her, looking up, the daughter so small in stature, or followed her, skipping to keep pace, her mother's black coat disappearing along grocery aisles, corridors, slushy streets. Dimly, she heard the words her mother read: *Long miles of road then opened out before my mind* . . . Good-bye was not so simple as a kiss. Good-bye went on and on.

"Mom, wait," Kate said softly.

Her mother stopped speaking and raised her eyes, startled.

"I'm sorry," Kate said. "I wasn't concentrating and I missed the part I really wanted to hear. Can you go back a bit, and read the underlined paragraph?"

She glanced at the book and moved her chair closer to the bed, then half stood, remembering the compress, reaching to touch the cooled cloth that lay across Kate's breast. But Kate gestured to leave it be, and nodded, encouraging her to go on.

"*I went away,*" her mother read, "*loving you. I stayed away, loving you. I returned home, loving you. And now I tried to tell her of the struggle I had had, and the conclusion I had come to. I tried to lay my mind before her, truly and entirely.*"

There was a hush in the room. Kate's mother looked back at the lines once. Then she leaned forward and touched her open palm to Kate's face. Kate touched her own hand to her mother's wrist and inclined her head as her mother stood to embrace her. Listening, she heard the beating of her mother's heart as snow brushed the windows in sweeps of wind.

*No barriers. A broad metal gate barring the airfield from an out-
door waiting area swings open. Kate sees her mother walk out to meet
her in the small crowd. She wears tailored white shorts and a bright
yellow shirt and clutches her square white purse. How quiet it seems
after the noise of the plane, almost as though sound is suspended.
Katherine moves toward her in the calm, flat hush; at the far edge of
the runway, crows lift and settle. Kate thinks of the airport in Udai-
pur: same black birds, same time of day, the cluster of small buildings
and the low wall. There, massive begonias with fuzzed, protruding
tongues overran the bricks, and the guards crossed their rifles to hold
back those waiting, who made no move to surge forward save with
their eyes. But it was the same long approach at low altitude, the
same murmurous auditory blur on arrival, and heightened visual detail.
Kate saw her mother's hands on the purse as she came near, the tense
curl of her fingers and the bright metal clasp. Oh, the sound of that
clasp, open and shut, crisp and official, a tiny echo of emptiness; as a
child Kate would pull out a bottom dresser drawer and open all the
purses. Each wrapped in tissue paper, one folded linen handkerchief
inside smelling faintly of Tabu. Kate reaches for Katherine, smiling,
embracing her. She's looking her best, too thin in her polished white
sandals.*

*"Katie," she is saying, "I was so afraid I'd be late. They've just opened
two lanes of the new highway, and I was dumb enough to try it. The traf-*

fic was bad but none of the exits were open until this one, so everything crept along toward the airport."

"Very Sartre," Kate answers, "right here in River City."

"I could see your plane coming in," her mother goes on, relieved. "It was nip and tuck."

"So we circled, waiting for you. See, your timing is perfect. You look classy, Mom. You're tan already, and no wonder, it's real summer here."

"Well, of course. They're putting up flags on Main Street for the Fourth. Where's your bag?"

"That won't be complicated. I see them unloading. The plane is so small, it's faster than unloading the bottom of a bus. Now, don't try to carry my bag for me."

"Absolutely not. Be my guest."

"And I hope you'll let me drive home."

"That's going too far—you know how I love your driving. And I really am fine—I tire out a little earlier in the day, is all. My only problem now is, just, knowing I'm sick. But sometimes it's like a mirage."

Kate reaches to put an arm around her. "<u>Be Here Now</u>. Remember when I bought you a copy? That oversized purple book, written in wavy script?"

"That's not all that was wavy about it. Heavens, that was so long ago, in your hiking boots phase. Well, I'm certainly here now, and happy you are." She puts on her sunglasses, pats her hair. "Here come the bags, courtesy of our small-time airport. They put them on the pushcart, shove them in our direction, and leave us to our own devices. See how simple and uncomplicated life can be?"

"I've got it," Kate says, bending to grab her shoulder duffel off the cart.

"And Matt's coming day after tomorrow?"

"Yes, and he'll love that plane—a little adventure. He'll be looking out the windows for black bears and alligators."

"Alligators?"

"He gets us mixed up with Mississippi, and the swamps of the Carolinas. I try to tell him this isn't the South, but he's still hoping. It's good and hot, though." She takes her mother's arm. "Let's go home. Let's take the old road."

"If you insist. With all the highway construction, it may be faster."

. . .

Kate drives. The old road home is a two-lane winding past clustered houses and abandoned coal tipples. Closed roadside gas stations still wear the weathered, upright jewelry of their empty pumps. No trucks rumbling through, no travelers stopping to buy sandwiches and soda pop. Here the same battered green metal signs are peppered with BB holes, lettered with the names of settlements and the legend "Unincorporated." Across the hilly yards of the houses Kate sees chickens strutting, laundry hung out. A kid with a wagon. The air, the sky, the leaning buildings, all seem less dusty, the land more green, the storefronts preserved and oddly alone, as though they will vanish beyond this deserted grace into a future that already exists, shimmering where the heat meets the road.

"I suppose people will begin to leave these places now," Kate says.

"Oh, eventually," her mother answers. "But the school buses still bring plenty of kids in from these hamlets, and from hollows farther in, the ones up dirt tracks. That will disappear in another generation. Everything will be paved, after a fashion."

"I love this road," Kate tells her mother.

"It's nice," her mother agrees, "now that no one drives it. But, my God, how I used to gnash my teeth if I had to follow the whole length of it behind a coal truck. And your father! Waylon would drive right up behind them, so you'd choke on exhaust. Creeping along in smoke, ready to floor it the minute he got a broken line."

"In those big white Pontiacs he drove"—Kate laughs—"on these curves! No seat belts back then. And no air-conditioning—the wind whipping through the windows. I don't remember being scared, though. We thought it was exciting."

"I'm sure you did. I'd be holding on to the armrest in the front, both feet pressed to the floor. Of course I couldn't say anything. That would only get him fuming worse."

"The motor would ratchet up, just as he pulled out to pass. Sometimes you could see another car headed at you, a curve or so ahead. Dad's cars were like big boats—they seemed indestructible, and they gleamed. You've got to admit, he took great care of them. Who was that mechanic he always took them to, at the first squeak or backfire?"

"Oh, Brownie Cogar. Lord, if that man had a brain, it would rattle. How he fixed cars I'll never know."

"Wasn't he a cousin of Dad's?" Kate looks over at her mother mischievously.

"A distant cousin, you'd better hope." She pauses. "Your father will want you to phone him the minute you get home."

"I already phoned, just before I got on the plane. I'm seeing him tomorrow for dinner at the Elks Club." Kate smiles. "Dad called the acceleration 'pickup.' He'd yell at the car, 'Pick up, you son of a bitch!' while he tromped the gas. The boys bounced up and down on both sides of me, miming the sound of the engine. Egging him on. I guess it was a guy thing. Why did I always have to sit in the middle? Answer me that."

Her mother shrugs. "You were born in the middle."

"Yep," Kate says, "that's how it was. Summers seemed endless. We wandered through the field to the creek and back. They played baseball in those awful hot uniforms. What did I do?"

"You read books," her mother says. "You lay in the glider on the breezeway with a pile of them. I took you to the library twice a week. Yes, they were long summers. Now the days fly by. I can't believe how fast. From the time I got out of the hospital, in April, to now, it's as though each day just—vanishes."

And she lifts both hands from her lap, opening her palms in one fluid motion.

Kate aligns her fingers perfectly to the ridges of the steering wheel and drives smoothly, centering through curves. They seem alone on the road, and the big, solid car moves them along like a sealed capsule. "You and Dad are so alike in some ways, and so completely unsuited to each other," she tells her mother.

Katherine makes an exasperated noise. "I don't know how I stood it as long as I did, and I certainly don't know how I'm like Waylon."

"Oh, your big cars and your exact opinions. Very different opinions, but held so absolutely. Your histories. Neither of you had a father, really. Yours died young, and his didn't raise him. He had no mother, just his aunts, while you had yours to yourself, when she'd lost so much. You were so close, almost like sisters."

"Now, we weren't like sisters at all. I was her sixth baby—goodness, she was in her late thirties when I was born—old, then, to have babies.

She'd lost those three before me, one to diphtheria and two to stillbirth. She confided in me, yes, but that's natural between women."

"I just mean that you were raised by a confidante, only to move in with a man who didn't talk at all, and then she died."

There is silence in the car. Kate wonders why she spoke so plainly and immediately regrets the words. But her mother only sighs a calm, small sigh. "Move in?" she says softly. "What do you mean, 'move in'? We were married; no one 'moved in' then." She smooths the pleats of her shorts. "And what man talks? Very few of them, at least in my experience. Men weren't supposed to talk, until recently."

"Some of them talked, surely."

"None you'd want much to do with." Her mother smiles. "Does Matt talk?"

"Of course. Though I suppose I ask a lot of questions. I suppose I push him sometimes. But yes, he talks. He kept scrapbooks from the time he was about nine—his birthday cards, newspaper clips about Little League and the time his father survived a plane crash, his grandmother's obituary, with a little heart drawn beside it. All of it a narrative. I think he's unusual." Kate pauses. "It was the heart that got to me. This little boy, drawing a heart in red pencil. And you know, Mom—we're buying a house together."

"You are?"

"You know he's been living at my place for several months, since we asked the upstairs tenant to move out. It's been good. He and the kids have a private space."

"But if you buy a house together, they won't have a private space."

"You're right. I may have to get lost on a regular basis. Think I can do that?" Kate glances over at her.

"Lost in your own house?" Katherine looks doubtful.

"They do need time alone together. I sort of do the entertaining—puppet shows, treasure hunts, Easter baskets. We barbecue in the drive-way. I even mowed that tiny square of grass behind the house, cleaned up the dog debris, to make a croquet course."

Her mother laughs. "You mean back by the high fence, below the barbed wire? So where does Luna do her business?"

"Well, there, but I clean up before the boys come over." Kate lives at the top of a steep dead-end street in Boston on the wrong side of the

Orange Line, a rather notorious elevated train whose tracks shadow the run-down business districts and housing projects of the city. Her neighborhood is mostly working-class Irish Catholic and Latino. The owner-occupied triple-deckers and two-families are well kept up, but Kate knows better than to walk down by the trains at night, past the bars and little spas and bodegas where people buy Wonder Bread and Devil Dogs and lottery tickets. "Did you know I have our old croquet set?" *she asks her mother.* "Sam and Jonah love croquet, especially since I let them win."

"You do?"

"Sure I do. It's bad enough someone has to win. I'm no idiot." *Kate takes the clip out of her hair and feels for her sunglasses in her pocket.* "I wanted him to bring them with him so you could meet them, but their mother would never have agreed to it, and there's no point antagonizing her while the settlement is being worked out."

"Oh." *Katherine looks over at Kate and raises her brows.*

"It's a bit delicate with the kids. They know she left first, or at least I assume they remember, but they don't know she was involved with someone long before Matt met me."

"Why not?"

"She chooses not to tell them, and Matt feels it's her decision."

"But doesn't this impact rather badly on you?"

Kate takes a breath. "My point is that Matt has what you always called character. He treats her with consideration, when he might behave differently. You always used to say, 'A dog that will bring a bone will take one.' Wasn't that one of your famous expressions?"

"But what must the children think? Their parents are apart and Matt is with you. I'm surprised they talk to you."

Actually, lately, Kate thinks, they sometimes don't. "It's a hurdle, I suppose," *she tells her mother,* "but life is full of those. You were always saying that too, as in, 'Get a running start, because life is full of—' "

"All right, all right," *her mother says.*

"Matt and his wife are their parents, and what they're told is up to Matt, and to her. They'll never be my children, even though I wish they were."

"You do?"

"Well, yes. I thought at first it was going to be like adopting children, but it's not. Not at all."

"As long as you understand you're in for a long stretch of 'not at all.' "

"I think I do. And hopefully I'll have my own kids. They'll probably keep me pretty busy."

"Standing aside on a regular basis can hurt, though," Katherine says quietly, "and I know you. Your name may be Tateman, but you're like Mother, like me. I know it's going to grate on you."

"I suppose it will." Kate realizes she is driving more slowly. She looks over to meet her mother's gaze. "And if it does, shall we say it's your fault? I was always . . . so important to you. Maybe my expectations are too high."

Katherine shakes her head, smiling the small, sad, slightly rueful smile Kate imagines on her face during their phone calls. Now she touches her finger to Kate's wrist. "Expectations protect you," she says. "There's nothing wrong with them, unless they're never met." Her finger moves, a brief caress. "You're a good judge. If you're ready, buy a house. There's time for all the rest. You're in no hurry."

"I suppose not." Kate looks back at the road, but the expression in her mother's eyes stays with her. Such brown eyes. Black brows, short black lashes, and her dark, full hair, beginning to silver just at her temples. She'll be fifty-nine at summer's end. The ocher light in the car seems to reveal a paler cast to her skin, what lies beneath the burnish of sun she's encouraged, sitting in her chaise in the backyard, forgoing the shade of her screened-in porch. She's trying hard to look healthy. Kate reaches to turn off the air conditioner. "Let's open the windows. I want to smell things."

"Smell things?" Katherine rummages in her purse. "Wait, at least let me find a scarf. I just got my hair done this morning, in your honor."

"You still live here. But it's so far away from me." Kate pushes the console button to lower all the windows in a rush of air. "Mmm, it's different, moist, a little bitter. The hay used to smell pale green, and dry—"

"The hay is growing, it's June. You smell alfalfa, it's all in bloom, and manure, and wild thyme and mint and the hot tar they've poured in the potholes of the road, and a dozen other smells." She laughs. "Not much of a country girl anymore, are you? You weren't so easy to entertain when you were hell-bent to get out of here."

"But maybe I'll regress. Back to my roots. You always said it would happen." Kate looks at her mother through her own windblown hair. "You don't realize how different it is, at least here, in these left-behind pockets where there are no chain restaurants or billboards. It all still seems what I thought it was."

"And what did you think it was?" Katherine pulls her scarf tighter.

Kate shrugs. "I thought it was mine, that it would stay mine and not disappear. You never left home, so you couldn't tell me how it would feel to go. When I think of a place, I think of here. I'm from this place, no matter where I am. But it doesn't really exist anymore. The highway bypasses what's left."

"There's an exit ten miles or so out of town. Why would we want it any closer?" Katherine shakes her head, peering into the road. "The noise and those tractor trailers. And the coal trucks, what trucks there are now, take the big road. That's good."

"Yes," Kate agrees slowly. In summer, black dust had filmed the windows like powder. Touched, it left a smudge. Sleep dust, Kate had called it; she feels drowsy, remembering. Just now dense woods fan out on both sides of the road. She focuses on the faded double line in the center of the curving asphalt.

"I thought we'd stop for groceries once we get into town," Katherine says. "You can help me carry the bags. By the way, my friend Rip is coming for supper. He thinks it's so intriguing that you write poems and work for a publishing house. He's pretty intriguing himself."

"I think you've mentioned him. Or I've seen pictures. Who is he?" Kate asks. "A suitor? And what sort of name is that?"

"Heavens, never a suitor—I'm far too straitlaced for Rip. And the name is a nickname. Maybe it refers to his height—he's always been tall and skinny—or his sharp tongue or his escapades. He was in high school ahead of me, and college, the two years I went before I married. He's traveled all over the world, married and divorced, then come back and taught grade school, way down in rural Kentucky. Now he's retired here and has a house in Rock Fork full of antiques. I knew you'd want to traipse around to look at antiques."

Kate nods, watching sunlight play in sparkling, isolated patches across the surface of the asphalt. There's a stream, a band of cold like thrown shade; Kate smells it before they round a turn to cross the narrow bridge. Suddenly her memory of the road deserts her and the rumble of the car, the clatter of boards under the wheels, seem utterly new. They could be anywhere. She's with her mother, and they move forward in darkening glitter.

3

Amy was the only one who answered the ad that Kate phoned in to a student agency in February. She had the blond freckled good looks of a contemporary Doris Day. She was wholesome, an elementary ed major at Lesley College, and, as it turned out, she was a stepchild.

"How old are you?" Kate asked.

"I'm twenty," Amy answered.

"What experience have you had with children?"

"I helped with all my brothers, all three of them. Now the youngest is six."

"There are four in your family?"

"Well, my mother died when I was five and my sister was four. Then my father remarried and they had the boys." She smiled cheerfully.

A veteran, Kate thought. "Is your sister in school in Boston too?"

"No. She's at home. She has CP. She's in a chair."

"Oh."

"She goes to school part-time. At home there's a van to pick her up, different services she needs." Amy smiled again, a smaller smile.

"It must be a challenging situation for your family. And for her, of course." Kate paused. "You know, it's part of our situation that my mother is very ill. That's why she's living with us."

Amy nodded.

"It's very hard for her . . ." Kate's voice trailed off. "Well, for everyone."

"My mother died of cancer."

57

"She did?" Kate wanted to know; she wanted to know everything.

"I don't remember much about it. She was just in bed all the time." Amy spoke matter-of-factly. The naked blond lashes of her eyes would look spiky if they were wet, like the fringe painted to frame the eyes of dolls. She frowned just slightly. "I think I was mad at her. You know, for never getting up much."

Kate was conscious of a hush in the room, a stillness that seemed to have risen from where the girl had been, from where Kate was going. "Do you mind if I ask you, Amy, what kind of cancer it was?"

"I don't know," Amy said, her expression unchanged.

Then she'd never asked. Kate was envious. She wished she knew less, would remember less; she wished she were five, a savage orphan playing in the yard. Someone who would grow up able to survive any blow and not know why, someone whose past had turned placid and unmoving. Amy's eyes were unarmed, undisturbed. Whatever she'd witnessed had vanished, pulled under by its own immense weight. Now there was a scar, Kate thought, like a depression in a landscape. She imagined a deep crater at the center of an island. Rain had fallen for an interminable season, perhaps for years, fallen and fallen. The crater had become a lake and the lake was wide and heavy. Now the sun shone down on a living surface that was vast and still. Is that how it would be?

"The ad said your baby is a boy. I love boys. How old is he?" Amy sat up a little straighter in her chair. She really did have a nose that could be described as pert, and freckles, and blond bangs.

"He's nearly two months old. His name is Alexander, but we call him Tatie."

"Tatie?"

"His middle name is Tateman, my family name, but he was so little at first, his names seemed too big. Now, of course, he's a giant. You'll be his first baby-sitter." Kate smiled hopefully, then she paused. "I should tell you too that Matthew has two boys, Sam and Jonah. They're eight and six. Their mother lives nearby, and they're here on Wednesdays and Fridays and Saturdays. But you won't have any responsibility for them. You'll just be helping with Tatie."

"I was listening for him," Amy said. "It's so quiet. Is he asleep?" She widened her eyes in a questioning expression and Kate noticed the starry clarity of her irises. Blue, with gray facets, like silver radiations.

"Yes, he's sleeping," Kate said, aware her tone must betray wonderment and relief. "He's happy most of the time," she hastened to add, "except when he needs to sleep. That takes a lot of walking and singing. On our part."

Amy nodded, as though this were perfectly normal. "He likes to travel while he thinks about sleeping."

"That's a good way of putting it," Kate said. It *was* very quiet in the house. Kate could hear the tick of a clock, and a car passing outside on the street seemed unnaturally loud. "Anyway, he's asleep, and my mother is resting. We're the only ones here. Believe me, when Sam and Jonah are around, you'll know it. But I guess you're used to—" What? Kate thought. Kids who can't believe what their father's gotten them into? Kids whose mother complains to them about the terms of her divorce agreement? "—Boys," she finished.

Amy nodded. "Tomorrow's Saturday. Would you like me to come over for a while, when the baby's awake? Give him a chance to get used to me?"

"Sure. We'd be glad to pay you to do that." She's great, Kate thought, or she has pressing bills. "It's pretty lively around here on Saturdays, but if you don't mind, we'd be glad to have you. And you'll get a chance to meet Matthew as well." She smiled. "Otherwise, it might be quite a while before your paths cross."

Amy nodded. "And what hours would you want me to work on weekdays?"

"How about three hours each afternoon? You choose the hours. We're always here." Kate made a gesture with her hands, the gesture in which the fingers open to show the hands are empty.

Kate had never been much of a singer, but Tatie liked songs. He wouldn't go down for a nap without being walked, his head drooping onto someone's shoulder, and whoever walked him had to sing. Kate thought he must feel the vibration of someone's voice, like a purring, when he was too asleep to hear. The walking went on and on until said caretaker tried to deposit him gently in his crib. Often he woke up at this juncture and the process had to begin again. Kate sometimes thought she would drop from fatigue. Her mother was still well enough to help a little in the daytime; she was the only one who could get away with sitting in a chair and "dandling" the baby on her knees, subtly bouncing or swaying him as she sang. Tatie seemed to know she was too weak to walk about with him. He lay on his stomach across her lap, and when he was asleep Kate would pad soundlessly over the floor and try to lift him into the old-fashioned iron baby bed that Matthew had recently set up in a corner of their bedroom. Today Katherine sang words to the tune of "Always," stroking the curve of Tatie's velvety head with one finger. *I love you, I love you, I love you,* she sang, for phrases whose real words she'd forgotten, then, *It's a sin to tell a lie.*

Kate sat on the bed, leaning back on the mound of pillows she used to prop herself up while nursing, and listened, adrift in a haze of genetic memory and hormones. She knew she'd heard the same words as a lullaby, all those long nights, earaches and hot-water bottles, when she was small enough to be held by someone as petite as her mother. Her childhood past had washed away from her, and the more recent past, between home and Matthew, was gone too. Nothing but now: her mother and Tatie in the blue armchair. The process by which the chair had come to rest in a house she'd bought with Matthew in Boston seemed a mystery not worth bothering about. The mystery seemed in motion still, as though they all bobbed and circled on some watery surface. Living on the lake, Kate thought, the lake that covered such endless depths with forgetfulness. No, that was wrong. They were only just approaching the lake. Or the lake didn't yet exist, only the island valley in which they lived, completely vulnerable, in the middle of nowhere. Slowly, inexorably, the rains would begin and the water would rise, but today there was such a blue sky above them. Her mother sang, a soft, unremarkable tunelessness, and arched her brows at Kate in a signal it was time. Kate knew she should get up and take the baby, but she couldn't bear to move, or to separate them.

Her mother broke the spell. She stopped singing and whispered, "Did that girl take the job?"

Kate nodded. "Amy. She seems perfect."

"When does she start?"

"Tomorrow," Kate mouthed.

"I'd still like to give him a morning bottle," she said softly. "I'm part of his routine." She patted Tatie with one hand and held up the plastic cylinder they referred to as a bottle with the other. It was really just a holder that served as a receptacle for tubular plastic bags of breast milk. The bags, marked in red milligrams, came in perforated rolls. Kate filled one twice a day, fastened it with a twist-tie, and froze it. The freezer portion of the refrigerator was full of elongated plastic bags of frozen breast milk, each carefully dated with a grease pencil. Kate had a system: she nursed Tatie from one breast, then emptied the other into a portable plastic pump. The pharmacist at the health plan had referred to it as "a traveling pump, small enough to keep in your briefcase." Kate had never owned a briefcase, even during her stint as a university lecturer, but she was sure that not even an astoundingly successful corporate mother could outdo her as bovine producer. Accustomed to "nursing on demand," she had only to attach the pump's gentle suction and milk poured into the clear tube in three distinct threads, a full eight ounces so forcefully expressed it frothed.

"I never saw a baby eat like this one," her mother said. "He must be healthy."

"Of course he's healthy," Kate said.

There was a pause, a kind of lag in which they collaborated. Kate's mother worried about Alexander. When Kate had taken him in for his two-week checkup, the pediatrician sent her directly to Children's Hospital. The baby was "a bit jaundiced." They'd kept him under lights for the rest of the day while Kate walked back and forth between the lounge and the ICU, waiting and nursing, nursing and waiting. Matt had phoned Katherine to reassure her that the problem, more usual just after birth, would resolve; they would "pink Alexander up" and monitor his bilirubin afterward to be certain. When mother and baby were released at dusk, Matt was still at work. It was Kate's mother who met her at the door. I was so afraid they wouldn't let you bring that baby home, she'd said tearfully, embracing Kate with Alexander between them. In her mother's arms, Kate forgot the abundant medical reassurance with which she'd left the hospital and grew tearful as well. Not bring him home? The winter twilight in which they'd stood seemed for a moment the advance flank of a darkness that might not lift, a darkness so blue it wanted all of them. There. The thought was where Kate touched bottom even now. She visualized swimming back up hard and fast as a watery surface danced above her. A warm surface, lit with summer. Why not? Hadn't someone, somewhere, advised directing one's fantasies, even the dark ones? The pediatrician still looked carefully at Alexander's color each visit. That's his job, Matt would remind Kate. Things can develop with any baby. If it happens, we'll deal with it then. So far, he's fine.

Now Katherine changed the subject. "Are Sam and Jonah coming tonight?"

"It's Friday," Kate reminded her.

"Take this baby then. I'd better go and rest, so I can help you with dinner and stand the ruckus."

"Mom, you don't need to help get dinner."

"Sure I do. I'm happy to, as long as I can."

When Kate's mother came to live with them, Kate had been seven months pregnant and they'd only been in the house—the "respectable house," Kate called it—for two weeks. Her first house in Boston, the first house she'd ever owned, had been a two-family on a hill in Jamaica Plain. She'd bought it for her own thirtieth birthday with money from an artist's grant and with salary from the two-year teaching appointment her second book of poems had engendered. The house didn't cost much. The neighborhood was not yet gentrified and domestic squabbles took place on the sidewalks, escalating until the police came. The couple across the street, who'd once threatened Kate when she had their broken-down car towed from in front of her driveway, were prime offenders. Now Kate lay in bed at night in an enclave called Pill Hill, because doctors had built these expansive houses a hundred years ago, and heard her former neighbors' voices tearing through the soft dark. Kate had never known their names. The woman would stand on the second-floor porch and scream down at the man, *I've called the cops! You betta get outa heah!* and he'd yell up at her for all the world to hear, *You're an unfit motha! Everybody knows it! He oughta be taken away from you!* They had a child, a son, who looked to be seven or eight, and the mother screamed at him from the same porch, up and down the street. His name was Mark but she pronounced it "Mack." "Mack!" she yelled in her shrill Southie accent, "Mack! You! Mack!" Kate saw the boy in dreams now, scuffing along down the hill in the narrow street, frowning and woebegone, and then she'd wake with her breasts like rocks, aching and full.

. . .

Matthew had taken a week off from his medical practice when Tatie was first born. Very briefly, he'd been Kate's doctor. She joked that it wasn't too late for her to file a sexual harassment suit, but in fact his harassment had seemed reticent and endearing, given the courtships to which she was accustomed. Her other relationships, with musicians, writers, academics, and the odd photographer or painter, could be more properly classified as firestorms or conflagrations, intense and short-lived, though she had to admit a substantial number of them had resulted in enduring friendships once the ashes had cooled. Matt had merely interviewed her, as required by the health plan that employed him. Kate had never belonged to a health plan, but she couldn't receive a salary from her teaching job or process her papers until she took the required physical. Signing in at the lobby desk, she'd noticed a man in a trench coat watching her. She got onto the elevator, on her way to Matthew's office, and the man observing her got on as well. He was about her height, and certainly looked nonthreatening, but she didn't often return the smiles of men she didn't know. She looked away, went where she was told by yet another person behind a desk, and slipped on the paper gown she found obligingly provided in examination room one. She sat on the table, waiting, and then Matthew, who was, of course, the man in the trench coat, walked in. He wore a white coat now and a stethoscope, and they both laughed, and he sat down to interview her. *Here at the Mayflower Plan we try to encourage more personal, informed patient-physician relationships, and I wonder if you'd mind if I take your history and ask you a few questions.* Kate supposed someone who admitted being a poet must have seemed exotic to him.

She would not have seen him again, at least not soon, except that she was invited to teach in India for a month and had to be inoculated. When she called to schedule the shots, he told her on the phone he did remember her, that he'd found her books in a Cambridge shop, and there wouldn't be any problem getting the shots in time. Later he told her doctors didn't take time to do inoculations, the nurses did them, but she received her shots from Matt personally. After the last one, they went into his office as he filled out a card for her to carry in her passport. Nervously, he said he'd never made this request of a patient before, and he'd certainly understand if she didn't think it was a good idea, but he was wondering if, when she got back from India, they might have lunch. Sometime. Kate told him she really didn't date, and she sort of had a boyfriend, but, well, yes, they could probably have lunch.

Then sixteen weeks passed in which life changed utterly. By the time Kate got back to Boston, she felt as though she'd been dipped in a vat of acid. She looked like herself, though dark with sun and thinner, from the dysentery, but she had changed forms, molecularly, within the shell of her body. There was all that had occurred in India and Sri Lanka, and then the weeks, later, on her own in Nepal, and there was flying back to the States, where an emergency message, relayed through her publisher, awaited her. Apparently her family had been trying to contact her without success: her mother was at Cleveland Clinic, the large medical center closest to her hometown, where she'd undergone surgery for lung cancer. Kate went back to the airport immediately, her bag still packed with inexpensive cotton dresses purchased at open markets in Madras and Delhi. Her parents had been divorced for twelve years. Even before that, since adolescence, Kate had been her mother's confidante. She would be her partner now, in this long dance, this last boat trip, a trip in which they seemed to drift and drift, hearing at intervals the terrible roar of the rapids they approached.

It had been summer in India, summer in Sri Lanka.

When Kate thought about India, she was afflicted with a kind of mind's-eye blindness. It occurred to her that India was the real world, and this one was a dream. The real world was not knowable; it was an immersion in sounds and smells, in different, ancient air, in death that burst with color. Metamorphosis was actual; there were orchids in the streets, in the gutters that ran with shit and grainy water. She couldn't see the gutters anymore, she only heard the sound of the water rattling in them. Now, when she finally got Tatie down for his nap in the afternoon, and the house was quiet, she'd sit, drifting and paralyzed, watching him sleep. There was always the same picture in her mind, not of India, which had eaten all its pictures, but of Sri Lanka, where she first went when the teaching in Madras was over. She saw herself at the lake in Sri Lanka, the lake in Kandy, by the Temple of the Tooth. Within the massive temple, encased in caskets within caskets, lay a tooth of the Buddha, though no one had seen it for centuries. Lines of pilgrims stretched along the stone terrace, winding through the arching outer doors. But Kate was walking around the lake on the wide dirt path where the same boy always crouched with his cloth-covered jar. For a few rupees he would play his pipe, uncover the jar, and mesmerize the cobra inside into rising, tensile, its hooded head erect and sexual. But each version of her daydream was the same: Kate walked past the boy, and he didn't ask her for money anymore. She walked around the lake and it was dusk, and the bats began to swarm above the trees, and the lake turned colors. Tatie was there with her; somehow, he was the water itself, and Kate simply walked, waiting to know what was next.

Now, she thought, making dinner is next. Then Matt and the boys would arrive. Sam and Jonah would be thoroughly engaged in what Kate's stepfamily manuals termed "transition." Stepfamilies needed manuals. The boys often fought, and Matt often let them, as though they were voicing what he couldn't. Jonah would bring his roller skates and rumble through the downstairs rooms, leaving long black streaks across the wood floors. Matt might suggest they all go outside, but Jonah's myriad needs (a glass of water, his red football, a bathroom stop) required numerous reentries. Sam was happy to stay outside, but Jonah seemed intent on goading him into an indoor chase, perhaps because Jonah could be faster in the living-dining-entryway arena, where he could negotiate the turns on wheels. Lately he arrived with the skates already strapped to his feet, and Sam already mad at him, due to some altercation in Matt's van during transit.

"Katie? Should I peel some potatoes?" Kate's mother was peering in at the doorway, whispering. She wore one of the velour sweat suits Kate had bought her at the Gap: the same suit in five colors, so she could mix and match. She'd grown so thin she was always cold, and she lay down so frequently it didn't make sense anymore to wear the tailored clothes she'd favored before she got sick. She'd taught elementary school while she compiled advanced degrees, then risen through administrative ranks as a reading specialist. Soon after the diagnosis, she'd had to retire early from her job as director of a federally funded remedial reading program in Kate's hometown.

"You can if you want to, Mom. But sit down while you do it, okay? If you do too much, you won't feel like sitting through dinner." Kate moved to get up but her mother waved her away. Katherine had consented to chemo in Boston, so she could "live to see the baby." And she had; she'd even taken care of Kate.

"Take it easy," she told Kate now. "I'm fine this week. It's my good week, before they zap me again. Next week I'll be flat on my back, and you'll be carrying that tray up and down with my meals. As though you don't have enough to do." She took an ever-present Kleenex from her sleeve and wiped her nose. "At least you found that little girl to baby-sit. That should help." She dropped her voice again, until Kate could barely hear her. "Oh, look. He's waking up. He doesn't see us. Look how beautiful he is."

Kate moved toward the head of the crib soundlessly; she loved to watch him when he thought he was by himself. Tatie lay completely still, only memorizing with his eyes. He was always happy when he woke, wholly intense and contemplative. For long moments he looked out the second-story window by his crib and watched the top of a tall pine tossing in the wind. What was he seeing? What he looked through was not defined in his mind as a window, and the shape was not a tree. The icy tips of the pine's long branches scratched the cold outer pane lightly and then were tossed away again. Through them the faraway sky was brilliant winter blue, the crystal blue of air made hard and pure by cold. Above the room and the house, above Pill Hill and High Street, where traffic never ceased, the inverted bowl of the sky deepened and deepened; for miles, the sky filled with swirled cloud and vapor and emptied into blackness. The water of eons, Kate thought, the lake above the lake. She watched Tatie see the colors and the motion; he never seemed excited or afraid. He lay quietly, his eyes moving as the branches made their round circuit on the glass.

Dinner was late. Kate's mother got nervous when meals were late, when schedules were unmet.

"Should I turn the potatoes on yet? Katie? Should I set the table?" Katherine sat perched in her straight-backed chair. The heavy ironstone plates, five of them, sat in the center of the table beside the folded tablecloth, stacked cups, silver. Every evening Kate had to move everything to the counter to put the tablecloth on, then put everything back, but her mother liked getting things ready. They both knew she took the plates from the cabinet one by one, and then she sat down to rest.

"No Mom, I'll get to it. The meat's not done." Kate had Tatie in the Baby Bouncer, a front sling that Matt and Kate had rechristened the Mommy Bouncer. The sling was the butt of assorted sarcastic jokes—Kate called it "the only bouncing Mommy gets," and Matt called it "the only bouncing Mommy wants or understands"—but in fact it was a lifesaver. Tatie could reach Kate's neck and chin and jaw if she faced him toward her; he was temporarily sated with Mommy smells and tastes and he might be happy for fifteen minutes if he'd nursed recently. Now he latched on to Kate's chin with his warm wet gums and sucked her voraciously as she tossed salad.

"Did you use my recipe for the meat loaf?" her mother asked.

"Yes, I did, to the letter," Kate lied.

"Are you going to let him do that? Your face will be black and blue. Here, let me hold him."

"No, he's so heavy." Kate turned the gas on under the potatoes and washed her hands, then she slid her smallest finger carefully into Tatie's mouth. It was important not to break his concentration; he turned his face to the side and settled in by the curve of her throat.

"His eyes are closing," Kate's mother said. "Look out, here comes Jonah."

There was a rumble as Jonah sailed between them on his skates, hit the kitchen wall and turned to sail away.

"Jonah, not in here." Kate stepped quickly to the left. "You need to stay out of the kitchen. Or how about using the driveway? Skates belong outside."

"I can't turn out there," he said, jumping the threshold.

"Babe! Babe!" Sam called from the living room.

"What's he talking about?" Kate's mother asked.

"He brought his gerbil," Kate said.

"Good Lord. I hope the dogs don't get hold of it. Sounds like it's loose. Is Matt out there?" She reached for a dish towel and held it up to Kate. "Here, bend down and I'll wipe you off."

"Oh, don't bother."

"You're covered with saliva."

"So what. I'm always covered with something. I drip. It's my new vocation. I drip and I dry and then I smell funny."

"Oh, you don't at all. You're just beautiful."

"Sure, I know I am." Kate picked up the tablecloth with her free hand and slipped it unobtrusively into a drawer.

"What are you doing?"

"I'm putting this cloth away. I don't want to use tablecloths anymore."

"Well, they just make the table look so pretty and—prepared."

"Preparation isn't everything. We've reached saturation point here. I don't need to launder tablecloths."

"You sound angry," her mother said. "I know it's hard, but you've got to try to be patient."

"Screw patience."

Her mother pointed at the stove. "The potatoes are boiling over. They're going to be pulpy."

Kate lunged back toward the stove, dimly aware of an approaching rumble, and Jonah hit her broadside. Tatie woke up and began a betrayed wailing as white speckled froth cascaded down the front of the oven.

"Jonah!" Kate said. "I asked you not to skate in here! Matthew? Matthew!"

"She ran into me," Jonah said. "Dad, Kate ran into me."

"All right, all right." Matt appeared in the doorway, holding the gerbil in one hand.

"Where have you been?" Kate asked.

"I was chasing the gerbil. Here, give me the baby."

"I can't get dinner in all this insanity. You're going to have to take this baby and walk him in the stroller."

"I'm *trying* to take the baby. Give him to me."

"Well, take him! And Jonah, get those skates off. If you wear those skates on your feet in this house again, I'm going to bury them."

Matt looked at Kate's mother. "Your daughter sounds like Khrushchev. Next thing we know, she'll be banging her shoe on the table."

"No!" Jonah said. "No! I want my skates!"

Matt handed off the gerbil to Jonah and then lifted Tatie from the Mommy Bouncer as the wailing increased in volume. "Jonah, come out with me and you can hold on to the stroller and skate on the sidewalk.

Take Babe and put him in his cage. Don't drop him! I just spent ten minutes finding him in the couch."

"Good!" Jonah chortled. "Good! I'm still skating! I'm skating with Babe!"

"No," Matt said. *"Put Babe in his cage.* Right now."

"Sam," Jonah called, "I'm skating with Babe!" He rounded the corner with the terrified gerbil in hand.

"Dad," Sam called, "where's Babe?"

"He's skating to Babe's cage, that's all," Matt said. "Come on outside. We're going for a walk."

The screen door slammed three times. The din receded. There was silence. Kate turned off the burner and sat down. Froth continued to run onto the floor. "Oh, my God," she said.

"I didn't appreciate that crack about your shoe," her mother said. "He could control those children a little better. It's very hard for *you* to do."

"He's afraid they'll be unhappy," Kate said.

They could hear the clock ticking. Her mother sighed. "You certainly have a full plate, little girl."

"I'm not full," Kate said. "I'm starving."

"There, there," her mother said.

"If I can't wear them on my feet," Jonah said, "I'm going to wear them on my hands. My skates are gloves now."

"As long as you don't walk on your hands," Kate answered. They were sitting on Kate's bed. The boys were watching television and Kate was perusing Alexander's baby book. The baby book had been a present from friends and seemed destined never to fulfill its function. It still cracked when Kate opened it and the snowy pages were untouched.

"How come you only have one TV?" Jonah asked. "How come you keep it in your bedroom?"

"Oh, I don't know," Kate said. "I never used to watch television much."

"Our TVs are in the living room and the kitchen and my mom's room," Jonah said, "and they're bigger than yours."

"Dad likes to watch cartoons with us," Sam said. "How come Dad is doing the dishes?"

Because he's no fool, Kate thought. "Because it's good for everyone to help out," she said, "and I cooked dinner, so your dad is cleaning up."

"You could clean up," Sam said.

"I could," Kate said, "but mothers who are up at night with babies don't get much sleep, and I'm a little tired. Besides, I like to watch TV with you too."

Sam didn't take his eyes from the screen. "But you're not watching," he said.

"Sure I am," Kate said. "I can do two things at once. I'm looking at TV and I'm looking at this book."

How would she ever catch up? Every time she picked up the baby book, which was composed in the style of a luxurious fill-in-the-blanks test, she felt she'd fallen farther behind in life. Already it was too late to remember all the details about the pregnancy (under "What Mother Liked to Eat" Kate wrote "Whatever") or paste in pictures of "Mother and Me, Month by Month Before the Birth." Mindful of her own interest in artifacts about a past she couldn't remember, Kate persisted carefully through "Family Tree," leaving blanks for the lost ones in Russia, names Matthew and his parents didn't know. Under "First Baby-sitters," she wrote "Granny," and then she remembered Amy. Amy, Kate thought. She and Amy would have talks, and she would take a photo of Amy and Tatie to put into this book. Maybe next week she would do that. Feeling encouraged, she pressed onward through "Comments on Baby's Looks," writing appropriate phrases but remembering that stark moment when the doctor had chanted, *There, there, the head has crowned. Now push! Push! Don't stop—* His voice continued for her against the *Bam! Smash!* backdrop of a cartoon laser fight on television. Sam and Jonah lay with their legs entwined, Jonah cradling the offending roller skates. They lay in his arms, identically marooned, their orange rubber wheels upturned. The wheels suddenly looked incongruous and sad, bright and overly large, the wheels of skates not quite real, but they were scratched silver in the centers with use.

Jonah felt her glance and looked over. "What's that book?"

"It's Alexander's baby book." She turned the page to "Advice to Baby from Family Members." "Here it says to write down our advice, so Tatie can read it when he grows up."

Jonah slid off the bed, headfirst, wearing the skates on his hands.

Their wheels creaked a kind of rubberized grinding as he pulled himself along the floor to Kate's side of the bed. "I have some advice," he said, peering up on all fours, his face at her elbow.

"Okay. I'll write it for you." She took up her pen hopefully.

"Get your own roller skates," he chirped, "because you can't use mine."

"You really want me to put that?" Kate asked.

"Will you?" He sat up on his knees, the skates held in midair as though poised for applause.

"Yes, if you want me to."

He dropped to his hands and knees again, beaming. "No, just put 'Be sure to have roller skates.' "

Sam had edged closer on the bed, and he watched as Kate wrote the words. Then Jonah put his skates down to print his name on the page.

"Sam-I-Am," Kate said, "what's your advice to Tatie?"

He thought a moment, then raised his eyes to hers, smiling. "Don't get a divorce."

"You can't tell him that," Jonah said flatly. "If Dad wasn't getting a divorce, Alexander wouldn't have a father."

"Well—" began Kate.

"Yes, he would," Sam said. "Dad would see him on Saturdays."

Jonah looked back at the television, where red fires were erupting from ray guns shaped like trumpets. "He would not, stupid. He always sees us then."

Sam shrugged and looked down at the empty page.

Kate sighed. "How about, 'Try not to get a divorce'?"

Sam leaned over near her, looking at Jonah's signature; the *J* was very large and resembled a sailboat whose sail had turned upward in some aberrant wind and now existed parallel to the sky. Sam touched it, leaving a smudge of silver. "Yeah," he said. "Okay. Put 'Try *hard.*' "

"I will, Sam," Kate said. They were both satisfied. He sat close as she wrote it down, and then he signed his name in script.

"You know," Kate said softly, looking at the words, "it's just about time for you guys to get ready for bed."

"Not yet," Sam said. He leaned away, back into television position.

"Not me," Jonah said. He pulled himself out into the hallway, scooting along on his arms and elbows, pushing the skates in front of him.

Kate felt she could sleep forever. She leaned back on the pillow and closed her eyes. The skates squeaked. She could still hear running water downstairs in the sink, the sound of dishes. She listened for baby sounds, Tatie crying from the downstairs travel bed they kept in the dining room. She heard only the memory of his cry. But she heard, truly, behind the halting lament of the skates, her mother's slow progress up the stairs, and the little groan of the banister as Katherine leaned on it with all her weight, resting halfway up. Soon it would be dark, it would be night. They would all sleep. Kate would fall into the narrow two- or three-hour crevice her baby allowed her. It was a deep crevice, sheer, with walls, and Kate longed for it as though it were something she could eat or touch. She wanted to be inside it. *Don't stop.* She knew how to push. She pushed until the ripping pain came to a point and then she had pushed all the way. *Again. You waited so long. Now do it.* She wasn't sure anymore there really was a baby; she almost forgot she was giving birth; she was just trying to stay alive. *We've been here thirty-six hours. Almost there. Push.* They'd made her go to sleep, that was why. The sun had come up and gone down and come up outside the big window; doctors came on and off shift. The new one said, "Put the monitor on her. I don't like the way this labor is progressing." Kate nodded at her midwife and her midwife said, "No drugs. She'll do it. She's on top of it." "I understand that, but she's tachycardic and the labor has slowed. This will let her sleep for an hour so she can make it the rest of the way." "We need an IV here." "Get the monitor." No drugs. "She's on top of it. Let her do it." Excruciating to lie down. The panting and the counting was a lie, none of it worked. Just breathing. When she was a child and dawdled, her mother had prompted, "What are you waiting for, Christmas?" Kate stood up, breathing. They held her up. She sat on the birthing table, tilted all the way up. *There he is, to his shoulders. Reach down.* She did, and pulled him out. It was dawn of Christmas morning. She'd delivered her baby with her own hands and he gazed at her with open eyes.

He was crying. "Sorry," Kate heard. "You asleep? Someone's hungry. Jonah! Into bed. I'll be right in." The television was off and Matt stood over her. Alexander leaned toward her from his father's arms and she sat up to take him.

.   .   .

It really was night. She made her way to him along the sleep wall. She could hear him breathing and the side of the wall felt warm in the dark, soft with growth or dust; it smelled of earth and the sweet tang of her milk. She came out along the passage where the slippers and sandals were piled and saw moonlight rising from the lake like smoke. She moved toward the water and he beckoned her close; it was Amrit, with his coarse black Prince Valiant hair and broken teeth, though she'd not met Amrit then, in Kandy. Later, after Sri Lanka and India, in Kathmandu, he would speak to her in German, then French, when he said things he didn't want her to understand or remember, when he wanted to excite her. The mist from the lake was all around him. She was too far away to touch him but she felt the fullness of his mouth on her face, along her jaw, and her eyes welled with tears. He shook his head impatiently and spoke faster in his Heidelberg German, as though time were short; *Kathmandu,* she heard, and *Ist es weit zu gehen,* and he gestured toward the pilgrim walking near them, a woman swathed in cloth. She was pushing a cart in the shadows and the wheels creaked in the dust; she was dirty and her face was streaked, but the headpiece of her sari pulled away to reveal her bright hair. Kate saw that she was Amy. The cart was smaller, a stroller now, barred in front like a cage, with two high, flared handles for pushing; it rattled savagely. Whose child was trapped there? Amrit would understand; he was in engineering; all foreign-educated Nepali men studied engineering or hotel management. Hadn't Amrit said so? Kate felt his arms beneath her hips as though he were lifting her to embrace her, but he turned to look at Amy: Amy saw them and moved toward the water. It was a wheelchair she pushed now, a small one sized for a child, and the chair was empty, and she walked into the lake. The chair was hard to push and it tilted and listed, bobbing like a boat, then the water took it, rippling. Amy stood still, watching, her hands in the silvery lake. *Namaste.* Amrit turned Kate's face away and she saw the temple, its grainy walls glowing pink. A child wailed, inconsolable.

4

Though it was March, Amy the baby-sitter proved adept at Christmas carols. She walked Tatie tirelessly, singing "Jingle Bells" softly and slowly, so slowly that the words took on a sorrowful tinge, like the coloring of someone's lost memory. Kate supposed that babies all over America were being sung to in a language of artifacts and extinctions. Now there were no horse-drawn sleighs; perhaps someday there would be no horses, but the song would still be sung. Kate herself tended to sing cowboy songs—"Red River Valley," or the theme from *Rawhide. Rolling, rolling, rolling,* she sang in low tones, thinking of Jonah on his skates. But kids didn't watch cowboys on television anymore; Rowdy and Wishbone and Gil Favor, the boss man, had given way to animated superheroes and spacemen. The popular imagination seemed to have given up on Earth: if anyone was saved, help would come from beyond the stars. Outer space was where our interests lay. Popular culture taught children to believe in UFOs whose inhabitants were collectively wise and physically luminous, a cross between robots and angels. Even so, wars were not obsolete; they were galactic in nature and required sophisticated weapons, also luminous, metallic, and preferably glowing. Space seemed to exist as a paradox of arena and New World, where there were no memories at all.

Now that Tatie would stay with Amy, Kate found herself with an hour or two free in the afternoons. The baby slept; Amy cleaned up. Kate's mother rested in her room with the door shut. The dogs slept; Kate's fox-colored mongrel lolled in the brick entry and her mother's dog napped on newspapers by the kitchen door. Kate first thought she'd use the time to work, but the little room she'd intended to use as an office was full of baby gear and clean, unfolded laundry, and anyway, she was too sleep-deprived to think clearly. Every day, she took herself away from the house, on foot. She thought of herself as brain-damaged, all her edges softened. She didn't read, she didn't write. She walked along, hearing her boots on the pavement. She never went far, only to the little row of shops at the bottom of the hill. Today she planned to stop at the second-hand store and look at a European pram she'd seen in the window, with the idea that it would, someday, be spring. They already owned a practi-cal stroller, a long-considered, state-of-the-art Perego: a pram seemed a luxurious fairy tale, a story with a happy ending. The pram was English, no doubt; Americans didn't manufacture prams. Prams didn't fold up and required boulevards or wide sidewalks; ideally they were managed by a person whose job it was to push them along in a luxuriance of spa-cious time. In fact, Kate felt she had entered such a time, a time when every moment was limitless and fluid and heavy, drenched in sensation and fatigue. It seemed this time would never end. She passed the dry cleaners, she passed the fire station, she passed the convenience store. The secondhand shop was just next door; it was run by a ladies auxiliary of unknown origin and seemed always to be open. There seemed to be just one lady present at any particular time, and she was never obvious, but materialized from somewhere in the back after a subtle, peaceful interval.

The pram was not in the window. Kate turned the ornate knob of the heavy door and went in, hearing the attenuated tinkle of the bell. The bell had a shivery, melodious sound, like a reminder, high and gone; sometimes Kate heard it in her sleep. And there sat the pram, off to the side; perhaps someone had purchased it. What a boat of a thing, with its big round wheels and silver fenders. Kate felt weak even to think of pushing it along. The bed seemed large enough for a smallish, cramped adult in fetal position, and Kate was tempted to crawl inside. On a shelf of used toys above it Kate saw a perfectly intact Millennium Falcon, one of the original *Star Wars* spaceships. Though she disliked plastic toys, Kate was attracted to the thing, to its shape and the fantasy of what it represented. She thought of buying it for Tatie and saving it. Then she thought of Sam and Jonah. Matt's boys lived with Matt three days a week; they didn't exactly live with Kate, not yet, though she cooked their meals and made their beds and hoped for their approval in some far-off sphere, a sphere in which they would stop bickering long enough to notice her. They were only safe with one another now, and so their constant argument continued, a series of trusting, mildly varied refrains that woke and slept according to their need. One Millennium Falcon would inspire them to hostile negotiations, at which Sam would triumph, and then outright battle. It seemed to Kate that Sam and Jonah fought more than any other mortals on earth, completely unfettered by any regard for adult authority. It's the age, Kate's mother liked to say.

It was the age, Kate thought, the age of wonders. She reached up toward the spaceship and felt someone approach her from behind.

"Let me get that for you," said a voice. "Things are piled so haphazardly around here, I'm afraid everything will fall on you." One of the auxiliary ladies had appeared; Kate hadn't encountered this one before. She was at least seventy, her hair was permed and blue, and she was quite short. She produced a folded metal step stool, positioned it, and climbed four neat steps to reach the shelf. Elevated, she tilted her head back to gaze through her bifocals at the Millennium Falcon. "What is it?" she asked Kate. "It's been up here a long time, looks like."

"Oh, well," Kate said, "it's a toy, a spaceship, sort of."

"There, I have it. Those masks were piled on top. They've shed glitter all over everything." She reached down to give the object to Kate, tilting it in the shine of light from the window.

The ship was about the circumference of a large pizza, layered in shape, like a cake, with two short, propellant protrusions at one end, like atrophied legs; it was marked all over its gray plastic surface with numerous minute indentions. Windows, thought Kate, for very tiny travelers. Specks of gold and silver glistened as she turned it in her hands, but the older dust layering each crevice was softer in aspect, a subtle fur. Kate traced its lines with her hand and found a little slot, half as broad as her forefinger, that pulled down. A little door. Unaccountably, her heart leapt.

"I'll take it," Kate said. "How much is it?"

"Five dollars?" said the lady. She had climbed down and stood at Kate's elbow.

"Would you have a bag I could put it in?" Kate asked.

"I don't know about that, dear. It's such an odd shape, isn't it? I'll have to look around here."

"It's just, I don't want the kids to see it. In case I want to save it for a present—"

"Oh, you have children, of course you do. And there must be a baby in the picture." She leaned closer conspiratorially and dropped her voice. "I saw you looking at the buggy. Isn't it quite something?"

"It is," Kate agreed.

"The hood folds all the way down, like this," she said, demonstrating, "for sun, or all the way up, for shade. And there's even a plastic piece, in the same blue, that snaps across for rain. And you see these little handles?" She looked up to be sure Kate did. "You just *depress* them, and the whole thing comes away. See?" She lifted off the entire bed of the pram, a contraption shiny and velvety at once, and nearly as big as she. She stood holding it a few inches above its empty chassis and looked at Kate expectantly. Was she a little out of breath?

"So handy," Kate volunteered. "Definitely."

"And the original mattress and pillow." She replaced the bed on its frame. "Oh, they built them to last, and someone's taken very good care. Now, let me wipe off that—toy. It's going to get you all dusty." Kate handed over the Falcon and the auxiliary lady began to rub it vigorously with a towel, nodding her blue hair. "Not many things in here are as clean as that buggy. It was in plastic till we put it in the window. It's English, you know."

Kate took the Falcon back, and shut the little door. "It must be expensive."

"Fifty, dear. I can't take less than fifty." She touched the broad white handle of the pram and bounced it softly on its wheels. "Try it out while I go and look for a shopping bag."

Kate put the spaceship in the pram and began to wheel it down the wide main aisle of the shop. Nestled into cushions, framed by the regal hood, the Millennium Falcon looked odd, like a strange, flat, satisfied baby, or important and dangerous, like a bomb. The pram moved along smoothly on level ground, sighing on its broad wheels. It seemed the most solid object Kate had held on to in weeks, and big enough to hold anything.

The lady from the auxiliary was back. "My, I'm afraid I can't find any bags wide enough," she said. "We only have the grocery sacks that we bring in from home."

"I guess I'll take the pram," Kate said.

The lady smiled. "Then our problem is solved." She picked up a folded blue baby blanket from the counter and placed it over the space-ship. "And take this as well, for being such a good customer."

"Thanks so much." Kate reached into her shoulder bag for her wallet.

"Not a bit, dear. And we do accept checks with ID." She stepped back and folded her hands benignly, nodding once.

Kate found herself outside the shop with the pram, as though she'd always stood in front of a secondhand store holding the broad white han-dle of a noble conveyance. She considered continuing her walk down-town into the village, where she might have a cup of tea. Perhaps today was the day she could do that. If she went to the tea shop she could drink something herbal and bounce the pram with a subtle touch as she gazed out the big front window. The Millennium Falcon certainly wouldn't complain. Kate moved the pram experimentally back and forth, thinking it over. Other nice auxiliary-type ladies or professional mothers might lean to peer into the pram, inquiring as to the age and fortitude of its young inhabitant. Kate would smile serenely and adjust the blanket, tucking in the blue satin edge. Five years old at least, she'd say, maybe more, and such a good sleeper, I never hear a peep. He actually requires the company and animation of others; he's that type, a born performer, and really into fantasy.

But no, not today. She'd come to her usual stopping place, standing in sight of the big intersection where High Street bisected Route 9. She wondered if she was going crazy, just now, when she had so much to do. She'd always been afraid of going crazy; what a strange term it was, any-way. *Them cattle are loco,* Wishbone had said to Rowdy. Kate liked that episode, when the entire herd had eaten some sort of psychotropic plant and stampeded. "Loco" was a fabulous word, actually, with its intimation of movement—locomotion, locating, finding a place and moving on from that place, all at once. No, Kate thought, as long as I can think about words, I'm not crazy; it's just that I'm not strong. Whatever she had got used up at home. The rest of the world was too much for her; she could only go to this corner. In a car she was safe; she could drive past this spot with just a shadow on her shoulder, but on foot, herself, she only looked. Crossing at the big intersection meant walking across five lanes and a concrete island. Somehow the island was most frightening. Kate was afraid of being marooned there, with cars whizzing by before her and behind her. She imagined tilting backward into traffic, *straight as a board,* as her mother would say. Or tumbling forward. Or simply walking across without looking, against the light, like an angel. Not even loco cattle would pull such a stunt, and they were high on something, probably jimsonweed, which used to grow in the fields of the long-ago land where Kate was born, where her mother had been healthy and completely, continually capable, a pillar of her community, a pillar turned to salt in a long, loveless marriage that finally ended as the children went off to college. Kate, flush with hippie feminism, had welcomed news of the divorce; she'd carried the burden of her mother's confidence for years, and even before words were spoken, her childhood had unfolded at the strained boundary of her mother's entrapment. In the yard of a ranch-style brick house on a rural road, she'd watched cows on the rumpled hills across the two-lane. They were somnolent heifers who scratched their necks on the barbed-wire fence through the long summers and bunched in a corner of the field. Occasionally one bawled like a big needy supplicant and the others slung their heads about as though to look for the sound, switching their long tails at the bluebottle flies on their faces. Sloe-eyed Virginia Jerseys, they were the same shape and size as those in the restless, grounded cloud of the herd on *Rawhide,* but they bore little resemblance in spirit to what the cowboys managed. It was in those grade-school years that Kate rode the school bus home and watched reruns of the show each day at four o'clock. She remembered dolly shots of the stampede, with Wishbone driving a Conestoga wagon overrun by cattle, and Rowdy coming alongside on a horse to rescue him just as the wagon catapulted down a ravine. They knew ravines, those *Rawhide* guys. Rowdy got most of the heroics and ended up a movie star, but Gil Favor, the boss man with the tight, mournful eyes, was Kate's idea of a man. With him, she thought she could stand on that concrete island, right now, today. What was it about him? It was as though he'd already been where Kate was going, when so many others around her were innocents. Steadfastly, they looked away from what she sensed was ahead for them all; they refused to acknowledge what approached, or to feel its chill breath hovering near them in sleep. At night it passed its thin dry lips along the narrow planes of Kate's collarbone and down, to the cleft of her breasts, and then she woke, lunging sharply away to keep it from where the baby put his mouth, from poisoning her milk and turning it black as blood. What's wrong? Matt would ask. You wake up like something's after you, he'd say then, making light. Do you have a guilty conscience I should know about?

Now Kate heard the unexpected sound of a bell and raised her eyes to see the auxiliary lady looking out at her from the doorway of the shop.

"Did you forget something, dear?"

"Oh, no. Sorry if I—"

"Not at all. Just wondered if you needed anything."

"No. No, I was just thinking." Kate tried to smile reassuringly. How long had she been standing here? How much time had passed?

"Of course." The auxiliary lady nodded. "Yes. I often do the same. Take stock, so to speak."

"Exactly," Kate said.

"Come back by, now. We often get in wonderful equipment. Children's things."

"Yes, I'll stop by," Kate said.

"Take care, then." The door shut. Her blue-tinted head, which barely cleared the window, faded back into the drowsy confines of the storefront.

Kate turned toward home. It seemed a shame to go back early, as though she'd failed in her mission to get away and return refreshed, or at least hydrated, aerated by cold brisk air. But the sky had darkened and was gray and bruised, like snow might dust the slush again with new powder. Kate reflected that she should have asked for the plastic covering the auxiliary lady had mentioned, for whatever had kept the pram so pristine in the shop. Never mind, she had the rain bonnet, and she snapped it on. *Dashing through the snow.* No wonder Amy sang Christmas songs; spring would never come. *O'er the fields*—that phrase made the song sound so old. Kate walked back past the long windows of the convenience store and saw herself reflected in watery chiaroscuro. The point of leaving the house for an hour or two was to walk about unencumbered, not nursing anyone or carrying anything, and now she had a large something to push up the steep hill of High Street. The slush was still considerable on some sections of the old sidewalk, which buckled and heaved in any case, toothsome bricks at angles. Kate knew every outcropping from staring at her feet each day, and she tried to steer accordingly. The pram, however, seemed less fragile than expected; each big wheel appeared to have an independent suspension, and they all moved smoothly along. Kate felt absurdly happy. The Millennium Falcon lay secure under its blue blanket, barely jostled. The edge of its platform peeked out and the little door in the side seemed to peer at Kate like an eye. She still wasn't sure what she would do with it when she got home. She could give it to Matt's kids, to whom she often gave presents in her transparent attempts to gain favor. They would know how to bang and smash it; plastic was meant to be smashed. But this toy was so untouched, unscratched, as though no one had ever played with it. Surely there was a reason someone had revered it so. She would keep it safe, Kate thought, put away somewhere, like an escape vehicle she might fit into when they were all through with her. *There's no such thing as a blended family,* one of Kate's stepfamily manuals intoned, *and if there is, it's the woman who gets blended.*

For a time Matt's boys had stopped speaking to her. Their mother had let them believe Kate was the reason their father had left. He'd lived in an apartment for a few months and taken nothing with him but his clothes and a kitchen table he'd made himself. Even the removal of the table had engendered tears and recriminations from his spouse, who had halted a long liaison with her married lover in hopes Matt would renounce all others as well. But her affair, which predated Matt's alliance by nearly a year, had allowed Matt room to maneuver. He bought a new bed, a couch, a table, bunk beds for the boys. Kate bought him a set of dishes. But, Dad, Jonah asked him, what are you going to do with all this when you move back home? He's not moving home, Sam had said. Sam faced things squarely, before they faced him. He hadn't worn glasses since the age of three for nothing.

Was it all for nothing? No, Kate would take hold of it all. She would push it all uphill in this royal pram, all of it but death. She could not support death, or hold it or configure it, or carry it with the rest. Death was a barely heard melody behind her, down the hill where the sky glowered;

it was the same secretive creeping that had begun in her mother's cells nearly two years ago.

At first, Kate's mother had stayed home and taken radiation therapy at the little cancer hospital near their rural town, but she grew worse, unable to live on her own despite help from a well-organized circle of friends. When she'd arrived, Kate had watched her wheeled up an airport walkway in a US Air wheelchair. Kate had spoken to her daily on the phone in the four months since she'd seen her, and the strength of her voice had belied the sudden advance of the illness. It might be too late, Kate had thought. Her mother sat erect in the approaching chair, abysmally thin, her face a set mask with anguished eyes, holding on her lap the small pet carrier that enclosed Katrina, her toy poodle. The dog had slept on Katherine's bed atop its own pillow for fifteen years. Deaf, nearly blind, drugged for the flight, Katrina only scratched feebly at the floor of the carrier with her sharp, miniature nails. Kate's mother said, in weakened tones as the chair came closer, "I know Katrina's a terrible bother, but I couldn't leave her behind." "Of course not," Kate said. "Haven't you baby-sat my dog lots of times?" "Well," Katherine had sighed, "I told her she'll be in Luna's territory: she'll just have to know her place." "Oh, they'll be fine," Kate said. She moved to take the carrier and her mother gestured to leave it be. Then Matt was beside them, greetings were exchanged with the family friend who'd come along, ostensibly to visit the city, and they'd moved on at an efficient momentum calculated to get Kate's mother prone in bed as soon as possible, and set up for treatment with the oncologist Matt had recommended by the next day. The birth of Kate's baby approached and her mother consented to chemotherapy, consented to leaving home, consented to never going home again, where she'd lived all her life. She crossed all those lines in her wheelchair, without a whimper, moving down an airport walkway. In its cage, her little dog made a sound. "Hush," she said.

Kate conjectured that all lines of transit came together in a starry radiance too bright to observe. In that adjacent dimension all was known. There, icons and realities and the figures of populous dreams and histories existed in equal importance, in true relationship, each according to its nature. In that place, manly cowboys glanced away from death and rode on through big-skyed plains and sage. Those who populated Millennium Falcons didn't recognize lines or points of location. Space was a continuum and they floated through it, ignoring boundaries, attached by tubes to what they breathed. There were no low valleys or red rivers, no wind to hear blow. No animals to feed and rescue, to pray for. *Hang your head over.* There was the black wonder of space pocked with stars, with intense, consuming fires. Inside their silver suits, the spacemen were alien to all they encountered, each an enclosed system, away and apart, and that was death. They lived in it, each of them alone as Kate's mother was alone. Death made the body alien as one tried to keep living inside it. Kate's mother had a new language, now that she was sick. She spoke always in the royal we.

Dr. Jansson says we try this new regimen for six weeks, then we check the X-rays.

We have to be at chemo at two o'clock.

We're doing well with the morphine—five teaspoons yesterday but only two today.

We couldn't sleep at all last night.

Kate stopped pushing and stood still. From here, halfway up the hill, she could see her street and the stone wall that edged the lot of her stucco house. Tatie must be awake by now, and Kate might return before Amy needed to make him a bottle of defrosted milk. Almost before the thought was complete in Kate's mind, her nipples stung sexually in a radiated pulsing and her milk let down. Her blouse would be wet through the harnesslike bra and absorbent nursing pads before she could get home. But there would be plenty left for the baby. The wind whipped at her coat, and she turned to look behind her down the hill. Traffic moved at the intersection; the lights had just changed and so it all surged forward, like energy held captive and released at once.

Kate rolled the pram up the short circular drive and over the brick stoop to the accompaniment of high- and low-pitched barking. As soon as she opened the big front door, the dogs jumped at her in tandem. The little poodle, whose rheumy nose was literally the size of a penny, dodged the footfalls of the larger dog via some instinctual sonar, yipping frantically. Kate's dog barked happy, booming entreaties, pausing to snarl sideways at the morsel underfoot. Amy appeared; she scooped up the poodle in one hand and grabbed Luna's collar with the other. Kate got the screen door open and pulled the pram in after her. Immediately, the big dog hung her front paws over the edge and stood there, balanced precariously on her hind legs.

"No, Luna, that's not what it's for," Kate said. "Down. Down right now."

"What a commotion," Amy said. "Good thing the baby's awake."

"Where is he?" Kate asked. "I'm absolutely dripping. I was hoping you hadn't fed him."

"No, he's all strapped in his sling chair in the middle of the kitchen table. I just came to open the door. I'll run and get him. He hears you—listen to him."

And Kate heard him, vocalizing what seemed his triumphant version of Luna's name, a syllable he associated with festive pandemonium. He would shout even louder as Amy unstrapped him, and croon anticipatory phrases. When a relatively new neighbor questioned Kate about the makeup of her household, she referred to the ages of her charges as "fifteen and twelve, those are the dogs, they're constant, and eight and six, those are the boys, they're three days a week, and three months, that's the baby, he runs the show, and there's my mother, and then us, and Amy, the baby-sitter, who's twenty." Here Kate paused for breath as the neighbor, invariably a matronly female with a perfect garden and coordinated designer lawn furniture, nodded encouragingly, and then Kate added, "Amy will only work for us three hours a day, on weekdays. I'm sure you can understand why. She won't come near us on weekends, and then we nearly go crazy." The neighbor would chuckle and nod, as though Kate were kidding, and make some reference to her own long-grown children.

In fact, the kids in Kate's house were the only small children on the street, and the dogs were the only dogs; luckily their house was on the corner of Glen Hill, a dead-end enclave of beautifully manicured houses, and High Street, a busy main thoroughfare that functioned as a clogged superhighway every rush hour. The upscale village Kate walked to nearly every day lay at one end of High Street hill, and the housing projects lay at the other, near the border of a more mixed community, the community in which Kate had lived until she and Matt had purchased this house, a house big enough for all of them. Here on Pill Hill, there were few black people, there were no gay people, there were no Latinos, there were no mangy cats sunning themselves on trash can lids, there were no unleashed dogs skulking along for scraps and cats, and there seemed to be no kids. Kids who played with chains, Matt liked to remind her, and matches, whose parents got arrested for beating up on each other. And how about those gay tenants of yours, like the one in the basement, in the in-law apartment, the one with the huge pornography collection who kept forgetting to eat until you made dinner for him? I miss him, Kate would say, what's happened to him? He used to call me a Southern belle and he loved my mashed potatoes and gravy. Sure, Matt said, and he liked you to look at those pictures. How could I help it, Kate would laugh, they were amazing. And he was careful never to show me the ones that would have made me mad, or scared for him. He adored me, now you know he did. No question, Matt would say shortly and roll his eyes. Well, Kate would argue, there has to be room for people like him, there has to be, and there sure isn't any room on Pill Hill. But that's the point, Matt would remonstrate, that's why we're here. We've circled the wagons, like any other couple who can afford to, because it seems the safest way to raise a kid. You're the Queen of Safety. You want every-thing absolutely tacked down. Do you really want to live back there? No, Kate would say, *no hon,* in a defensive parody of housewifely agreement, you're absolutely right, they would have stoned my Perego, and then where would I be, on Pill Hill without my Perego? Right. And Kate could pass here; as Matt said, she had a look about her; she could pass anywhere. But she felt like an interloper, someone in disguise, with her perfectly dressed blue-eyed baby and her Perego stroller and Rock-A-Bye and soft blocks in educational black and white. In fact, Kate liked to remind Matt, I'm an unwed mother, and you're married to someone else. I'm not married, Matt would say, I'm separated, and I'm waiting for my divorce. In fact, he'd been divorced since January; it was Kate who refused to marry now, in some office, in this season of snow and slush and cold and mud. She insisted they wait until spring, until things bloomed and she wasn't always wondering if the baby was warm enough, feeling his hands and his silken feet. Marrying now would assume gray skies—threatening skies, skies that both thundered and snowed on Perego strollers, skies that never lightened—for all their lives. It had been a terrible winter, the worst in years, everyone said so, all the neighbors, and they knew, they'd been here forever, growing their gardens while police arrested this one and that one back on Kate's old street. You talk as though you belonged there, Matt would tell her, but I'd like to remind you that you were there for three years, and you moved there from Cambridge, a stone's throw from Harvard Yard, where you also belonged, for two years, completely so. That fellowship you won over so many others, the one that helped you become a landlord with such diverse and interestingly needy tenants, was Harvard money. How many people on that street owned their triple-deckers? And how many bought them with Harvard money? A lot more should have, Kate would reply. That house cost practically nothing and it's still going up in value. Spoken like a true WASP, Matt would charge. I'm not a WASP, Kate would say, I'm from Appalachia. You've heard of it, coal mines, desolation. How could I be a WASP? You're not, Matt would admit. You look like one, he'd say, but thank God you don't think like one. How can you be so sure how they think? Kate would counter. What is a WASP, anyway? Let's hear it. Look around you, Matt would say. Where do you think you are? Well, Kate said, you're here. You're a doctor, like most of them; they've all got a doctorate in something, even the women. I'm a *Jewish* doctor, Matt would say, *I bought in.* Oh, that, Kate responded. There are plenty of Jews here. No, Matt would correct her, there are some Jews. And they bought in, just like I did. Though I may be the only one who bought in with help from an unwed mother. I doubt it, Kate would say.

"Our baby loves these dogs," Amy said now. "The louder they are, the better." She was back with the baby, and Kate took him in her arms and danced him around the entry, a circular route mostly defined by the pram; she loved putting her face in his neck and making noises that set him crowing his happy, exuberant sounds; his neck, his tummy and thighs, even his upper arms, were folds of sweet flesh; he was round and bald and the smooth skin of his head was velvety with down; he smelled of baby powder and the warmth of his sticky saliva.

"Alexander! Mr. Tatie!" Kate said to him. "How do you like the pram? Look, look at your limo. What a kingly apparatus! You're going to love it!"

"Gosh," Amy said, "it's amazing. What's inside, under the blanket?" She stared, looking slightly confused. "At first I thought it was a doll, the way you've got it covered, but what is it?"

"This?" Kate balanced Alexander on one arm and pulled away the blanket. "It's a Millennium Falcon, in mint condition. Did you see the *Star Wars* movies?"

"I think I did," Amy said.

"You must have. You're American, aren't you?"

Amy looked up as though she might answer the question in all seriousness, but she asked, "Is it cold?"

"Is what cold?" Kate said.

"That thing." Amy smiled. "Why is it all covered up? So neatly, as though it were a baby or something?"

"Oh, the blanket. The lady at the shop gave it to me, as a bonus. It's a decent blanket. We'll wash it and use it."

"Sure," Amy said, "I'll throw it in with the bibs. Should I do that now? Do you want to nurse him?"

"I do, but where's my mother? Hasn't she come downstairs yet? She's usually up by now."

"No, she's sleeping longer today. She called down for you a couple of times, but I said you weren't back quite yet. I asked if she wanted some juice or something, but she said no."

"I'll go check on her," Kate said. "Tatie will be fine another few minutes. You take him and I'll be right back."

"Mom? You'll never guess what I bought." Kate approached her mother's door, which was unlatched, and pushed it open. Usually Katherine dressed and sat up for a few hours every afternoon downstairs with Kate or Amy, but now she lay in bed. The stricken look on her face nearly stopped Kate's breath; Kate saw that she was weeping, propped on her pillows, her neck tilted at an angle as though she hadn't the strength to raise her head. Kate felt her own hand at her throat. "What's wrong?" she said. "What happened?"

"Oh, I'm in such pain, but I was afraid to take any more of the morphine." She tried to turn her head and couldn't.

"But Mom, the medicine is for the pain. Why didn't you call Amy? If I'm not here, Amy can always call Matt, or Dr. Jansson. You know that."

"I knew you'd be back soon. I wanted to wait for you. You never stay away long. It just seemed long."

"Where is it? Where's the pain?" Kate leaned over the bed and touched her mother's temples. Her face was moist and warm and creased, as though she'd been crying in her sleep, in the low fever she ran continually.

"Across here, all through here and into this shoulder, and my back. I just could hardly get my breath. I put the heating pad on—that helped. I think I slept. But when I woke up, a few minutes ago when I heard the dogs, oh, it was worse than ever."

"Here, let's pull you forward and sit you up. Let me fix these pillows better, and then we'll see to the pain." Kate sat on the edge of the bed and put one arm carefully behind her mother's back, supporting her head with the other; she tilted Katherine forward gently and took her weight against her own chest. Now she could reach the numerous pillows and turn them and fluff them—Kate's mother had brought her own feather pillows from home—but she had to move the heating pad aside; the pad had folded among the pillows and it felt too warm. "Mom," she said gently, "you must never go to sleep with the heat turned on. I'll fix this for you from now on, okay?"

"I had it on 'low,' with a towel over it," she said in her strained voice. "Isn't it on 'low'?"

"Yes, but if you lean on it, it can get too hot. Here, sit here just a minute while I take a look." Kate moved behind her mother. The shoulder of Katherine's cotton nightgown had slipped aside and Kate moved to pull it up, but stopped. The cloth, a pale blue strip edged in lace, was in her fingers; beside it she saw a dark lengthened slash on her mother's shoulder. For a moment she couldn't think, or comprehend what she was seeing. The burn was a puffy, oval shape three inches long; a dark blister filling with fluid; it would fill up tight and burst and weep, and it must hurt; it must hurt terribly. It was Kate's fault. Her stomach turned with hatred of herself, with shame. She should have checked on Katherine just before she went out; she should have urged her to take her medication, even if she thought she didn't need it; she should have warned her again about the heating pad, not to put it between herself and any other surface, not to use it in bed, not to anything, anything; she should have asked for a forecast, asked if today was the day another plateau would be reached and moved beyond, below, because they were descending, after all, in their progression, their transit. Kate traced around the burn with her forefinger, careful not to touch it. "Does it hurt here?" she asked. "Is this where it hurts?"

"Where?" her mother said. "Back there? No, it hurts in the front, and inside. I don't feel anything back there. Why? Is it red?"

"Yes," Kate murmured. "It's red." She made her voice stronger. "You can't use the heating pad anymore, all right? Unless I'm with you. The big pain keeps you from feeling the small pain. It could be dangerous. See? You can't feel back here at all. You can't feel me touching you, can you?"

"I—I can," her mother said weakly. "I can a little, now."

"Your nightgown is all damp," Kate said. "I'm just going to put the pillows in front of you for a minute, so you can lean forward on them, and I'll get you fresh things—" She moved the pillows and got more pillows, and a clean towel to put over them, in case the blister broke; she got her mother's gown off and put another on her, a baby doll gown with thin straps that wouldn't chafe the burn. The burn will heal, she told herself, it shouldn't be bandaged, I'll keep it clean and it will heal, I'll keep the blister from tearing too much and it will heal. I won't let her have that heating pad again, and nothing like it, either, ever again. Damn it, damn it, damn it. "There," she said to her mother, "let's lean you back carefully. Oh, there."

"That's better," her mother said. She flinched. "But this pain. I can't imagine what's gone wrong. I was doing so well."

"You'll do well again. You've let the pain get ahead of you. Remember what Dr. Jansson said when he was here just last week? You don't have to ration the medication." Kate reached for the bottle of liquid morphine, a brown glass bottle, like one that might contain cough syrup, and she picked up the clear plastic medicine spoon, the same tubular kind used for babies, and she poured in one teaspoon. Kate had marked the spoon with a thin strip of red adhesive tape, and again with a long black line of permanent marker, marker that would never wash off, so that Kate would never, never, now or in the future, use this spoon for her baby, her little boy. Not for cough syrup, not for grape decongestant, not for bubble-gum-tasting antibiotics. This was her mother's spoon, her mother's morphine spoon. She would have this spoon long after her mother was gone, and she would keep it here, in the drawer of this table, the table crowded now with bottles of medicine, the bud vase with its single marguerite daisy, the hospital Styrofoam pitcher sent home with

Kate after childbirth, glasses and cups, flexible straws. The medicine spoon was kept just beside the morphine bottle on a folded paper towel, near the small pad of paper on which every dosage was noted. Kate held the spoon to her mother's mouth. "Take this now," she said gently, "don't give me trouble."

Her mother leaned forward and closed her lips around the circular spoon. She swallowed with a grimace. "Maybe they need to move up our treatment, not wait until next week."

"Or change the regimen," Kate said. "I'll call Dr. Jansson. Meanwhile I'm going to give you an extra dose, because we're playing catch-up. You need to be comfortable enough for me to bring you in, if he wants to see you."

"No, nothing extra."

"Oh, you stint so," Kate said in frustration. "How can you pass up medication they say you can take? Why do you suffer? I wouldn't, I can tell you."

"I'm sure not," her mother said. "You'd have taken the bottle by now."

"Yes, and they'd have given me another. You don't need to be in pain, Mom, you don't."

"Kate," she said, "I have to pace myself with these drugs. Who knows?"

"Who knows what, Mom?"

"What I'll need later. How bad it will be."

Kate kept her voice even. "But they promised us, remember? When Dr. Jansson was here, just the other night. He told us they can manage your pain, no matter what." She paused. "You've been on chemo six months. They have another regimen they can try. Remember? He mentioned making a change. If the new regimen works, you can always cut down again on the morphine, like you did before."

"I don't know," her mother said.

Kate heard the wind rattle at the pane of the window. A little shake, like a tremor. It seemed to her the light outside had brightened and dimmed, as though clouds were being blown back and forth across the afternoon sun. Still holding the spoon, she moved a straight chair close to her mother's bed and sat down. She could do this. "What is it you don't know?" she asked quietly. "Are you afraid you can't cut down, afraid you won't be able to?"

"No." She moved her hand slowly across the border of the sheet that

Kate had turned neatly down over her blanket. "I know you think I'm afraid of being addicted to the morphine and you think that's silly—"

"Not silly, Mom," Kate began. "Of course I don't think—"

"Given my situation," her mother finished. "But it's not the pain medication I wonder about. I'm going to do that my own way." She waited a moment. "It's the new regimen. I don't know if I can go through another one. All those weeks."

"Oh." Kate put the spoon down on the table. She took a clean washcloth from her mother's drawer and stood to open the lid of the Styrofoam pitcher. She dipped the edge of the cloth inside and wrung it out over the basin. The cloth felt cool but not shockingly cold; she moved it gently over her mother's face, along her hairline, over her brow, across her eyes. It was like wiping a child's tears, but there were no tears. She touched the cloth to her mother's mouth and throat, careful not to move her. "Why don't we talk to the doctor about that?" she heard herself say. The cloth was barely cool now, only damp. She did her mother's hands, her wrists. She did each finger. "We'll talk to him. But I want to give you one more spoonful now, for the pain. We may need to drive over to the health plan."

"Half a teaspoon, then."

"I don't think that will help much. You need to get ahead of it."

Her mother said nothing.

"You know how hard things can seem in the dark, at night. Pain is like the dark. It's hard to think when you're in pain. And we have all these important things"—Kate paused—"to consider."

"All right," her mother said. "I'll take it, and you call the doctor."

Kate folded the cloth and hung it over the basin. She unscrewed the cap of the medicine bottle, picked it up, and began to pour the dosage into the spoon. At the window, the rattling wind murmured, moving in the branches of the trees.

"March has come in like a lion," her mother said. "Surely it won't snow."

"Don't worry," Kate told her. Again she held the spoon to her mother's mouth. *A draught of forgetting,* she thought, the words so Victorian, like an old valentine. "If we need to go out," she said aloud, "we'll bundle you up. Just let me call the doctor, and nurse the baby."

"I gave him a bottle before his nap. Amy brought him up to me." She spoke with effort, as though wholly exhausted. "As soon as he was finished and she took him, the pain really came on. Out of the blue, the pain just—had such weight."

"Maybe he's too heavy for you to hold now."

"I didn't put him up to my shoulder, or burp him. Amy did that. It's not the baby, or holding anything. We know what it is."

Kate went to her mother's table to straighten the bottles and rinse the spoon in the basin. "I'll go phone Dr. Jansson."

"We won't have to go in," her mother said. "When he knows about this pain, he'll come by, or tell us to wait until tomorrow morning."

"He'll try a new regimen," Kate said. "He'll try something else."

"He always does," her mother said dreamily. "Doesn't he."

"Can you feel the medicine," Kate asked, "so fast?" She put the flat of her hand lightly on her mother's head. Her hair had been so thick and black. Now it was much thinner, but she hadn't lost it: that was a blessing. Her Black Irish blood gave her an Italian look; her olive skin, black brows, wide-set brown eyes. *I didn't get one brown-eyed baby,* she liked to say, *not one.* Kate had placed photographs of her—as a young woman, her hair in a French twist, as a young mother with Kate and her brothers, as a teacher with one of her classes—on her bureau, near the lamp. When the lamp was on in the evening, the pictures were bathed in light. What are you bothering with those for, she'd asked Kate, and Kate had said, I like them.

"The pain is still there," her mother said now, "but I get farther away from it, farther from everything. That's why I hate the stuff, the medicine, even when it helps."

"Well," Kate said, "I'm here. Are you far away from me?"

Her mother gazed up at her. "Yes. I see you from farther away. I see us both. The way I might later, I suppose."

"Not yet," Kate said. "We're both here now. We're both right here."

On the question of what was seen later, on what any of them would see, Kate maintained a silence even of thought. She tried to think only of what was in front of her: the bottle of morphine in her mother's room, the spoon she kept beside it. Baskets of the baby's clean clothes; stacks of bright cotton Kate folded, Amy folded, but Kate liked to put away herself. She had lined the drawers of his white bureau with paper patterned in pastel teddy bears as small as polka dots; anonymous voyagers, they floated on a white field, through and across an emptiness of white. Sometimes Kate opened the drawers and straightened the clothes, glimpsing the paper, understanding as she did so that nothing needed straightening; she'd only wanted to open the drawer and see the clothes in their perfect, enclosed space, stacked neatly in piles: undershirts and shirts folded inside coveralls, vanilla woolen diaperwraps with their Velcro edges tucked, footed velour playsuits in red and green, in crayon yellow. One was bright blue, with clouds. *Out of the blue,* her mother had said; people spoke of blue in that way, meaning the sky, a forgiving, limitless sky that threatens no darkness yet descends, blue air laden. *The pain had such weight.* Pain did have weight; Kate carried it downstairs in her chest, in her arms and shoulders, in her abdomen, in the cage of her ribs, in the soft press of flesh above her diaphragm. *I like how small you are here,* Matt had said to her once. But the ache was columnar, circular, opening through her. Its bitter edge was the sick clutch in her throat, and this pain was only awareness, thought, fear. Yes, there; she felt terror draw near to her. Her mother lay upstairs, inside it, as Kate descended the carpeted stairs. Katherine's physical pain, so intense when there was a lapse in medication, when the disease took a new turn, when a regimen seemed no longer effective, must consume all attention, all thought, like a fire, or did she feel terror even then? Terror acknowledged that space and ease were past, that time diminished and was canceled, that lives moved through her and beyond her. Kate caught sight of the pram, all deep royal blue and silver chrome, luxurious lines and curves; Amy had parked it just by the front door, flush with the wall; it seemed to squat on its high round wheels and the little black poodle lay beneath it, waiting. The dog didn't see well, the dog couldn't hear, the dog had trouble climbing steps and was so incontinent everyone had agreed it was better she stay downstairs, and so she waited for Kate's mother in the entryway, a prone flop of combed dark curls, ears erect. On the landing sat an overflowing basket of clean, tumbled clothes, Tatie's clothes, snaps and ribbon ties outflung, and through the angular windows of the big front door Kate glimpsed Amy's pink jacket, Amy's blond hair, Tatie in her arms. The door opened and they came inside; Amy walked the distance to the stairs in three long strides and smiled up at Kate. She'd distracted the baby as long as she could.

"Did you sing him Christmas songs?" Kate asked.

"I sang him three," Amy said. "We did 'Jingle Bells,' 'We Three Kings' and 'Silent Night,' twice. He's tired of them."

Now Alexander flung his arms upward, fussy and bedraggled. His red corduroy coat was zipped to his chin; Kate loved its padded texture, the black piping across the front, the hood that flopped to the side now, as she reached for him and pulled the zipper down. She touched inside the folds of the coat to take him and lift him close. "Oh, poor darling, waiting so long. Do you know you were born on Christmas, but it took days and nights, it took forever, did I tell you? Let's go in the kitchen. I'll have to use the phone as soon as you've nursed." She was hoisting her shirt as she moved, unhooking the cups of her bra. "Grab his jacket, can you?" she said to Amy, and Amy pulled it from his arms as he nuzzled under cloth to find Kate's breast. His weight in her embrace was known and solid, a practiced longitude; he lay across her, closed his eyes, and settled in. Kate sat in a kitchen chair and unbuttoned her damp shirt completely, pulling it away from his face; she nodded at Amy to hand her the pump and she affixed its plastic mouth to her other breast, maintaining the slight suction needed with one hand.

"As you may have noticed," Kate said, "any modesty I ever had is gone. My body is something I use."

Amy leaned back against the counter and stood watching. "You're so—" She shrugged. "Coordinated."

Kate began to laugh. "I guess. And so thirsty. Out of habit. At the hospital they told me always to drink as I nursed, replenish fluids, God pouring into God, that kind of thing."

"God?" Amy said. She was already moving to the fridge, pouring a glass of juice. She took a flexible straw from a box they kept handy for Kate's mother and put it in the glass, bending the straw toward Kate with a little flourish of her hand.

"You know, God, the elixir of life, pouring from one thing to another, in a circle. They got me with that. Every time I nurse, I'm ravenously thirsty, as though everything were pouring out of me."

"It is," Amy said, and held the glass close.

Kate took a drink, a long, cold swallow. "Um, so good. What would I do without you? Just put it on the table." Amy did, and Kate noticed the little moons in her fingernails, which were naked of polish and filed short. She sat down on a kitchen stool, content and comfortable, like a girlfriend. Was there a flush of pleasure in her cheeks? She admires me, Kate thought. She doesn't know I can't get myself to cross the street, that I let my mother burn herself. No one should admire me, she wanted to say. Don't be fooled because my baby is beautiful, because I have so much milk.

"It's filled," Amy said. She got up to take the pump from Kate, and held it to the light. Inside, the white liquid swirled. "The milk is warm, even through the plastic. He must love the taste."

Kate was fastening the cup of her bra. "Haven't you tasted mother's milk? Not that you remember. It's sweet, thin as water. That's why they love it. Taste it. Pour some out."

"Well—" Amy said. She poured some into the palm of her hand and looked at Kate as she licked it, then smiled her tentative, slight smile. "Actually I have tasted it before. Yours, I mean. When I defrost the bags of milk, I test the warmth on my wrist. Whatever little beads are there, I drink. I mean, it seems a waste not to. I know you have a lot, but still, you make it with your body . . . it seems wrong to just wipe it away . . ." Her voice drifted off.

Kate was unsure what to say; she found herself merely nodding an acknowledgment, but something moved in her. Whenever Kate spoke of Amy, Matt would shake his head and testify as to Kate's "unerring instinct" for complications; who but Kate would end up, in this situation, with a baby-sitter whose own mother had died of cancer when she was five, who'd grown up as a stepchild? She found me, Kate would remind him. Despite the stepmother, the three younger half brothers, the seemingly happy family life, Kate thought of Amy and her sister as foundlings, foundlings of sorts. Amy had lost too much before she knew what loss was. The foundling had grown up. In some recess of herself, she remembered everything; of course she did.

"I wonder if your milk tastes different from anyone else's," Amy said quietly.

"I don't know," Kate confessed. "There might be shades of difference, but I think all mother's milk is sweet."

"Your mother," Amy said. "Is she not so well today?"

"No. She's better now, she's medicated, but I need to call the doctor."

"She didn't seem to want me to do anything for her—"

"Caring for her too isn't in your job description, Amy. I need to call now, though. You know where the number is posted, there on the cabinet. Could you dial it for me?"

"Yes, sure."

Kate watched her dial. Alexander shifted in her arms and his mouth trembled at her nipple. He was sleeping and waking, conscious enough to nurse and nurse until Kate could disengage without startling him. His eyes moved under their opalescent lids, a rapid, subtle motion. Dreams. Amy gave her the phone. "Oncology," Kate said into the receiver. "Dr. Jansson." Then, to Amy, "I'm on hold." The baby, wakened slightly by her voice, stirred. His hand began to drift up and down on Kate's skin, palm curved to touch. Up, down. A lover's touch, completely satisfied.

Amy looked away from them. "I'll go down and put in the laundry," she said, and she was gone.

Kate heard her on the basement steps. Carefully, she wet her smallest finger and slipped the tip between her nipple and Tatie's mouth. She turned his face up, warm against her, then took her finger away as he slept on, lips pursed. Against her ear, the phone made its blurry hum, and a voice came on.

"Oncology."

"I was holding for Dr. Jansson," Kate said.

"Dr. Jansson is in conference for another hour. Is this an emergency?"

"Not exactly," Kate said, "but my mother, who is his patient, is worse. Her pain is more severe. Could you give him that message? Please have him call me as soon as he can."

"Your number?"

The line wheezed and hummed as Kate repeated the number, as though Kate and the voice she spoke with drifted into separate spheres. Kate wondered if the interference was only on her end; she didn't want to speak loudly enough to wake the baby. She said, in a normal tone, over the crackling, "Did you get that?"

"Yes," said the receptionist. "He'll call as soon as he's free."

He'll never be free, Kate wanted to say. How did he do this work, juggling concoctions, prolonging lives, comforting the anguished, facing facts. Didn't it reach him? Wasn't he ever afraid? He was Swedish, but his voice had no lilt; he'd left his own land long ago. The receptionist had hung up; in her hand Kate felt the vibration of a dial tone.

Amy was back, leaning close to her. "Should I take him?" she whispered.

Kate nodded. The baby's weight was lifted from her, expertly, soundlessly. Amy wouldn't try to get him all the way upstairs. Kate knew she'd put him in his travel bed in the living room, and then she'd let Kate's dog out into the yard, and put the poodle, who was so small she could walk between the rungs of the black iron fence, on her chain; Amy would minimize disruptions, noises, outbursts that might wake Alexander, and then she'd sweep the kitchen floor, retrieve tossed rattles, clean up crushed pellets of dog food the poodle could barely masticate and dropped everywhere. Kate's dog walked into the room now and yawned, stretching, blinking her yellow eyes. She looked like a cross between a weimaraner and a retriever; in fact, her mother had been a beaglelike mutt. She wagged her gold flag of a tail and came close, nails clicking on the wood floor, and put her chin firmly on Kate's knee.

"I remember you," Kate said, and kissed her between the eyes. "You're going out now, and I'm going to launder the spaceship."

In the basement, the companion washer and dryer thrummed in their watery cycles. Kate stood at the old-fashioned double sink, scrubbing the Millennium Falcon with a toothbrush. She took care to keep the little door shut and rinsed sparingly; it wouldn't do to have the thing sloshing in its minute chambers. A spaceship should navigate soundlessly through depths of black, through the only infinity of place accepted in the scientific mind. Silent night, indeed, and holy in its cold brilliance, its ability to hold suspended so many worlds and burning stars. Glows in the dark. Like candles in the dense forests of Europe, through longest nights: the early tribes and clans had lit evergreens, built bonfires, danced in circles to celebrate the solstice, the turning of the year. Kate had gone into labor the night of the twenty-third and endured two days of travail without drugs. Her baby was born Christmas morning, alert and awake, but Kate was taken away on a table, intubated and sedated; the placenta hadn't detached at all and had to be scraped away. In prehistory, in the days before operating rooms and D&Cs, Kate was one of those mothers who would have died; the tissue that fed the baby, that breathed for him, would have rotted inside her. Mothers died. Kate's mother would die. *Someone's taken very good care.* The words hung in Kate's mind, terrible and softly luminous. No, they had not abandoned her mother, yet she was alone, a creature trapped and hurting. She was right about the morphine, yet the morphine was all they had. As the pain increased, Kate would have to send her mother farther and farther away, so far she couldn't feel, she couldn't think. She would hear Kate's voice in patches, as disembodied sound, and the words would float, untethered. What was space but a rolling of time, dimensional and deep, in which words were lost? Kate held the dripping spaceship in a glowing nimbus cast by the naked bulb on its cord; beyond that circle the grimy basement windows let fall their powdery daylight. Millennium Falcon: such an effective name; the words denoted a thousand years in which to forage, and the hawklike vision of a bird trained to hunt. Kate put the toy on the ironing board to dry, then touched the top of the washer to warm her hands. Amy knew to wash the sheets in hot water, on the long cycle. Leaning against the machine, Kate felt a circular, external vibration, a warm and mindless hum. She lifted the lid and peered into a wet maw, skimmed with bubbles; instantly, water stopped sloshing and the machine clicked impatiently. Kate took off her shirt and dropped it in with the white sheets and bibs, with colors laundered so often they wouldn't fade, then shut the lid and leaned across the machine, her face and chest flush with its warmth, its smooth throb. She put her face in her crossed arms and thought she might sleep, but she closed her eyes and wept.

The world Kate knew is gone. Kroger's Grocery, down by the old train station, closed years ago. Main Street has emptied out, the locally owned stores replaced by chain franchises and a new mall. Open fields between town and the high school are now parking lots fronting warehouse-size concerns with floodlights: Kmart, Pizza Hut, Bonanza Steak House, CVS, NHD, Blockbuster, a vast Purity Supreme open twenty-four hours. The giant lights stand storklike on gargantuan poles, their flat, rectangular faces downturned and glowing pale yellow in the ocher afternoon. Kate wonders if the timers are off as she follows her mother into the bright market, with its air-conditioned aisles and piped Muzak. People who worked downtown have taken jobs at the huge new stores, her mother has told her, and that is a good thing. Even though the stores are so much bigger, you can still buy from people you know.

"I'll have those three filets, Herb, just those," Katherine says, pointing over the meat counter, "but don't trim them. It ruins the flavor."

"You're right." The butcher nods approvingly. "People are always asking me to trim their meat, and I do, but it dries the texture. Meat is meant to cook in its fat. Good cooks know this." He looks over at Kate, who mans the cart. "Your mother is one of them, I'll bet."

"She certainly is," Kate answers. "From way back."

"You can tell by what people choose," he says. "You gotta take the bad with the good, that's the way with life. A little fat with the protein. Your mother knows." He holds the meat up to Kate on an open sheaf of pristine white paper. "Look at the marbling—that's how you tell tender meat."

Kate assents, noting Herb's spotless apron, imagining him a fake butcher, perhaps a public relations person. The filets are uniform in size, neatly red and white, nearly heart-shaped. "They don't look like meat," Kate says.

Katherine shakes her head. "What are you talking about? She just got off a plane, Herb, a small plane."

"I mean," Kate tries to explain, "they're so compact, almost pretty."

"Of course they're pretty," the butcher says, wrapping the paper expertly. "Nothing prettier than a good piece of meat."

"Thanks, Herb." Katherine takes the folded package as they move off toward dairy. "I had his kids in school," she tells Kate.

"Quite the morals lesson. And why is his apron so clean?" Kate steers the cart around a tower of Cocoa Puffs boxes and small stuffed toys that match the illustrations on the boxes.

"What lesson?" Katherine peruses her list.

"Good with the bad, life, all about marbling. People really don't think about slaughterhouses, cows in pens, with the meat all packaged up in plastic trays—that's what I meant. It seems amazing they really cut meat behind those swinging doors, doesn't it?"

"Oh, he cuts meat. He worked at the market downtown for years, before it closed. They change their aprons, of course, before they come out to the front. You could ask to see his other apron, if you like." She leans closer to Kate and says more quietly, "Actually, I don't eat meat often. I'd cook fresh fish every day, if we could get it. All the fish here is frozen. It's not good enough for a special dinner. For Matt, when he's here, I'm making pork roast, with cider glaze, and fresh rolls."

Kate laughs. "He's Jewish, remember? But that's all right, he's completely unobservant, he does eat pork, and it's one of your best meals. But he doesn't eat eggs."

"My mother used to say an egg was the perfect food," Katherine protests.

"Cholesterol. But your pork roast will be a treat; he'll know he's in a different country. And the rest of it: kraut with brown sugar, mashed potatoes, that rich gravy."

"And Waldorf salad," her mother continues, "but I make it differently *now, no mayo, just lemon juice, and chopped walnuts I roast with honey. Much healthier."*

"Oh, health! You're making me hungry! But I'm relieved you still love cooking."

"Well, I don't cook much for myself. And in the heat—I've been making aspic, that's my new thing. It's supposedly very chic. Actually, I'm making a little book of my recipes." She stands over the dairy case, lifting out narrow cartons of skim milk.

"Better to drink whole milk now, Mom. It's not as though you're dieting. I'll have that. You have this." Kate gets a large container, realizes it might be too heavy for Katherine, and exchanges it for a half-gallon carton. She steals a glance at her mother. It seems to her Katherine stands differently, bent slightly forward, her shoulders rounded. As though to protect her chest, Kate thinks. "You're making a book?" Kate asks.

"Just handwritten, on recipe cards—you can read my writing. I'll make copies for your brothers, and a couple of friends, have them bound at the Xerox place. It's one of several things I'm doing. Things that need to be done, some more fun than others." She turns to Kate, holding the milk in her arms, her thin face oddly radiant. "So much. I run out of time, every day."

She's undiminished, Kate realizes. It's as though her enormous energy is banked and contained in a body more fragile than she, a body she attends reluctantly, and cajoles. During the radiation treatments they gave her prednisone, a type of cortisone that delivers a sustained, mild euphoria. But she's off meds now, off treatments. This is her own force of purpose. Kate can almost hear it surrounding her, a blurred hum of constancy and power. Just above it she imagines she hears the faint whine of her own fear—fear for Katherine. She is Kate's to protect.

"I'll show you all my projects," her mother is saying. "We have everything. Let's go."

Kate takes the milk. "How do you usually shop, Mom? I mean, how do you carry things?"

"I have them put two or three things in each bag. I take the cold things in first, then the rest. It's not a problem."

Kate nods. They all know her, just as they knew her before, years ago, when the smaller, family-owned stores lined Main Street, and butchers' aprons weren't so clean. Kate remembers a Frigidaire case with a curved glass front. There was a wood counter behind, with a cleaver in a slot, and above that, a broad window where a slab of meat hung as though displayed. The white, knobby tendon where the hook poked through was flecked with red, and the nude, flayed-looking chickens lay below, across a porcelain sink top, their scrawny necks flung back and their pronged feet sticking up. Six or seven years old, Kate couldn't help staring; it seemed otherworldly to be so naked. The butcher's window was a framed study: all things reduced farther and farther. Seeing her daughter's face, Katherine had taken a quarter from the cracked red leather billfold she'd carried in those years and told Kate to go to the front and buy a pretzel. Kate went; pretzels were in the jar with the metal lid and she was tall enough at last to get her own. Then she stood facing front, chipping away each glasslike shard of salt with her thumbnail before she put the pretzel in her mouth. Refusing to look back.

"Want to have a seat somewhere," she asks her mother now, "while I go through the line at the register?"

"Don't be ridiculous," her mother says.

The groceries are put away, the aged toy poodle let out and in. Kate goes to the upstairs of her mother's house to unpack, but in the end she only opens her suitcase and arranges it on a window seat. The drawers in the bureau are full, and she can't bring herself to empty them. She'll do it before Matt arrives. They will stay in this room, where Kate slept at seventeen, in the double spindle bed her mother refinished with steel wool and linseed oil. She refinished furniture in the garage of the old house in the summers, a hobby, a pastime, before she moved the family into town and asked her husband to leave. She'd always said the antiques were for the children. All three second-floor bedrooms of the house she owned alone held high antique beds fitted with bedskirts and shams she'd sewn, Eastlake bureaus and bedside tables, platform rockers, all in satiny walnut she'd hand-rubbed to bring out the sheen. There were two or three quilts for each child, all cross-stitched Early American patterns whose symbolic language seemed to Kate reminiscent of hieroglyphs or cave paintings. Prehistoric man had his bison and mastodons, colonial women their birds and sheaves of wheat, their red apples and crossed palms.

Kate leans against the bed, then crawls carefully onto it. Never sit on quilts, she's been told since childhood, or even sleep under them; tension breaks the stitches. The old beds are "turned down," the quilts folded down in even bands like broad flags, tucked to the footboards. But quilts are made for warmth, Kate said once, surely people slept under them. Of course they did, her mother told her, that's why there are so few antique quilts left, when every household then had a dozen. Katherine keeps the quilts she's made wrapped in plastic bags in the walnut blanket chests; she puts them on the beds for special occasions. Kate knows without looking; all the rooms are "done up," for Matt's sake. The beds themselves have names, like monuments.

Katherine sleeps in "the Grandmother Dodd bed," where her mother and grandmother slept, a bed all the more cherished for the gnawed decorative ball on the footboard, reminder of a beloved cocker spaniel, long dead. Dogs and their women, Kate thinks. Katherine likes to say she "didn't know and wasn't told" where her grandmother died, "but Mother died in that bed, where her babies were born." There was the implicit assumption Katherine would die in it too, one day. But now Kate will have a baby, or Kate will be pregnant, about to give birth—she will need to be with Matt in Boston, near the obstetrician she's seen twice thus far. How will they manage? Kate will care for her mother: that is understood, but how or where remains uncertain. How far in the future will it all occur, on which terrain? Birth and death are unfamiliar landscapes; Kate imagines she walks a border between the two and marvels she's grown to flagrant adulthood with so little firsthand experience of either.

On the plane from Madras to Kathmandu, Kate sat with an American girl and her silent Danish boyfriend. He spoke no English, the girl explained, she knew some Danish; after all, she'd been gone from Illinois ten years, but she didn't communicate with her family. Her mother? No, it wasn't necessary. Was she cruel to you? Kate asked. The girl shook her head. They'd just stopped seeing eye to eye. One can't care, one moves on. But she's your mother, Kate said. Then, abruptly, everyone stopped speaking. Kate turned to look as the Himalayas came into view, suddenly close, as though a world had exploded and flung its hot depths so high that each giant, broken piece had turned to ice. Miles of snow. The plane seemed to fly into jagged white, then banked and dropped lower. The peaks grew ever more massive, into vertical fields and gleaming, tipped sheets, dwarfing all creatures, timeless, implacable. There was silence save for a removal of lens caps, a clicking of shutters. Furled air rose in swaths from the peaks themselves, and the plane leveled off so that it seemed to fly a nether region veiled above and below. The bases of the mountains were obscured in cloud, their heights in shifting vapor.

Stepping out of a history seemed as cold. Kate found in her mind a clear image of her own mother, sitting in her chair in this house, counting back through her knitting to see where the pattern was off, to find the mistake; clear back here, she lamented, undoing rows of tight, clean stitches. The picture was startling in its clarity and intense aura, when Kate hadn't thought of home for weeks. She understood clearly that her mother was right; it wouldn't work to throw the pattern itself away. What was the meaning, then, of anything? Now she knows Katherine's odyssey into illness began about the time she herself was flying into Nepal, unreachable, out of touch. Why hadn't she called home even once during those weeks?

Rattling in a taxi rickshaw through darkened streets delirious with music, shouting, singing, the one month in which astrologers decreed certain days fortuitous for weddings, Kate had let her former life recede. Through weeks in Sri Lanka, India, Nepal, she slipped into a pocket of time familiar to her from other travels, a time in which the blasted days grew tranquil and no life but this existed. On hiatus from a teaching job, she decided not to seek reappointment. She could go back, see to things, do some freelance editing for a small publishing firm that sometimes employed her, and return to Nepal. The friend who was house-sitting, caring for her dog, would be happy to sublet while Kate lived here on very little. She spent her days alone, walking or writing, numbering drafts of poems on yellow legal pads, and her nights in company, long evenings with friends in the inexpensive restaurants by Durbar Square, or drifting with Amrit through the bead market at Indrachowk. Wedding parties began to congregate each afternoon; by night they roamed squares and narrow spoked streets lit by the blue-rimmed stare of Bodhnath stupa. Fruit overflowed on altars rife with offerings; rats thumped benignly along the wood and earthen passages to the shrines, so well fed no one feared them. At the Hindu sites all life was sacred, all pilgrims welcome: Kate saw the American girl just once more, at a shrine to Shiva, on the last long night before she left Nepal. When she thinks of that night, Kate feels an alert watchfulness, a patience she cannot entirely enter, as though she grasps the enormity of what she might apprehend, yet has not understood.

The open door of the room moves. Katherine's little black dog skitters through and stands still, sniffing the air.

"Katrina," Kate says, "it's me."

The dog coughs its miniature cough and sneezes mightily, which Kate interprets as an expression of doubt, then peers at her with its bright, tilted gaze.

"Are you completely blind now, Katrina?" Kate inquires softly. The dog bumped into Kate's suitcase an hour ago, and stumbled over Kate's feet, but stands quite still now, as though to disprove all theories.

"Never mind," Kate says, and closes her eyes. She is so tired. Every late afternoon, it's as though a spell is cast over her and she simply has to sleep. The baby is a wet bud, curled or moving, but her own body demands she forget herself, lie down in sounds she can't hear. She drifts, hypnotized, the quiet float of image and phrase almost a dream. <u>Natural between women</u>, she hears, and <u>like a mirage</u>. Stone lions on the Nyatapola steps stand sentinel in their hard, curled manes, ten times stronger than the elephants below them, ten times weaker than the winged rams above. <u>All my projects</u>, murmur the Buddhist nuns in their saffron robes. They cover their shaved heads and shop two by two in the markets, live at the monasteries, never roam, supported by alms, like the men. Pressed to accept money, they tuck the coins in their cloth bags and bow discreetly. <u>Nip and tuck</u>. None of them are beggars; to give to them is blessed. Now Kate walks with Matt through Harvard Square at night, where people drop money into jugglers' hats: Americans give to entertainers. Panhandlers who merely beg are obliged to invent a variety of attitudes, while those who are ill invent nothing; they whisper and gesticulate to themselves. In Nepal, there were no beggars; only ascetics supported by offerings. One, dressed in monk's garb but filthy, his thick hair matted, wandered or sat in the square, demanding nothing, subsisting. Was he pretending to be a monk, or was he a monk who'd become ill? She asked Amrit, who was home on break from engineering studies in Heidelberg. He opened his hands and looked upward in the universal gesture: who knows? Either way, the ragged man was treated as a religious person. <u>Each day vanishes</u>. Kate stands with her mother on a silvery plateau whose level plain extends, end-

less, into the line of the horizon; the outcast holy one stands with them, barefoot, garbed in orange silk, his skin rubbed white with ash. Katie, her mother is saying, Katie.

Kate wakes abruptly to see her mother at the bureau, pulling the top drawer carefully, soundlessly open. "Mom?" Kate asks.

"Oh, you're awake. I was getting these out to show you." She turns, holding a pair of small white baby shoes in her hands. "You need to know about these."

Disoriented, Kate wonders if she's told her mother about the baby. No, she hasn't, not yet.

Katherine laughs. "You look so confused. They belonged to you—your first leather shoes. I'm having yours done in porcelain, and your brothers' in bronze. I've always wanted to. It takes three or four months, and I'm sending them off tomorrow. It may seem silly, but I want you each to have them." She moves toward Kate. "In case anything should happen, suddenly—you'll know I sent them off. It won't seem absurd that preserved baby shoes are arriving on the doorstep."

Kate balances one of the little shoes on her palm. It was scuffed and soft, worn on one side. "Seems a shame to cover it."

"I know. But otherwise they get misplaced or lost, broken down in some box. People don't really preserve them for the shoe, but to save the shape of the little foot inside." She pauses. "You walked early, and you haven't stopped since."

"I think the same might be said of you," Kate answers softly.

"Oh, no. I was a late bloomer. I'm just now . . . making my way."

"What do you mean?"

"I was so preoccupied when I was young, losing Tom, that boyfriend of mine who died just after high school, then Mother being sick, then the years raising kids, and just as you left home, the divorce. It's only in the last few years I've really felt—on my own. There've been your brother's troubles, his divorce, his financial problems—"

"Most people who divorce have financial problems," Kate says quickly. "Anyway, it seems to be getting better."

Her mother nods. "Or at least he doesn't tell me anymore."

"He's working it out. He'll be fine."

"Well," Katherine says, collecting the shoes, "I'm going to box these for mailing tomorrow. I think I heard the doorbell, so Rip must be here.

Come down when you're ready, and don't mention to him that I'm bronzing baby shoes. I'd never hear the end of it. Is that the phone?"

"I'll get it up here, on this extension. I'm sure it's Matt. You go ahead. I'll be there soon." Kate turns, reaching for the phone as she straightens the quilt on the bed. Cradling the receiver to her neck, she hears her mother sing out a greeting as she descends the stairs. "Hello?" Kate says.

"Hey, it's me. How was the trip? How are you feeling?"

"Matt, the trip was actually good. Small plane, but the weather was, well, glorious. I've just wakened from my afternoon coma, and we were discussing baby shoes."

"You told her?"

Kate laughs. "No, they were my baby shoes. We'll tell her together, as planned, when you get here."

"And how is she? As well as you hoped?"

"She seems very well." The receiver buzzes. Kate speaks a little louder. "It's a good time for you to come. She's so excited. She's got the meals all planned. It's as though you're a hero, or a dignitary."

"No," Matt says, "I'm just yours." The connection clicks repeatedly. "Kate, look, I'm sorry, but I can't—"

"The line is suddenly so fuzzy." Kate strains to hear. "What was that?"

"—I said I'm sorry, but I can't leave tomorrow. Jonah is acting out at day care, and it's getting worse." He went on to describe the most recent incident. "It's just"—he broke off, then finished—"We're going in to meet with his teacher tomorrow morning."

"But your flight isn't until noon."

"I know, but I really need to spend some time with him. None of it makes any sense to a five-year-old. I just can't leave right now."

"I know you're worried about him," Kate hears herself say. She looks out the window at her mother's flower garden. The buoyant faces of the marguerite daisies are nodding.

5

Kate thought it great fun to dress up and go next door to Camille's for a glamorous meal on Easter. Now that Dr. Jansson's new protocol had taken effect and Katherine was better, they could all actually go out together, as long as they didn't go far. Sam and Jonah were traveling too, visiting relatives with their mother for the holiday. Kate had already given them baskets of chocolate rabbits, books and trinkets; she knew better than to buy them clothing. But she included new clothes wrapped in pastel papers with Matt's basket, for her mother, for Alexander.

"You Christians," Matt said. "You and Camille just got your Christmas decorations put away a few weeks ago, and now there are china rabbits and ancient chickens."

"I know. Aren't they beautiful? Look at this one. My mother put this in my Easter basket every spring for twenty years." Kate held a papier-mâché chicken in her hand. Its knobby surface still sparkled with old glitter and its head wobbled on a short spring; Kate pulled it apart to reveal its inner compartment, a cardboard oval lined in rickrack. "For an egg. What's sexier than an egg? Eggs move us through the long dark. Those insistent yearnings in our blood, the need to couple, and finally it's spring. Safe to give birth."

Matt raised his brows. "And there's nothing sexier than birth. We know that."

"Stop complaining," Kate laughed. "You're getting yours lately. Maybe you need me to bite your tongue." She leaned forward to lick at his lips, kissing him, then murmured into his mouth. "Didn't we have enough snow this winter? Don't we deserve a festival? It's not Christian anyway, it's pagan. Celtic fertility rites and ritual."

"Camille's got ritual, and plenty of spectators. How many people will be there with us and our four-month-old? He's not great at waiting for course changes."

"He doesn't have to wait," Kate answered, flexing her fingers at her breasts. "And there will be a nice crowd, not too big. You can wear your new linen shirt, and the yellow vest I gave you. Don't be a killjoy. Don't you want to go?"

"I like Camille, but her crowds make me antsy. Does she always have to tell everyone what everyone does? It drives me crazy. It's like you have to be somebody to stand in the room."

"She's just a good hostess. Trying to start conversations."

"Let's take your mother's dog for dinner."

"What? That's not funny."

"I don't mean as an appetizer." Matt laughed. "I mean as a guest, a relation. We can say, 'This is Katrina. She barks.' "

"Everyone on the street already knows Katrina barks. Though 'barks' is a misnomer. It's more correct to say Katrina yips. Real dogs bark. *My* dog barks."

Matt fixed her with a serious look. "You know, you're jealous of your mother's dog. And I can't fathom why. I mean, you're taller. You're smarter. I personally think you're better-looking than Katrina. Just because your mother keeps mixing up your names—"

"I mentioned this to Mom the other day," Kate said. "She pointed out that both our names start with a *K* and said it was an understandable mistake."

"I say again, let's take Katrina. She's small enough to adorn a platter; she could impersonate a baby Easter rabbit of the black chocolate variety. If nothing else, she can sit at the table on your mother's lap, stare at the food, and shake."

"True," Kate said, "but I'd lose my appetite immediately." She paused. "Oh, I'm bad. I shouldn't talk like this about Katrina. After all, she's my sister, more or less—an adoptee with a pedigree."

"Adoptees have concerns. Maybe she's upset about the mystery of her parentage."

"What mystery? My mother is her mother. Do you know her official name, the name inscribed on her papers? 'Katherine's Katrina Kay.' "

"No wonder the dog shakes."

"Now you're overstating it. She doesn't shake. I'd say she . . . trembles. I think it intensified a couple of years ago when she had most of her teeth pulled. Then too, being barricaded in the kitchen here every night hasn't helped her mental health."

"Or her incontinence," Matt said. "Every morning, while you're nursing Alexander, I'm down there cleaning. Katrina doesn't mess in one spot, she messes everywhere, on the papers, off the papers, for spite."

"Matt, it's not for spite. Katrina used to tremble with excitement; now she trembles with anxiety. She senses what's coming."

"I don't know about that," Matt said gently. "I'm not sure Katrina senses much of anything. I mean, she's old, and overbred, and miniature."

"She's a toy," Kate said.

"What?"

"She's a toy," Kate repeated. "In poodle parlance, 'toy' is smaller than 'miniature.' Toy poodles have to be small enough as puppies to sit in teacups. Or are they supposed to sit in teacups full-grown, as some sort of standard? I don't know if Katrina did, or can, now that she's fifteen. My mother got her before her divorce, when I went off to college."

Matt feigned wonderment. "Katrina's divorced?"

"Very funny."

"I admire Katrina. For a toy with few teeth, she tears up a lot of newspaper. Katrina could make short work of all those things Camille displays that children can't touch."

"You're right," Kate said. "That settles it. Katrina stays home. All the dogs stay home. Camille would never have a dog. She likes her house too much."

"My point exactly. Camille's house is perfect. I'm always a little nervous when I'm over there with my kids, any of them, even Alexander. And he can't even crawl yet."

"Camille adores Alexander, and I adore Camille. I don't care what you say. I think it's reassuring sometimes to see something perfect—a perfect world, lively and interesting, put together with so much care."

"I'm not arguing," Matt said. "I adore Camille too. Well, 'adore' may be putting it strongly—"

"You do adore her, don't you?" Kate said. "It's just that you use Camille as a mother-in-law. She's twelve years older than me, more of a big sister. But you can't have any 'issues' with my mother—she's too sick. So you have them with Camille, though thank God you don't tell her so. You tell me, and I defend her as though she *were* my mother."

"You sure do." Matt looked over at her and smiled. "Maybe *I'm* jealous."

Kate paused. "Maybe you are." Then she continued, more softly, "I mean, of course Camille values things. That's one reason she's good at selling real estate. But her possessions have spiritual connotations to her. They aren't just things. I understand it perfectly well."

"But why are all her spiritually meaningful things so one-of-a-kind and delicate? Why do they all cost so much money?"

"You don't know what they cost," Kate said, irritated. "Anyway, they're good things, well-made things, old things. Shouldn't well-made things have value? And shouldn't someone who will care for them and respect them own them? And what's wrong with asking others to respect them as well?" Kate sat down on the bed. She lowered her voice. Soon they'd wake Alexander, and then he'd be fussy at lunch. "And Camille has always supported herself. She bought most of those things on time, because she cared about them, with money she made in her own business. After her rich second husband bounced her. She didn't even get alimony."

"Bounced her for infidelity," Matt said.

"Yes, for one night, an adventure. I suppose you'd bounce me for the same."

"You bet I would." He frowned at her in mock anger.

Kate sighed and shook her head. "Why should you sympathize with Camille's ex-husband? Is *he* here helping us, driving my mother back and forth to chemo, staying with her in the infusion room because I can't stand to be there?"

"I do appreciate Camille, and I respect her. She's a self-made man." He smiled gently. "It's just that I feel almost as vulnerable about my kids as you do about your mother. And anytime I've had Sam and Jonah over there, there's so much to respect, I can't move. I have to get the kids out onto the patio as soon as possible."

"That's your own paranoia. Anyway, isn't it possible that Sam and

Jonah need to learn to tone down in certain circumstances? Maybe it's them, not the circumstances, that need to change, or, well, evolve."

"Sure," Matt said, "evolve. You just wait till you have kids."

"I *have* kids," Kate said through gritted teeth.

"I mean big kids, kids their age. They do move suddenly and fling their arms out and lurch into objects, especially in a house like Camille's."

"And Camille has kids too, in case you haven't noticed. Kids she basically raised by herself. And now she takes care of Lannie's kids practically single-handedly when they visit."

"Single-handedly?"

"Well, he goes to work, she picks them up from summer camp and entertains them and washes their clothes and talks to them and there they all are for dinner, which she cooks. Meanwhile Lannie keeps adding to his personal glassware collection." Kate took a breath. "Those kids are not much older than Sam and Jonah, you know, and they seem to manage in Camille's house."

"Yes, and they make fun of her constantly."

"If they do, it's fondly, with a kind of amazement. You might ask for as much from your kids someday, let alone your stepkids, if you ever have any. Don't you suppose they'll make fun of you? Don't all kids make fun of their parents?"

"I suppose so," Matt said. "Look, do you really want to fight about Camille before we go to her house for lunch?"

Kate sat down on the bed. "No, I don't want to fight. I want my mother to wear the pink silk suit she brought up here in hopes she'd wear it another spring, and I'll put on my pale blue jacket, and you the linen, and Tatie his cloud suit. It'll be one spring day."

Matt sat down beside her, lay back on the pillows, then pulled her down close to him. "Okay, so it will. Roll away the rock." He sighed. "By the way, why didn't Camille get alimony?"

"I don't think she asked for it," Kate said.

"Then what did she ask for?"

"Forgiveness, I assume."

"Oh," Matt said.

.   .   .

It really was a cloud suit, a white jumper and snap onesie printed in small blue clouds, with a blue cap to match. Kate dressed Alexander, who cooed at her as though delighted. She hummed a song to him, a song she thought was a mindless tune until she recognized the melody. *Daisy, Daisy, give me your answer true.* In her small-town grade school, the music program had consisted of forced singing every morning before classes, and the songs were folk songs: "She'll Be Coming Round the Mountain," "Charming Billy," "A Bicycle Built for Two." Kate had thought them boring and silly but lately recognized them as unforgettable; she wondered if her classmates had been similarly imprinted with their tunes and phrases. The words seemed plaintive to her now, and nearly frightening. *I'm half crazy, all for the love of you.* People did go crazy with love, Kate knew, and each kind of love seemed to offer its own strain of craziness. Strain? Stain, thought Kate—stain of love was a more apt description. Love did that: it left a mark.

Carefully she pulled on Tatie's white crocheted socks, took his pale blue leather shoes from tissue paper, opened them to encase his chubby feet. The softest leather possible, like the kid gloves her mother had worn to church, leather culled from baby goats. If people were only mindful of where things come from, Kate thought, we'd know ourselves for the savages we are. Love was savage, surely. Kate saw her little obsessions with Tatie's clothes and toys as ridiculous, yet she clung to them; all mothers clung to detail, for good reason. Attention was a hedge against fortune, a registration of love and fear specific as the moving needle on a compass face: true north. Families bought layettes or passed them on: christening dresses, silver rattles, teddy bears in pastel colors, the white ribbon ties Kate knotted now in perfect bows. Mothers clung to the illusions of control, nurture, benign providence. Anything to forget how easily the satin cord could snap, or the bough break. How much, how constantly, babies needed.

Kate leaned close to Alexander, breathing in his powdery smell. *"I wish I was an apple,"* she sang to him, *"hanging in a tree . . ."*

He smiled. He was so big now. He'd found his hands and liked to clasp them. He liked to shout vowel sounds. Now he grabbed Kate's hair with both fists and held on.

"And every time my sweetheart passed," she whispered, *"he'd take a bite of me."*

Ravenous, Kate knew, this need to birth babies, to hold one's child. The fact was, birth dwarfed sex, swept sex before it. A woman had sex to get this, to be here, to smell the clean smell of her child tended by her hands, to drink him in, consumed. Kate sometimes imagined herself a flat meadow ravaged by wildfire, an unsuspecting meadow; for years, she'd avoided babies, which was easy, because most women she knew didn't have them. Most women thought they were looking for men, not babies. Kate thought now that they were wrong: they were all looking for babies, even those who said they didn't want children, or didn't like them. Kate knew only a few women whose disavowals she took seriously; they were often artists who had suffered through childhood with no allies, and even they sometimes changed their minds. When they met the right man. When they wanted the baby badly enough. When time began to announce its finite nature, gently at first, in their bodies, in their minds, on their faces. The desire to be beautiful or powerful was not so much about the need for admiration or control, Kate conjectured; it was about wanting babies. Determined women might be determined to have babies, or not have them, but the idea of control was an illusion. Gestation progressed, labor progressed, birth progressed, opening and driven, and once life existed, threats to life progressed. Mothers tied ribbons on baby shoes and baby shirts, and for a while the ribbons stayed tied.

"Alexander," Kate said.

Startled by the slight alarm in her voice, he released her hair, pulled his hands to his chin, and frowned.

"Tatie," she said then, "oh, Mr. Tate, sorry. Sorry, hon."

Down the hall, Kate heard her mother's footsteps, and just behind, the tick of Katrina's nails on the wood floor. Matt must have left the kitchen door open: Katrina had liberated herself and made her slow way up the stairs. Kate's mother had put on her heels, so she was undoubtedly dressed in her suit, the pink suit; she was ready to go to Camille's, and now she would lie down to rest, composed, heels aslant so as not to dirty the bedspread, with Katrina on her lap. She'd wait for Kate to collect the baby and the baby bag and the baby things, and be totally, finally, ready to go. Are you ready? she'd say. Are you sure you're ready? That morning she'd sat downstairs in her vanilla robe with the pink satin collar, exclaiming over the Easter basket Kate had filled for her. She took things out and put them back in again, a pleased, determined look on her face. Kate's mother was nothing if not determined, and strong, but her illness progressed and determined she live with Kate. She would never leave Kate, not now. She would not grow well or grow strong; Kate raged against this insane fact even as she tried to comprehend it. She could not save her mother; she feared she could not even allay her own apprehension firmly enough to offer real solace. Kate looked directly into things; she could not lie or deny; sometimes she could not believe or hope, and so she looked for solutions, she grappled and persisted. She could be someone's strong advocate or stalwart defender, as, beneath their differences, her mother had been hers. But now she confronted each new problem, phoned each doctor, studied the intricacies of each new chemo protocol and vitamin regimen, and saw her mother plateau and decline, gain ground and decline, a mysterious spiral downward that dragged all the mundane, celestial detail of the everyday into its slow turning. All were impelled by this movement, this progression. Death was so much like life, Kate concluded, except that it seemed to offer only darkness.

Kate's mother had no partner to care for her; she had Kate and Kate's brothers, who were far away in their Southern lives, engaged in their own struggles. Her weight had stabilized; she had actually put on weight, but she had done so before. It would take a miracle, and rocks didn't roll away, not really; they were shifted by seismic forces, or worn down elementally. No one had that kind of time. Time was so short, so brief. Kate viewed time in a controlled panic, yet a part of her stood back from her anger and the various shades of her despair. Why be disturbed, she thought in a still version of her own voice, a voice far from alarm. Countless lives came and went. Wind passed over the grass. Drought, fire, flood decimated vast meadows, replenished in their turn, a cause and effect of weather and circumstance linked across centuries and solar systems, eons, star nebulae. Kate imagined a gear in space, a great cog to which the faithful prayed, turning, grinding on. Never mind, said the still voice.

"Kate?" her mother called now. "Katie? Is Alexander dressed yet? I can't wait to see him."

"He is dressed," Kate called back, "and he looks fabulous."

"Oh, bring him in here. Let's see."

Kate leaned down and nuzzled Alexander, lay her face against him, hearing the pump and peppered skittle of his heart, the sound behind the cloud suit. Then she scooped him into her arms, one hand cradling the back of his velvety head, and moved toward her mother's voice.

She lay on the bed, almost exactly as Kate had imagined, but more comfortably, still in her stocking feet. Surprisingly, she'd opened her window wide, and there was no screen. The room, shut up for so long, seemed pierced with cool, spring light, suffused with pure air. Kate thought her mother's face almost translucent but for the spots of high color in her cheeks. Was she feverish? No, makeup, Kate decided. She'd rouged her skin with a remnant of the red lipstick she wore, and knotted the collar sash of her blouse. Katrina was a circle of dark smudge on her pastel skirt. The dog's brown eyes, milkily overcast with blue shine, looked inquiringly toward the commotion of Kate's entrance. Katrina read movements, thudding footsteps; she no longer heard sounds, though Kate's mother still talked to her. "Move, Katrina," she said. "Here comes that little boy. He does look wonderful. Those eyes of his, and just the most beautiful skin. Pearly as apple blossoms." She reached for Alexander as Kate settled him carefully in her lap.

"I hope he has enough Black Irish in him to tan beautifully in the summer, like you do," Kate said. "That warm pink color is so pretty on you, Mom. Is the blouse silk? You should wear it to the wedding."

"It's not pink, it's apricot, and I will wear it—it's the best thing I have with me. But I'm not going to put on my shoes today till the last minute, so tell me when you're really ready to go."

"Don't tell me you're going to wear shoes that hurt your feet."

"I didn't bring spectator pumps up here to have them sit in the closet. And they used to fit. Who would think my feet would get bigger just as every other part of me is shrinking? Swollen, I suppose." She followed Kate's gaze to the window. "I got my window open. The air smells so good I don't mind there's no screen. Can you believe winter is over? No wonder we love spring. Don't we, Alexander? Sure we do." She looked back at Kate. "It's his first," she said softly.

She seems so well, thought Kate. A stranger, seeing her, wouldn't know at first that anything was wrong. True, she was seldom on her feet and held herself carefully, her shoulders more and more rounded, as though she was always cold. But a stranger wouldn't know how quickly she'd always moved. Purposeful. Forging ahead. A million things to do. Kate had never been able to keep up with her on the street. *Time is time,* she'd tell the child, the girl, the teenager lagging behind. *Don't woolgather.*

"Time is time," Kate said aloud, smiling. She sat on the edge of the bed. "Remember what you used to tell me? About woolgathering? I was just thinking how often I was warned—"

"The things you think about," her mother responded.

"Woolgathering must have to do with lambs and sheep," Kate went on, "but why does it mean someone is distracted, as though wool is gathered slowly, in a kind of daze?"

"Woolgathering doesn't have to do with shearing sheep. It's more to do with the aftermath, the way puffs of wool drift along the ground after a shearing, you know, when the air catches them . . ." She laughed. "Or maybe you don't know. I did, as a kid. I took care you didn't."

"Why?" Kate asked. "We lived in the country, after all."

"Hardly. By the time you were born, the road was paved. School buses and ranch-style houses, like ours. But there were still farms. I always took my children to see the lambs in spring, out that dirt fork near home. But no, not the shearing."

"I don't know why not. Seems educational."

"It was terrible. Like when I was little. The ewes would bawl and bleed. The men didn't like to get the wool bloody but it was okay for the sheep to get cut and knicked. They bucked so, it was hard for the men not to cut them. Now they use electric shears."

"Progress," Kate said. She stood to look out through the open window. The pickets of the iron fence framed a carpet of crocus and snowdrop in Camille's elaborate garden. Luna strode along Kate's as yet unplanted strip of dirt, dancing in and out of the yard, waving her flounce of a tail, prancing and tossing her head. "Look at that crazy dog," Kate said. "You thought I named her for the moon, but no, Luna is short for lunatic."

"What's she doing?"

"She's biting the air, or the wind. I used to think she was snapping at flies or gnats, but there aren't any flies. She feels the air move and she tries to catch it—a sign of optimism, I think. Listen, you can hear the snap of her jaws. What a nut. Luna, you're a nut." Kate smiled at her mother and leaned forward to pick up Katrina. "We better get going. Can you just hold on to Alexander while I take this one downstairs? Then I'll be up to get you both." Kate held the dog up to the window. "Sorry, Katrina. You can't come to the party. But be consoled. Your compatriot out there isn't coming either, and she's not concerned." Katrina stared, intensely attentive, though what she saw was undoubtedly a blur. Her upright ears quivered. Kate stroked her back. "She's as soft as fluff after you work on her with that comb."

"Poor Katrina," Kate's mother said. "What a point in life to realize she's a dog."

Kate nodded. "Those newspapers we keep thrusting under her are a dead giveaway."

Kate's mother smiled her slow, wry smile. "You ought to make peace with Katrina. When you're an old lady, maybe someone will have patience with you."

"I'll never be an old lady," Kate said.

"Let's hope you're wrong," her mother said. "Let's hope you're not like me."

Kate gave Matt the baby and took her mother's silk-sheathed arm as they ascended the stone steps to Camille's house. Camille's door was usually open; often she didn't even lock it at night. In this day and age, Kate's mother liked to comment, in a big city like this.

"Yoo-hoo," Katherine called, as though she were home, and then she caught sight of the sumptuous table. "Oh, Camille," she said, "you've outdone yourself."

"You certainly have," Kate agreed.

"Katherine! Matt and Kate!" Camille called from the kitchen. "I'm just tossing the salad. I'll be right in. I'm so glad you've arrived—it's just a gorgeous, gorgeous day, isn't it? So sunny and bright—"

"She will be right in," Landon said. "She promised me."

Kate saw that he'd grown his ash blond hair longer. He wore a loose beige sweater—cashmere, probably—and white linen trousers; his clothes were usually soft, like these, but they looked expensive rather than casual, understated, as though elegant camouflage were part of his seductiveness. Women intuited some hurt in him, and he deflected their concern even as he inspired it. He nodded at Kate now and indicated the dining room with an open palm.

The long table behind him was set for fourteen. There were name tags and little gifts wrapped in iridescent paper at each place, and miniature paper Easter baskets to hold glossy, hand-painted eggs, each with someone's name. The spiky centerpiece was a great silver bowl of flaring pussy willow branches, each soft nub concealed by a blown eggshell, meticulously painted. Kate turned to look at her mother and saw that Katherine's eyes glistened with tears. "Sprays of Easter eggs," she said carefully. "They're so delicate, aren't they, Mom?" She touched her mother's shoulder. Small and hard, bones that seemed to fit Kate's rounded palm.

"She's done them in the Russian way," Kate's mother said softly. "They shine so."

"I hope Alexander can't reach them," Matt said.

"I hope not too," Landon said. "Do you know how long it takes Camille to do one of those?" He raised his brows at Kate, a smile playing at the corners of his mouth. "A lot less time than it would take you or me, but still—"

"I couldn't do it at all," Kate said, "in any amount of time. And look how beautiful the colors are, with the chairs."

Years ago Camille had needlepointed the seats of each high-backed chair in bright Southwestern designs that reminded Kate of Appalachian quilts, quilts from the mountains Kate had left. Camille sometimes seemed to her a more sophisticated version of women Kate had grown up watching, women who plowed through whatever distress or complication life offered, who sewed and cooked like artists and raised kids. Women of her mother's generation began to have careers and earn money; in rare cases, most of the money. Unlike Camille, unlike Kate, they never left home. They lived where their mothers had lived and certainly never collected art, or trusted themselves to recognize it. Women of good family added to a legacy of antiques, made their own quilts, raised flowers, perfected a trove of recipes. They were the backbones of their families, put up with men and survived them within the confines of marriage, but they never lost their heads as Camille occasionally seemed to, or picked up the pieces with such élan. Camille was ultra-capable but allowed herself to veer sharply off course "once a decade," as she put it, "for better or worse." Certainty, Kate thought, and strength. Impulse, her mother would say. Dangerous.

Now Camille herself strode into the dining room, resplendent in a full white dress and lapis jewelry. Kate recognized her mother's apricot jacket in Camille's outstretched hands.

"Here we are," Camille called out, "the finishing touch. Katherine, you look beautiful. Isn't this color perfect on her? Kate, let's help her on with this."

Kate reached to assist. "Mom, why does Camille have your jacket?"

"Didn't you notice I wasn't wearing it? She offered to iron it for me."

Kate laughed. "Isn't it enough that Camille cooked dinner for all of us? I could have ironed your jacket. I do iron, Mom."

"Yes, you do, when absolutely necessary, but Camille offered—"

"Of course I offered," Camille interrupted. "I was ironing anyway, I love to iron."

"She does love to iron," Landon said. "Ironing is absolutely tops with Camille. You know, the weight of the iron, the heat and the steam, the repetition; she gets into a rhythm. No doubt it's sexual."

"It must be," Kate said, "I mean, in the sense that everything is."

"Oh, everything is *not*," Kate's mother said. "That's just *you*."

"And we love you for it," said Matt.

"I should think so," Landon said.

"Well, I love all of you, and I'm so glad you're here," Camille rejoiced, kissing each of them. "Let me see that baby," she said to Matt, and reached for Alexander. "Oh, you're so handsome today," she told him. "Why, you're dressed as a *cloud*. Like Winnie the Pooh when he tried to steal the honey from the bees!"

"And look what happened to *him*," Matt said.

"Camille," Kate said, "keep his hands away from those eggs."

"Oh, his little hands are nowhere near the eggs. Matt brought his sling chair over this morning and it's right here—in his own spot *on* the table, just by his mom. Look, darling, do you want to have a seat? Of course you do. Here's the new squeaky bunny I bought you. What a pretty bunny! And your teething rings and your little bear and your plastic books from home. Look at all this—you're going to be busy for hours! Lannie, pour the wine. Let's have some while people arrive."

"Yes, ma'am." He winked at Matt and Kate.

"Thank you, darling," Camille said.

"Go get that corkscrew," Kate told him, "before she replaces you with someone faster."

"What do you care?" he asked Kate. "You won't drink any."

"It's the spirit of the thing," Kate said, "and anyway, Matt will drink mine."

"It's a tough job," Matt said, "but someone's—"

"Got to do it!" Camille chimed in. There was undifferentiated, silly laughter as she fastened Alexander's sling chair straps. "Do let's have some. I'll get Kate some fresh orange juice. Nursing mothers don't need wine. They're naturally magnificent—"

"Vivacious!" Kate added. "Bubbly! Effervescent!"

"—and they're always in good spirits," Camille finished. "Am I right, Alexander? Katherine, dear, have a seat in the living room and put your feet up while Lannie pours the wine. He says he's brought these perfect Italian wines! Kate, come with me into the kitchen."

"Absolutely," Kate said. "I'll help. Matt, watch Alexander?" She fastened the sling chair straps a little tighter, checked to see that the chair was secure, and followed Camille into her small, crowded kitchen, a kitchen hung with copper pots, cooking accoutrements, photographs and utensils, whose every surface stood crowded with jars, cookbooks, serving trays, baskets overflowing with breads and fruit. All six burners on the stove were occupied. "What are you cooking?" Kate asked. "Is it the whole menu from *Gourmet* again?"

"I *love* doing the whole menu. It's fun, a project, always different. But those appetizers, the lamb tarts with chèvre and mint preserves, were so time-consuming—I was all day on them yesterday. It's this pastry dough with bits of chopped, roasted poblano chiles—"

"Oh, my God."

"—they're going to be delicious. Sit down there, sweetie. I'll get your juice." She was slicing oranges even as she arranged the tarts on a cooling rack.

Kate sat at the small round table, just by the sliding door to Camille's porch. "Camille, I don't require fresh juice. Don't you have something so plebeian as a carton of Tropicana?"

"Don't be silly. I'm too spoiled by the real thing. I keep a big bowl of oranges and the juicer right here on the counter"—she fairly threw the

oranges onto the spiraled blade as the whir of the machine burst forth—
"and I make juice all day, whenever anyone wants it. There. This is so
much fresher. You need the freshest, best things now." She brought
Kate a tall glass of still frothy liquid and dropped her voice. "Kate, she
looks so *well*. Remember how bad she was just a few weeks ago? She
could never have come over here for a meal. Every day now, she walks to
the end of the street and rests on the bench. Then she comes back, and
we chat while I garden; I bring a chair out for her. These new treatments
are worth the agony. She really has good time between them."

Kate drank her juice. "There's that word again."

Camille turned back to the stove, stirring, moving pots. "What word?"

"Time. The time word."

"But, Kate, you've got to try to enjoy these weeks when she's doing
well. You do seem so— Is it something else?" She fixed Kate with a look.

"It's a little something else." Kate turned her glass a half circle on the
marble tabletop. "I have to have a test tomorrow morning at nine."

"You? What sort of test?"

She turned to face Camille and spoke quietly. "They're going to aspi-
rate a lump in my breast. An office procedure, but I'm a little nervous."

Camille stopped what she was doing. "You must be nervous, with all
that's going on. When did you notice this?"

"Just recently, but they want to test it quickly. Apparently if you're
nursing or pregnant and there's a problem, it becomes quite virulent, the
hormones . . . It's probably just a blocked duct, but they want to be sure."

"You mean a milk duct, from the nursing." She paused as though to
encourage Kate's affirmative response. Kate only nodded. "I know you
won't tell your mother," she said then, "but have you told Matt?"

"I'm not going to tell him until it's over. It's his birthday in two days.
If something was wrong, he'd always connect first hearing of it to his
birthday—that would be awful, wouldn't it?"

"Oh, honey." She sat opposite Kate at the little table. "You're right to
be checked. But I'm sure you're not sick. That wouldn't happen now, not
to the mother of a beautiful little baby like yours."

"It does happen. That's why they know the statistics. And please,
don't say you're sure. It's bad luck."

Camille grasped Kate's shoulders with firm hands. "Your luck is going
to hold, Kate. It's your mother who is sick, not you."

Kate glanced away from Camille, out the glass door into the garden. The soil bordering the patio was thick with blooming crocus. Lavenders, blues, pinks. A blooming, specific trail wavered the garden's length, though Camille's rhododendron and potted fruit trees still wore protective burlap. Quiet emanated from the still forms of the shrouded trees. They were like penitents, with hoods. With secrets, Kate thought, and prayers. "I like the way you dress your trees," she said aloud. "They look so sheltered and spiritually experienced. Can you make me a cloak like that? A little burlap, a little rope?"

"You were going to go alone, weren't you," Camille said. "Don't. I'll move my appointments and go with you. You don't need a cloak. It's going to be fine."

Kate gazed quietly at Camille, whose eyes were very blue in her strong-boned face, then touched the broad lapis stone of Camille's bracelet, as though taking the pulse of a talisman. "That's what I like about you, Camille. You work so hard, you're experienced, and you're still an optimist."

Camille sighed apologetically. "I know, but otherwise . . . life is so various. Who could stand it? And I've got to have plenty to do. At least then I feel I'm having an effect, even if it's only in my own garden or my kitchen, with the people I bring together for a meal." The sounds of boisterous greetings grew louder. "Which reminds me"—Camille suddenly bolted from her chair and peered through the lit window of the wall oven—"the soufflé. Oh, it looks nearly perfect. I'll give it exactly sixty seconds."

Kate laughed. "Or else. Really Camille, let me help. I'll take the tarts out. I'm sure everyone is here. Use the cut-glass plates?"

"No, let's save those for dessert. Use the majolica, the flower plates." She rose to move napkins and magazines strewn on the counter and uncovered a stack of bright plates. Their irregular borders were a chartreuse pattern of porcelain petals. Camille moved them to the table and placed them in front of Kate like prizes. "Just the green of baby grass. I found them in that church auxiliary shop, down past the firehouse."

"I know all about the auxiliary shop," Kate said. "The plates look old. Are they real majolica? The color is so muted and bright, all at once."

"They are, from some estate, and the ladies knew what they had. But I didn't mind—it's a good cause. That auxiliary funds everything from hospice care to homes for teenage mothers. My firm makes a donation every year. They're a whole network of shops."

"Teen moms to hospice care," Kate agreed darkly, "that does just about cover it. As an unwed mom myself, I pronounce these earthenware flowers perfect for chèvre tarts."

Camille laughed, but shook her finger at Kate. "Their stories are desperate. Yours is romantic. It may be hard, but yours is a wonderful story. Don't forget that. I bought these plates because you were coming to dinner, and I know I'll think of you and Katherine every time I use them, forever."

Kate ran her fingers around the bright edges of the plates and smiled. "Flowers and eggs and plates. We do get a kick out of it all, don't we? Let's just eat and drink into next week."

Camille nodded emphatically. "We'll roar in and out of your appointment, and then spring will be here."

They feasted on chèvre tarts, garlic croissants, salads of baby greens and pears, peppered turnips, horseradish-and-onion potato gratin, English peas with chives and bacon, roast rack of lamb with rosemary beurre blanc. Alexander, lifted into and out of various contraptions, was the hit of the party. He sat crowing in his swing chair for hors d'oeuvres and appetizers, chortled in the reclining position of his stroller during the long toasts that followed, demonstrated chiming rattles from Kate's lap during the main course. He did manage to reach Kate's plate and throw a few empowered fistfuls of gratin and vegetables at her feet, but she scooped up the mess in napkins and wiped the floor before anyone else walked through it. The assembled crowd commented with gusto on the strength of his pitching arm and the accuracy of his aim; they were all a little drunk, Kate realized, and she felt nearly drunk herself, a contact high of sorts, composed of forgetfulness and company, the dizzy, welcome intersection of *so many lives that knew each other not*. That was a line from an old poem, a beautiful poem Kate had known well but could no longer remember; she would have to look it up, what were the words just before? But now there were plates to clear and the peach cobbler and berry pie to warm, and glazed oranges to smooth with crème fraîche. As she flew back and forth from the table Alexander finally began to cry.

He needed nursing, and Kate gave Matt her jobs to finish as Camille went to the kitchen to beat whipping cream with vanilla in lieu of sugar (by hand, she said the electric mixer ruined the texture) and Landon followed her to retrieve the last, best bottle of red. Kate's mother looked at her in mild consternation, no doubt hoping she would nurse modestly rather than open her shirt, and so Kate settled into the same armchair her mother had earlier occupied, and put her feet up on the hassock. She lifted her shirt and nestled Alexander underneath, baring only a ribbon of abdomen; he was so hungry he didn't complain at being covered. There, she thought, I'm certainly decent, and Mr. Tate might even sleep through dessert. She thought of her baby as Mr. Tate when she was happiest, as though she knew him through and beyond time as a personage, a grown man and compatriot, delightful and beloved, original, a bit eccentric, as though he fulfilled her instinctual knowledge of who he was, separate from her, temporarily present in this warm, compact form, smooth skin and new bones.

She looked up dreamily into the dining room and caught Matt's eye. A knowing glance passed between them; Matt knew the locus of her thoughts. The baby against her breast was his as well.

Landon was back with the wine, making a show of opening the bottle as guests milled around him. Matt helped clear the table as her mother sat watching, pillows at her back. The arch into the dining room seemed filled with voices and shifting presence. The small, full rooms of Camille's house were layered with pattern and color; somehow crowds fit into them comfortably. Kate heard her mother laugh at Landon, who was, after all, charming; he was only six or seven years younger than Camille but seemed kiddishly mischievous and sophisticated at once; he'd married money, Camille said, big money, and so wasn't hampered by alimony and child care expenses. In fact he seemed unbowed by care; he came and went, always lightening the atmosphere; he made Camille happy, seemingly, appreciated and benefited by her talents even as he joked about her penchant for control and ducked out of photographs, engagements, commitments, causes and work details he found less than enthralling. Surely the resistance Camille termed his "boundaries" increased his attractiveness to her, or perhaps she was only putting a good face on it all; perhaps she was in love with him, and hoping. But could she love him, be more than enamored? Stupid question. Sex felt so like love, Kate mused, dispassionate, as though her own memories of besotment, the configured ups and downs of her checkered course, were ancient history. In fact there was nothing ancient about history, any history; countless, simultaneous images seemed to Kate to coexist, dimensioned sound, smell, textures; *all we breathe and live within,* ran the lines of the poem she couldn't place, *all that is vanished from us.* Not vanished, Kate thought, moved from sight. Any of them might inhabit again the forms and structures they had once composed, certainly they might, but the shapes would seem changed or wholly new in the intense, sensual present: new snow, new flesh, new place, new child. Kate saw her mother stand, move the pillows at her back, sit again. Pain was not new; pain got old fast. I must finish and get up, Kate thought; she needs to rest or she'll be too tired to stay for the end of the meal. And then we'll all go home, because I won't let her go home alone. "Mom," Kate said, "you must come in here, as soon as he's nursed."

"Just a moment," Landon said. "Let her attend to this wine." He fixed Katherine with a playful look as he poured her a glass, then cocked an eyebrow at Kate.

"Ah, yes." Kate laughed. "The wine to end all wines."

"*You* are not to be spared." He turned from the long table and moved toward Kate with a goblet and the open bottle. "This you must have. Resurrection. In the name of all that lies stored, dormant, waiting to approach perfection . . ."

"Lannie, you know I can't drink anything alcoholic. Give it to the others."

"You don't understand," he said seriously. "This wine is very special. Katherine, tell her."

Kate shook her head. "What about my darling here?"

"He won't know," Landon stage-whispered. "He appears to be *sleeping.*"

"He'll know," Kate whispered back. "He knows everything."

"She's tough," Matt interjected, passing through the dining room with a dessert tray. "Try talking her into wine, or anything else."

"Not one glass?" Landon persisted. "Not a swallow? Suppose he sleeps an extra few minutes. Is that brain damage?"

Kate sighed. "Lannie, maybe I'm a purist. In any case, why tempt myself? Not a drop of alcohol or caffeine has touched my lips these many months. Suppose I drink a whole glass and want another, and then more?"

"You're hardly the type to go off the rails, unless I'm missing something." He spoke quietly, in his most convincing tone. "Listen. Hold the wine in your mouth. Just . . . savor it. Taste it and spit it out."

"That would be a waste. And I'm not sure I want to know what I'm missing."

"But you could *taste* the wine. This has an aged, beautiful bouquet." He poured the wine, leaning near, and held the crystal globe of the wineglass to her face. Kate smelled the clean cotton of his shirt and coat, a tinge of musky aftershave on the back of his hand, and then the shadowy glow of the wine. She closed her eyes and inhaled. "Years in the dark," he said. "You can smell them."

"I can," Kate murmured. It was a deep, black purple smell, murmurous and heady.

"Kate," her mother said teasingly from the dining room, "now that he's had his moment, I have to tell you, you've got smeared potatoes all over the bottoms of your shoes."

"How typical," Kate said.

"Katherine," Landon sighed. "I was making progress. You've distracted her."

"Take them off," her mother told her, "before you track vegetables all over Camille's rugs."

"I will, Mom. My arms and hands are occupied at the moment."

Landon shook his head. "Mothers. You're all impossible." He put the wineglass on the mantel and bent over Kate's feet. "I'm taking them off . . . never fear," he said into the dining room.

"You're all overreacting," Kate said, surveying Camille's Turkish rugs for signs of her passage.

"It's all right, Kate," he told her seriously. "You didn't know you were doing wrong." As she began to laugh he took her ankles and made a show of inspecting her shoes. "These aren't shoes, they're little boots, old lady's boots. I'll have to unlace you." Then he was kneeling, working at the shoes. "What happened to women in high heels? None of you care anymore."

"Not true," Kate said. "My mother is wearing her spectators at this moment. And I won't apologize for my shoes. I admit they're a lot of work, but there's no need to remove them. Whatever damage I've done is accomplished. If everyone will wait until I'm finished here, I'll clean them off myself—"

"No, no," he said, "I think we'd better do as we're told. Luckily our Italian ambrosia has prepared me for this task, but I can imagine how you're suffering." He gazed up at her, smiling, a coconspirator.

Kate looked at him a bit ruefully. "Tell us, Lannie, while you're on your knees there, how did you purloin this wine of the gods?"

"Dusty little shop near my office. Connections."

"Where is your office?" Kate looked into the dining room at the others. The guests had brought out the crumble and a lemon tart, all heaped round with blood oranges and crème fraîche. At Camille's, there was always too much. Time slowed down; people lingered.

"Little Italy," Landon said. He'd pulled off her shoes, and held her feet in his hands. "Great restaurants, small streets. You should come by. We'll have lunch." Stroking the arch of her foot, he said more softly, "You should, you know. Do. Say you will."

Kate looked away, into the dining room. Coffee was being poured. Kate's mother began to serve from her chair, encouraging everyone to have a little of both desserts, they were so perfect together. Now Camille appeared with her gardening catalogues and lists. She spread them out on the table near the silver tray of cups and saucers, the bowl of frothy whipped cream. "There are several dedicated gardeners here who might give me suggestions, so I want to announce my gift of a wedding garden for Kate and Matt. When they get married in their backyard in June there's going to be a beautiful little garden running all along the land and fence between us."

There was a smattering of happy applause. "Oh, Camille," said Kate.

"Lots of blue," Katherine said. "We've spent hours planning."

"There'll be a blue corner, for Katherine. And pinks and rose and peach, and green, green, green, all summer long." Camille reached for her goblet, its round globe dark with wine. "To all of you."

"Hear! Hear!" Landon said. He stood and raised his glass.

It was evening. Dark had fallen, colder than the day. Kate heard her mother walking from her little bathroom to her bedroom. She would be holding Katrina under one arm, touching the wall for support with the other. She was stronger, but at night she moved as though she were still her weaker, sicker self. Kate would have to go and get the dog soon, put her outside on the chain, then wait to exile her in the kitchen. She shifted the laundry basket on her hip and wondered if she had time to fold the sheets before her mother started for the stairs herself, knowing Kate would intercept her. Perhaps. Kate stood in her own room, with a view of the hallway; Alexander was sleeping and Kate liked being near him, working at something without the faint white noise of the monitor she used when she was downstairs. Now she heard the shower come on. Matt was luxuriating; he didn't wear deodorant or cologne, he showered, and his skin smelled good, always. How to describe his smell? Like the faint scent of strong stalky flowers, fallen down clean and powdery.

The radiators hissed softly, coming on all over the house as the warmth of the day's sunlight utterly disappeared. The forced-air hiss was so like the sound of Kate's old apartment, the first-floor walk-through of the two-family she still owned in a very different neighborhood. That barbed wire strung along the tall back fence might have given some women pause, Matt liked to say, but Kate had moved right in, a bachelorette. A grown-up, Kate had corrected him. That house had been her place, but she thought of their new house as a necessity for Alexander, for all the kids. She'd liked the similar vintage of the houses, and the familiar, sibilant hiss of radiator heat, which they'd left on this far into spring for Katherine, who got cold so easily. Moving-in day last October, six months ago, seemed years past; Kate had entered the final trimester of pregnancy but was only reasonably huge. Jonah had found an old black silk shirt of hers in a box and ceremoniously donned it; he ran up and down the stairs to the boys' new room with trucks and Twister and the Classic comic books Kate had bought for the occasion. She'd loved Classic comics and purchased anew the most masculine ones—*Kidnapped! Prince Valiant, The Jungle Book*—wistfully imagining the boys curled up on a couch, poring over pictures and words while the hoisting of furniture continued unimpeded around them. Kate had been that kind of kid, nose in a book, unconscious, but Sam and Jonah were drawn to balls and missiles, action, any action. Sam played outside with Luna, throwing balls hard against the fence and shooting water guns, but Jonah was enthralled with moving in. More stuff! he kept shouting, opening boxes marked "Toys" before anyone could move them, dodging up and down the stairs around and between big men and their burdens, the unbuttoned shirt flapping wildly behind him. Shrunken from repeated bouts at the dry cleaners and purchased to fit another self—a self smaller, Kate mused, in every way—the shirt nearly fit him and the collar, minutely beaded in shiny blue-black jet, was still intact. Jonah wore it all day and begged to take it home. Of course he could take it, Kate said, but would he really ever wear it again? Every day, he assured her, his new shirt.

Weeks later, she played marbles on the floor with Jonah; Kate asked if he still liked the shirt. I like it, he'd told her poker-faced, but my mom says she won't hug me if I wear it. Kate took her turn without comment. Then she'd suggested he bring the shirt back. He could wear it here, anytime. "Yeah," he'd said, considering, but the shirt never made another appearance.

Kate hadn't mentioned the exchange to Matt; it seemed too terrible a story, a story that was her fault, Kate's, that she was so disliked and resented. Possession of her possessions was betrayal and mention of her name was not allowed, yet the kids were supposed to like her. They were kids, therefore Kate must somehow elicit their goodwill over an enormous chasm. Better for them if she'd disappeared into that chasm as the earth closed over her, but it was too late; she stood her ground, holding her child, buying them presents, planning puppet shows and scavenger hunts and filling Easter baskets. Someday, surely, they would all move on. Kate and Matt and his ex were young and healthy, weren't they? Time would allow and demand jointly celebrated occasions, graduation dinners, even weddings. Years from now, they would stand together, proud lookers-on in large or small crowds, sharing the same explicit hopes, relieved the boys were grown strong and accomplished, undaunted, full of their own lives, no longer subject to any custody but their own. His ex would have a new partner—a good person, a fourth parent; happily, they would toast the boys' success. Now Kate folded sheets: white flannel for Alexander, bright yellow for Sam and Jonah, pastel stripes for her mother. She'd folded them all, and there was no more putting it off. A custodian herself, she had to go and get Katrina.

She always felt vaguely guilty when she took Katrina from her mother, as though she were forcing a separation, or depriving Katherine of comfort. No one expected Kate to take the dog outside twice during the night in addition to being up with Alexander, but still, every night, she put off exiling Katrina downstairs to the kitchen. She started up the hall with her mother's sheets. She could change the bed if Katherine was sitting up in the chair; Easter night seemed so clearly a darkness in which to stay awake and keep watch. Kate hadn't taken her to church: another demerit. They'd always gone to Easter services at home, but Kate didn't have a church. She'd offered to find one, pick one, for today, but her mother had only shrugged. Kate had books and friends and traveling; years ago, she'd told her mother the world was her church. The world won't baptize you, Katherine had answered, or counsel you or bury you.

Kate paused at the door of the room. "Mom?"

A small sound. Katherine was already in bed. She opened her eyes drowsily and looked at Kate, almost without recognition. But she smiled. "That was a nice day, wasn't it?"

Kate nodded. "I wondered if you minded not going to church."

"I've gone to church plenty. Anyway, if it's not my church at home, what does it matter?"

"But you've always gone. You might want a minister to talk to. You did that, at times, didn't you?"

"I'll talk to you," Kate's mother said. "And to Camille. Don't you love the idea of the garden?"

"I do." Kate put the sheets on the chair. She could change them tomorrow while her mother bathed. Now she stood close the bed. "You know, Mom, Dad needs to come and see the baby. I won't invite him to the wedding—it's too complicated—but the month after, I want him to visit. He could sleep in Sam and Jonah's room."

"Of course. Waylon should visit. Of course." She touched Kate's hand. "Sorry I'm so drowsy. I can't stay awake. I've taken my medicine."

Kate smiled. "No wonder you're so agreeable."

"Of course Waylon should see his grandson," she said in a sleepy, slurred voice. She closed her eyes. "Don't worry. It will all be fine."

Kate stepped back from the bed. Her parents had divorced nearly twelve years ago; they'd begun speaking to one another again only recently. When Kate told her father of Katherine's terminal diagnosis, he'd shaken his head and referred to his own bout with prostate cancer soon after the divorce. People do get over this, he'd said, I did. But

Katherine wouldn't. Kate looked at the notebook her mother kept by the bed. Yes, the night dosage was checked off. It was all she'd taken this week—just the night dosage. Already her breathing was measured and steady. Her lips parted slightly and she sighed, unaware. Katrina stirred at her side and Kate picked the dog up. The little animal moaned, a tiny creak of a sound, and blinked her filmy eyes. Kate shut off the lamp, turned on the night-light. She did worry; she worried that her mother would get up in the night and fall. But she wouldn't fall on the stairs. Kate did the stairs after dark.

"The chain awaits you," she whispered to Katrina as they started down. She ran one hand along the banister and reflected that holiday nights were always melancholy. When she was a child, Bible movies had described CinemaScope extravaganzas around the Passion: earthquakes and darkness the night of Christ's denial and arrest, flaming rents in the earth of Gethsemane. Lightning and shooting stars attended versions of the Crucifixion in which Christ was denied, humiliated, a criminal scorned except by those who wept for him: all a prelude to the rose light of dawn, the empty tomb and the appearance of angels. Even then, Kate had never believed it, but she believed in those Technicolor earthquakes, the sliding of rain-tossed, eruptive earth as the guilty tried to hide from sight. Kate thought of their personal chasms as represented by similar images: divorce a pitched melodrama of feeling involving shirts and infidelity, and beneath it all, a silence—a long slit in the earth emitting steam, the vented heat of pleasure and guilt. Whose guilt? As with the loaves and fishes, there was enough guilt for all. Miraculous, that quality of guilt, its warmth and weight. Kate was an afterthought in *their* story: Matt and his wife had evolved a relationship fraught with difficulty before Kate knew they existed. His ex had pursued someone or been pursued, then Matt had pursued Kate. Kate had turned to meet the both of them; now they shared their guilt with her. This seemed to Kate a reasonable deal, characterized as it was by negotiation, bargaining, insecurity—all hallmarks of life. But the chasm of death dwarfed guilt. The depths of death were blacker and darker than guilt could ever be, with all its quirks and shadings and degrees.

She stood at the back door and set Katrina on her feet. The dog skittered sideways in simultaneous anticipation and dread as Kate latched the end of the chain to Katrina's collar. She'd meant to buy the little poodle her own lightweight chain instead of using Luna's hardware. Maybe Matt was right; Kate's good intentions were clouded by jealousy of a canine. But she often couldn't remember all she meant to do. She opened the door and stepped out as Katrina danced over the grass in her awkward, hopping gait, dragging the chain. Kate saw Luna busily digging at the border of the naked garden, a blond form moving her flag of a tail, then the big dog turned and bounded toward them, into the arc of the porch light. She tossed her head, snarling at Katrina, yet prancing, showing off. She had something in her mouth.

"Luna," Kate said, "come here. What are you eating? What is that?" She grasped the dog's ruff and stroked her head, held her jaws still. "Let go." She pulled a mangled mass from the dog's mouth, something crushed and yellow, with a spring and a few wet feathers. "Oh, no," Kate said. Her Easter chicken, considerably beyond repair, fell to pieces in her hands, goggle eyes and glittery beak attached by shreds.

Katrina came closer. Luna only fixed her greenish eyes on the ruined mess in Kate's palm and growled. "Here, then, Luna," Kate said, "finish what you started, and bury it." Luna stood very still as Kate held the smashed toy out to her, then took it gently into her mouth and walked with controlled grandeur back into the dark. Kate heard the drag of the chain as Katrina made for the kitchen. Kate followed her inside and stood looking dully for a moment at the back door, then she put newspaper down and bent to unchain Katrina. She closed up the room, latched the toddler gate into the pantry and stepped away. The little dog stood looking at her, vibrating, and Kate turned out the light.

Amy had agreed to come early to baby-sit. Kate told her mother she was going shopping with Camille to look at stepping-stones and a bird feeder for the garden, but she sat with Camille now in a waiting room of the crowded health plan.

"My mother told me not to bother about the bird feeder," she told Camille in a low voice. "She said, 'You think you're going to have any birds with Luna running around out there?' It's like one mother pointing out the deficiencies of another mother's child. I told her the birds would be fine as long as they maintained altitude."

"Katherine has a point. How long have you had Luna?"

"Ever since my last, crazy year of college. Luna's been to California and New Mexico and graduate school, without benefit of leashes or tags. She led a great life until I settled down. When she was a puppy, my friends actually said I should take her because she looked like me."

Camille paged through an issue of *Smithsonian* she'd brought along. "That's silly. How could a dog look like you?"

"I don't know—light eyes, narrow face, long thin nose, lots of hair. I hope it wasn't her tendency to walk sideways, or her, well, rather high-strung demeanor. Matt says he doesn't know that my maternal relationship to Luna bodes well, as though I'm the one responsible for her racy metabolism. I think Luna is just smart."

Camille laughed and rubbed Kate's knee. "Yes, of course she is."

"Anyway, Katrina makes Luna seem Zen-like."

"That's true. I'd have to agree with you."

"I'm sorry to be jabbering, Camille."

"It'll be over soon. They'll call us soon." She dropped the pretense of reading her magazine and looked at Kate straight on.

It occurred to Kate that Camille was nervous, not so sure today that all would be well. The health plan complex buzzed with dim urgency and the monotonous tension of waiting. Across the hall, from the pediatrics wing, sounded the panicked wailing of a child. The wailing rose and fell, pathetic, horribly alarming, and then ceased.

"Probably a baby," Camille said, "getting a polio shot."

"Polio is a drink now. Anyway, let's not think about what the baby is getting. What were we talking about?"

"Dogs," Camille said. "I never had a dog once I came east. I mean, we always had dogs on the ranch, but they lived outside with the sheep, with space and room to run. Even on the coldest nights, they slept with the animals, and they were just fine. It doesn't seem natural to me to pen dogs up in a house. I suppose if you do they get very domesticated."

"To their detriment, you mean. They absorb stress."

"Well, yes, but they elicit good feelings too. Look at your mother and Katrina. I know that dog is a nuisance, but your mother would be so much lonelier without her."

Kate sat back in her chair and they leaned closer to one other in an attempt at privacy. "She is lonely. How could she not be? She's so alone. I can't make that up to her."

"No, you can't. But you've done what you can—"

"Anyway," Kate interrupted, "I'm not sure she's ever really wanted a partner again, a man, since her divorce. Once we were talking and I said something about men's bodies, how much I liked them, and she said, 'Oh, how can you, those awful, hairy legs,' and shivered. Can you imagine? She's one of those women who prefer men stay dressed. When they've got their clothes off, she doesn't want to look."

"But that's what girls were supposed to feel, certainly in her day. She just never unlearned it. How much experience could she have had?"

"It's terrible to think she never slept with anyone but my father, in all her life."

"It is terrible. Maybe there are secrets about her you don't know."

"I wish there were."

"She has other things," Camille said seriously.

"I don't know what other things there are. I know I'm isolated now, and sleep-deprived, but it seems to me there are men and there are babies. And there are books. Yes, there are certainly books, and language of every description."

Camille laughed. "And food and flowers and wine."

"Architecture and photographs. Films. Music. But all these things—when they're wonderful—prime you to want intimacy, connection. Sex."

Camille shook her head. "Maybe your mother feels this way now for her own protection. It's hard being alone. I can't do it. I was so alone as a child. We were educated at home; I never went to school until I was twelve, or played with anyone but my sister. I've told you how my parents were—artistic, Socialist, back-to-the-land types. When I finally got to be among people, I couldn't get enough. I've put up with things I shouldn't."

Kate nodded sympathetically. "I know."

"You mean Lannie," Camille said. "He's been better lately, he really has. Lannie can be marvelous. After two years, we're finally getting to the point that we understand each other."

"That's good," Kate said.

"You and Matt have been together how long?"

"Well, eight months, before I got pregnant. Alexander is four months old now, so it's nearly two years. It's amazing we're still at it, given the state of siege we're in."

"Babies do miraculous things. There's a half-life that goes with babies, like a radioactive momentum forward; it gets you through nearly anything in the first year."

The nurse appeared behind the desk. "Kate?" she called out.

Camille and Kate stood up.

"Two Kates?" the nurse said brightly.

"No," Camille said, "but I'll come in with her. We're together."

Kate lay on the table, naked to the waist, covered with absorbent green cloths arranged strategically to bare one quadrant of her breast. The nurse had injected her with a local and swabbed her skin with orange disinfectant, then left the room. The doctor arranged his instruments on a steel tray as he explained the aspiration and what to expect. He indicated Camille with a nod and asked if Kate wanted her to be present.

"She's here to hold my hand," Kate said.

"Well then," the doctor said, "get busy. This is the appropriate moment."

"Exactly," Camille said, and took Kate's hand in hers.

He picked up the long needle and attached a syringe, tapping it with his finger. "It's not really such a large needle. But I'm extracting fluid, so it has to be large enough to drain off some of whatever material is in there. If we're lucky, it will drain relatively easily. If it's denser material, we may need a larger needle."

"Denser," Kate said. "That would be bad."

"Let's just go ahead," said Camille.

"Is she always like this?" the doctor quipped. "You two are quite a team." He touched Kate with the needle. "Can you feel that? Other than the pressure?"

"No."

"All right. I'm inserting the needle. You shouldn't feel any particular discomfort. Now. We're in."

Kate looked at the ceiling. The circular fluorescent light had an odd corona, bright and white, but as Kate stared its outer radius grew darker, more blue, as though its true qualities became apparent only under close observation. She felt her fingers gripped hard and wondered vaguely if Camille was afraid of needles. Somehow the table, the light, the close stance of the bodies on either side of her, the pressure of the needle pulling something from her while pain stayed muted, cottony and thick, reminded her of another procedure, years ago, when she'd journeyed out of state from her university town to a clinic she saw only once. The awful sound of the machine came back to her, and the nurse's anonymous voice, "There now, hon, almost finished, just a little longer . . ." *It's more to do with the aftermath,* Kate thought now, in her mother's voice, and it was true. Kate hadn't understood what an abortion was until her own had begun, and the knowledge was a total surprise. She had certainly believed in "choice," and still did, but she knew now what choice cost, the spiritual burden it imposed. She knew the word to be a euphemism for an experience never approximated by verbal description, or talk of political issues. Kate had thought of it rather often, for years, and then rather seldom, as though she'd bargained with someone or something to let her forget. Now that she had a child, she understood again. One's first encounter of an experience could seem, in retrospect, almost as flat as a picture in a book. Then it became real, and more real, resonant, until psychic movement toward it was no longer necessary. One stopped resisting or approaching it, and stepped inside. *This is the appropriate moment.* Kate's gaze moved to the needle in her breast; she saw the plunger slowly rise as the syringe filled with fluid.

"I have a good angle," the doctor said quietly, "so I'm going to drain it completely."

Yes, completely, Kate thought. She didn't breathe. The big clock on the facing wall made an electric stutter; Kate saw the jerk of the second hand. She felt the pressure intensify, blur to the edge of pain, then withdraw. The doctor held the needle up, directly over her. The syringe was full.

"Milk," he said. "Clear milk. Look." He depressed the plunger slightly and a clear, light fluid sprayed widely from it in a fanned, delicate arc. Kate felt it fall across her face and hair. Camille reached to wipe her off but Kate stopped her. "It's all right," she said, "it's fine. You could even do that again."

"Not necessary," the doctor said.

"It's milk?" Kate asked. "You're sure?"

"We'll test it, of course, that's routine. But it's milk." He smiled. "The stuff of life."

"Yes, it is." Kate found she could barely speak. "It is."

Camille let go of Kate and put her hands to her face. "I'm sorry," she said, and began to sob.

Kate sat up to embrace her; green cloths fluttered to the floor. As though hesitating at the sound of tears, the light overhead abruptly ceased its hum and flickered two slow blinks of darkness.

She touches her fingertips to her closed eyes. Sleeping in the middle of the day has always unsettled her, and the voices downstairs in her mother's house have grown quieter. She pauses on the landing. Rip and her mother are still talking, but their laughter and cheerful, raucous tone have changed.

"It was tragic that he died," her mother is saying, "but we were so young—seems rather romantic to think we would have stayed together. How unlike you to have a romantic thought. You must be growing addled."

"No, I'm cynical as hell. I'm thinking he'd have left you a widow long ago, what with his heart ailment, and we'd be sitting right here, possibly in this very house. About to eat aspic."

"This very aspic."

Delighted, loud laughter. "The hell of it. We'd look the same, along with the aspic; your kids would look a little different."

"I wouldn't mind looking different," Kate says, entering the room, "as long as I get to be a new, improved version." Rip stands; Kate thinks she recognizes him from old pictures in her mother's forties photo album. He's bald now, mustached, but still tall and thin. His blue eyes and the look of his face—gleeful, smart, obstreperous—resemble that boy with the shock of hair over his forehead. Even in black-and-white Kodaks, he had the look of a redhead, the pale brows and skin. He reaches to shake her hand, his wide palm warm and enveloping. "You still look like your pictures," Kate says.

"*Different, however. And hardly improved.*"

"*Of course you're improved,*" Kate says. "*You've taught, you've traveled everywhere, Mom says.*" She sits next to him, in the chair her mother has pulled up beside his. "*You knew Tom.*"

Rip looks at Katherine. "*She's direct, isn't she?*"

"*She's my daughter,*" Katherine answers.

"*Yes, I knew him. He was a good boy and I was a bad one. We lived together at the boardinghouse, just by chance, down by the bridge, his last year of high school. I was in college. His parents were dead, both of heart attacks, his older brothers out of state in medical school, and I was a hick from way out in the country whose dad had run off long ago. My mother paid tuition and I got a job to pay rent. We were right across from one of the college sorority houses, which I found a great advantage.*" Rip crosses his long legs and reaches in his pocket for rolling papers and pouch tobacco. Expertly he begins rolling a cigarette.

"*She lets you smoke?*" Kate asks.

"*We've discussed it,*" Katherine says. "*He's powerless to stop. But he doesn't actually smoke in front of me. He rolls them and puts them away.*"

"*It's completely wrong,*" Rip says. "*I should have problems, not your mother. She hasn't smoked for twenty years.*" He tamps a line of tobacco into the fold of thin paper, rolls it tight, licks the edge to seal it, puts the cigarette in his pocket, along with the papers and pouch. "*When your mother invites me, I stop in, then smoke what I roll on the way home. I give myself a good cursing and smoke like a fiend all the way back to Rock Fork.*"

"*I'll make you another drink, take your mind off it.*" Katherine stands and reaches for his glass, moving into the kitchen. "*I just have to slice some limes,*" she calls, cracking ice in ice trays.

Rip leans nearer Kate, speaking softly in mock secrecy. "*You've been back nearly two hours. Have you written your coming home poem yet?*"

"*Definitely not. I don't write here. You realize she keeps my books in the piano bench.*"

He nods. "*She showed me. But don't let that stop you. You should write here. I'll give you titles: 'Duress, Re-visited.' 'Desist, Traveller.'* "

"*Those are awful. But 'Traveller' is a good word. You probably know it was the name of Robert E. Lee's horse.*"

Raised brows. "*A distant relative of yours, I understand. The general, that is, not the horse.*"

"Very distant."

"There was a bloodthirsty bastard, all for God," Rip says mildly.

"Well, his horse loved him."

"Not surprising. Thousands of men laid down for the good general, didn't they? Fell asleep at the portals, never having seen much but the farms they marched off of."

"You're not a military man."

"God, no. They wouldn't have me."

"I can't think why not," Kate says.

"He was a medical curiosity." Katherine is back with his drink and three little plates. "Here's the aspic. Our gin and tonics are coming."

"Are you still a medical curiosity?" Kate asks.

"Yes and no. Those were the war years. I was sitting behind the little curtain after my draft physical, and I could hear the nurse call to the others, 'You'll never guess what's walked into the clinic—a twenty-three-year-old Hirschsprung! Come and see!' She was excited. Hirschsprungs typically drifted off into the cosmos as skinny tykes."

"Pilgrims," Kate says, "wise beyond their years. But what does 'Hirschsprung' mean?"

"Congenital gut problem. No nerve endings, intestinally speaking. They cut out pieces now and then. Jesus, it's fabulous cocktail chat."

"We need the cocktails, though. I'll get them." Katherine looks at Kate, amused.

"No drink for me, Mom. Here, you sit down, let me—"

"No drink? What's gotten into you?"

"I know the very plane ride you survived," Rip says. "Better have a drink."

"I'm purifying my system. Let me bartend. You two can get sloshed." Kate rises and goes into the kitchen over her mother's protests.

"Sloshed?" Katherine goes on. "Hardly. I'm not known for my alcoholic tendencies."

"Maybe you should be," Rip chides her.

The big Tanqueray bottle is out on the counter, along with the tonic and limes. Her mother has organized everything—drinks, appetizers, salads, food. The bottles are ice cold from the fridge. Perhaps Katherine drinks now. Drinking, for her, would be one drink every afternoon, at this time. Yes. Her friends, her house, her garden. The long wait until she had these things. All the years her parents were married, Kate doesn't remember adults coming over, other than relatives. Or meals out in restaurants. Or laughter. She hears Rip cursing good-naturedly against the backdrop of her mother's relaxed gaiety. How odd to meet someone who knew Katherine and the boy who died, someone who has returned home after successful escape. Rip married his best friend's wife after an intrigue, her mother has said, but they divorced a few years later in Europe, then were "associated" long after. What's "associated," Kate asked. They shacked up when they got together, her mother answered wryly, shaking her head as though the idea of sleeping with an ex-spouse was complete, insupportable lunacy. In fact, people do it. Doesn't Kate wonder, in the shadow-murk of her anxieties, if Matt will, given the pull of former hearth, home and recrimination? As though the inevitable recriminations in a present, evolving relationship aren't enough to keep one occupied. But haven't Rip and his ex ever committed to other people? Kate asked. Rip didn't, Katherine answered, out of selfishness, he says, not longing. He wanted nothing more to do with wives, period. Kate pours gin over ice, adds tonic, squeezes limes and runs the bright bits around the rims of the glasses. She takes the drinks in; Rip sits laughing, his head thrown back, eyes shut with mirth.

"No one knows this about the Japanese," he is saying. "There I was, in the fifties, head and shoulders taller than anyone, pale white skin, bald, riding the already excellent trains, and the little kids would crowd around me, looking at my smooth shiny head and the red hair on my arms and the backs of my hands, then run away giggling." He displays the hairy backs of his hands. "To them, I was a sort of furred creature. I thought they were amused. But one day there was an accident—the train ran over a drunk. There he lay, maimed and bloody, and I was appalled to see people laughing, quietly, behind their hands. It was anxious laughter. Japanese laugh when they're stressed, in this quiet, nervous way, just as the kids had laughed at me." He shakes his head. "I was scaring them, scaring children," he says. "Luckily, my students got used to me."

"You taught in Japan?" Kate sits. Her mother hands her a small portion of tomato aspic. Dark, dense, studded with olives, it trembles on the plate. Kate feels her stomach quail. Though she's skipped morning sickness, she is not currently an adventurous eater, or a drinker; soon Katherine will know why.

"Germany, too," Katherine answers. "And where else? France?" She cuts into her aspic with a sterling fork. "This recipe is supposed to be <u>très chic</u>. I got it from a magazine called <u>French Cook</u>. Rip subscribes. Kate, did you taste?"

"Not yet." Kate glances through the dining room to the screened porch her mother added on to the house after her divorce. Antique white wicker, bountiful plants. Kate thinks the green outdoor carpeting resembles Easter grass or the surface of a fake putting green, but her mother attests to its waterproof perfection. Katherine has set the porch table with sterling, crystal, good china. Flowers. The little marguerites, muted against baby's breath and pale sweet peas, are a milky dream, not brave, not strong. Kate feels a heaviness in her chest, a softening knot. The women, the silver, the china. Later they will wash each piece by hand.

"Try it," her mother urges.

Kate looks back to meet Rip's gaze. It's as though he can read the moment in which she finds herself. Her mother has fastened on something else, denial, her own hopes; Kate sits motionless. The plates, the sterling in its wooden box, will pass to this child she carries, and the space that child will claim in her life moves now before her, all emptiness and contours, a spacious gravity pulling all it touches into itself.

"You're looking a little stunned, suddenly." Rip leans forward deliberately and takes Kate's plate. "You're thinking 'better not,' and you're right. Aspic and travel aftermath might not agree."

"Are you still queasy from the plane?" her mother asks.

"A bit," Kate allows.

"You'll just have to get over it," Katherine says. "We've got to go take a look at the furniture in Rip's barn, tomorrow, before Matt gets here. Katie's got her own house," she tells Rip. "She's stockpiled a rocker and bookcase in my basement to take there, eventually. Kate, what turns your head lately? What's your heart's desire?"

"I don't know," Kate says. "A bed, maybe." She was about to say, "a cradle," but stopped herself. She feels Rip looking at her. He might suppose she is lovesick. Or just maladjusted, like a poet. She is not maladjusted. She is, probably, lovesick. Her mother. Her baby. Her man, who loves his own babies.

"Dinner's ready when we are," Katherine says. "Rip, are you still working on that aspic?"

"I'll finish Kate's. It's great, actually. I don't know where you get off, Katherine, mastering French cooking. I never have."

"It's not as though the recipes are in French. Oh, but the photographs—" Katherine regards Kate. "I don't know why you want to travel to places like Nepal, where nothing is clean and you can come home with a disease you never get rid of. If you were wandering around in Paris, I could understand."

Kate shrugs gently. "But, Mom, everyone goes to Paris."

"And why do you suppose that is?" her mother asks rhetorically.

"Let's go to Paris, then," Kate says. "Let's go together."

"She has you there," Rip interjects. "Kay and Kay Jr., the Tateman twins, off to Paris."

"Yes, Katherine as Kay," Kate laughs, "a new you."

"Brighter shoes and teased hair," Rip suggests, "both of you."

"The Kay Tour," Kate says. "It's imperative. Travel is so broadening."

"It is in those restaurants." Rip is rolling another cigarette. "For weight control, we recommend the Third World, which Kate frequents."

"I knew you two would get along," Katherine says airily. "I recommend we move to the porch now. No more aspic, just basic, delicious food. Kate, you'll be fine."

"I am fine," Kate says.

Kate washes her face in the little bath off the sitting room. Dinner is over, the dishes are dried and put away, and Rip has gone home. She can hear Katherine through the wall, talking to the dog, gathering needlework from a basket she keeps near the daybed. Her office, she calls the little room in which she spends her evenings. Antique lift-top desk, her bills and papers, family photos. The street beyond the window quiet, winter and summer. Kate hears a car pass. And cricket sounds, soft pulsing beats Kate remembers growing up, each throb distinct as a round, winnowed bead. She refolds the careful guest towel and goes in to her mother.

Katherine looks up brightly. "What time do we need to leave for the airport tomorrow to pick Matt up?"

"We don't need to leave, Mom. Matt's not coming."

"What?"

"One of the boys," Kate says, "the youngest one, is having some trouble at day care."

"What kind of trouble?"

"He peed in the classroom sink, apparently."

"Jesus wept," her mother says. "So Matt's not coming because Jonah peed in the sink."

"Right."

"Little girl, you may as well forget about him."

"Think so?"

"Yes, I think so."

"I don't think I'll do that," Kate says.

Her mother looks at her.

"Mom," Kate says, "let's sit down for a minute."

Her mother turns and sits in her chair by the window. The little room is so small that Kate is four steps from her: the chair and low footstool; the braided rug, the daybed where she lies at night and watches television news programs with her dog on her lap. In winter, to keep the heat in, she shuts both doors through the long evenings, knitting in her chair, her work on her raised knees. <u>Washington Week in Review</u>, <u>The MacNeil/ Lehrer NewsHour</u>, <u>60 Minutes</u>. Heat rattles in the register at her elbow. She gets up when the dog stands at one of the doors and wants out, looking back over one shoulder to bark its imperious little yip. Maybe it was the hot air from that open register that had made her sick, radon or old dust adrift in the closed room through so many winters, sighing into the blue glow of television, meeting the nimbus of light around the one lamp.

"Kate," Katherine says, "what is it?" She puts her hands lightly in her lap, as though steeling herself requires little effort.

"It's just as well Matt's not coming," Kate begins. "I need to tell you something."

Her mother sits quietly. The little room seems to tighten or clarify. Kate is conscious of the framed newspaper clippings on the walls, a series of yellowing photographs and words in black plastic frames. Her brothers' graduations and Eagle Scout awards. Kate, presented with undergraduate awards at college ceremonies. Announcements of fellowship grants. Reviews her mother has insisted Kate send her, small print and grainy photographs from literary magazines. Never the poems themselves, but praise for the poems. Success.

Kate sits on the footstool at her mother's knees, close to her.

"What is it, Kate?" her mother says.

"I'm pregnant," Kate says, and bursts into tears. She holds her face in her hands and sobs.

Her mother touches her shoulders. "But you should be happy."

"I am happy," Kate says raggedly, "but I was afraid you'd be unhappy."

"Oh, Kate."

"You need to know I won't be married," Kate tells her. "Not until later."

"I suppose he hasn't told his wife."

"He doesn't want to tell her now, while they're working out the settlement. He thinks it will just make her more recalcitrant."

"Or it might have the opposite effect," her mother says. "It would if it were me."

"None of them are us," Kate says.

"Matt had better be, if he's going to be a father to this baby."

"It takes a while," Kate says, "for him to be us. All these other people were there first. But this baby is mine. I've given this baby a good father." She wipes at her eyes with her hands. "I'm sorry if you'll feel bad about the timing."

"No one here will know the difference. Just say you're married."

"You want me to lie. Does it matter so much?"

"Here? Yes. It matters to me. I don't want people talking about you."

"I don't care if people talk about me."

"I care," her mother says.

6

The dogwood tree was in full bloom, a riot of frothy pink. If they'd waited any later in May, the blossoms would have dropped, but now the tree stood like a big, stalwart nosegay in the center of the backyard. The iron pickets of the fence and their fleur-de-lis caps were wound with pink and white peonies, tendriled ivy, baby's breath. Camille had cleared the garden of spent daffodils. Tall, belled stalks of white hollyhock nodded above pale blue phlox; the hydrangea and iris, the cloudy lavender, had all bloomed just in time. Kate watched her guests from the second-floor window of her bedroom; they sat or stood among white, beribboned chairs or milled about along the border of the garden. There stood her older brother and his new, second wife, her younger brother and his girlfriend, and Matt's uncle, who was showing them all a rather strange sculpture of rusted metal he'd brought as a wedding gift. And there was Amy, pushing her sister's wheelchair across the grass. She stopped in front of the dogwood and turned the chair so that her sister had a good view. The mimes had arrived with Raphelo, the magician. Very tall, handsome in his fuchsia jacket, he stashed his bag of tricks behind the white azalea bush and stood near the fence looking pleased, which Kate took as a great compliment. After the ceremony he would do his "subtle, milling spectators show." Hoops, balls, juggling pins, he'd told Kate—rabbits and doves got nervous in crowds. Noticing her disappointment, Raphelo had shrugged so regretfully they both laughed. Now he seemed content to find himself in this evolving festival and waited opposite the dogwood in silent correspondence, as though it were his calling to match the salmon throb at the center of the blossoms with the dark pink of his jacket. Kate saw him nod at Amy and she fantasized that Amy might run off with him, elope with the magician, based on one magical day! The Renaissance trio commenced playing a lyre, a flute, and a blond mandolin. The lyre sounded of melodious rain, but it was a clear day, a beautiful spring day. Amy gave her sister a flower from the dogwood, and Kate's memory tugged at her, as though she'd seen Amy before against that shade of pink, in some other place or time. But it was unlikely. Amy had arrived in their lives, like Alexander, but Amy would depart. She'd been their baby-sitter for four months now, but summer would come; Amy herself would marry and move near Parris Island. Her fiancé had enlisted in the Marines; he'd start basic training in July.

"What's wrong with Amy's sister?" Jonah asked.

"She was born with cerebral palsy. It means her muscles don't work right. That's why she uses a wheelchair." Kate smoothed Jonah's collar. Matt owned a forties-era tuxedo, but he'd rented them for Sam and Jonah. The boys wore shirts with pleated fronts and jet buttons, black satin cummerbunds, dark pants striped in grosgrain. "We're already dressed, and I forgot the boutonnieres," she told Jonah. "They're downstairs, in the fridge." She called through the open door of the adjoining bathroom. "Matt?"

"In a minute. We're just finishing." He was helping Sam into his tux. "Am I hearing you correctly?" he asked then, teasingly. "We've withdrawn for dramatic effect, and you don't have the boutonnieres?"

This morning, early, as soon as the shop opened, Kate had walked down to the village to get them. Moira, who'd quit cooking for mothers and newborns to start her own catering business, would bring corsages for Matt's mother and Katherine, but Kate wanted to give Matt and the boys their flowers. Crossing Route 9 on foot was a task she'd set herself on her wedding day. The simple white dress she wore was, in fact, her nightgown; she'd slipped on her sandals and set out, on purpose, with no further adornment. The flowers were paid for; she needed no money, no purse. Her hands were free; she was just . . . herself, a brand-new veteran. She strode across three lanes. Then the light changed, stranding her on the very concrete island she'd felt compelled to avoid for months. Perfect. She stood very still, just touching, shoulder to thigh, the

T-shaped aluminum pole that supported the traffic lights. Attention! The pole buzzed within, its vibration against her subtle and electric. Cars whizzed by. Kate gazed steadfastly over the passing blur.

In a florist's cooler midway down High Street, the boutonnieres lay visible through cellophane in their small white boxes: fern, baby's breath, a single white rosebud whose delicate petals curled tight. Those boxes, neat as rectangular envelopes, were small prizes. Kate would carry them back up the hill to Matt and Sam and Jonah. People didn't always need to know what a gift meant; really, how often *did* one know? The giver knew the gift. She would put the careful boxes in a plastic bag and swing the bag each step, gently shifting the flowers in their green tissue. Little fists, each with a pearl-tipped pin. So armed, she would cross Route 9, twice in one day. This day.

Through winter and hesitant spring, her inability to cross this juncture on foot, with or without Alexander, had become the first secret of her life with Matt—a secret she acknowledged only to herself. She'd never been phobic. How surprising to discover such a definite, inarguable avoidance in herself, which nonetheless tucked into life so neatly. After all, she could easily avoid crossing Route 9, and it wasn't as though she was becoming afraid of other things. She wasn't, was she? She'd thought she was coping well. Somewhere, across the bleak chasm of her mother's illness, she was even hopeful. She supposed she was battling the idea of passage. Some days, she'd stood at the crosswalk a few minutes with the stroller, fighting her dread of noise and blur as she doled out zwieback, entertaining Alexander by counting cars in the singsong he seemed to consider their private language. Those days seemed long past; another day had arrived. All days arrived, dressed themselves, and departed.

The self was specific, Kate believed. Motionless now in her wedding dress, her hand on Jonah's collar, she reflected that the self moved along an evolving path defined by boundaries. The boundaries broke down as the self changed or dissolved. Buddhist and Hindu mystics tried to push the envelope, which they represented as anything but square and neat; they tried to live inside the dissolution itself, to practice within a voluntary pilgrimage. Her mother had begun an unsought, unexplained journey. Despite concerted efforts to interrupt or impede her progress, Kate was merely a witness, unwilling to enter into death, unable to cross beyond it, careful not to violate any limbo that might hold Katherine fast. This much Kate recognized, and the rest was mystery.

Jonah looked up at Kate. He was tired of waiting. "I can get them. They're in white boxes, right?"

"Wait, we're kidding," Matt said teasingly. "We have the bouton-nieres in here with us, don't we, Sam? Sam remembered them."

"You told me to, Dad," Sam said.

"Doesn't matter," Matt answered, "you still get credit. Where's that shoehorn?"

"Are his shoes too tight?" Kate asked worriedly.

"No, they fit perfectly. Really, Sammy." He was talking to Sam. "You're used to your sneakers. These are supposed to fit tighter."

"If my feet had mouths," Sam answered, "they'd be screaming right now."

"Oh, come on," Matt said.

"Okay," Sam admitted, "they don't hurt yet, but I can tell they're going to."

Jonah drew closer to the window. Kate leaned down beside him. They watched Amy and her sister turn halfway around; one of the mimes knelt before them, offering a branch of dogwood flower as if it were his own bouquet. "I like those chairs," Jonah mused. "Maybe I'll get to play in hers today. If she gets out of it, and takes a rest or something."

"I don't think that will happen," Kate told him. "Maybe if they were staying over—but Amy is just here for the afternoon. She always wanted us to meet her sister, so she brought her along." College classes were already over; Amy had moved back to her parents' house in New Hampshire a week ago, but Kate hadn't done anything about finding another baby-sitter. It was too much to think about right now, with all the preparations for the wedding and the party. Matt had written the invitations by hand, and Moira was catering everything; she'd rented the gold-rimmed plates and white folding chairs, brought flowers, food, serving baskets and trays, her own cleanup crew. Kate heard the chime of pans and plates below in the kitchen, and running water. Would Sam ever be ready? The day had begun with running water: Camille, spraying the garden at seven a.m., drenching it, she said, so that everything in bloom would be dry and beautiful for the wedding.

Kate wished the ceremony were over; she could be standing in the garden, talking to people, no longer nervous, her own glass full to the brim. She'd pumped extra bottles of breast milk for Alexander so that she could drink champagne with the guests. Amy had driven down from New Hampshire, her sister's wheelchair folded in back, to baby-sit during the wedding and the party. "My present," Amy had said, "will be myself, and can I bring my sister? It would be a nice trip for us, and she'd love to meet you. She likes weddings." What sort of a girl in a wheelchair liked weddings? Kate wondered. Hannah was the smart one, Amy had said of her sister; as soon as they'd got her into her special school, where computers did so much of what she couldn't manage, she'd done very well. She was finally starting college, in religious studies. According to Amy, Hannah was devoutly Christian, though the rest of the family only observed holidays. And she wanted to hold Alexander; she'd heard so much of him from Amy, and seen pictures.

Kate checked her watch. He was asleep but due to wake soon. Everything might go according to plan, and everyone looked wonderful: the window framed a tableau of such charm and safety that Kate touched the wooden sill to remind herself it was all real. Camille's wedding garden was an impressionistic swath of nodding pastel. She'd planned well, concealing little piles of spent flowers under newly blooming plants. Nourishment, she said, and it was true. The bright jonquils had dried to powdery husks, invisible now as summer flowers burst forth in bouquets and long sprays. Camille contemplated her handiwork in a mid-calf-length, yellow linen dress, broad-brimmed navy hat and matching dark net gloves, the only one to understand the wedding as a garden party. Amy's sister wore light pink, a color diaphanous as seashell against the black wheelchair. Blond, like Amy, she wore her hair in braids, twisted round and pinned. A milkmaid, pale, round-shouldered, her hands in her lap. One hand was turned. Possibly her features were delicate behind the dark frames of her glasses; hard to tell from this distance. Amy herself wore white. Maybe she was practicing. In any case, Kate decided, white made her bridesmaid designee; together, in the old pagan style, they would confuse fate.

"These shirt buttons are way too little," Sam said from the bathroom.

"Should we stand back," Kate asked Jonah, "so they can't see us if they should happen to look up?"

"Why are we hiding?"

"We're not hiding, but we're sort of saving ourselves. Then we appear, right before the wedding, all together. It's a custom, usually for the bride. But we're all getting married, so we're going to walk downstairs together."

"Dad too," said Jonah.

Kate nodded. "In this ceremony, you men are as special as the bride."

"Look at the mime," Jonah laughed. "He's pretending to drink for the minister."

Kate watched the mime fill an imaginary glass, drink it down, fill it again, then stumble backward into what became an adept handstand. The mimes were a male/female team dressed in white leotards and medieval-style silk vests. The mime and musicians were totally separate concerns, but they'd arrived in similar costumes, as though they'd stepped off the same movie set. Kate supposed she might have tried to look more Renaissance herself; then again, it wasn't good to be too thematically obsessed. Her own dress was a Victorian ankle-length gown, simple except for the embroidered silk of the fabric. White on white. *The bride wore a sleeveless, vanilla silk gown embroidered in white, with a white net and lace jacket, all created by hand somewhere in the world, long ago.* Kate had bought her dress from Alyssa's Antique Formal Wear, where the phrase about the world graced the broad store window in white script letters. As a child, Kate had read newspaper accounts of weddings, but she'd always imagined herself being the writer describing the clothes rather than the bride. The one sitting in the back, taking notes, wishing she'd been assigned a gangland war or a high-powered political scandal. *The bride arranged her own hair, a simple chignon with a flower crown of rose and delphinium. She wore no veil because all was known to her, and she had nothing to conceal.*

"There's the girl mime," Jonah said. "She's climbing a ladder."

They were called Jim & Julie, professionally. It seemed such a waste to deal in fantasy, in illusion and pretend, and not christen one's endeavor more suggestively. Kate wondered if their real names were Letitia and Sylvester, or Cleopatra and Mandrake; perhaps they'd gone undercover with white-bread names in quest of posh children's parties and Yankee suitability. Kate was aware that her wedding, in fact, was not suitable, in Katherine's opinion; she'd realized belatedly that her mother's barely discernible hesitation at planning food and flowers arose from a conviction that brides who were mothers should marry with less fanfare. Kate had resisted debating the point. She considered Matt and herself proven quantities. Conception, birth and infancy were behind them. And divorce, of course—Matt's divorce. If Kate prayed, as Hannah must, she might pray they never experienced their own legally sanctioned separation, that they married now for good, not ill, though she resisted ever thinking of divorce as failure. Divorce was acknowledgment, she'd told Matt, and new combinations. Divorce is chaos, Matt had replied, and the paperwork, my God. I forbid you ever to divorce me unless you can accomplish the entire thing while I'm asleep. Then, if I wake up in a good mood, I'll be willing to see you off. See me off? Kate had said. So I'm the one put out to new pastures? Exactly, Matt told her. He might bless her excursion, but he'd packed up his last care and woe; he was staying put. Kate found his ironic statement so moving that she immediately disrobed and agreed to the deal, which was why they'd finally fallen asleep last night at two a.m. as the camouflaging drone of a late, late movie rose and fell. Kate had dreamed, nearly conscious, of white tents and circuses amidst the odd phrases of anonymous whispered dramas: *Shall we go? undeniably reprehensible . . . Madam, your arm! ah, beloved melody.* All day she'd wondered intently if "Melody," in this unknown context, were a name or a song.

"We're ready," Matt said softly. Sam preceded him, carrying the boutonnieres in their compact boxes as Matt reached for Kate and kissed her forehead.

"We are." Kate turned with Jonah to form their lopsided circle. "We have kids, waistcoats, flowers." One by one, she took the boxes from Sam and began pinning rosebuds to lapels. "I award you each the rose of valor," she said.

"What's that?" Jonah asked.

"A special, brave love," Kate answered.

"Like knights," Sam said.

Jonah fixed Matt with a cheerful conspirator's look. "We're staying up late on this one, right, Dad?"

Kate caught Sam's eye and smiled. "We certainly are, but first I'd better see about Mom. She wanted to go down just before us."

.   .   .

Katherine had put on her corsage and sat waiting in her rocker. "You look lovely," she told Kate, then glanced, musing, out the window at the crowd below. "Everything does. You and Camille have made it all so natural and beautiful, with the flowers, and that tree is glorious. I don't know how many pink dogwoods I lost, full sun, no matter. I planted one nearly every year."

"I think I remember. Little white wire fences around them, ankle high."

"They never took. I used to blame your father, for running into them with the mower, but I think now the earth was just wrong. Who can say?" She sighed. "Look, Amy wore white. Alexander is too young to miss her, but we sure will. What could possess her to marry at twenty? She's so young."

Kate envisioned Amy holding Alexander. A week ago, when she'd come to say good-bye, she'd nuzzled him happily, skin to skin, as though she weren't leaving at all. Now Kate touched the flat of her own belly, smoothing the skirt of her bridal gown, and suddenly knew Amy was pregnant. Warmth moved in her like dappled light, as though she herself expected another child. She'd wondered at Amy's seeming ease of detachment, not from the family, really, but from Alexander, when she'd always said how hard it would be to "lose" Kate's baby. She'd planned to stay on through next year, until her recent announcement. But she wouldn't go away without them after all. Amy had lived in their world of baths and milk, sleep and baby spoons, winter to spring; now her body would carry it from them. Kate had noticed her obliviousness, her lack of appetite, the mild, wan look she'd worn lately, but hadn't wondered about pregnancy, even when Amy said she was getting married. Industrious, self-determined Amy, when birth was a matter of choice and mothers might not marry at all? Perhaps she'd miscalculated; more likely, she'd decided. No stranger to life's vagaries, she never seemed to have wavered from an early alliance with her grammar school sweetheart. Kate hadn't met the boy, but Amy said they'd been children together, like siblings; he came from a family of five, like her. He'd helped put himself through college. Now, graduated, all of twenty-one, he'd enlisted in the Marines. Maybe he'd stay in, Amy told Kate; it was a way to afford law school. They weren't buying an engagement ring, she'd confided, just wedding bands, like Matt and Kate. She admitted she was old-fashioned, someday she'd have a diamond, but just now there were so many ways the money was better spent. Easy to imagine Amy married to a lawyer in uniform, serving canapés on a porch while kids dashed here and there. Modest sling heels and a dressy apron with one frill, older, with glasses. Or a lawyer herself? No, not likely. She was a caretaker, not an explorer. Fate had explored for her, without so much as a by-your-leave. That was how women would put it in the town where Kate was born, where Katherine had been a child, a high school girl, a bride.

"Well?" Katherine said now. "Shall I pull myself together? Are you ready?"

Kate looked at her mother. "You know, I think Amy is pregnant."

Katherine nodded slowly. "Could be. Though it doesn't seem out of character for her to just quit school and follow that boy."

Kate smiled. " 'Follow that boy'? Mom, you're too much."

"Isn't he her first and only? All the more reason to follow him now. Some women get next to a baby and that's just about all it takes." She fixed Kate with a fondly approximating gaze. "You're not thinking of starting in again right away, are you?"

Kate laughed. "Well, no. Alexander's only five months old. Why would you ask?"

"That look on your face. You were just his age, a babe in arms, when I found I was expecting your younger brother."

"No, it's just—Amy. And it is my wedding day."

Katherine shook her head. "That's not a dewy wedding-day look," she said softly. "You kind of skipped that, didn't you. You look as though you've seen deep in, way beyond where you're standing." Then she added, almost to herself, "Well, how could you help it."

"I was always the deep, beyond type," Kate chided her, undeterred. "It's my calling. May I remind you that today is a *party*, Mom? Time to make your entrance. Look, here comes Camille to escort you. She gets everyone outside, then you appear and I follow you—just like life."

Two days ago, her brothers had arrived from the airport, Richard with his new wife, Doug and his most recent girlfriend. Kate's mother sat in the kitchen while Kate made lunch for them. "I worry that Doug will never marry," she'd confided. "He seems such a confirmed bachelor."

"Do you think so?" Kate remembered visiting one or another of his beach apartments, how he'd stood at the top of the carpeted stairs, bare-chested, kicking off his shoes. He'd brought home a giggly blond wait-ress from work and they had to be back at the restaurant within the hour. They were literally throwing their clothes off as they ran into the bed-room when Doug came back to give instructions on keys and locks; Kate was headed to the beach. He was laughing, Kate was laughing, but he looked flushed and tense, his smooth torso a tawny silhouette against the window behind him. "He'll marry eventually," Kate said. "He's been too busy to concern himself with all that."

Sailing tourists on his catamaran in summer, ski-instructing in winter, moonlighting as a bartender year-round, Doug liked to characterize his work as highly pleasurable and devoid of security. He described himself as a migrant worker: the shore in summer, the mountains in winter. Kate's older brother, who'd married just after college graduation and gone to work in a bank, had always envied Doug's lifestyle. Now Richard supervised loans to corporations and liked to intone, expressionless, on the subject of Doug's prospects: Great life for a young bachelor. Then he'd follow up, in or out of Doug's hearing, with the observation that Doug wouldn't be a young bachelor forever. Young at heart, bro, Doug would grin, and chide Richard to come for a sail in the glorious Caroli-nas, he needed it, slaving away all these years, the kids, the job, the wife. Of course, he hadn't made such comments recently. Richard had left his first wife over a year ago and moved four states away with Lynette, whom he'd hired at the bank as a secretary. Richard and Lynette had children nearly the same ages. Now they lived six hundred miles from them; Lynette had left hers with their father, until she and Richard "got on their feet" farther south, where Richard had found a new job. I couldn't take those kids away from him, she'd said of her ex-husband. Then why not stay in town, Kate had asked Richard, keep your jobs and see your kids? But someone had offered him a partnership in a new ven-ture, an offer he might never get again; it was now or never: start over. Lynette was a legal secretary in a law firm, paying her own child support as Richard paid his. They'd taken almost nothing from their respective marriages, and they were struggling. Kate had sent them plane tickets to come to her wedding.

"I'm just afraid Doug will concern himself with a career too late. And

Richard—" Katherine shook her head. "Oh, that will never come right. Four children, growing up without a parent."

"Mom—" Kate began.

"I'm sure it's hard for Matt's boys, too, but he sees them three or four days a week. He probably spends more time with his kids than some married fathers do."

"Matt is a married father, Mom, or he will be, in two days."

"You know what I mean." She paused. "Doug is thirty. He should have stayed with the park service. He had that job with the state."

"Sitting in an office all day, miles from snow or coastline? He may have worked his way up to a fire tower and a set of binoculars. Doug knows what he wants, or doesn't. It is amazing, though: fifteen years of serial girlfriends, and he's managed to evade ever moving in with one. But look at me. It took a baby to get me to marry."

Her mother gave her an exasperated look. "I wouldn't boast about it."

"I'm not boasting," Kate said seriously.

"How many men have you lived with? No, don't tell me."

"Two, before Matt. Not many, over so many years. And don't act as though you don't remember them. You met them."

"I suppose I set you all a bad example of a marriage."

"You set a good example of a parent, a relationship—one reason I had the good sense to fall in love with Matt. Anyway, I wasn't thinking of anything *you* did, Mom. I was thinking about Dad. You were young, but wasn't he nearly forty when you married? Talk about a confirmed bachelor."

"And he should have stayed confirmed. I should have known better."

"That's fine talk from the mother of the bride." Kate leaned over and kissed her on the cheek. "Were you going to raise three kids sans husband?"

"I basically did," Katherine murmured. "No," she said then, "I should have married someone else. It might have turned out better with just about any of the others."

Kate knew she was probably right. "Dad was the best-looking. I'll bet you won't deny that."

"Movie-star handsome should be avoided like the plague. That's what I'd like to tell our hardworking neighbor."

"You mean Camille. I'm on my way next door now; I need to borrow some Parmesan, for the salad. Maybe I should convey your advice. Lannie would be thrilled to hear himself described as dangerous."

Her mother nodded. "I'm sure he would. But don't you go over there. She's working on tomorrow's rehearsal dinner, and she's making something special she doesn't want you to see."

"Only Camille would put on a rehearsal dinner for a wedding party that's not bothering to rehearse. Or you might say we've already rehearsed." Kate laughed. "I wouldn't worry too much about Camille. She loves a charmer, and she's a bit of a movie star herself."

"It's different for a woman. Women run into trouble no matter how beautiful they are. But men who are that good-looking never learn a thing. Why should they?"

"Karmic advancement," Kate said, poker-faced. "This life, after all, is but a moment, a ripple on the waters."

"I don't know why you should find that such a delightful thought."

"Because it puts us all in sync, Mom, sort of like spawning salmon, working our way upstream against the current. Flashes of color, a rush of rapids."

Life, a moment? Why had she repeated such a phrase to her mother? Though she supposed Katherine had said as much herself, in various ways and more seriously, numerous times in the past months.

Now Kate heard the clock strike one: the wedding hour. Matt was organizing everyone at the top of the stairs. Jonah, then Sam, then Kate and Alexander, awake and alert in his white suit, aware something was up. Kate held him in her arms and signaled Amy, who stood on the landing below, smiling up at them and waiting to receive him. Kate and Matt had memorized their vows; they'd wanted to do it all themselves and use Zachary as official listener, but he maintained he would say a few words. Zachary, a doctor of divinity and one of Matt's Adams House roommates at Harvard, was fully sanctioned as a representative of the Judeo-Christian tradition, but he fondly referred to himself as a founding member of the Black Buddhist Party. In fact, he'd been a Panther briefly in California, years ago, but the temple in which he practiced now was largely Korean. Mostly, he was standing up with Matt and Kate, triangulating the proceedings, he'd joked, a trinitizing, black Buddhist mother of a presence. Today, watching Alexander sleep, he'd opined Mr. Tate was a fortunate man, both in aspect and in personification: "He is the moment and he attends the moment."

"Here we go," Matt said, as they started down the stairs.

Kate felt his hands on her shoulders, then Amy took Alexander. The caterers came to stand shyly in the dining room as the wedding party passed through open double doors to the garden. How bright and wide the day was, nearly blinding, and the guests were all standing! Only their mothers, who sat together under the trees, watched from white-draped chairs as Kate and Matt and the children walked through the quiet, smiling crowd to Zachary. Then he was speaking of marriage before the blossoming dogwood, *honorable estate, ancient times, gather together,* talking, it seemed to Kate, and talking, as the blossoms behind him stirred, moving like sea stars in a breeze. *No longer alone,* he continued, *symmetry of passages.* She caught Matt's amused eye and felt a stab of panic; Zachary had never mentioned he planned to deliver a homily. Sam and Jonah would get confused; at a particular moment, they'd been told to give Matt and Kate the rings they'd exchange, and then be seated for the actual vows. Though it made a pretty picture to include all the children, Alexander might have cried or fussed, unwittingly cursing them forever, and it seemed unfair to involve Sam and Jonah in the actual ceremony when they were already dealing, more than half the time, with their mother's unremitting disapproval of the whole endeavor. Besides, it was Matt and Kate who were setting forth, casting off, trying to float this amphibious conveyance to ferry them all over hill and dale and ocean of separation. *Sorrows and joys of a various past,* Zachary was saying, *certain glorious future.* What possessed him? Filaments of her drifted: Richard's first wedding, Kate a bridesmaid and her parents divorced just a year. Katherine had refused to be photographed with Kate's father; she'd asked her brother, Kate's uncle, to stand with her in the ensuing, professionally rendered family compositions. Wedding-party roulette. Her father had left immediately after the ceremony; perhaps Kate's painful memory of his exclusion was why she'd refused to hire a photographer today. Ironically, her father was excluded again. It was nearly a year ago now that Katherine had requested permission to tell hometown friends Kate was already married. Kate's trip home to tell her mother she'd decided to have a child, regardless of Matt's marital status, was transformed into a wedding announcement. Shortly after returning to Boston, Kate received wedding presents from far-flung high school girlfriends, all informed of her news by their mothers. She'd written back announcing her due date, but couldn't bring herself to blow Katherine's cover. Hence she could not invite her father, or those oldest friends, to a wedding that in Katherine's version of events had already taken place. Her father would be absent, and her parents' discomfort with one another would cast no shadows. No one would ask or answer the wedding question Kate had always considered most, well, remarkable: Who gives this woman to this man?

No one would obligingly surrender Kate. She and Matt would marry in the garden of their own jointly purchased house. Camille and Landon were taking pictures, as were Matt's sister, and both Richard and Doug. Just an informal album, please, not the staged books Katherine had created of Richard's ceremony; books packed away now in whatever boxes held mementos of failed marriages. One day the children of those marriages might open the dusty boxes like time capsules, peering at images of their parents as couples they couldn't even remember.

Kate's own parents had lived in the same house her entire childhood and rebellious adolescence, but they were never a couple. In her acute teenage remembrance, they were smoldering adversaries, all their sadness layered over. Her father's lone silence and Katherine's striving were the magnetic poles of existence. That any of their children married was amazing, stubborn, willful. Richard had immediately established a family, while Kate and Doug spent a decade in the cultivation of independence. Just now Katherine's suit, a glimmer of promissory pink, floated in Kate's peripheral vision. Doug and Richard stood stalwartly behind their mother, hands on her shoulders as though to support her in whatever bittersweet avalanche of emotion. Second child, second wedding. Katherine had not attended Richard's recent nuptials, which had taken place in an office, with clerical support as witnesses. She wouldn't live to see Doug married. Doug! In the midst of her own ceremony, Kate prayed fortune would present him with the right woman. In the year after Katherine's death, he would marry; Kate was certain. Katherine was that important to them all. Her loss would require strong ballast. The sea would be tempest-tossed, and Kate would become whatever mother any of them had.

Dearly beloved, Kate heard. Ah, here was the melody, and Matt was taking her hands. Kate had a sense of déjà vu so strong and unexpected that she gripped his hands in a gesture that was more than warmth and welcoming; she hung on. It was as though she could see them all from high above and far away, wedding party and guests, each in place on a green leaf of garden strewn with flowers, mimes and musicians in their costumes, children in play clothes and party dress. In the shelter of the house lay the wedding feast and Moira's delicate tiered cake, all aslant on the turning globe. Ballast! Altitude! The storm was below them, and Matt was saying his vows. In offices and gardens, the words were the same. *Sickness, health, richer, poorer, till death.* The words moved through her as a humming enlarged over them all, louder and more insistent. Kate spoke into it, unable to hear her own voice except as underscored vibration. She stepped closer to Matt, until their faces nearly touched. As the sound abated, lifting away, she realized its source; Sam and Jonah were peering into the sky with great interest. Zachary made the sign of the cross in the direction of the departing airplane, encouraging discreet cheers from the more lighthearted guests, but the cub plane and its motorized *om* looped back over as Matt and Kate exchanged rings. Then it disappeared, lifting away. Bride and groom kissed in a dramatic wake of silence and turned from one another to applause and music. Luna and Katrina, beribboned, formerly restrained, dashed into the crowd excitedly, barking in concert. The smooth trill of lute and lyre, distilled, pure as water, enveloped all. People moved about and Raphelo performed with pale blue scarves and hoops he let the children touch; the mimes began serving imaginary food, expertly balancing invisible trays. The dogs took refuge among the tallest flowers in the garden, sank to their haunches, and made no further comment.

They were married! People surged toward them. Matt's mother leaned close as though to express congratulations, but she told Kate pointedly, "I couldn't hear what you were saying to my son."

Doug, beside Kate, put his arm around her and spoke as though in confidence. "You're referring to that fly-over outfit I hired. Good timing, but they forgot the banner. I'll have to speak to them about that."

"Banner?" Matt's mother made a quizzical face.

"When you ask for a banner and pay for a banner, you should get one," Doug said with conviction.

"Oh. Well, I suppose so. What did the banner say?"

Moira was at her elbow with a glass of champagne. The crystal champagne flutes were adorned with satin ribbon and blue forget-me-nots for the wedding party. "Mothers first," Moira smiled, then reminded them, raising her dark brows, "the wedding toast. We're nearly ready."

Matt's mother accepted her glass. "More flowers," she told Matt, who'd appeared with his own champagne. "You certainly know how to throw a party." Nodding in Doug's direction, she said, "He ordered a banner."

"What banner?" Matt asked.

"This one." Doug lifted his glass. "Congratulations, Doc and Kate. Heights and depths, and most important, latitude. The bridge over beautiful waters. To this day, always!"

Amy stepped close with Alexander. "To health and happiness," she said, eyes glistening.

Kate embraced her and then took the baby, balancing him on one hip. Alexander, as though exultant at having found her in the crowd, raised both fists over his head, then opened his hands and crowed. "You tell them," Kate said. "To Mr. Tate, and to Sam and Jonah and Matt."

"Her brother hired the airplane," Matt's mother interjected, increasingly mystified.

Doug winked at Kate. "Did you notice it was blue? To match the garden."

"The airplane was an interesting touch," Matt answered. "Fortunately, I lip-read. Kate said what she was supposed to say. It counts."

"That's a relief," Matt's mother said. "Mazel tov!"

"Mazel tov," his father added warmly.

Kate turned toward her own mother. Across the lawn, at Katherine's side, Sam and Jonah, forefingers jointly extended, took upon themselves the glittery golden ball Raphelo offered. He gestured up, up, as they raised the spinning globe higher. Smiling, Katherine raised her glass.

For a moment the gathering swam in Kate's misted eyes like an impressionistic reflection of modern life. Or perhaps it was just that modern life seemed a process of continual transformation. Together, apart, together, here they all were in their various configurations: Doug and his girl, a pretty blonde, trading sly insults and knowing looks now that the serious moment was over; Richard and Lynette, slightly at odds, having wakened near noon from a late night on Newbury Street; Lannie, ducking assigned photographic duties to mingle as Camille recorded them all in detail. Lannie gave Kate a congratulatory kiss on the cheek, then took Lynette's hand, mock chivalrous, inspecting what he called "the only diamond solitaire in close proximity," implying, out of Katherine's hearing, what a much-divorced, largely unmarried crowd they were. Camille put down her camcorder long enough to respond with the observation that commitment meant all the more when one knew what was at stake.

Kate threw Lannie a jokingly reproving glance as Camille moved away, camera in hand, but she had to admit Lynette's ring was puzzlingly substantial, given Richard's circumstances and the fact they'd never actually been engaged. Lynette was pointing out that it matched her filigreed wedding band; they were antique rings, she said, as though this were consistent with having gotten a bargain. Kate shifted Alexander from one hip to the other and watched as Katherine, across the lawn, pulled her pink jacket closer about her shoulders; she would be marveling to Matt's mother about the garden or the perfectly presented food Moira was setting out inside. Kate knew her mother was determined to "be nice to" Lynette, whose tight, stunned smile, when Lannie wasn't disarming her, resembled that of an actress playing an actress. Later, Katherine would ask how in the world Richard had afforded that diamond. Kate might speculate that personal priorities ranged widely—the rings were probably a symbolic necessity for Richard and Lynette, even if they did without furniture. Hope was a necessity, after all. Kate watched Camille film Sam and Jonah as they stood by the wrought-iron fence that enclosed the garden. Quickly minus their shoes and socks, ties askew, they peered through black pickets at the rope swing Camille's children had long ago affixed to a tall oak shading the narrow hill between the two houses. So oddly adult they looked, in private consideration of plans or wishes, bereft, Kate thought, and possessed of something else. Between them, almost magnetically poised, they held experience jointly, like a bubble they balanced and battered; no parental relationship could ever rival who they were to one another. Their parents were caretaking, demands, safety, and divided, complex shadows; together they were plenitude, fed and lit. Who would be Alexander's comrade, counterpart, alter ego? Kate could not hold him so close, not for always. In the shadow of the trees, she saw Matt offer their mothers more champagne. Alexander kicked his feet as she held him against her. Soon she would have to buy him real shoes, not these glovelike slip-ons with barrel bells to keep them tied. She stroked his velvety leg. The thrill of chiming each time he kicked or moved would probably never be equaled in later, more prosaic locomotion along grown-up avenues and boulevards. He kicked in time to Kate's movement through the crowd, chuckling to himself. "All right, Tate," she told him, "let's tour the wedding."

Landon, pouring champagne, looked up as he topped off Lynette's glass, then raised his own to Alexander. "A symphony of sound," he marveled, "but how do you ever expect that kid to catch any birds or get his fist into a cookie jar?"

Lynette protested, dimpling. "*My* babies wore bells. Babies *love* bells."

"First intimation of cause and effect," Kate agreed.

Landon nodded. "On these our Kate is an expert."

"Expert on which," Kate queried, "intimations or effects?"

"Intimations *of* effect, of course," Landon said seriously. "Causes are beyond even your scope." He turned to Lynette. "Camille and Kate keep me honest. They keep the whole street honest."

"Is that right?" Lynette winked at Kate. "How so?"

"Movement is carefully tracked here," he confided with a slow smile. "I'm always untangling jingle bells from the laces of my Reeboks. Tiny ones, dozens—much smaller than those ascribed Alexander here. I speculate Matt has the same problem, though we've never actually discussed it."

"Confess, now," Lynette teased, "didn't your kids wear bells, especially the girl, on hair bows and zipper pulls?"

"No way," Landon swore, grinning at Kate as she turned away from them. "Run silent, run deep," he said, pitching his voice to follow her. "Those were my watchwords, right, Kate? Hello? Kate?"

"You're just as crazy as a June bug," Kate heard Lynette giggle, her buttery drawl distinctly relaxed.

Kate looked for Matt in the crowd, glad to escape yet thankful for Landon's court jester persona. Lynette's sojourn here had to be difficult.

Richard had declared bankruptcy and moved away with Lynette just six months before Katherine was diagnosed. Devastated, Katherine mourned in the interim, cried easily, couldn't "face her friends," as though it were her life unraveling, not Richard's. When Kate phoned him from the clinic, after the first oncologist conference, he'd said brokenly, "It's my fault, isn't it." No, Kate had protested, no, never, she wouldn't believe people victimized themselves with their own sorrows. Especially not Katherine, who'd followed all the rules for years, and lived by them! She'd *taught* rules to hundreds of children, supplied them with phonics readers and construction paper Pilgrim hats, math, language. *I before e.* All rules.

Clusters of children jostled Raphelo in happy confusion; he looked up at Kate, smiling, as she made her way toward Katherine and Richard. Camille was filming them, angling to allow for the shade of the dogwood, her face all but obscured under her big hat. Landon was work, no doubt, but Camille excelled at work; she stepped back adroitly to allow her subjects more privacy, or perhaps to get a better shot. Matt's mother had vacated her seat and Richard sat close beside Katherine, their knees touching; he'd taken her hand; they seemed almost unaware of Camille, who put her camera down now and turned to help Amy with Hannah's wheelchair. As Kate reached them, they were discussing dogwood. Camille was saying hers were a dwarf species, just tall enough to trail along the garden fence.

"But all dogwood are dwarf trees," Katherine said. "That's the legend of dogwood. My grandmother, even my great-great-aunt, another generation back, told the story."

"What legend is that?" Camille asked.

"There's no scientific basis for it, of course," Katherine said in her practical way, "but it was a spring story about Easter and the Crucifixion."

"Ah, yes," Kate said, "you used to have a postcard, at least when I was little, with the story on the back. How the blossoms had four petals, each notched with a wound, and in the center, the yellow crown of thorns."

"I remember." Hannah bowed her head slightly, in focus or concentration, before she spoke, pale lashes brushing her cheeks behind the glasses. "They used to tell us in Sunday school . . . how the dogwood was once a full-sized tree." There was no stutter, just a hesitation between phrases, on occasional words. Hannah's lips, slightly lax in musculature, appeared soft and malleable as flowers, darkly pink inside. "But the cross was cut from it." She hesitated. "And ever after, the tree grew small and gnarled. So it could never be used again for . . . such a sorrow." She looked over at Katherine. "Is it that story?" she asked carefully.

"Yes, but I've only heard the symbolic explanation of the blossoms. Your version is much better." Katherine smiled, but Kate saw in her eyes that she was tiring.

"Goodness!" Camille said. "The things churches tell children."

"But churches should tell children things," Hannah said gently.

"Everyone else does," Matt joked.

Kate shifted Alexander in her arms, then put him on the grass and let him lean against her. Hannah's manner of speaking made words sound different, so that one didn't automatically assign the usual meanings. Listening to her, Kate could believe in a realm underlying meaning, a realm in which things happened by generally beneficent, mysterious design. Aloud, she said, "It's an animist take on adaptation, isn't it? I mean, as grief or penance, it worked. No one builds anything from dogwood." Alexander grabbed her hands as she spoke. "Dogwood only stands and flowers. Instead of ceasing altogether, the tree rendered itself ornamental, and survived."

Hannah smiled. "More than ornament."

"Beauty is Truth?" Kate asked.

Hannah gave a little shrug. "The stories religions tell—find reasons. Churches aren't so bad."

"There are worse things," Matt agreed, "and none of them were invited to this party."

"Absolutely not," Kate agreed. Alexander had found Hannah's wheelchair, and Hannah's white ankle. "This baby wants to meet you," Kate told her.

Hannah looked down at him. Her eyes focused slightly to one side, and the lenses of her glasses magnified her gray eyes. "Oh, I'd love to hold him. I wish I could take him for a ride. Could we squeeze him in right beside me in the chair, nestled back so that he's safe?"

"If you like," Kate said. "I'll push you, just to the end of the street.

There's a little circle of garden at the end, and a bench. Mom walks up there nearly every day."

"It's really Katherine's street now, and Katherine's bench," Camille added.

"If you're worried that he's too squirmy for you, I can put him in the Baby Bouncer, my front sling, and carry him." From across the yard, Kate saw Jonah rapidly approaching with Raphelo in tow.

"Dad, Dad," Jonah was calling. "Raphelo kept a secret trick for last. It's the best magic, and I saw!" He'd jettisoned his small tuxedo jacket and now pulled his ruffled shirt over his head. The shirt fell away, streaked with grass stains, and his bow tie hung from its elastic like a necklace. Cheeks purely pink, he struck a muscle man pose.

Kate laughed. "Hannah, this is Jonah, Alexander's brother, stripped down to his power suit, and you've met Raphelo. Jonah, we were talking about taking Alexander for a ride."

"In the wheelchair? Can I ride too?" He gave a skip of excitement. "I could hold Alexander."

"That would actually work well," Hannah said. "I think we can fit you in, and you can hold Alexander more securely than I could."

"You got it, buddy." Before Kate even had a chance to brush off grass, twigs, crumbs, Matt lifted him carefully into Hannah's chair, and she rested one arm around him. "A perfect fit," Matt said.

Kate leaned down and put the baby squarely into Jonah's lap. "Show me how tight you'll hold on," she told him, then tucked his hands more firmly around Alexander. "Don't let go at all until I take him from you, okay? Promise?"

"I got him," Jonah said seriously.

"I'll watch," Hannah said. "Off we go."

They were through the gate, down the driveway, and onto the street when Kate paused behind the wheelchair to look back at the party. Music, running trills of sound. Slow, pointillist colors. White balloons drifting in bunches, nodding over their tethers. The group had grown smaller. Most of the guests had gone inside to the buffet. Only Amy stood near Katherine, with Raphelo, watching Hannah and Kate and the children through the fence. Katherine looked tired, but she waved. Raphelo held up one hand as though to signal a pause. Smoothly, with professional flourish, he swirled a cloud of white scarf across Katherine's empty lap. The scarf seemed to hang in midair, elongating, then fell away as a white bird fluttered from it, wings beating a startled staccato.

"There!" Jonah called over Alexander's head. "The surprise!"

"For the bride," Raphelo answered, "one dove . . ."

Surprised and breathless, Katherine cried out as the bird rose, circling higher and higher above them.

She lies awake late in her high school bedroom, looking into the dark. All known objects recede equally—the table, the chair, the footboard of the high spool bed, the bulletin board once tacked with mundane trophies, her mother's precise, needlepointed cameos in their oval frames. The high Victorian mirror of the marble-top dresser stands up like a gleam of ice, furred with shadow. What have they come from, she and Katherine? A place where women held still, having accomplished what was possible. Self-destruct buttons were not part of the mechanism; no one gave in or admitted despair. No, it was a long measuring-up and then a slow unfurling, a dance, dawn to shaded dusk, faces averted from the edge. Legions of pilgrims, cast long ago from the living, drifted beyond that edge like smoke and cloud. Supple leather might hold the form of a baby's foot, but the body changed, moment by moment, a relief of itself, a record of its own metamorphosis. Which struggle has ensued, and where? Kate wants one of Rip's cigarettes, warm from his shirt, so thin it burns quickly and makes a tiny fire.

In Kathmandu that last night, ropes of firecrackers exploded on long poles, sparks flaring in staccato runs above the crowds. This last, biggest wedding night seemed Kate's personal send-off, too bright and loud; after all, she was coming back, wasn't she, she'd found a monastery in which to stay, a mendicant's hours to keep, postulant for a year, out of touch with any world but this. She'd write messages; she'd written Matt, who'd signed her vaccination certificate and asked to see her when she returned. She would see her mother too, explain this plan, this veering off onto the flank of Asia, into the terraced foothills of the Himalayas. Time enough, higher into the long-closed cloisters of Tibet, Bhutan, and this world would change her view of what she'd come from, mix it up, stoic Protestant ethic and Christ as bridegroom crossed with the dharma whirl of prayer wheels, *om madne padne om* behind the words of hymns. Western women learned to sing alone among the dewy roses: *he comes to me and he walks with me and he tells me I am his own*. Expectation only God could meet, the Word made flesh. It was all wrong, and that was the point, flesh blooms and fails. The fireworks popped like guns, singular little stars, and Kate stood in the entrance of a Hindu shrine to escape the crowded street. The carved wooden doorway marked a passage, a small dim room of earth and stone; those on pilgrimage might sleep on a shelf of earth along the dim back wall. Someone lay there now, a fellow journeyman with birthright to this particular sacred; Kate glimpsed the soles of his hand-sewn boots as she crossed into the courtyard of the shrine. Flower leis adorned the stone visage of dancing Shiva, and the altar lay strewn with fruit. Scented mandelas cut open, and sweet banquet breads in flower shapes. Wedding guests had come in daylight; those paying night homage were the local devout or pilgrims from the mountains. Their simple offerings of palmed rice bore little footprints. Satisfied vermin slid discreetly past Shiva into the dark well of stones at her feet. Brother rat, keeper of the dark well, puja warrior. No mansion here, no Father's house. Behind her thoughts Kate imagined she heard the Himalayan wind, wild as tsunami, tear across the remote Tibetan plateau to the northwest; Tibet, she dreamed, moonscape, snowvast ceiling of heaven, hear my prayer.

She found herself standing before the dirt shelf of the passage in the dim anteroom without really remembering having left the shrine. The pilgrim was there still, unmoving. She went closer. In the near dark, he was not sleeping. Dressed in the bulky clothes of the high country, hand-woven vermilion jacket faded to dull scarlet, he lay full length, a small cloth bag beneath his head.

There was murmuring behind her; a small group had paused. Kate turned to see the American girl from the plane. A frisson of recognition passed between them, but no surprise; the street beyond flickered with sound and light. The Danish boyfriend stood silently as though revering *the stolid prayerful weight supine before them. In dappled illumination, the broad, lined face and workman's limbs appeared to have arranged and abandoned themselves. He was not a small man. A crescent of belly showed among layers of cloth; the body had begun to swell. One or two other foreigners murmured comments . . . he was there two days ago . . . at least two days . . . it happens, they come around with a cart. No, Kate thought, no cart could remove the imprint of this form. As she stepped back, looking hard, her eyes tricked her; she saw a movement of light across the body, a lifting of shadow. The confusion of the festival, she told herself later, dappled bursts of the fireworks outside, casting a run of glow. But she felt in her gut it was more: he lay revealed to her, his passage completed, and then the light turned off.*

Kate thought of Katherine. She made her way to one of the four-star hotels to try to phone her mother, but the international operator informed her the lines were jammed. Kate went on to meet her friends; the rest of the wedding night unwound like a bolt of spinning cloth. She had packed her bags. Without having slept, she flew out of Kathmandu through Abu Dhabi and crossed the black desert in a mauve Atlantic sunrise. Came home to an emergency message and went back to the airport.

Now she goes to the window of her mother's house. The town looks worn and twilit, layered in new, American time; square boxy roofs, straight streets and alleys, steeples, pale concrete that shone. Smooth, gleaming. She thinks of rough Nepali wool, with its interwoven bits of wood and husk. Bargains and debts, promises kept. Traveller. Surely the horse soldiering on despite its deluded rider and the pilgrim lying down to sleep share some unerring, indisputable instinct. Tomorrow she will drive into the country with Katherine. They will look for a baby's bed, an object made here from hard woods carved and scrolled as Appalachian myth.

Kate sleeps. In her dream the cradle is an oracle whose turned, pegged wood and scalloped edge are spiritual braille, read by the soul itself, but there are no words in that language. She hears the hard, ragged breath of her mother's last weeks and watches a horse the color of rain, immensely strong, pick its way riderless across a field of corpses. Then she forgets the sounds and pictures; sleep puts them deeply away.

7

Each morning of her father's June visit, Kate came downstairs to see her parents sitting together at the kitchen table. Matt made coffee early, before he left for work; Katherine and Waylon sat with steaming cups before them and spoke of this or that street paving in Kate's hometown, or the vagaries of the last mayoral election. Today they discussed how bad traffic was on Kanawha Hill, and then all the way out Tennerton Road, now that the chain restaurants had gone in.

"My God," Waylon said with conviction, "you can't get anywhere five o'clock of a weekday, all up and down that strip."

"But aren't they widening the road out by the high school?" Katherine asked.

"That won't do a damn bit of good, except to help the buses turn around. There's still too damn many people driving the same place at the same time. And where the hell are they going? Raytheon up there shut down two years ago." He chuckled, shaking his head. "I tell you."

Kate stood in the pantry for a moment, listening, just to hear again the timbre of their conversation. The tone was friendly, not noticeably effortful. In fact, they spoke with a careful eagerness surely afforded by relief. Their actual words could be described as gossip concerning place rather than people, though names occasionally surfaced. They didn't look up when she entered, as though well accustomed to breakfast at the same table.

"Oh, I think Perry will close the store when he retires," Waylon was saying. "Why, he must have been there fifty years. Started it just after the war."

"You don't think his son will take over?" Katherine sipped her coffee. "Bill has worked with Perry a long time."

"Bill does the books for several businesses. He'll probably stay with accounting, or move over to Central National, next door." He was speaking of the bank, one of three on Main Street. "Nah." He gave his trademark curt dismissal, a mix of exhalation and forceful sigh. Considered resignation, everyday grief. "Men's clothes, the stuff Perry sells, don't pay now," he asserted. "It's quiet downtown. Only the ones that still like to walk downstreet shop there. Most go up to the mall."

Kate set the table with bowls and spoons. "But you've always bought your clothes at Perry's, Dad." Year-round, Waylon wore woolen or rayon pants of the same big cut. Wide legs, single pleats, long enough to cover the tops of his wing-tip shoes. She'd never known him to own a pair of sneakers or sandals, or sports clothes of any description. He wore Pendleton shirts in winter, conservative woolen plaids. In summer, he wore white button-down shirts with short sleeves, Arrow shirts he ironed himself.

"Hell, I don't need any clothes," he chuckled. "Anyway, if Perry goes out of business I'll have plenty of time to buy a few pairs of pants. No one else buys the kind of thing I wear." He reached down to pet Katrina, who stood cowering against a rung of Katherine's chair. The little poodle stepped tentatively forward.

Waylon claimed he had no use for animals, but he unfailingly acknowledged or tended to them if he happened to encounter them, repeating phrases in a gruff singsong they seemed to recognize immediately as benevolent. Animals settled near him and waited to be touched. "Yessir, pup," he growled at Katrina, rubbing the dog's ears. "You know it."

Kate opened cabinet doors to pull out a box of Shredded Wheat for her father (two biscuits carefully broken up in just enough milk to make them edible) and All-Bran for Katherine (with Sweet'N Low for her diabetes, half a banana, whole milk to encourage weight maintenance). She set out milk and orange juice and grapefruit. Remembered phrases occurred to her like fragments retrieved from some loving, sorrowful cyberspace. *I suppose I felt safe with Waylon. With some men, you feel that way at first.* When Kate was a teenager, mother and daughter spoke most frankly when they were alone in the car, driving a worn route of hometown transits. Specifics and weathers were forgotten now. Only the words were left, as though years of life had existed purely to provide time and place for sentences engraved in indelible, flowing script, the daughter questioning, the mother driving. *You mean he never told you he loved you? Oh, he tried a couple of times, in his clumsy way.*

Clumsy? Kate couldn't recall ever seeing her father in an act or gesture of physical clumsiness, and the idea of him searching for words caught in her head. He ran machines, paved streets, built roads. When he ran a construction crew and actually poured concrete, his khaki clothes had stayed clean, his work pants creased. Never just a workman, always the boss. His partner might have complained that he let others do the dirtier work; Kate suspected that in fact he tended to personal details just as compulsively as he oversaw every effort in the yard and garage. She remembered him pulling on work gloves as he approached big trucks whose barrels were already turning, the heavy substance pouring out like gray inexhaustible lava. He kept a fresh set of khakis at the plant and never came home in spattered, dirty clothes. The square nails of his hands were always clean. His leather shoes and work boots shone; he brushed them quickly and efficiently at night, and kept a small wooden chest of implements and polish under the bathroom sink. Even Katherine would concur on the subject of his meticulous habits. *Oh, he was fastidious. He never left things lying around. There was no one cleaner than your father.* He was self-sufficient, preferred to do things for himself, and generally avoided social situations that didn't involve his own family. Kate couldn't imagine him as the ladies' man her mother described. *No wonder he married late. He never wanted for companionship.* After the first baby she had an excuse to stay home from Elks Club dances. *He'd have a drink or two and put his arm around some woman's shoulders, or dance too close to her.* Katherine always said Kate looked like her father. If she'd been a man she'd have acted like him too, and cut a wide swath. Of course, being a woman, she could do no such thing.

Now Waylon bent down and lifted the skittering Katrina to eye level on flat, wide palms and peered at her. "Can you see through that hair in your eyes?" he inquired. The dog only blinked, quiet in his big hands. He lowered her to his lap, where she sniffed the air in Katherine's direction and then settled, content.

"Would you like cream for your coffee, Dad?"

"Oh, I'd take some half-and-half if you've got it."

"Don't let that dog bother you," Katherine told him. "She can just as soon lie on the floor."

"Well, now, she's not bothering anybody."

And so they sat, nearly an hour after breakfast every day, while Kate went upstairs to Alexander, summoned by coos and babbles on the intercom. When she brought him down to them, bathed and dressed, Waylon was rinsing out coffee cups, wiping the counter, and Katherine was sitting in her chair, ready to lie down and rest. Waylon went with Kate for Alexander's walk and pushed the stroller. They took him down by the river to feed the ducks. After the first day, her father had a plastic bag of bread ready, torn into little pieces of amazingly uniform size.

It wasn't much of a river, really, more a stream that narrowed and widened, but the walkway along the water was paved, the brush cut to a pretty tumble of weed and wildflower. It seemed to Kate the bridal walk: seven days of a ritual whose significance, admittedly, was apparent only to her. Waylon had never walked her down an aisle. Last month, when she'd stepped across the grass of her own garden to her wedding, he hadn't known and wasn't present. He'd been told she was married a year ago, and his presence would have involved him in a lie that seemed large or small depending on what Kate considered in the same frame of reference. She wanted to undo the lie even now, but surely it was wrong to then ask her father to help maintain a fiction Katherine had requested. And so Kate said nothing. Each morning they were at the river by nine for their promenade, moving slowly through bars of sun and shade as the baby called out and river sounds masked the hum of far-off traffic. Each morning the whole dilemma lifted away. They talked of other things— Kate's brothers, the weather, the lay of the highway they saw in the distance—without referring to the house they'd return to, or to Katherine, who waited for them in her sleep as though illness were an enchantment that came and went. Sometimes they simply walked, amiably quiet, Waylon murmuring acknowledgment of Alexander's sounds and exclamations. This boy's a talker, he would tell Kate. Yessir, he'd murmur then, almost under his breath. My father lives in the unspoken, she'd told Matt, and when I'm with him I live there too.

Waylon steered the stroller to water's edge and stopped. "Yep, here's your ducks. They're looking mighty hungry today, buster." He lifted Alexander into his arms. "Where's that bread, Miss?"

"Right here." She gave Alexander a handful, which he proceeded to cast a few inches over the waters. "I've been meaning to ask how you tear bread so neatly, Dad."

"Why, I don't tear it at all, I cut it with a knife, on the bread board. It's just as easy." He nodded at the converging ducks. "Take a look. They can eat it quick and they don't fight over the pieces."

He was right. Harmony reigned among the feisty ducks. They moved soundlessly as dreams, barely rippling the surface of the water. All light and color and instinctual movement, Kate thought, a blissfully uniform crowd. She surveyed their domain. A strip of grass, thin woods, and a narrow dirt road separated nameless park from town street. Across the way, land had been cleared for a building project as yet represented only by a sign: MCNAMERA CONSTRUCTION. INDEPENDENT AND ASSISTED LIVING. Today Kate pointed out the words. "Look Dad, you could live near me."

"Bunch of old ladies," Waylon responded.

"Don't you like old ladies?"

"Not particularly."

The little park, which seemed an afterthought to the highway overpass dominating one end, was apparently slated for improvement. The dirt road would be filled in and seeded, the walk repaved, a gravel bike path added. Kate wondered if the ducks' overgrown habitat would be improved as well. Streetwise, amply supplemented city ducks, they abided on two brushy islands diverting the muddy water, oblivious to lone drivers who parked along the dirt road and sat in their cars. Occasionally a man or woman emerged from a vehicle and ventured to one of the benches dotting the long pathway. Who were these contemplative souls? Delivery boys smoking cigarettes, pizza signs perched atop their Hondas. Secretaries on break. Men reading want ads, their newspapers propped on steering wheels.

Waylon wore his summer hat, Kate her own wide pants and a halter top, the better to get some sun. She might have attired herself more modestly if not for her father's company. Recently she'd sat on the bench directly to her left, Luna's leash in hand, idly pushing Alexander's stroller back and forth as she watched the river, when she noticed a rhythmically shaking bush at water's edge. Someone crouched behind it, watching her as the movement of the branches intensified. There were no burning bushes in modern life, only bushes agitated by the morning labors of perverts. The idiot! Kate got up and walked away, only to find that the man stood up and followed her, half a block behind, on the opposite side of the street. She was angry at herself for not turning around and yelling at him, but suppose he was a pervert with a gun, rather than a mere bush-beater? And why pick a woman with a baby? Kate resigned herself to walking past her own house when they reached the busy High Street, but her pursuer turned back as they neared the top of the hill, perhaps to revisit the scene of his efforts. Not the kind of thing she'd mention to her father, though she'd made a call to the local precinct and reported the incident to Matt that night in derisive tones, incorporating every bush cliché that occurred to her. No, she wouldn't tell Waylon. After he left, she would have to come here in the late afternoon, when it was more crowded. The summer would grow rounder and sweeter, full of scent and blossom.

"This baby is quite a chunk, now, I'm telling you." Waylon put Alexander back in his stroller, where he crowed and reached for the bread bag.

"Eighty-ninth percentile," Kate said.

"Say what?" Waylon looked puzzled.

"On the scale of weight for babies his age," Kate explained.

Waylon adjusted the safety strap and straightened up as Alexander protested. "Hear that, mister? They're already keeping tabs on you. Don't fret now, those ducks will follow us. They need the exercise." Idly, Kate took her father's arm as they began walking along the water. For the first time, Waylon mentioned Katherine. "Your mother," he said, "how do you think she's doing?"

"Pretty well, don't you think?"

He nodded, circumspect.

"I mean, considering," Kate said then. "She does badly, then gets better. She fights her way back, but never all the way. She's always losing ground."

Waylon nodded.

"So far, I think it's bearable for her." Kate looked back at the meandering river. The ducks were, in fact, swimming along behind them, but Alexander had lost interest. The forgotten bread bag, upended now and smashed in beside him, trailed crumbs with every jostle; insistent pigeons settled and flew, settled and flew, squabbling like a crowd of hungry minions. "She talks about her mother," Kate told Waylon. "Well, she always has, but now she tells the illness stories, you know, her mother's last months. How long did she live, after you were married?"

Waylon reached up to adjust the brim of his hat. "Oh, about six months."

"Is it true there were never any difficulties between them?" Kate asked softly. "Her mother seems to have been so strong, so idolized, even when she was sick. And Mom seems to have been the perfect, able caregiver."

For a moment Waylon said nothing. Kate looked over at him, about to dismiss her own question. "Your mother always has her own versions of things," he said then, his mouth tightening. "You ought to know that."

"That's why I'm asking," Kate said. "What's your version?"

Her father looked away from her, toward the water. "Grace Tateman was a good woman, and she'd always managed on her own. They didn't have anything but that big house. After we got married Katherine could at least quit her job—secretary at the State Road Commission—and stay with Grace. She was bedfast pretty much."

They'd reached the end of the sidewalk and a view of a busy four-lane over a bridge when they turned to walk back. Kate took the empty bread bag from Alexander. The pigeons had dispersed and the ducks had retired to sun themselves on a knob of island. "Did she ask you to take care of Mom," Kate asked quickly, "I mean, after she was gone? The way people do?"

"No. She would have said that to the women."

"What women?"

"Women who came and helped. Mostly older women, neighbors, friends—several of them. May Snyder was a nurse. She moved in the last few weeks. I was foreman on a new job, thirty miles away. I left at seven in the morning and got back eight at night." He paused, then went on in a definitive tone. "Your mother had help. She didn't do it alone."

"No, I suppose not," Kate said.

"Who's going to help you?" he asked. "Now that this baby-sitter— what was her name?"

"Amy," Kate replied. "Her name was Amy."

"Now that she's left, who will help? I'll be too damn far away." He made a dismissive sound. "I could have picked up groceries for you, taken the baby for walks, that kind of thing."

"Camille helps."

"Yes, but Camille has a job. She can't do what you'll need. And Matt can't. He's got to work every day. And with a baby this young—" He shook his head.

They walked on, more slowly. The more civilized end of the little park lay before them, bright green in the sun. Here and there a stranger strolled unhurried. Far ahead, Kate saw Luna's yellow flag of a tail flash through the trees. She'd startled some mouse or squirrel and was on the hunt. Kate took her father's arm. She could have mentioned Hospice, or the Visiting Nurses' Association, or other groups she'd listed in her note-book along with medications and appointments. But she only said, "You mustn't worry. I've thought it through."

Birds wheeled above them, indiscriminate gulls mixing their raucous calls with the warble of pigeons. They wheeled and turned as though on an unseen plane. Luna came bounding back and Waylon paused to receive the muddy stick she gripped in her jaws. He threw it hard in the direction of home. The stick twirled end over end through blue air as Luna scrambled after it.

"You like dogs," Kate told her father. "Why don't you get one, instead of living alone?"

Her father grimaced good-humoredly. "Now, I'm not cleaning up after any damn dog."

Kate did laundry and tried to remember her parents' marriage, way back before she'd realized there was anything wrong with it. Vacation road trips were the only time the family spent uninterrupted days together, captive voyagers in the capsulelike space of the car. Katherine packed the backseat floor with coolers of food and drinks and arranged mattress and pillows overtop so the kids could take turns sleeping. Wherever they went—Myrtle Beach, Deep Creek Lake, Atlanta to see friends—Waylon drove straight through. They stopped at rest stops for picnics, never at restaurants or motels. Waylon had a habit of reading highway signs aloud while driving. "Rest stop, two miles," he would announce, or "Danger, falling rock." Rocks fell onto highways only in Appalachia, Kate assumed, from the sheer stone cliffs blasted apart for roads. He read signs in a tone of mild amusement: "Wheeling, 25 miles," as though he knew worlds the terse words represented.

Her mother would have wanted communication, intimacy, shadings and distinctions, even stories. But maybe she didn't much expect them—from a man like Waylon. He didn't hold with yakking, to use one of his expressions. What he did say was direct, unembroidered—a shorthand of nearly elegant brevity, studded with mild curses that were almost conversational. Always hell this and damn that, her mother would complain, and his grammar! He spoke with no self-consciousness, as though his phrasing and choice of words were honorable allegiance to who he was. To Kate, the cursing seemed manly punctuation, reflecting good humor as readily as anger. "I'll be goddamned," he'd say to express surprise or bafflement, "son of a gun."

At eight or nine, Kate asked him what it meant.

"What does what mean?" he answered.

"Son of a gun."

He'd laughed. "Who the hell knows."

When he was angry, his breathing changed, his fists clenched; he yelled, his mouth inches from their faces, breathing hard as though he might explode. Kate learned to stand her ground yet never meet his gaze. Unflinching, pulse pounding, she stayed silent, motionless, until he backed away. A couple of times, she remembered seeing him cuff her brothers with the flat of his hand, quick whaps to the back of the head that conveyed more insult than physical damage. He left discipline to Katherine. She administered whatever spankings they received, and never in anger. She talked to them first, then they had to bend over her lap, which Kate found far more humiliating than being struck. I had to handle all that, she told the kids when they were grown, your father couldn't trust himself.

He operated in certainties. Men were men and women were women, work was paid and leisure was not. Those in power, men in government or business, were usually sons of bitches. Difference was suspect; people understood their own and should stay among them, yet half her father's background was mystery. His mother had "gone back to her people" after he was born, and his father had passed the baby on to his three sisters to raise. Loyalty to family was unquestioned: raise him they did. Childhood on the farm, before it was sold and marriages separated the sisters. Phases of life marked by transfers from one aunt to another: grade school in Ohio, junior high in the West Virginia Panhandle, high school in Kate's hometown. It seemed the aging aunts doted on him, that his numerous, much younger cousins were like siblings, yet he was never quite anyone's son, anyone's child. A retiree of sixty-two, divorced, he moved back into the small wood-frame house he'd lived in as a high school boy, off and on as a young adult, then as a veteran between war's end and marriage. Aunt Raine, the last, longest-lived of the aunts, widowed for thirty years, was the one he'd taught his children to call "Gran." She'd been his first caretaker; now he became hers. She was able to stay in her own house partially because Waylon had "come home." Last year, at ninety-seven, she'd died in her sleep. In her own bed, Katherine had repeated to Kate, as though the words represented hard-won victory.

The aunts, all alive at the time of the divorce, blamed Katherine. He had more equity in that house than she gave him, they said of the financial settlement, in which Katherine had paid Waylon a cash amount. For her part, Katherine thought it incredible a woman should pay a man for a divorce. Wasn't it enough she'd been the financial mainstay of the family all those years? He doesn't need to think he's going to sit in a chair while I keep him, she'd told Kate, as though to convince herself she had it in her to fight this final battle and remove him from the trim Cape he'd never wanted to live in to begin with. *I told him I was going, with or without him.* And so they'd moved into town. If he refused to sell the rural ranch house they'd lived in for twenty years, the bank was willing to lend her the down payment *and* the mortgage. Her credit was good, whatever she needed. *Of course, we weren't talking a million dollars. They knew I wouldn't borrow a penny more than I had to.*

When the aunts said she'd cheated Waylon, Katherine was bitterly insulted. They'd sold her family home to buy that acre of land and pay for most of the construction Waylon supervised. After the kids were born she'd finished college and then a master's on loans she repaid herself while she taught. It was she who scrimped to take over bills when Waylon was between jobs, as the jobs themselves dwindled to commissions only. When she moved the family he'd refused to include his name on the new loan, which meant she assumed the debt alone, and he was no longer responsible for whatever they still owed on the first house. How, exactly, could she owe him money? I don't know, Kate had told her, and I don't want to know. No sense asking why she'd married him in the first place; Kate knew the litany. He was older, handsome, had a good job, and Katherine's mother was dying. When Kate was planning her own marriage, her mother lay on the daybed and said airily, "The parallels don't escape me."

"What in the world are you talking about?" Kate demanded in a low voice. She'd still had a baby-sitter then; Amy was folding laundry in the kitchen.

"You've had the baby, you've bought the house. Why get married?" her mother said.

"To make an honest woman of *you,* in part," Kate reminded her. She felt her face flush with anger. "Are you saying that now you *don't* want me to marry?"

Katherine shrugged. "I'm just saying, you never bothered with convention before. Why start now?"

"For *fun,*" Kate told her pointedly. "We could do with some around here."

"Oh," Katherine had replied. "Well, then."

Katherine had raised her daughter to believe a man needed bread with a meal. Waylon certainly did. He ate methodically, buttering his bread bite by bite, sopping up the juice from his steak with each carefully torn piece. He ate like a workingman but sat and moved like a king, broad-shouldered, solid. Broken blood vessels across his sun-darkened face gave his skin a healthy flush and set off the silver of his hair. Years ago, in the wake of the divorce, when he was in the hospital after his prostate cancer operation, Kate had helped him shave, running a battery-powered electric razor carefully over his high cheekbones and down along the angle of his jaw. As a young man, he'd had an almost Roman profile, big masculine head and strong, finely drawn features, but his straight nose had been broken more than once in his twenties. "Fighting," was the only explanation he'd ever offered. He didn't refer to childhood or youth, and his responses to direct queries were brief or monosyllabic. His years of living with bone-thin, upright Aunt Raine, driving her on her errands, doing the shopping, taking over the cooking as she grew more infirm, had actually mellowed him, as though living again with someone who loved him, approved of him, depended on him, had smoothed out the tension and flares of rage Kate remembered. Now that she saw him only intermittently, she noticed his courtliness; next to a woman, he walked on the street side of any path or sidewalk; he automatically took parcels or grocery sacks from her; at the store, he pushed the cart, and kept the baby supplied with zwieback. His grandchildren called him Papaw; when Alexander "talked" to him he threw one hand in the air as though paying homage to a colossus. In fact Waylon was just under six feet, but he gave an impression of heft, even in his seventies. It was the walk, Kate thought. Standing at the airport when he'd arrived, searching the approaching crowd for him, she first saw the movement of his shoulders, the top of his hat, the heavy, elegant gait that had once seemed to her so sad and ponderous. Then she could see his face; he was looking down in the same thoughtful way she remembered, a blocklike strength concentrated in his chest and upper arms, like someone tensed to lift a burden. Holding Alexander, she began walking forward, her lips pressed to her son's temple. There's your grandfather, she whispered, look, there he is.

His masculinity was like an elemental gravity. All day, he "helped out," wiping the counter the minute anything spilled, washing any dishes in the sink. He swept the flagstone patio and the front stoop every morning, wielding the broom expertly in corners. The first day, he swept the basement laundry room too, and cleaned the dried detergent out of the well of the washer. It was a hell of a mess, he'd informed Kate; this machine would last twenty years if she took better care of it. What time did they eat of an evening, he asked then, shoulders squared, one hand on his hip; he always ate at five. Impossible, Kate told him. Matt didn't get home until seven, later on nights he picked up Sam and Jonah. Waylon nodded; households should revolve around a man's work. He adapted by having coffee at the stroke of five, and a thick slice of bread with butter. The aunts had made their own bread twice a week, fat loaves Kate tried to approximate by patronizing a bakery. Evenings, Waylon gravitated to Matt and Matt to him. Together, they had a beer before dinner, outside on the patio. They sat in fold-up plastic armchairs Kate had bought at Kmart the day before her father arrived. Waylon sat with his back to the house, just at the edge of the flagstones; Matt sat facing him and the open kitchen windows, his chair at an angle. The chairs were a set piece; Waylon moved them onto the grass when he swept and then replaced them in exactly this configuration. Since he'd begun tending to Katrina, he sat in his chair several times a day while the little dog picked her way through the grass on her chain. Katrina stopped her usual outdoor yapping and actually lay at Waylon's feet, alert and trembling, cowering when cars passed. Luna sat in the garden, mauled tennis ball at the ready, waiting her turn for his attentions.

Inside, cooking supper in the evenings, Kate saw her father's broad back and Matt in profile; she heard conversation concerning the pitch of the roof, the weather, traffic, cars and sports. It was as though Matt joined him in a sanctuary apart from the house and the women. Kate chopped vegetables, marinated fish or chicken. When the food was actually cooking, Katherine came down to set the table, carrying Katrina, who was allowed upstairs for pre-dinner rest. Kate and her mother sat at the kitchen table while Kate made salad and the men's voices murmured outside. Wasn't it strange? They were like a little family.

"You won't believe it," she told Katherine. "They were selling homemade shortcake at the bakery today."

"I wondered where you got them."

"But it's his favorite, isn't it? There they were, in the case. Just seems odd, on the last night of his visit."

Katherine appeared to consider. "It *is* berry season. Maybe they make them every year." Then she leaned forward, conspiratorial. "We won't tell."

Kate was tearing romaine for a Caesar salad. "Tell what?"

"That you bought them."

Kate laughed. "Okay, Mom. But if anyone asks, I warn you, I'll confess."

"I'm sure you will." Katherine smiled, shaking her finger at Kate. "I've always said, you miss so many good chances to keep your mouth shut."

"Think so?" Kate sliced tomatoes as her mother got up to get silverware and plates. "Wait, Mom, I'll do that. We're going to eat in the dining room tonight."

"I believe I can walk to the dining room." She was on her way, holding forks, knives, spoons to her chest.

Quickly, Kate stacked plates, napkins, glasses; she carried them to the dining room and placed them almost surreptitiously on the table while her mother's back was turned, then returned to the kitchen as though she had pressing duties. But she stood at the counter and did nothing, looking absently out at the garden. Katherine wasn't in pain, wasn't nauseous, but she was weaker. It really would have tired her to walk back and forth from kitchen to dining room—as she would have, with each ironstone plate. What tremendous will each day demanded of her, to speak and smile, lift a plate or bowl and carry it from here to there, walk up and down steps. If only Kate had a bedroom on the first floor, or an elevator. If only someone knew which free radical or chemical or virus would prove disastrous in the first place, knew what mix of minute, crosshatched phenomena would lead to disease waged in the body like a battle, and years of second-guessing the invader. Katherine's initial medical team had asked if she lived near a plastics factory. Power grids were bad. Microwaves were bad. Over the hum of the window fan, Kate heard words and phrases from the patio. There was a reference to smoking. Matt's voice, like a radio signal innocently tuned to her frequency.

"You smoked, Waylon?"

"Started when I was sixteen. Two packs a day, forty-five years. I quit, oh, couple of years before Katherine's trouble."

Kate tried to remember if that was true. When had he stopped?

"How did you manage to quit?" Matt asked him.

"Woke up one morning and couldn't breathe. Yessir. Quit that day. Never had another one."

Matt, who seldom drank beer, took an appreciative swig of his Budweiser. Waylon cleared his throat, a raking, guttural sound reminiscent of the smoker's cough ever present all the years Kate was growing up. Childhood nights were punctuated with the sound of his rumbling hack and lit with the yellow light that spilled under the closed bathroom door.

For what seemed hours at night, he smoked and read mysteries. Summer evenings he'd mow their acre of lawn or sit on the porch; Kate couldn't remember him ever helping with meals, doing dishes or cooking, until the last years of the marriage, when he wasn't working much. She would return from high school in late afternoon and find him already home, frying potatoes in the big iron skillet. Gray March days, then the little chartreuse leaves on naked branches and a cold, pewter spring. Waylon and Katherine argued for weeks about moving to town. Perhaps it was that spring Katherine locked herself in the bathroom away from him, shouting, *There are laws to protect me from men like you*, while he stood cursing and seething, both hands grasping the door frame as though to prevent her escape. Or perhaps it was earlier; Kate remembered her mother's voice with the cornered apprehension of a much younger child, as though she'd sat alone in bed and listened in the dark, knees clutched to her chest. By day, those early summers had seemed luxuriously benign; they ate outside on the roofed, concrete patio that ran the length of the house, looking out on fields and a range of hills. The heat broke at dusk, and Katherine served cold baked beans, fresh corn, homegrown lettuce wilted with a hot dressing of bacon, vinegar and sugar. Barbecuing was man's work. Waylon cooked, tending the coals in a long ritual before he assumed a hand-on-hip stance, turning meat with a long, bone-handled fork.

Tonight, Matt was grilling. They didn't have an outdoor table; Kate had never even thought about getting one. Suddenly it seemed a necessity. She opened the French doors in the dining room onto a view of the flagstones and the garden blooming against Camille's fence. The plastic armchairs and Katherine's nearly matching recliner would attend, empty until dessert, when Kate thought they could all go outside and linger. She'd equipped a big tray with bowls for the shortcake and berries, and moved Alexander's high chair from kitchen to dining room. When she collected him from his nap upstairs and put him in it, he seemed perplexed. He'd taken to frowning when confronted with change, as though mighty concentration would meet any challenge. Kate put his plastic keys and pink teething ball on the tray. "Steak and potatoes," she told him. "Boys love them." He guffawed, eyes crinkling, then fixed her with a tilted, aptly timed "I-get-it" grin. Kate smiled but thought she shouldn't. He seemed to pick up on tone. Was he drinking in an appreciation of irony with mother's milk? How would he ever find the way to his own plastic armchair? He stopped the knowing smile as though reading her thoughts, and scowled pensively.

"Katie?" Katherine stood in the kitchen doorway. "You know how he likes to eat early."

Kate thought her mother was reproaching her. "He did eat. I fed him before I brought him down."

Katherine looked at her with patient exasperation. "Your *father*," she said pointedly, and nodded toward the patio. "You'd better take the steaks out to Matt."

Dinner seemed more formal simply because they were eating at a bigger table, in a bigger room, bathed in late-afternoon light. It felt like a holiday, as though they were meant to celebrate more than good weather. Kate couldn't bring herself to mention Waylon's departure, or to toast his visit. She almost regretted making the dinner slightly special, as though any little acknowledgment was too much. Too much for her— she was the weak one. They were amazingly strong; Katherine in her frail body, honed inside herself like some concealed brilliance; Waylon with his deliberate quiet that was stationary as a field. Kate tried not to think about them lest her desolate gratitude at their commingled lives show in her face. Luckily, Matt played host.

"Waylon," he asked, "more steak? I can put another on the grill."

"No, no, I'm fine. Good meat. Where'd you buy this, Miss?"

"Little butcher shop, down in the village at the bottom of our hill."

"Delicious." He looked past her, out the open French doors. The coals in the grill on the flagstone patio glowed. He seemed to look into a middle distance that was empty, neutral space, uncharged and receptive. Kate tried to follow his gaze. Then he looked back at the ear of corn on his plate and began meticulously cutting off the kernels in neat strips. He would push the white corn into a mound with his fork. Salt, pepper, butter.

"Dad," Kate asked, "remember that big wooden picnic table we used to have?" She'd always assumed the broad weathered table was some vaguely illegal remnant of Waylon's years at the State Road Commission, when public parks were equipped with massive tables whose immense weight discouraged pilferage.

"You mean at the old house?"

"Wasn't it an old park table?" When she was small, the whole bench had lifted under her when her father sat down. "How did we end up with one?"

"Oh, the state decided to replace those wooden tables with metal ones that bolted into concrete, so they told the motor pool if they'd just go and cart them off, they could have them. Talk about a waste of tax money! We must have spent a week hauling those tables around to every little hollow any of the crew happened to live in. Took four strong men to lift one." He laughed, pushed his plate away. "Brother, they built them to last in those days."

"I don't know how many splinters from that old wood I took out of you kids," Katherine said.

Kate remembered; Katherine had kept a needle in an empty pin box for the purpose. She'd sterilize it with Waylon's lighter and move it back and forth over the skin, a hot, silky feeling, until she could grasp the minuscule end of the splinter with tweezers and pull it out. Then she'd put her mouth to the hand or finger or knee and suck the speck of blood. A version of a kiss, Kate thought now, for succor, for protection, to take the pain away.

Waylon only shook his head and chuckled, addressing Matt. "Those were wild days when Miss was little, with the three of them." He pushed his plate slightly away and leaned a little back in his chair. "They'd all be at the breakfast table. One brother would look at the other and ask whose side he was on today. Yessir! The boys were a little tough on Miss."

"After all these years," Kate said, "you admit it!"

"Now, it was nothing you couldn't handle."

"That's not exactly what I remember," Kate replied.

"You should thank them," Matt said. "Dealing with men early strengthened you for the struggles ahead."

"I definitely encountered resistance."

"On a daily basis," Katherine interjected.

"All the better," Matt said agreeably. "No princess treatment for you."

"That's not true," Katherine said. "She was always my princess."

Everyone laughed. Kate took her mother's hand in joking, congratulatory solidarity. Matt and Waylon exchanged a look. Just for an instant, Kate saw their gazes connect, as though a glance could traverse the distance from where she'd started to where she sat now. Her father touched his temples with his fingers, a habitual mannerism she'd vaguely associated with worries or troubles when she was small. Alone at the dinner table, outside on the porch, household activity swirling around him, Waylon would touch his fingertips to his forehead or his closed eyes, a pause like a lonely prayer.

Men she knew weren't like him. It was as though his kind comprised a vanished world, a time when sexuality was mute stored power and isolation. Men like Waylon lived by touch, and wordlessness, and custom so ingrained it seemed instinctual. Language blurred instinct, made it harder to find, allowed for variation, illumination. Men entered language and became more obviously complex and expressive, like women, though with a different edge. And Waylon came from working people. Working people were the town then, and Aunt Raine's family figured prominently. Education was apprenticeship. Vocation was blood ties when men worked with their hands, brought family into a business. Kate remembered some of those men, or thought she did, from photographs and stories—her father's uncles, and Raine's husband, and the husbands of the other aunts. Big men of Welsh and English descent, they'd seemed a singular tribe possessed of quiet dignity and understood beliefs. Men Kate knew talked, existed in a range of options, deliberated, vacillated. Workingmen from home had shared fraternity rather than freedom; they made of necessity a respected code. She watched her father cross his silverware on his plate and remembered tables of workmen at modest outdoor cafes in Madras. She thought of their ease and silence, their nearly orchestrated movements as they ate with their hands, folding chapatis shared from a copper bowl piled with the thin, hot bread.

Waylon had glowered at her when she told him she was going to India. Why the hell would she go to such a place, cattle in the streets and filth everywhere. Couldn't she find a job in her own country for Christ's sake? From every city she passed through, she sent him the most beautiful postcard she could find; she wanted him to know that in some strange way this was her alarming country, an alternate, completely opposite, directly sensual place, but in the message space under rows of exotic stamps she only wrote of the heat and the museums; she never said she was sick. Later, from her Nepalese two-star hotel, her high narrow room with its alcove desk and squat toilet, its window flung open on Durbar Square, she stopped writing to any of them, as though in addressing her own notebooks she canceled the need to speak to them, to call out or say where she was.

Alexander began to fuss. Kate lifted him out of the high chair and held him. He liked to roll around in her lap like a bald, brightly clad Buddha. Sometimes, holding him, she felt as though she held all the words she was not writing, warm now, tended and alive, sprung at last from their as yet unformed shapes and configurations, their flat, two-dimensional boundaries. Loving him was a terrible seduction, Kate thought, flowering continually while she persisted in thinking he was hers in the way words were. She discovered him deeply and more deeply in their continuous physical communion, in the dressing, cleaning, feeding, caressing that fed and exhausted her, while writing necessitated a deepening loneliness. Writing happened in sustained, hopeful anguish, like the pain of separation, as though one's counterpart existed in some denied spiritual realm, urgently signaling over a vast distortion of distance while the writer tried to hear, tried to speak. Alexander raised his arms and threw himself back against her, head nestled between her breasts, the better to view his audience. Smiling, he opened his arms to them all.

"Mr. Round-bottom," Katherine said. "Mr. Happiness."

Kate put her face to his neck. He smelled deliciously of baby powder but was undoubtedly wet. She would change him quickly and then appear with the shortcake, babe and whipped cream in hand. Mistress of the house, freshly cleansed of bodily fluids! Her mother should rest; the men should enjoy the equivalent of after-dinner cigars in the library. *Your father never changed a diaper,* Katherine always said of Waylon. *He didn't know much about you until you were older.* "I thought we'd have dessert outdoors," Kate told them all. "You can put your feet up, Mom. I'll clear things later." She nodded at Matt. "You go ahead, Matt. I'll bring everything in a minute. Mr. Tate and I will be right out."

.   .   .

Here in the city it was never truly dark. Lights of cars cast ghost beams that came and went across the ceiling, and the sky Kate could see from bed was gray dark mauve, like a healing bruise. Tomorrow her father would go home as planned. He wouldn't see Katherine again. Kate thought about cigarettes, years and years of smoke, thin wafting threads of smoke, restive and seeking, curlicued in rooms and trapped by ceilings. Cigarette ads were wrong to feature cowboys and western vistas. They should feature women in bed in rooms like hers, thinking and smoking. Cigarettes were hot, bit back just a little, breathed down your throat. No wonder people couldn't stop.

Matt stood in front of his bureau, taking laundered shirts from boxes and putting them in his drawer. He'd picked up the laundry today, the shirts he wore to work. He'd used the same dry cleaner for years predating Kate, a Greek-owned business near the hospital; he took his shirts, picked them up, paid for them, as though it were part of work ritual. Whenever Kate did it for him, Irena, the wispy matron at the counter, pretended not to recognize her before launching into a song of proprietary praise for Matt: oh, that man, such a wonder, he was Irena's man too, Kate might as well know. How surprising Kate was the doctor's wife, so tall, for one thing. Not right for Matt, was the implication, no better than the last one, who likewise had left dry cleaning to Matt's devices. What decent wife would let her husband pick up his own shirts, and why didn't she iron them herself? Those thoughts were Kate's, Matt told her. He pointed out that dry cleaners would go out of business if all wives ironed their husband's shirts. Of course, if Kate insisted on picking up the dry cleaning, he'd forgo his relationship with Irena. I'll stick with the laundry in our very own basement, Kate had replied, after all, she and the washer-dryer had their own evolving alliance.

Their bedroom was quiet once rush hour ended and the traffic stopped. Matt was folding cardboard shirt boxes into little squares that fit in the wastebasket. "I won't turn the light on," he said, his back to Kate. "I feel you in deep meditation. Thank God it's not so hot tonight. Your parental week can end on a balmy note."

Kate watched him. This is what marriage was—a man moving near her in almost dark, someone so known he could never be a stranger. The days ended, jeans or trousers, zippers, cuffs. Whispers, nesting. She barely remembered being alone, everything sharply defined, the only sound at night her dog turning in sleep. Really being with someone for years was a feeling of such completion she thought it had to be wrong— a mirage she helped create. Even through her fears for Katherine, she planned and tended life with a vengeance, as though the everyday were immortal protection. She spun chores and rituals and meals around them all like gossamer webbing mixed in her own mouth. The days were that delicate, vanishing one after another, while fear was the fiery solid she stood upon. How odd that real life should seem to her unreal even as she lay back into it, stretching her limbs in close warmth as though she'd always slept just here, in this fluffy, layered bed. People wanted this, it was natural. Yet she'd never been "people" before, or wanted what people wanted. She'd been someone else, someone in league with her mother, who lived alone, someone who looked like Waylon and Waylon's vanished parents, parents who'd left their baby. Was there a gene for aloneness, for standing apart, an inherited magnetism that attracted only to turn away? Kate imagined a smoky, glowing vapor on her skin, a secret aura that marked those afflicted and blessed by separation from other people.

Matt was people. Student council president: the stamp of it never left. What part of him desired a person like her? When he'd stared at her in that elevator, she'd looked away; when he spoke to her, she'd walked away, but he'd slipped on the white coat and read his schedule, become her doctor and pressed his advantage. You were unattainable, he'd told her, beyond what I thought I could have. Have? Yes, live with every day. There you were in your own self-made world, and it wasn't a small world. You seemed to keep everything you'd ever made or defended with you. You were fierce—that's the word that comes to mind. Certainly he had grounds for some sort of truth-in-advertising lawsuit, Kate observed, now that he knew her for the uncertain, skittish creature she really was. He'd agreed, smiling. What's more, he told her, in the headlong rush of it all he'd ignored the fact that he would have to fight his way in once he caught up to her, then fight twice as hard to *stay* in. Kate remarked that he sounded awfully embattled, but he only shrugged. Some guys liked a good fight. Was that it? Kate asked a little sadly. Or could it be he'd thought she was fierce enough to protect *him,* when no one really had before? After all, it was the one thing people like her were good for. Matt had looked at her meaningfully. Don't sell yourself short, he'd cautioned, you make a mean omelet, and you're good at lining drawers. Every drawer in this house is *lined*.

Now he took change, keys, wallet out of his pockets. The back of his neck under his longish hair was whiter than his burnished arms, shy-looking. Coins touched, chiming metallically as he put them on the bureau.

"I love the way men empty their pockets before they undress," Kate said. "It must be the modern equivalent of taking off armor."

"The only armor left to us." Matt turned to her. "You know, it's felt good having your dad here. Though at times I wondered if I was being a classic enough male compatriot. Stacking my dimes right, so to speak."

"Your dimes are fine," Kate said. "His pockets are deeper, though, in the karmic sense. And darker and emptier."

He lay down beside her. "Waylon gave Sam and Jonah a football. Did you see him yesterday, throwing it to them? 'Put a spin on it,' he tells them, and the ball flies halfway down the street. They were thrilled. Soccer is so suburban-approved, they've never owned a football."

"Soccer is a civilized European import. Real men play football."

"While the princess cheers." Matt pulled her close. "It's been an interesting week."

Kate put her face to his throat. "Now, there's a neutral statement. They've been good, haven't they? They've done well. Say so, will you?"

"They have. It's been this heavy, set-aside time, with lots of space between sentences. The house feels different when I come home in the evening. Pulling into the driveway, I have this mental image of a stucco castle completely enveloped in layers of invisible vines, all grown up in the hours I've been gone." He pulled away to look at her. "I have to say, though, I'm not so sure anymore whose princess you really were. He's the one who calls you Miss, as though he's deferring to you in some old-fashioned, formal way."

" 'Miss' may be old-fashioned, but it's short for 'Missy'—as in 'little miss' or 'pipsqueak.' " Kate traced the line of his jaw with her finger, touched the soft pulse in his neck. "When I was twenty-five, I forced myself to stop calling him Daddy."

"Why?"

"Sylvia Plath. Surely you remember. Her Daddy poems—all the sarcasm and evil and longing she heaped on the word." Kate sighed. "I did want a daddy, someone big and manly, proud like my father, but understanding, sensitive, educated. Someone who expected great things of me."

"Hence your older-men phase," Matt said. He was rubbing the backs of her thighs under her nightgown, always a preamble.

"I never wanted to marry them, though. I wanted them to adopt me. Lead me into the world instead of trying to shut it down with warnings and foreboding. My own father was like a man of a century ago, when men and women in the mountains stayed within fifty miles of where they were born."

"Oh, those mountain breezes," Matt whispered against her face.

"Yes, we need a breeze. A little camouflage. Breeze will do." Kate was up, turning on the window fans. One after the other, they blurred into efficient, rapturous humming. She crept back onto the bed beside Matt, opening her hands as though she'd performed a magic trick. "White noise is right noise. The baby's asleep. Surely *everyone's* asleep. Quick, while the spell lasts—"

They were pulling off the rest of their clothes, snuggling under sheets in manufactured, fragrant air. "Don't rush," Matt said against her face. "We have a few minutes. Let me introduce myself." He was moving his hands over her, circling her legs in his.

"Ah, foreplay," Kate whispered. "Do that tighter, and talk to me. Tell me what you thought about all these evenings with my father, out there in the moat of the castle."

He moved his mouth along her collarbone, smooth, quiet touch to slow them down. "Tonight I thought about the year my father left my mother, for that woman he met at work."

"You were away at college then." She cupped his face in her hands and looked at him. "Why did your father go home?"

"At the time I didn't ask. Years later he told me he went back because he didn't think he could support two families." Matt smiled wistfully. "So he sent me to medical school, and now *I'm* supporting two families."

The words plunged through Kate like little stones. She whispered, "But you can do it. I'll help you." She closed her eyes, tilting toward him, easing him inside her. Later, turning under him, bound up in him, enveloped in the deaf dumb blindness sex almost brought her, she wondered if she'd said the words or only thought them. His muscular thighs pulled her deeper in; the soft dark pushed, contoured with ridges and nubs, hot radiations that pulsed. They were two bodies clinging to the same ship or sled, alternately steering and plummeting, and this was enough, enough . . . a word like a heartbeat. She let the word go, riding her own feeling, hearing Matt's name whispered before and behind her, continuous as the ticking of the fans. People shouldn't ask more than temporary haven, or assume power won't change hands in whatever cycle of years was allowed. No matter what happened between Matt and her, it would always be the two of them, floating this interlude of years between them like a bubble the circumference of their joined arms, magical and dangerous. Brimming, invisibly full, it kept them afloat even as they supported it. She felt herself reach him inside it, holding him tighter each time he ground to the center of her, each time they pulled back to push deeper. *Nothing but that old house . . .* Kate pushed the phrase away from her; she wouldn't hear it or see it; still she refused; she pushed away into her own sensation and heard Matt cry out as though he were her voice.

Falling asleep, she saw her father's face in specific photographs, pictures she'd taken years ago, visiting home alone—Waylon looking dead into her camera, a softened battler, beautiful colors aged into his face. Or that picture of them standing together, Kate in a button-down white shirt similar to his, their heads at the same angle, their awkward-looking elbows. One of her brothers must have taken it; Waylon had squared his shoulders in masculine solidarity, but he always did that for photographs, drew himself up like the lieutenant he'd been in the Pacific. Kate's guardedness was in her eyes. Who had bequeathed her that watchfulness? She slept; she thought she slept. She drifted at the borders of sleep, blunt and eyeless, nudging a phantom coast of inlets and jagged depths. Something was wrong; there were fumblings of sound, muffled noises. She slipped her gown on and stood even before she realized they were real sounds. Not Alexander's cry; she would have heard sooner. Wetness trickled along her inner thighs as she opened their bedroom door and moved into the hallway, toward the landing at the top of the stairs. Dimly, she saw Katherine's form in her white robe, kneeling by the stair rail, and Waylon's dark bulk bent over her. Kate heard a whimpering. "Mom?" she was saying, beads of panic in her voice. "What's wrong, Mom?"

"Your mother fell," Waylon said. "The damn dog—"

"Did I fall on her?" Katherine asked in a crushed voice. "Why is she crying?"

"Just scared, I expect." He reached to lift Katherine up, his arms encircling her. For a moment, he held her. She cringed as though in pain as she tried to stand, and reached for Kate.

Moving to help, to receive her from him, Kate smelled the clean, detergent smell of her mother's robe, tinged with a ranker smell of fear or despair. Katherine leaned heavily against her as Waylon turned from them. Reaching down for the poodle, he trolled the floor with blind hands like a man pulling in a net. The dog darted in and out of reach, piping her cries of distress with increasing confidence.

"Come here, now," he said. "Here, pup." His bare legs beneath his brown terry robe were white and thin, an old man's legs, nearly hairless, pure. His leather slippers looked pristine and oddly feminine. He'd probably worn them for fifteen years—they were the sort of thing Aunt Raine would have given him for Christmas.

"Are you hurt, Mom?" Kate helped her into her room, toward the bed. She seemed to walk without difficulty, but she'd be sore and bruised, or worse; she should lie down.

"I realized Katrina was up here," Katherine said, "and I was going to take her back to the kitchen before she made a mess. But she got under-foot and I fell. Then I couldn't get up, I just—couldn't."

"The dog is all right," Waylon said behind them. "I'll take her down-stairs. She'll probably want a visit outdoors."

"Be careful on the steps, Dad." Kate had reached behind her to flip on the hall light switch as she helped Katherine into her room. In the glow from the hall, she saw her mother's glistening face. "Mom, did you hurt your back?"

"I take so much medication, I probably wouldn't know if I did." She squeezed her eyes shut as though denying tears. "No, no, I'm not hurt. Just . . . angry at myself, waking everyone. Angry at everything! I try not to be." She turned away, but her face was wet.

"Don't go near the stairs if you're up at night," Kate begged. "If you'd fallen down the steps, if Dad hadn't been here . . . You must call me. I'm up anyway, with Alexander—"

Painfully, she eased herself onto the bed. "Of course you are, another reason not to—"

"Oh, *don't!*" She gathered Katherine into her arms. There. Like holding the form of a child, knobby and slender, filled with distracted humming and a wild electricity of hurt. She whispered desperately, without thinking, "How much longer do we have? Think of all the nights I won't hear you! You won't be able to call me—"

Her touch on Kate's hair lingered like a passage of shadow. "I won't need to then. I'll have gone, just as full of hopes for you." The recognition seemed to comfort or exhaust her utterly.

Kate helped her lie back on the pillows, supporting her shoulders and the back of her head as women support infants. "Just promise you'll call me," she heard herself say quietly. "Then I won't worry. Otherwise I'll have to listen for you at night, as well as for Alexander. I won't bother going to bed at all."

Katherine didn't answer, only nodded. She slept so suddenly and completely, as though sleep were a version of drug that altered, orchestrated, read her body, and the only true translation was unconsciousness.

Kate arranged the sheets over her, went to the door of the room, and turned. "Dad leaves very early tomorrow, Mom. We won't wake you, and I'll be back before Matt goes to work. All right?" She waited, gazing at the form on the bed, but there was no reply.

Before driving to the airport, Kate pulled into the parking lot of the construction site opposite the river, at the bottom of the hill. "Look," she told her father. "There's a new sign up now, with a picture. See? They're going to be nice apartments."

He shook his head. "Honey, I don't think I want to be living with any bunch of old people."

"You could have as much or as little to do with everyone else as you liked."

"I'm used to being on my own, Miss."

"I could find you a place of your own, then, but here. None of us are living at home anymore, Dad. I hate for you to be there by yourself."

"Why, it's what I'm used to. What would I do here?"

"What do you do there?"

"I make the rounds. Coffee of a morning with the fellows at McDonald's. Couple of cousins I still see—you remember Nella, lives in a trailer over by the river. She's near blind now—since her husband died, she don't get out. I do her shopping."

The air conditioner continued emitting its gradual hum, breathing into the small space of the car. Beyond Waylon's profile the little river shone, nearly coppery in bright sunlight. The light was incongruous, Kate thought. There was dusk all round him, the hour when gold light darkens.

Waylon took his hat from his head and placed it on his knees, smoothing the taupe brim with his fingertips. "Everything's there," he said, "houses I built, streets I laid down, Raine's grave. You'll be bringing your mother back. I've been in that town sixty years. It's home, no matter who's left it. Your home too."

"My home is here, Dad," she said gently.

He turned to look at her. "This is where you live. Home is where you come from." He reached to cover her hand with his. "Don't you worry. I'll be up to see you again before too long."

She was back in plenty of time. It was still early and the street was quiet, as though the neighborhood had not wakened. She got out of the car, locked it and stood by the open garden gate. Dew swathed the grass. She walked through fragrant wetness to the empty patio and sat down in her father's lawn chair. Here he'd waited like a dowager in the sun, watching over Katrina as she picked her way across the grass, stepping over bare spots as though they were holes replete with darkness, dragging behind her the little chain Kate had finally purchased. Waylon betrayed no impatience but sat with his hands clasped, calling an occasional encouragement or just waiting for the dog to wend her way to his feet in her own time. "Oh, well," he'd say then, "I suppose you're finished. You're certain, now?" Lifting the dog up, unsnapping the chain, he might murmur a benediction. "Yessir, time to go." If Kate had told him, if she'd explained about the wedding, and the whole family being there but him, he would have sat with his eyes cast down as she spoke, as though considering. Then he would have shaken his head slightly and said, looking up at her, lapsing into the workman's grammar her mother had once disparaged, "It don't matter, Miss. Why, it's all right. It don't matter at all."

8

Kate won the boat at Big Boy Sports' July Super Sale, where she'd gone to buy Sam a birthday present. Big Boy Sports was famous for the apple-cheeked-boy-faced balloon that floated above the oversized marquee of the store. Big Boy's extremely friendly clerks and clerkettes all wore the same red baseball cap as the boy-faced balloon, and red shirts with name tags sewn above the right top pocket, like gas station attendants. A mixed metaphor of some sort, Kate concluded, baseball and gas stations, all very American, but still, baseball was not gasoline. Baseball wasn't merchandising, or it shouldn't be. She thought of buying Sam a baseball glove, supple brown leather; he would be nine years old; he should have a glove at their house, Matt's house, even if he already had one at home, his house, his mother's house. But no.

"Nerf," she said to Alexander as she strolled him toward the store, across the parking lot.

"Bye," he said back, "bye bye bye."

He was too young to say words, of course he was; they were sounds listeners heard as words, sounds he liked, sounds as sensical as the sounds he heard, sounds hands, mouth, skin that touched him were pleased to make. Kate paused once they made the sidewalk to let down the back of the stroller. Alexander, seven months old and full of milk, lay back in drowsy mid-swoon. Kate had nursed him the moment she found a parking space, motor running, air-conditioning on full-tilt. "Something Nerf," Kate told him, "something new and just invented." All things Nerf were Sam's desire, plastic accoutrements and big spongy bullet/missiles; they were just the ticket, just what the doctor ordered. Kate followed doctor's orders frequently, but she drew the line at guns.

"Get him what he wants," Kate's mother had told her.

Kate and her mother often held opposing opinions. In such instances, Katherine signaled Kate with small silences or fondly directive remarks that she, Katherine, was still senior partner in their mother/daughter enterprise.

"I can't buy him a gun," Kate told her. "I don't plan to buy my own son guns."

Her mother looked up with a faint smile, eyes tired behind her glasses. "Boys like their guns," she counseled.

"I'll find some other Nerf thing," Kate assured her, "a big sports toy."

And she went off to Big Boy Sports, where she'd never been, having helped her mother into bed, turned on the window fan, and filled the Styrofoam pitcher with ice water. She had good days, good weeks, but this week was not one of them. She'd had lunch, she would stay in bed, she would call Camille if she needed anything before Kate got back. She would be fine. "Get something good," she'd told Kate, as though step-mothering were an enviable task. Not task, Kate thought, challenge: enviable challenge, rife with spiritual surrender, preparation for any-thing, certainly preparation enough for Big Boy Sports.

Driving while Alexander gurgled, car seat fastened backward on the passenger seat, Kate had considered her destination; generally she avoided consumer megastores, places miles out four-lane highways whose sites involved vast acreage, whose products were saturation-advertised on network television she never watched and pictured on Day-Glo boxes of sugar cereals she wouldn't let anyone eat. Already, in addition to being the stepmother, she found herself the bad guy, censor of Twix and Kix and Twinkles and Sugar Pops. At the health food store, she bought the brightest boxes she could find, but the boys ate bagels. That was all right. Bagels were good for them, she told Matt, especially with cream cheese or (natural) peanut butter. They wanted to bring their own Jif and Sonic Booms from home. After three discussions with Matt, Kate prevailed; they left behind their rations and guns with sound effects; they brought their sponge ammunition and Nerf weapons, as long as they shot them outside. Inside, despite Kate's discouragement,

Jonah roller-skated room to room, cradling his RotoRetro-launcher. What did RotoRetro *mean?* Kate wondered. Did the gun shoot forward and backward, exist in simultaneous time, create a vortex of motion or emotion? Yes, absolutely.

Sam would have none of it. He brought his gun in his father's car, then left it strategically placed across the front passenger seat, as though to reserve the best seat for the ride home. It was one more detail that wrung Kate out, as though it were about Matt; no matter how much they had of Matt, it wasn't enough—until she remembered how her own brothers had fought over shotgun, the shotgun seat, singular even before bucket seats, when the broad front seats of Mercurys and Chevrolets were like big couch cushions, indestructible and bedlike, with no seat belts, as though there were no wrecks, or big curved windshields to fly through. Wrecks. She'd reached over to check the belt threaded through Alexander's car seat and nearly missed the exit, though the Big Boy balloon was clearly visible from the highway, wafting moored and bright in sunlit air over hundreds of cars whose baked rooftops shone like glinting knives.

Chimes rang as Kate walked through one of numerous sets of double doors; she wondered for a moment if some metal on the stroller had set off an alarm. But no, the chime, melodious, detached, mechanical, rang at every entry, rang now, as others entered, as a girl in a red baseball hat approached Kate and Alexander. The baby stirred. "Shhh," Kate murmured, moving the stroller back and forth, back and forth in place. She put her finger to her lips as the clerk reached them.

The girl smiled. Red lipstick. Beautiful teeth. Aquamarine contacts; decidedly unnatural, but attractive. "Raffle ticket?" she whispered. "Just fill it out and drop it in the barrel. Part of our July Super Savings. Lots of sports articles. Beach and playing field."

They both looked down at Alexander, who closed his eyes and sighed. Kate shot the clerk a glance of grateful collusion, then asked, "All toys for boys?"

"Oh, I get it," the clerk said, lifting an expertly shaded brow. "You mean, do we have toys for *girls.* Well, you know, girls *love* buying toys for boys. It's *just* about their favorite pastime." She leaned a little closer and dropped her voice. "You wouldn't believe the groups of girls we get in here. They rove around and try to lift things—tennis balls, water pistols."

"All for boys, no doubt."

"No doubt," the clerk said.

Kate frowned dramatically. "Or maybe they're feminist guerrillas, protesting the whole enterprise."

The girl looked at her blankly, but Kate caught a whiff of patchouli oil, which was odd. Perhaps the makeup and perfect hair were a disguise. Kate herself had gone back to wearing her long hair in a ponytail, the better to keep it out of Alexander's mouth. "I'm Kelly," the clerk said now, as though to get them back on track. She touched her name tag with bright red nails, then, practiced as a stewardess, performed an ever-extending, fluid gesture to indicate the barrels beside every register, the alphabetized aisles, the entire world of Big Boy Sports. The vast ceiling provided its own arc of horizon, a world aglow with fluorescent light and banners. "Here's your form," Kelly said musically, "keep your stub. Next drawing in twenty minutes. You must be present to win!" She leaned closer, still sounding rehearsed. "I'm not supposed to tell which barrel we draw from next, but it's 15—my station."

"Oh, sorry," Kate said, "I'm in a rush. I won't be here for twenty minutes."

"Really? You never know." Kelly extended her perfect manicure, a form, and a tiny pencil. "He's asleep. Take you a minute." She turned. "Use my shoulder."

Kate did, writing. "You're good at this. Do you get a commission?"

"We're supposed to pass out every ticket of every book we're assigned, but nobody checks. A lot of them"—she wrinkled her nose—"don't bother. They toss the tickets at the end of the shift. But I figure, why not get in the spirit? Somebody's gotta win."

"Not me," Kate said. "I absolutely never win anything. Born on a Saturday."

Kelly looked perplexed.

"Works hard for a living. Remember the rhyme? Which day are you?"

"Monday, I think."

"Monday's child is fair of face. There you go. Who needs astrology when we've got nursery rhymes?" Kate returned the pencil and resumed motion, calling back over her shoulder, "Drop it in 15 for me. By the way, where would I find Nerf sports things, big things? I need exact directions—I'm new here."

"Nerf? All of aisle 21. We've got everything! Balls, blocks, bowling sets, parachute men, sports, small weapons, big weapons—"

Kelly's voice faded. Strolling quickly, Kate reflected that she'd come to the right place. Sam's present did need to be big. Stupendous. Impressive. Compensatory, said her shadow voice. Yes, all right. Something he would fasten on, revel in. Something to seduce him completely and blur the boundaries of the transition he and Jonah were always making, here to there, there to here, even on their birthdays. Perhaps Kate had more trouble with the coming and going than they did. Then again, how would she know? They didn't exactly talk to her. She talked to herself, or to Matt; lately she just tried to be helpful, like an assistant. Helpfulness was her new mode on Wednesdays, Fridays and Saturdays: cooking, making beds, picking up, doing all the Alexander and Katherine work so Matt could be with the boys. Mondays he took them to dinner in their suburb and came home late. He said divorced dad was a full-time career, in that he thought about it even when he wasn't doing it. Second wife, by contrast, now that she was one, seemed to Kate a rather murky situation, not quite legitimate, at least not in her case. Matt couldn't relate. After all, he'd been a first husband twice. There were stepfamily counselors, Kate knew, and an actual Stepfamily Association, with an 800 number. Kate wasn't quite ready to call. They were newlyweds, she reminded herself, all of them, she and Matt and the three kids. Even the dogs were suffering. Kate's mutt, Luna, liked Matt's boys but visibly drooped in Alexander's presence, venting her distress on Katrina, who was constantly distressed and distressed everyone. Almost sweet sixteen, Matt joked of Katrina. When truly exasperated, he referred to her under his breath as a three-pound deaf mute. Katrina, whose haphazard incontinence seemed to worsen by the day, suffered her exile in the barricaded kitchen rather stoically except at night, when there was no one to carry her back and forth to Katherine's bed. Big Boy Sports was miles of back and forth; Kate found herself in Pool Appliances, which seemed limitless. Were there really so many swimming pools in stony New England? Where was Nerf? She kept going.

Suddenly, at last, the 21 sign was directly overhead and they were enveloped in spongy forms as far as Kate could see. IT'S A NERF, NERF,

NERF, NERF WORLD!!! proclaimed arched banners in red, white and blue, and HAVE A NERF FOURTH OF JULY! They would spend tomorrow, the Fourth, at Matt's uncle's house, north of the city. It was a beautiful house with a private beach. Her mother would love to see the ocean. Somehow, Kate had to include her, though the ride was nearly an hour. She perused the weapons, thinking. There was Jonah's RotoRetro-launcher amid SubAtomic Uzis and rows of something called a Mack-Ack-Ack; Kate had to admit the guns were fabulous, in the sense that they were full-fledged fantasies. Perhaps Matt was right—time for her to join the mainstream. He pointed out that her brothers had played with guns, guns Kate cherished now that they were cast aside. Didn't she display, in the room she called her office, a leather Roy Rogers holster with metal studs and fake rubies? The two six-guns had once held metal bullets in barrels that really turned, but nothing came through the gun, and the only sound effect was a jewellike click when the trigger was pulled or the hammer cocked.

Cock the hammer. There was an interesting phrase.

Guns were different now, Kate told Matt. There were toy submachine guns and missile launchers and Gatling Grinders. Why not a weapons-detonation computer board, she suggested, on which a child pressed one red button to detonate a simulation loud enough to level the house, the city, even the state and the eastern seaboard? Now, now, Matt would say, there were bombs when we were kids. Back in the placid fifties, the early sixties, bombs had seemed closer to home. So close, Kate agreed, that toys had to do with cowboys and detectives. Radioactivity was not a selling point when people were building bomb shelters and schools held drills. Everyone into the bathroom! Crouch by the toilets! There sat the third-grade girls with their arms over their heads, amazed at their first sight of a urinal, a whole wall of urinals: the windowless boys' room was centrally located and big enough for all three primary grades. Ah, me. The men on the Nerf gun boxes still dressed in battle fatigues, like old-fashioned warriors buffed up on steroids. As though to compensate for their silence, the relatively safe Nerf projectiles were ridiculously oversized circles, spheres and tubes dyed the shout-it-out colors of psychedelic sherbets. How satisfying to blast away with them, running and jumping and bouncing off walls, and how deluding, as though people could simply blow apart whatever didn't work. A therapist had once told Kate to close her eyes, visualize the problems she'd mentioned, mark them with visual *X*'s and explode them. Kate refused. I'm just trying to get you to clear your mind, he'd explained patiently. Kate told him she didn't want to clear her mind; she wanted to figure it out. So typical, commented her then boyfriend, a computer whiz–social activist. Typical? Sure, you poets like to be up against it, he said, permanently grinding away. Hmmmm, Kate had murmured, pulling him toward her by his jeans pockets. Leaving Nerf weapons behind, she heard his breathy voice admit into the past the deep benefit of her personal flaws.

Here were sports at last. She and Matt had different games, more like play than combat. Daily life was already so full of demands and sched-ules, many of them negotiated between Matt and his ex when Kate was not present. Matt tried to be accommodating; his ex was alone with the kids; she had them more often than he; he said she was moody and emo-tional. Not like Kate, was the implication; despite her "artistic tempera-ment" and present vocation as a stay-at-home sometime writer/editor, Matt considered Kate self-contained and calm, someone to whom he could turn for talk and advice, a really equal partner. Rephrase, Kate said. When a man talks about equality, it usually means a woman is get-ting the raw end of a deal. Matt protested that he meant it, it was true; regardless, he couldn't imagine Kate and a raw deal occupying the same planet. Kate tried to warn him that she seldom wept or ranted, but got quiet when she was hurt or angry; she'd been known to specialize in some of the very silence she currently required of boys' toys. Or, Matt reminded her, she could be funny, ironic, even—horrors—sarcastic.

Matt told Kate that his ex had said she still loved him when they went to get their divorce papers. She didn't want to, she said, but she did. Good move on her part to say that, Kate observed. You don't believe her? Matt asked impishly. Kate shrugged. If she loved him so much, why had she treated him so badly? What was all that with her boyfriend, in the year before Matt met Kate? Why did she only get clingy when she realized Matt had met someone, namely Kate? Matt paraphrased, mock-dramatic: she *just* couldn't decide, she needed *space*. So now she has some, Kate had quipped. Afterward she castigated herself for her lack of empathy. Of course it was hard, with the kids, but hard too to be sympa-thetic, when Matt's ex made it so hard on Kate. The kids still weren't allowed to take home anything Kate gave them. If they brought things from their house to Matt's, they weren't allowed to take them home again unless the transport back and forth occurred that same visit. If an object was left behind to exist in Kate's sphere for a while, it had to stay, as though it were tainted. Maybe that was why Jonah held on to his Launcher and wore his roller skates; he was afraid he might forget some important thing that would have to remain behind forever, along with his father.

"Ma," Alexander said, awake now. "Bye." He gazed in seeming wonderment at the red, white and blue balloons wafting in clusters in the highest twenty feet of the arched ceiling.

"That was a brief nap." Kate adjusted him into sitting position. "You were due to wake up as we checked out. Now you can help shop." She wondered if she would have to worry about Alexander mouthing and sucking and inhaling filaments of Nerf, or perhaps Nerf was scientifically engineered never to break down, even under the warm assault of human saliva.

Time was of the essence. Alexander would be content another fifteen minutes. Kate moved along. Here were Nerf bowling kits, very strange; candlepins that fell over silently, with no *thwack* when the ball hit them. Then she saw the archery set, which was big and boisterous-looking, with a regular bow and a crossbow, a medley of Nerf arrows in various shapes and sizes, some tipped with Velcro. There was a bright nylon target, silk-screened in a surprisingly thoughtful way—figures meant to represent various ages of weaponry stood to the side of each target ring, frozen in the act of letting fly: a barbarian at the outermost ring, a medieval-looking figure, a Robin Hood–era hunter with a falcon on his arm, and so on, until the bull's-eye featured a modern Olympic archer. Sam would like shooting for points, adding up his score.

"Eureka," she said to Alexander. "Two bows, so Jonah can play, but one crossbow just for Sam, the target, and an extra set of Velcro arrows." Happily, Nerf toys were inexpensive. She was piling big, lightweight boxes atop the stroller and its fabric sunshade, negotiating a turn-around, peering from behind to steer back up the long, long aisle to check out.

Perfect, she thought, lots of boxes, lots of presents with big ribbons. Archery combined sport and weapons, and maybe she could find an age-appropriate book—*Weapons of Antiquity,* say, with pictures, or a story-book. There might be time to stop by a bookstore before picking up the cake. She'd already strung streamers and set the table—today was Sam's actual birthday. At this very moment his mother was presiding over a party for his class. Cupcakes, probably. It was Friday; tonight Matt was in charge of a cookout. Kate was in charge of the party and beach prepa-rations for tomorrow. "Are you down there, Tate? I'm up here. Don't worry. We're nearing the finish line."

Alexander crowed in response to their increased speed. Kate imag-ined the sunshade collapsing under its stacked cargo. Explain that one: I buried my baby in Nerf boxes. Thankfully, the Perego was nearly inde-structible. Kate sailed toward checkout. *We have a winner!* proclaimed loudspeakers from every direction. *Proceed to aisle 15!* continued a perky female voice. *Claim your prize, displayed in our Rafters of Prizes!* There was distortion, a loud squeak. Fine. Kate headed for checkout 1, likely to be least crowded. In fact it was deserted but for the clerk. Kate stacked the boxes on the counter and fell to surveying packages of plastic figures displayed beside the register. Boys loved bands of little men to set up and take down. She might find archers to put on the cake—

"Got a raffle ticket, ma'am?" The clerk addressed her as the register hummed and pinged.

Kate frowned. Where had she put it? "Do I have to have one?"

"You get a ten percent discount if you turn in a raffle ticket."

Everyone's a winner! insisted the loudspeakers.

"Never mind the discount." Kate folded back the stroller sunshade, got her wallet from the Babytote.

The clerk pointed to Alexander. "Is that it? It's bright red, like what he's got."

"Oh, God!" Kate bent down to pull a soggy scrap from Alexander's fist. Actually, it was soggy on one end and his chin was smeared red. She dropped the ticket on the counter and put her finger in his mouth, check-ing for detached bits, rubbing the red from his gums. Red dye number two, and her mother always said thick paper was made from filthy rags.

"You won," said the clerk.

"Won what?" Hurriedly, Kate handed over her credit card.

"The numbers match." She pointed to a number bleeping red on her register. "You get your discount, and you win. Just let me have you sign—" Already, she was handing back the slip, along with the ragged raffle stub. "Go right over to 15 to claim your prize. I'll bag your purchases. You'll need help out to the parking lot, anyway."

Alexander shouted as though he were responsible. They'd probably won batteries, or a set of golf balls. Kate pushed the stroller to checkout 15. There stood Kelly, enunciating into a microphone, her register line roped off. *"Big Boy July Super Savings!"* said her now eminently recognizable voice. She saw Kate with the stub in her hand and reached for the scrap of red. *"Oh my gosh!"* she called out, still broadcasting. *"Is it you? Did you win?"* Then she put down the mike and checked the stub. "You did! You did win!"

"Kelly," Kate asked, suspicious, "did you pick the ticket?"

"Nope, a machine picks them. You won, fair and square. Let's see. You won Prize Nine—there it is! You won the boat!" She flung both arms up, unrehearsed now, pointing directly above them.

Kate saw a lantern, skates, a portable basketball hoop, wading pools, bicycles, a pup tent suspended in perfect form, all labeled with big black numbers, dangling from red, white and blue bungee cord. The objects swayed in a barely discernible breeze of air-conditioning. It was clever, and Kate had entered beneath all this without even looking up. There was the boat, a bright yellow inflated rowboat banded in black, like a bumblebee.

"Gaaaaa," continued Alexander. "Dah!"

Kate suddenly heard him. Wonderful. He was swearing before he talked. "How will I ever get it home?" she said aloud.

"Comes with a pump, silly, folded up. And oars! That's just the display model." Kelly had a shopping cart all packed: black plastic oars, a heavy-duty pump that looked like a slim oxygen tank, and a square, plastic-encased bundle the size of a respectable suitcase. "Very heavy-duty, and big enough for two," she added. "Want to buy the baby a life jacket? We have them in all sizes."

"I wouldn't let him in that, life jacket or not, unless it was in the backyard. But his dad will like it, if he ever has time to inflate it."

"Takes a minute," Kelly assured her. "This pump is great—bike tires, air mattresses, whatever. The boat is the very best prize. You're lucky!"

Kate laughed. She supposed she was.

. . .

There were no archers at Party Cakes, but Kate bought a packet of tiny plastic baseball players—it was summer, after all—and they looked very engaged, turned toward one another, their miniature pedestals set in white icing on Sam's cake. His name was all done up in red and blue; at home Kate had got the whole confection out of the box onto a cut-glass platter, where it truly reigned supreme. Matt always said kids didn't care whether they ate their cake off cardboard or china, but surely any-one saw, over time, how care was taken for them, and things done spe-cially. Until they drop the glass plates and they break, Matt pointed out. Well, of course. For tonight there were paper plates and cups, all birth-day-embossed with red 9's and exclamation points. The Party Cakes sale bin had supplied hats and a paper tablecloth to match; modern parent-hood was full of thematic opportunity. Alexander was happy in his Play-yard, mouthing teething rings, so Kate wrapped one of the high-backed plastic lawn chairs in crepe paper and made Sam a crown. Surely kids' birthdays should always involve crowns. She'd thought of inviting one or two of Sam's friends for supper and cake, and to see him open his pres-ents, but it seemed too invasive. Unless, someday, Sam suggested it, which he might. Their only piece of Sam now was when he appeared, before he disappeared. If the kids were going to have one real home, which they certainly needed, wasn't the other relegated to a kind of limbo in which special occasions took place a second time? Kate decided against glitter. Glitter would be all over everything and Alexan-der would be glad to ingest it. She went with the tinsel pipe cleaners she found in the bottom of the art drawer she'd made for the kids: paper, crayons, Play-Doh, colored pencils, all pretty much underutilized, except by Kate.

"You certainly are having fun." Kate's mother stood in the dining room doorway. She'd dressed up in her white linen skirt and blouse.

"Mom, you look great. Did you see the cake? And how does this look?" Kate held up the crown, still unfastened. "I'd better wait until he gets here to tape it, so it'll fit."

"I wish I could have made you a cake. I always think it's a shame to buy one."

"Remember the train you did one year, with all the different cars, and the Raggedy Ann cake you made me—icing pinafore and Mary Janes and red hair? I can cook, but I could never decorate a cake that way, or make a fluted piecrust. Or sew, come to think of it, which always seemed so tedious. My fine motor skills are probably lacking."

"You compensated by developing other talents," her mother said sagely. "Dinner all set?"

"I made a salad, and the baked beans, and the rest Matt will do. Now, let's see." Kate stood over Alexander, looking down at him as Katherine joined her. He liked to throw everything to the net sides of the Play-yard, then demand someone pile it all in front of him again. "Mr. Tate, will you have a hot dog, or a hamburger?"

"Wouldn't he love that! Enough with the soft mushy stuff."

"Let's move him onto the porch. Can you hold him while I move this contraption? I've got the swing out there already. Let me lift him to you"—she bent down to swing him a time or two, a ritual he'd come to expect and greeted with squeals of delight—"but sit down, because it'll take me a minute, and he's so heavy."

"I feel better, really. But I'll sit if you insist. You're really going to move that big thing?"

"Sure." Kate gave her the baby, then unsnapped the metal hinges of the Play-yard, moved the fabric pad aside to grasp holes in the center of the fiberboard bottom. The sides came down, creaking as various Alexander implements fell into the netting. "It may be used," Kate said, "but it works. And no bars, I'd like to point out."

"Is that what you got at the auxiliary? Actually, babies like bars. They chew them and pull up on them. And play peekaboo behind them—"

"Okay, Mom."

"But I'm sure you're right. Play-yards are probably an advance."

Kate opened the screen doors to the patio. The dogs, taking their ease in the fenced yard, began barking at various decibels, providing one another competitive motivation. Katrina stood over her tiny chain, having stretched it to the limit, while Luna bounded in and out, showing off. Kate set up the Play-yard and went back to get Alexander. "Mom, come outside and try the recliner. Another secondhand find, and it has a cushion."

"My goodness, you got a recliner?"

"Yesterday, same source. It's nothing fancy, just one of those plastic ones." Kate situated Alexander.

"It's nice you have this for me," her mother answered, "but don't buy any more porch furniture down there. Someday you'll have the money to buy things that match. Then what will you do with these?"

Kate turned to see Katherine already in position against the dark green cushion, feet propped up, arms on armrests. "Well, look at that," Kate said, "a perfect fit, after you bad-mouth my eclectic style." She hadn't realized the recliner was exactly the right height; her mother could get up and down without help, and the cushion, which had come from some more exalted incarnation, was thick and comfortable. The whole thing was, yes, a stroke of luck—Katherine would spend more time on the patio for the rest of the summer, instead of lying on the downstairs daybed, indoors. So simple and so important. What else had Kate not considered, what else should she do?

"You know, I'm just realizing," she told Katherine. "You look so comfortable. Tomorrow, we'll take you to the ocean just like that. We'll take one of the seats out of the van and load the recliner in the back. You can rest all the way there."

Her mother looked doubtful. "And what will you do with me when we get there?"

"Matt says they have a beautiful enclosed porch, with a big window that looks right out on the ocean. I'm sure there's a chaise. Or we could walk on the beach, and I'll put the recliner just where the sand begins to dampen, so you can look at the waves. Wouldn't you like that?"

"It seems so much trouble for you." She looked down at her dog then, who yipped frantically in response. "Katrina, you simpleton," she said, "you've managed to wind your chain around that dogwood tree forty times. Now you're in a fix. No, I'm not coming over there to get you."

"I'll get her," Kate said, "if she'll stick with you and not run away."

"I know you worry about her taking off between the rungs of the fence, but really, she can't see a thing. Why would she run away?"

"Adventure. Excitement. How can you be so sure the raging passions of her youth are quelled? Katrina, it's me," Kate told the dog. "I'm just coming to unhook you. Why do all poodles have rhinestones on their collars?"

"It's a law." Katherine took the dog in her hands. Katrina nestled beside her, emitting the satisfied groan of the long-put-upon. "I can assure you," Katherine said, "she won't move until someone moves her. As for youth, well. Youth is so much of life, when you don't grow old." She laid her head back on the cushion. "I think of my mother; she was barely middle-aged."

"But Mom," Kate said quietly, "they didn't know how to care for her, then, in that place. If she'd had a hysterectomy, she probably would have recovered."

"A spot the size of a dime. They said they could cure her with radium. She was fifty-six. I'll be sixty this summer. Katie, you'd better get to living."

The baby began to fuss. Kate picked him up. She was living, wasn't she? Then why did she find it so hard, momentarily, to breathe? Her former "adult" existence—college, grad school, single life, thinking, writing, traveling, working—in which she'd interacted solely with adults, now seemed so luxurious in the vast time and space given over to consideration, thought, large and small decisions. It was a world in which no one was dying, no one was being born; a half-life, floating world, a bubble from which she observed and recorded and made of her observations an alternate world of association and image, a world as real to her, as present, as the food she ate. She was too busy now, too tired, too occupied with taking care and keeping up, too drenched in sensation, to think about living, to draw conclusions; she ate to keep going, to stay awake, to stay competent, to be healthy, to feed her baby, to get everything done. The interior world had receded, replaced by other lives and their attendant mysteries. She was the caretaker; she *took care,* waking every day within her own flat-out evolution. The events she lived inside shifted moment to moment over packed hours filled with detail and camouflage: meals and toys, shopping and baths, naps, doctor's appointments, conferences with doctors, and the double row of plastic pill containers with childproof caps her mother could barely manage to open. The diminutive bottles were the amber color of some transparent, primeval sap, identical but for their staggered heights and dosage schedules, and the complex content of their neatly typed labels.

Her mother asked, "Did you get the book you wanted for Sam?"

"Oh no," Kate said. "I forgot. I completely forgot about the books. Anyway, there wasn't time."

Books. Who was she without them? She called herself a freelance editor, but she hadn't actually accepted a project since Alexander was born. Life seemed work enough. As for her own work, if she were a writer, she would be writing, despite everything. She was no longer a poet; she didn't try now; she was a coward. Somewhere, on the other side of a terrible expanse, she would begin again. She had to think so. She read poems, other people's poems, the same ones again and again, as though she couldn't comprehend them but was focused and comforted by their very cadences and sounds, their voices in her mind, voices she could not hear unless she was staring at the words themselves. As though a door opened and shut, or a light went on and off; there was brilliance or darkness, and nothing in between but the free fall of time, its disappearance. There was so much to do, and there was not time. Kate walked the width of the flagstone patio and back, keeping Alexander in motion as he fussed against her. She'd fed him; he shouldn't be hungry. He rubbed his face and yawned, but he'd already napped. She should be tired, not he. In the garden, which seemed far away across the compact lawn, mounds of blue salvia were in rampant bloom, clusters and spears of blue against a pale textured green of ground cover her mother called lamb's ear. The velvety, overgrown leaves had climbed the fence; along the front of the bed, they spilled onto the grass. Kate heard voices, then a run of song from a car radio; Matt had pulled into the driveway. Alexander began to cry in earnest. "They're here," Kate whispered into his hair. "I'll check on things in the kitchen," she told her mother.

She sat at the table, nursing, as Matt came in. "Hey," she said, and lifted her face for his kiss.

"How's the boy?" He stroked Alexander's downy head.

"Fussy. He could be patented as a stress-absorber, but he expresses what he absorbs almost immediately. You might say there's a catch in the dynamic."

"There's certainly a catch somewhere." Matt loosened his tie.

"You don't look pleased. What's wrong?"

"He's in such a bad mood."

"Sam, you mean? Sometimes birthdays are too much. Maybe I did too much."

Matt looked around him, appearing truly puzzled. "He hasn't even seen what you did—they're still in the car, arguing over whose launcher is whose. The guns are exactly alike, but Sam is convinced Jonah switched them. The dining room looks great, by the way, and the presents. Sometimes no matter what we do, it's not right. There's no way to anticipate."

"Transition," Kate told him. "Sam will settle down in an hour or two."

"But will I?"

"Yes, you will. You're hungry. They're hungry. You'll feel better after you fire up the grill and throw the meat on it. Isn't barbecuing the modern equivalent of clubbing a mastodon?"

"I would like to club a mastodon."

"And you have to be satisfied with wielding a spatula. This is what we mean by modern distortion of basic urges."

"We're walking distortions, all of us but Alexander here."

"Speak for yourself," Kate said. "Gee, I guess you did have a rough ride. Matt and his rough riders."

"Up and down San Juan Hill," he agreed, "the twenty-minute ride that lasts a decade or so."

They heard Jonah's quick step—footsteps today, no roller skates—and his piping voice. "Sam! Sam! There's presents in here!"

"See? They've made it inside." Kate stood to burp the baby.

"Dad!" Jonah stood in the doorway, wearing sunglasses and a Jonah outfit—shorts, T-shirt, bat cape, unmatched socks and sandals, baseball hat. He held up the pump that went with the boat. "What's this, and the big present with no wrapping? Is it for me, since Sam gets all the others?"

"You sure did get a present," Kate said, "but not that one. The boat is for all you men, and your dad's in charge of it."

Matt turned to look at her. "What boat?"

"I won a boat, a blow-up boat, at Big Boy Sports. Can you believe—"

"Wow!" Jonah shouted. "It blows up? Let's blow it up! My friend has a race car that does that when you hit it with another race car."

"Not that way, hon," Kate told him gently. "You blow it up with air, inflate it, like a balloon. That's the pump you're holding."

His face fell. "Oh."

"I know it doesn't look very interesting right now, all folded—" Kate followed him back into the dining room, worried the boat would steal the thunder from Sam's presents, from Sam. Kate had left the oars outside and piled the rest in a corner; she should have put it all out of sight. But Jonah appeared to have lost interest. He was in the yard, throwing a tennis ball for Luna. He'd put Katrina, who looked alarmed, in the Play-yard, and Kate's mother was getting up to retrieve her. "But Katrina is a baby," he was saying. "She's my baby," Katherine was telling him, "but in dog years she's an old lady. That's why she has accidents sometimes." Not now, Kate hoped. Alexander could swing until she'd had time to inspect the Play-yard; she wanted to get supper started; Matt could take over once he changed his clothes. She heard him walking up the stairs, his step less buoyant than usual. There was Sam, standing by the fence in his jeans and sneakers and black T-shirt. He looked somber in his wire-rimmed glasses, watching Jonah. Maybe something had happened. Picking up the kids on holidays, Matt was always running into groups of former in-laws gathered in the big house his ex and he had shared. Matt had told Kate how numerous little cousins had set up a chorus last Christmas: Matt should come back home. "Well, he's not going to," Sam had announced flatly. Kate supposed Matt told her these things because they were hard for him to bear, and Kate was meant to help him bear them. She settled Alexander on one hip and picked up the plate of meat Matt had left on the table.

"Kate?" her mother called.

"Coming." She backed through the screen door to the patio and gave Katherine the plate. "Just let me get him in the swing. It's a perfect moment for swinging. Hello, Sam. Are you hungry for a hamburger?"

"Sort of," Sam said.

"Is it French fries too?" Jonah asked.

Was there time to make French fries? She'd need a full bottle of canola oil. "I'll make those for you tomorrow night."

"There's corn and baked beans for tonight," her mother told the kids, "but wait until you taste Kate's French fries."

"We like the frozen ones," Jonah said.

"Then you haven't had the homemade kind." Katherine held the plate high, out of Katrina's reach.

"I like McDonald's. I get my mom to go there every night."

"You're a liar," Sam said.

"Am not," Jonah said.

"Jonah," Kate said, "you like playing with the swing. Can you wind it up for me?" Jonah flew toward her, pleased to show how fast he could wind the lever, as Kate reflected on the several mistakes built into a god-send device. "Winding it requires two hands," she told her mother. "Isn't that a design flaw?"

It was true; the unassisted mom used both hands to put the baby into the swing, where he might begin crying before she could set the thing in motion. Said baby eventually drowsed, but the resulting pause that refreshed was limited to the life of the wind-up; the winding itself was a loud continuous ratcheting guaranteed to startle any baby within earshot into instinctual sobs if the cessation of motion hadn't wakened him already. The thing was obviously manufactured by people who hadn't used it.

"Beggars can't be choosers," her mother responded predictably. "Why don't I put the meat on the grill? I'm not helpless, you know."

"Hang on, Mom. Watch over the troops." Kate took the plate from her.

"I can do the music box. Sam is too far away." Jonah was already winding the smaller key, mounted on the side of the mechanism. Strains of "Rock-a-Bye, Baby" sounded, oddly pure and plaintive. Jonah liked to hold the key as it turned and make the notes sound one by one.

"It does sound better that way, Jonah. You can make the music box go at any speed you want, but don't change the speed of the swing, okay? It's just right for Alexander."

"The swing ticks like a clock," Jonah called over to Sam, but Sam ignored him and stayed outside the fence, like a wayfarer. Kate thought Jonah astute; the swing *was* a clock; she often measured time by its clicking, and she had ten minutes to get the food on the table. Jonah's perceptiveness could be wearying in a younger brother; Sam turned his back. Soon Jonah would be seriously importuning him, and cross if Sam didn't respond.

"I bet Sam wants to count his birthday presents." Kate stood at the grill. There. Under way. "You stay out here, Jonah. I bet Sam wants to go in and take a look."

"Take a look at these, you mean?" Matt was carrying all the presents onto the patio in a big pile.

"That's it." Kate's mother got up to help. "Bring the mountain to Mohammed. Can you see where you're going?"

"All those?" Sam watched through the fence.

"Come take a look, big guy. And guess whose chair this is, all streamers, and whose crown, on the chair?"

Sam opened the gate and came into the yard to stand by his chair. "My crown?"

"Have a seat." Katherine looked meaningfully at Kate. "Someone wants to fix that crown to fit you just right."

Kate left her post and flew inside for the tape. Where had she left it? Jonah stood by the swing, watching Alexander. Kate heard him say to Katherine, "Could I get in here?" "Oh, you're too big for that," came Katherine's voice. The kitchen. Kate checked the counters and the drawer before she found the tape in the sink. It was mostly dry. Through the open kitchen window, she saw Jonah at the Play-yard, fixing her mother with his sidelong, charming look. "Can I get in *here,* then? This has a lot of room." "It does," Katherine agreed, "but it's not strong enough for a big boy like you. Sit here, by me. There's just room, if you hold Katrina." "I'll hold Katrina!" he exclaimed. Kate ripped away the wet tape. How and why had she dropped it in the sink? She was hands and glands, no brain; it was probably better that way. Turning, she observed Luna, prized tennis ball in her mouth, slinking away into the garden.

Sam waited on the patio, holding the crown. "Luna is growling," he told Kate.

"Luna has to learn to share," Katherine said.

"I'll play with her next." Jonah was ensconced in the recliner with the trembling Katrina and a watchful Katherine.

Kate taped the crown to fit, careful not to catch Sam's long brown hair. For next time, she would find a dress-up cape. "Have a seat, Sir Sam."

"King Sam," her mother corrected her.

"I'm going to open all my presents right now!" Sam reached out with open arms.

"The hamburgers!" Kate said.

"This won't take long, believe me." Matt looked genuinely delighted.

It wasn't food he'd needed, obviously. Kate watched them from the grill as she warmed rolls, cooked the meat. "Wow," Sam kept saying, his voice drifting off as he applied himself studiously to each new parcel. Paper and ribbon fell away, piling up in sheets on the grass. Jonah had abandoned Katrina and dragged the boat outside in its plastic bundle;

now he sat himself atop its folded bulk and waited. It was too late to give him the extra bow. Sam had already opened everything and was meticulously arranging each object around his chair, minus cardboard trappings and packaging, in a kind of ready order, poised for use. He stood still, satisfied, then raised his eyes to his father. There was a lag of a few seconds in which Kate felt a tense apprehension; she heard the slow, occasional click of the nearly motionless swing in which her baby slept.

Then Sam threw himself against Matt and hugged him hard.

In the silence, Kate's eyes met her mother's. Katherine winked at her, and nodded.

Later, when Kate walked outside with the cake, it was just dusk, and the little flames shone. The plastic baseball men had sunk into the icing just enough; their miniature feet appeared poised on a sweet, snowy field. "Dad, it's a night game," Sam said, and blew out the candles.

They were en route, crossing the bridge above the naval yard, the city skyline behind them.

"Does your uncle have life preservers?" Kate asked Matt. She sat just behind him on the middle seat, Alexander's car seat buckled beside her.

"Of course he does, and yes, the kids will wear them if that boat actually inflates, and yes, I promise I'll take them one at a time."

"I still think I should have ridden in the back of the van with Mom," Kate answered. "The kids should all be belted. Traffic, holiday weekend."

"No, I'm in the way back. I don't need a belt. I'm on the boat." Jonah sat atop its bright yellow length, which he'd unfolded beside the recliner, roller skates in his lap. "Anyway, your mom doesn't have a seat belt. She's even lying down where a seat used to be."

"She's a grown-up," Sam asserted. He'd claimed the passenger seat beside his dad, but couldn't conceal his intense interest in Jonah's progress with the pump. Sigh and squeak, sigh and squeak; in the back with Katherine, Jonah had managed to affix the air tube; he held the cylinder of the pump between his feet and pumped air into the boat even as he sat inside it. Kate turned to see the boat swelling perceptibly, then alarmingly, murmurously inhaling as it grew. She'd once told Matt, back when they were first falling for one another, how she hoped she might "contribute something" to his boys' lives, something they wouldn't have had if they'd never known her. This wasn't exactly what she'd envisioned. The big yellow boat, taking form before her eyes in the elongated back of the van, suddenly struck her as funny.

Katherine was laughing as well. "Poor little thing," she called up to Matt. "He's really expending some energy back here."

"The boat is getting big," Sam said.

"It's going to be bigger than the recliner," Jonah claimed, "bigger than the van."

"You might have to climb out," Katherine advised him, "and turn it sideways, so we'll still have room to breathe."

Sam asked, "Can I pump now, Dad?"

"No," came Jonah's voice, "the boat is mine. The bows and arrows are yours."

"Kate said the boat is everyone's." Sam looked to Matt for arbitration.

"But we said he could take care of the boat for today," Matt answered, "since you brought your archery set with you."

"Today's *my* boat day," Jonah asserted.

"Who puts it in the water, Jonah?" his father asked sternly.

"You do, Dad. But I'm getting it ready, and I'm the one that pulls it to the beach. You said."

"Yes, I said. Kate, you're quiet. Still mourning your Baby Bouncer?"

"I can't believe he's outgrown it. I liked holding him in front, just next to me." Kate watched the shore beside them. She loved this vista, the seawall and the flats below, though the beach looked dirty, the water too polluted for swimming. There were no big houses here, only vinyl-sided bungalows and apartment complexes with metal awnings. Older pensioners watched the surf across a four-lane highway and walked their dogs along emptied sand barred with deep black streaks. But the spur of the coast was its own fluid crescent, curving away, free of whatever the water held. "The backpack is for big kids," she said aloud. "It's so restraining, with the metal frame and the straps."

"He is a big kid. He's almost crawling. We need something big enough to hold him still, don't we? The frame makes him feel secure enough to stay put and just look around."

"You're right. I'm glad you suggested it. And he does want to see, don't you, Tate, all Mom walks through. We'll stroll on the beach and see the gulls and the shorebirds. I promise we will." She reached over to

Alexander with his plastic book, his chiming rattle, and he grabbed her wrist with both chubby hands. "Bye," he told her, mischievous, holding on, not waving.

"Ten thousand byes," Kate said. "Monkey, you know what 'bye' means. Like this." She made the sign, opening palm and fingers. He watched her, smiling.

Sam sang with the radio, Jonah applied himself to his boat. Katherine closed her eyes. Kate sat up, leaning near to Matt. "What does your uncle do, living in this big house on his beach?"

"He's the one that owns the leisure wear company. You see his clothes in department stores, sweaters mostly."

"Handmade?"

"Factory made, I think, in the Philippines, and Argentina."

She leaned closer. "Where labor is cheap, and people disappear."

Matt threw her a glance. "I doubt he had anything to do with *that,* Kate."

"I'm sure not," Kate said quietly. "I mean, no more than we do, by not trying to stop it."

He looked at her in the rearview mirror. "Kate, we can't stop everything."

She sighed. "Ah, but can we stop anything?"

"We can stop thinking in those terms"—he looked at his watch—"for the next four hours, until we drive back from the ocean. Enjoy the day, the sea, everyone out of the house, your mother being well enough to come along." He fixed her with an inquiring look in the rearview mirror. "How's that? How's happiness for a big boy sport? Temporary, undeniable happiness."

She nodded back. "Yes, and tonight we'll see fireworks."

Jonah had paused in his labors. "It sounds like no more air is going in."

Katherine was holding the boat up with both hands. She'd helped Jonah turn it sideways; now she gave a little shove, shifting its yellow bulk to rest against the opposite side of the van. "That's what determination will do for you," she told Jonah. "It's as hard as a rock. Sit tight now and maybe we'll keep it from falling on you."

"Won't hurt me," Jonah said. "It's *my* boat."

.　.　.

The moment they arrived, Jonah headed down around the house toward the beach, clutching his skates in one hand and the rope in the other, dragging the boat behind him. Family members called out greetings as Kate and Matt unloaded: beach bags, a cooler of pasta and fruit salad Kate had made for the buffet, the backpack. Sam ran indoors as Matt's relatives milled around, commenting on the baby, on how big the boys had grown. Matt's aunt took Katherine's arm; she must come in and see "our view of the ocean," so wonderful Kate's mother could visit, would she like some lemonade while the food was set out, Matt was so fond . . .

Kate and Matt found themselves standing alone on the circular drive with Alexander. Katherine had disappeared inside.

"See?" Matt said. "I told you they'd take good care of her."

"And I *am* happy. I'm going to change Alexander over there on the grass, and go down to see the beach. We'll try out the backpack. They'll all be busy with the food, they won't miss me for a few minutes. Why is it July and we haven't been to the beach?"

Matt was taking the food inside. "You may not realize this yet, but infants and sand castles don't necessarily mix. And we have been, well, busy."

"Busy, he says." Kate knelt down with the baby and put him on the grass. The lush front yard had the look of a serviced garden, the grass cool in the shade, thick and tufted. Alexander kicked and squirmed; free of clothes, he wanted to turn over and go. Kate leaned close and spoke to him; he stopped moving to watch the words. "Smell the air," she told him, her face close. She brushed his forehead with her lashes. "Salt air. You'll live by the sea, Mr. Tate, I can tell by looking at you." She felt the expressions move across her face, reflections of his surprise, his attention, his laughter, interpretative back-and-forth between them to keep him interested, to keep her talking, only to him. "You'll know why waves run one way and not another, you'll see it all, the tides and the storms and the sea glass." She snapped his clothes back on, put the wet diaper in a bag, tucked it in the Babytote. She'd leave the bag until later; they were going walking, after all.

Now, into the backpack. They'd practiced this morning. Kate slipped him in, belted him tight, fit the straps to her shoulders, and stood. She felt almost guiltily independent, despite his considerable weight; no stroller before her, no head at her chin, nothing in her line of vision but the path she followed along the side of the house, then down, through beach grass and gorse, past broad rocks; a path as broad as Jonah's boat, and steeply descending. Kate kept her eyes on the ground, not wanting to see the beach until it lay before her. She heard the waves, then saw them, lapping foam along a broad beautiful sweep. The empty sand sparkled as though pearlized. Sunlight hit her eyes at a slant, nearly blinding her. Jonah must have gone back up to the house, but where had he left the boat? Absently, she looked at the ocean. There, on a gentle roll of surf perhaps fifty feet out, bobbed the yellow boat. Jonah was in it. He waved to her. One foot was propped up; Kate realized he'd put on his roller skates. In the bright sun, she felt a profound chill. The tide was going out. She ran far back on the sand, back to where the water wouldn't reach for hours, yelling toward the house, which sat silently above them on the cliff, betraying no sign. She couldn't wait. He would get too far away. She was calling Matt's name; she would have to leave Alexander here, strapped into the pack, upright and immobilized. "Mommy will be right back," she said to him, "right back." Her voice sounded calm, as though someone else were speaking. She slipped off the pack and jammed the metal frame deeply into sand to keep it still, even if he fussed, even if he screamed, and checked the belt restraint. There, by her foot on the sand, were the cast-away oars. She left them there; she couldn't carry them and get to Jonah in time. She pulled Alexander's hat more forward on his head and turned, stepping out of her shoes, running. The boat didn't appear to have moved; it seemed stationary but for its rise and fall on the waves. She was in water to her knees, to her hips. How had he done this, wearing skates? She'd hoped the water was shallow but it deepened immediately. She would have to swim; the distance was deceptive. She dove in as the shelf of sand beneath her feet suddenly gave way. A shock of cold, salt in her mouth. When she was a child and traveled to Carolina beaches with her mother, the water had been warm as bathwater, the strand beyond the boardwalk glittering with lights. *Our view of the ocean.* Katherine might be watching now, might see them from the window and send the men, send Matt. Alexander's swing ticked in her head, each slow click distinct. She heard Jonah call to her, his voice little and calm. "I got in," he was calling, "to wait for Dad, and the water came up." Of course, he'd sat in the boat, too near the waves, and put on his skates; he liked taking them on and off; he liked how they fit over his sneakers. Kate swam harder; he was farther away, ever farther than he seemed. "I know," she called back. "I'll pull you in." The water seemed turgid, intent on separation, but she was moving closer. She could pace herself. She could see the rope now, still tied to the front of the boat, bright yellow, trailing in the water. Swallowed up, appearing again. She was not a strong swimmer, but she would only need to get close enough to grab the rope and get back to shore. The boat was fully inflated. It could even hold them both, if she got tired. As long as he stayed in it, as long as he didn't fall out. It was a perfect day. The sky was absolutely blue.

9

Sam and Jonah loved the Pit. The boat became the Pit in the backyard, where it lay collecting rainwater and soccer balls, fading the grass beneath to a perfect chartreuse oval. Kate threatened to cut it up with garden shears and pack long shreds of PVC into the nearest garbage bag, out of sight forever, but no one would let her. One steamy August Saturday, when she fled to an air-conditioned museum with Alexander and his stroller, the kids hosed out the Pit, dried it in the sun, dragged it up to their room with Matt's assistance, and turned it into yet another hazard. Parked on the rug beside their beds, the Pit became an entirely new enterprise. They took turns jumping in from the top bunk. By the time Kate returned, there were Pit points and Pit rules authorized by Matt: one jumper at a time from the middle of the highest bunk, just where the guardrail ended. The kids had to shout "All clear" before each hurtle downward.

"It's relatively safe," Kate's mother said. "Broken arms heal. Legs, too." Then she added, as Kate's eyes widened in protest, "They're not jumping all that far. Consider yourself fortunate. As long as that boat never sees water again, we can all be satisfied."

"I should have stuck pins in it when I had the chance," Kate said. "Right afterward, when I was still a hero."

"You didn't quite get credit for your rescue," her mother told her.

"Mom, I was joking. What rescue? Matt and his uncle came and got us, remember?"

"They had a motorboat. Thank God they did, but you were the one who swam out there after Jonah. If you hadn't—"

"And if it weren't for me," Kate interrupted, "he wouldn't have been in the boat at all."

Her mother went on as though Kate hadn't spoken. "I'm practically blind without my glasses. When I saw the boat from high up on that glassed-in porch, I thought Matt must be in it with one of the kids." Her eyes teared up. She looked hard at the book in her lap. "Then I heard his voice behind me and saw you in the water. I couldn't imagine what you'd done with Alexander."

An aerial view of them all came to Kate unbidden—the half-circle inlet and strip of beach, the cliffs, the roof of the house, the drifting boat, the swimmer. The picture was round as a clock and a baby sat exact center, parked on the sand in his backpack like a dot in a sun hat.

"Suddenly all that moving water looked so wide and deep," Katherine said.

Kate reached over to touch her. Her hands were smooth, and surprisingly cool on such a hot day. "You couldn't see him, Mom," Kate said, "but Alexander was safe." In fact Kate had imagined various scenarios. Suppose she hadn't jammed the backpack hard enough into the sand and it had fallen forward, suffocating him against the beach. Suppose the only man-eating Labrador on the North Shore had happened along, or the Wicked Witch of the East, or a giant tidal wave. An efficient wall of water to embrace them all, motorboat, glassed-in porch, very nice oceanfront house! Everyone, vanished into the sea.

"I could see Matt and his uncle at the dock, hidden from you on the other side of the rocks, starting the motorboat." She abandoned all pretense of reading and shut her book. She held it, a solid dark rectangle, with both hands. "Oh," she said, "that was terrible."

"I know," Kate answered. "But it was weeks ago. The children are all fine, and so am I."

Her mother nodded, then managed a slight smile. "I didn't tell you before, but I promised God if he'd just not let anything happen, I'd thank him with every day I've got left. I took an oath, though I didn't have much to bargain with."

Kate smiled back. "Seems your promise worked, Mom, but is bargaining legit? I thought those negotiations were reserved for dealing with God's big bad opposite."

"Whoever," Katherine said. "When the chips are down, mothers worth their salt will talk to whoever listens. Eternity is a small price to pay." Her eyes met Kate's. "Poor Jonah. He's so intrepid. Was he ever scared?"

"A little, before I reached him. When he saw me swimming so hard, he realized the water was deep, that the tide had carried him out. I did convince him to take off the skates. It was a breakthrough—there we were in the same boat."

Katherine shook her head. "Afterward, he only cried when he realized one of his skates had dropped in the water. It never seemed to occur to him that his foot might have been in it."

"Or maybe it did occur to him," Kate said softly.

Ah, the myriad meanings of Jonah and his skates. Lost or found, their significance was paramount. While Kate blamed the boat for the whole misadventure, Matt seemed to blame the skates; he'd refused to buy Jonah another pair. Surprised at herself, Kate had questioned the decision. Jonah was so attached to the skates; couldn't they talk about this? Of course they could talk about it, Matt said, but no more skates. He couldn't see Jonah in skates again without attendant images of drifting boats and weighted feet. But could Jonah do without the skates right now, Kate asked, lose what they *were* to him, what they *symbolized?* Kate, Matt had remonstrated, listen to yourself. We lost a skate! Why fool with it? She knew what he meant: the fates had extracted a skate and left them all intact. She nodded acknowledgment, then remarked that Matt seemed to be taking on her view of the world, a view she counted on him to mitigate. Was she actually having an effect on him, and a bad one at that? Was it a bad effect? He'd shrugged, then smiled. He didn't think so. But having an effect, particularly on her husband, should make her *happy*. Otherwise she might reconsider before next wielding her powerful influence. But she'd *won* the boat, Kate reminded him; winning had nothing to do with influence. It was chance. A quirk, a curse. Or a gift, Matt told her. Then he hummed the first bars of the *Twilight Zone* theme.

A gift. Well. Kate supposed it was a gift of sorts that she now considered lost skates principally from Jonah's point of view. In terms of sibling rivalry, he'd lost literal, mobile advantage over taller, stronger, faster Sam. More important, he'd lost skating as spiritual verb: the ability to rapidly skim the surface of daily life, negotiate a morass that must occasionally seem to him as big and dark as the night Atlantic. What could she do? Let him jump. He needed to.

"All clear!" Jonah's soprano carried effectively from the boys' second-floor room, just down the hall from Katherine's. "Sam," he sang out, "I said *all clear!* Your knee is still in the Pit!"

Sam's lower-pitched reply sounded rumbly and understated as little-boy thunder. Jonah kept the remaining skate in a place of honor beside his pillow, where it might fall over the side of the bunk and brain Sam, who slept below him. At night, after the boys fell asleep, Kate had to go in and move the skate before she could sleep. Usually she propped it on the windowsill. It watched over them all in the dark, like an icon with round steel eyes, its long dirty laces hanging down.

Just now the boys were alternating games of All Clear with Pell Mell, an accelerated version of the basic game in which one had to scramble out immediately, yelling the appropriate word as the other hurtled downward. It was Game Over if one tagged the other on the top bunk before he could jump. Identities had to be switched before thuds accompanied by declarations of "Pell!" and "Mell!" resumed.

"They had fun setting it up," Katherine offered. "You'd never know it's ninety degrees in that room. Well, eighty degrees, now that Matt's got the fans on."

"Which prompts me to ask, why aren't you using your air conditioner?"

"I do, but I can't stand it for more than ten minutes." She raised her brows, peering at her book as though ascertaining her position. "I'm too hot or too cold, burning up or freezing to death. That's life."

"What are you reading there, Mom?"

"*The Daily Word.* My church sent it."

"Is there a word for today?"

"Of course there is, if you're really interested," her mother said evenly. "The word for today is 'fortitude.'"

"No!" shouted Jonah next door. "*I'm* Pell, *you're* Mell."

"Am not!"

"Are so!"

"We could all use a little fortitude," Kate said. "The Pit is demanding exercise, and loud."

"You don't use fortitude," Katherine answered, "you develop it. That's the point. As for the heat, I have the door shut, to keep in the cool air. I was just about to put the fans on when you came and distracted me. The jumping isn't loud then. It's more of a . . . vibration. You and Matt should put the air conditioner in your room; I told you it makes no sense to put it here."

"Pell!" Jonah shouted.

Sam's retaliatory response was partly muffled. Had he landed on his face? Kate considered supervising. No. She tried to imagine Matt's seal of approval hovering over the Pit like a protective cloud.

"Where's Matt?" Katherine asked.

"Alexander didn't quite fall asleep in the car, then I had to change him, and now Matt's strolling him up and down the street until he drops off."

Lately, it seemed to Kate that her mother felt safer when Matt was home. Was it due to the scare with the boat? If Kate had pulled off the rescue alone, would Katherine still be asking after him more frequently? She seemed more vulnerable, generally weaker, and at the wrong time. She was mid-cycle. "Rescue" was part of her chemo regimen. Kate had seen it written in her records: "Methotrexate with rescue." What was "rescue"? Probably a Leucovorin flush, Matt had explained, and the anti-nausea drugs. Aloud, she told Katherine, "The kids will be tired of the Pit soon. Matt promised to take them for ice cream. Then you can rest."

"I've rested," her mother said, determined. "Camille has a closing downtown, then she's coming over to get me and we're going to her house for tea. Ice tea and crumpets, she says. I'm sure you're invited too, but if I were you, I'd turn on that air conditioner you like so much and take a nap right here, while Alexander's asleep and Matt is out with the kids. You can lie down on my bed."

"The Pit," marveled Kate. "What a perfect name for the boat."

"A landlocked name," Katherine said gratefully, "for an object with no further marine use. Don't even think of it as a boat."

"Okay, Mom. You know, *your* birthday is coming up, this very weekend."

She smiled wanly. "I think a quiet celebration is in order."

"You don't want me to fly a bunch of your cronies up here in my private jet?"

"Why bother? I saw everyone just a couple of months ago when Camille went home with me." She nodded decisively. "We had a wonderful time."

"I just thought I'd phone a couple of people, see if they wanted to come visit."

"Where would you put them?" her mother asked. "I seem to be occupying your guest room."

"Sam and Jonah could sleep on the rug in my room, in sleeping bags. They'd like it. I'd love inviting someone up. Especially Rip. Be great to see him."

"Now, you know people from home don't fly somewhere on a weekend trip. It's a two-hour drive to a decent airport." She waved the suggestion away. "Of course, Rip would. I spoke to him just yesterday. I so loved seeing him back there, at home, in the place where I've always known him. Seeing him here, seeing any of them, would just be different."

Kate said nothing. Just after Easter, in a good spell as spring began, Katherine had wanted to visit home. Camille had volunteered to accompany her. They all seemed to realize Kate would find such a trip very difficult.

"It wasn't sad," Katherine said now, as though to reassure Kate after the fact. "We were so happy to see each other, and no one said goodbye. We said, 'We'll talk soon.' And we did." She gave a determined nod, peering into her book, and said musingly, "Now, it's so odd. When people call, it's as though their voices pour straight into me. Sometimes at night, I lie here and remember phrases and tones exactly. The words are clear as water." She closed the book, carefully marking her place with a pencil.

"The phone is very private," Kate said.

"Yes," Katherine said, "ear to ear, like a secret. You can't see the person, and nothing gets in the way."

"The only thing better is cheek to cheek," Kate said, leaning close, touching her face lightly to Katherine's. Against her skin, the line of Katherine's jaw felt fragile as porcelain.

"I have you for that," Katherine said.

Kate pulled away to look at her. "You don't want to see your friends?"

She met Kate's eyes. "I don't need to. And I don't want them . . . to see me now, or as I will be later. When I was home, I had such energy, a kind of false energy, probably. Of course everyone came to me—they had a schedule worked out, not to overtire me. And Camille and I never cooked a meal. They brought all the food—casseroles, breads, salads. The refrigerator was full, and the kitchen table. You can imagine."

"I can," Kate said. How many times, growing up, had she watched her mother make food when there was illness or death in a family? Food fed the survivors, nurtured the injured.

Katherine spoke almost to herself. "People used to call on weekends. Now they call more often. When I hear their voices so intensely, the distance vanishes." She looked up at Kate. "That's what you need to understand," she said carefully.

Kate nodded, unable to trust her voice.

Katherine leaned back in her chair, a signal she was finished with this conversation. "Good. Then you won't think anymore about importing visitors."

Kate took a breath. "How shall we celebrate your birthday, then?" she asked. "What would you like?"

"A nice pound cake, with fruit. And ice cream, for the kids. More ice cream, that is."

"Of course. But I was thinking we'd do something special. You've been through so much this year."

"Ah, well, necessity is the mother of invention." Katherine raised one brow, smiling. "Isn't that what they say?"

Kate reminded herself to take her cues from Katherine. Katherine knew. Kate was only reading along as this plot evolved toward an expected but unimaginable ending. She had better leave the room. "I need to fix Alexander's bed before Matt gets back with him," she said. "He's taken to ramming into his crib bumper at full speed, for the fun of bouncing off it. I got the biggest, widest extra bumper I could find."

"And you'd better look in on the big guys," her mother told her. "It's mighty quiet. They could be looking at that box of old kids' books I had Rip send up to us, but I'd check if I were you."

"I will, Mom." Kate was at the door.

"Those books were mostly yours, you know. You were the reader. You'll recognize some of them, I'm sure." She took up her own book, then paused. "You know, Rip always asks after you. And of course, every-one asks about the baby."

Kate stood threading the plump new liner bumper through the spin-dles of Alexander's crib. Across the hall, Sam and Jonah had in fact opened the box of books and found Magic Pads as well—lift-a-sheet drawing pads with pointed plastic wands attached by string. Lift the sheet and the drawing was gone. Far in the ancient past, Katherine had purchased them at the grocery store or five-and-dime in Kate's home-town. The world was far too sophisticated now for Magic Pads, but Sam and Jonah seemed to like them. Kate heard Katherine make her way slowly downstairs. She would lie on the daybed, waiting for Camille, gathering her energy for the walk next door. The front door opened and closed. Matt and Alexander. A murmur of voices, and her son's less than jovial sounds. Kate stepped up the pace, pulling and tugging both bumpers so that their gaps overlapped enough to withstand any onslaught.

"We're home, Mom," Matt called to her, walking up the stairs. "Unfortunately, we're awake."

"Almost finished," Kate told him.

"Finished with what?" He stood behind her, holding the baby, and pulled shut the door of the little room. "Interesting," he said in a rather confidential tone. "Here we have Kate Tateman, former hitchhiker, rec-reational drug user, sexual profligate—"

"A wild exaggeration," Kate answered sweetly, her back to him, "but I do thank you."

"For years, completely unconcerned with her own safety—"

"Not *un*concerned," Kate interrupted.

"All right then, *under*concerned?"

"Perhaps, yes," Kate allowed.

"All right, underconcerned with her own safety, now embracing bumpers and all manner of intense preventive measures with total, unadulterated passion."

She turned to look at him. " 'Unadulterated' is such a good word, isn't it?"

"You seem to think this is Lifesaving 101."

Kate looked at him aghast. "Wait. Am I in the wrong room? You mean this *isn't*—"

He put his free hand in both of hers. "I worry about that a bit. You know, you only save a life once in a blue moon. Even then, depends what you're saving it from."

"You would know, Doctor." Kate made a mental note to look up the term "blue moon." Probably a meteorological phrase having to do with lunar phases, harvests, woods rituals.

"Your mother tells me you two were revisiting a certain holiday week-end." Matt gripped her hand a little tighter and waited, as though he realized she required a pause in which to focus. "It was a little dicey and we were lucky, but we managed, didn't we? We had plenty of boats, and we had you and me. But it was only the ocean."

"As opposed to?"

"Jansson phoned me at work yesterday about Katherine."

"Why? Is there something he hasn't told us?"

"No, he doesn't do that. He just wanted to caution me, caution us. Your mother has come back from a couple of bad setbacks, and now, even though she's weak, her pain seems controlled. He called it a soft plateau."

"Plateau," Kate said. "I've heard the word before." Bargained and paid for, she thought, resisting the impulse to turn away and finish with the bed.

"A soft plateau," Matt repeated, "meaning it's fragile. A mirage, in a way. This far along, people can crash suddenly, and fail amazingly quickly."

"So her prize for doing well would be to crash fast."

He nodded. "Jansson was going to phone you as well, but I said we'd talk it over, then you'd call him next week if you had questions. Okay?"

Kate nodded back. This was a dispel-illusions discussion. Don't be hopeful or caught off guard. Did people think she wasn't paying atten-tion? One ending, with variations. We knew that. And now she wanted to push the words out of Alexander's room, away from his bed. Matt didn't know not to say these words here, while he held their son. She would not convince him that words were magnetized and full, powerful, that what he'd said even now attracted dark iron filings of contagion or despair: they were hard to tell apart and equally difficult to oppose. She felt a cut-ting flash of rage move off from her like a cartoon blur. Alexander cried out, distressed, and flung his arms toward her. She took him and walked past Matt, into the hallway and the sanctuary of Sam and Jonah, whose conflating voices rose and fell, Magic Pads cast aside.

Jonah was asserting primacy over the Pit. "It was my present on your birthday, and I was the one who rode it into the ocean."

"Yeah, like a dummy!" Sam burst out.

"Who's a dummy? You're the dummy, you *dummy!*"

"Hey, hey," Kate said.

"Out of here," Matt said. "The ice cream van is leaving, and if the fighting doesn't stop, one of you"—he bent down to address them at eye level, in a whisper—"is going to be staying here."

The boys were out of the room and down the stairs. Matt looked at Kate. "We're off."

"Mom still downstairs?"

"She was lying on the daybed, but she went out to meet Camille as I came up."

Kate sighed. She was wrong to be angry at him; it was not Matt's job to protect her mother. She clasped Alexander to her hip as he began crying in earnest. "I bet you'll be gone a while," she told Matt. "I'd head north if I were you, where it's cooler. I hear the ice cream in Nova Scotia is good."

He looked at her levelly. "I wouldn't abandon you, you know, even for less humidity."

Alexander's little room had one window and no cross-ventilation. When he was very young Kate had put him to nap in their bedroom, in the middle of the big queen bed. Now that he was alternately rocking and crawling, this was no longer an option. Crawling, too soon, at eight months! He was a disaster, pulling up but not standing on his own, possessed of tireless zeal, lacking any sense of balance. He had to be watched every minute. They were only safe when he was contained in one full-scale contraption or another: his bed, stroller, high chair, scooter. The scooter, a sling chair on a frame with wheels and padded, all-round tray, was a lifesaver. He could stand, move at will, and wham into walls safely, crowing like the proverbial banshee. Scooters supposedly retarded development, but Kate reasoned that if Alexander was crawling this soon a pause was in order. If he falls downstairs in that thing, Matt said, he'll do more than pause. Kate passed a law: the scooter stayed on the first floor. Alexander couldn't possibly fall *up* the stairs in it. Just now he pondered sleep on all fours in the middle of his crib, too tired to stand up any longer.

"Too hot for sleep, isn't it, Tate." Kate rubbed his back, exerting a gentle pressure she hoped might result in his closer proximity to the mattress. The window fan was set up to pull heat out; otherwise the cell-like room resembled a hot-air wind tunnel. These were dog days. Sweat dripped from her face. Alexander was moist and fussy; Kate had dipped him in cool water, dried and diapered him, but they were sticking to one another by the time he finished nursing. In the past week, central air had begun to seem an environment worth selling her soul to realize. She'd always regarded the various droning generator boxes of her neighborhood as ugly and morally questionable, emblematic of the resource-hogging, financial-might-is-right West. Moral responsibility: wasn't it one of the meanings of fortitude? She thought of rivers altered in their courses, mighty falls harnessed and tamed, not to irrigate crops but to run inground sprinkler systems and keep linen dresses from sticking to the shaved limbs of American women who could afford organic produce. Today she herself wished for a white linen sheath and the energy to iron it. Imagine a lifestyle suited to crisp, spotless clothes! Fair-weather friend to her own moral concerns, she envisioned victimized waterfalls and only wanted to stand in one. In New Delhi, she'd watched workers build five-story buildings in the wet heat by hand; men did the actual building and the women formed a human relay system, balancing boards stacked with bricks on their heads. Beneath the boards they wore saris, and necklaces, and silk scarves over their hair, the better to modestly balance fifty to seventy pounds. It was not a bad system, Kate's host had informed her; people needed work. More automation would result in fewer jobs, and these women made far better wages than they might as domestics. Their jobs were sought after; no one here debated the issue of stay-at-home moms, which would translate for some into stay-at-home starvation.

Alexander, full of milk, had capitulated to sleep clad only in cotton diaper and politically correct boiled-wool diaper cover. They may be bulky, she'd told her mother, but they breathe; even in this heat, no diaper rash. She angled the fan to blow across him, remembering the ayahs in Mumbai's botanical gardens. Broad, middle-aged women, dark and globular in their colorful silks, they fanned their wealthy charges in the shade of palms and parked various fancy carriages so the babies faced one another in a sort of baby terminus. The elliptical, frondlike fans moved like synchronized wings with handles; behind them wafted a music of easy voices and tinkling bangle bracelets. Kate, alien observer, had wondered if ayahs for affluent Indians were all issued the same fan, or if this group had settled on a particular brand through practiced trial and error. They were paid domestics adorned in gold, studs for their noses and rings for their toes; Kate was a glorified domestic with a gold band on her finger. Though she was technically co-owner of her domicile and had contributed her savings toward that end, she no longer provided her household with actual income. She did provide continual service, she and the Baby-minder.

Kate switched it on, willing India banished. She wouldn't get back there, not for years, not until she was someone else entirely. Alternate images merely toyed with her. Success was so attainable as a Westerner tasting the exotic, a temporary nun trying on spiritual practice, a drifting, artistic traveler with no ties but aging parents and happenstance alliances. Why not? They were all much easier than parenthood, running a house others lived in, facing up to the spiraling complications of intimacy with what felt to her like a whole crowd, some of whom were blood-related to one another but not to her. In finding her soft American life so demanding, she risked her own contempt.

But there was nothing soft about death, no matter where it occurred. Indians did death in blazing color and the Nepali embraced it as teacher and way station; Americans simply denied it until they stepped off the cliff and fell. Safety first! Americans held their collective breath and plummeted, angling their paltry limbs all the way down. Despite her wanderings, Kate was American to the core. She believed she had an effect.

Well, of course she did. It was what housewives had: home rule and round-the-clock effect. Alexander moved his limbs on his sheeted mattress as though floating in a tidal wash. Kate wanted to sit in roaring air-conditioning until the moisture on her face turned cool and tingly. She really did want to sleep, her senses shrouded in motor hum. If she turned the intercom on full volume, a sharp cry would wake her.

She went into Katherine's room and switched on the unit, then held the intercom to her ear like a shell to be sure it was actually working. Yes, there. Even in the hum of manufactured air its white noise sigh was audible, like a constantly exhaled breath. Kate put her face near the vents of the air conditioner and turned the knob to High. She longed to lie down in the cooling room but knew she couldn't bring herself to lie in her mother's bed. She only looked, and smoothed the covers. When Katherine had made her trip home with Camille, she'd told Kate on the phone how she "missed her nest" at Kate's. Surely that wasn't true. The bed was no antique heirloom; it was just their spare bed, a double mattress and box spring on a metal frame with wheels. Her pillows were the only headboard. Kate was arranging them, shaking them out, when a nefarious plan occurred to her. She couldn't get rid of the Pit, but she might transform it—now, when everyone was out. Turn it into something with appeal. Trick them, said her shadow voice. Maybe, Kate retorted, but only with their acquiescence. Sam and Jonah were absolutely capable of erasing her efforts if they liked; they could be counted on in that department. If nothing else, said rearrangements often kept them handily occupied.

The heat in the hallway assailed her as she stepped into it, shutting Katherine's door behind her. In the boys' room, books lay scattered around the Pit like stepping-stones; the Magic Pads were inside it. The bottom was already airless and flat, though the sides were holding up well. This was a shame, in Kate's estimation. If only the thing would completely fall in. She couldn't actually sabotage it, but she laid a blanket inside and topped it with a layer of pillows, then arranged various stuffed animals around the sides. It looked rather . . . inviting.

"What did you do to the Pit?"

Kate looked up, startled. Jonah peered in at the door of the room. "All the air was leaking out of the bottom, so I made it softer. What about your ice cream?"

He glowered. "Sam hit me, but Dad didn't see. Then I hit Sam and Dad made me come home. He said you were here and I had to come inside with you."

"Oh, no," she said in sympathy. He looked exhausted and wore a grimy smear across his cheek. "But I'll bet you a quarter your dad brings you a milk shake."

He shrugged as though he didn't care and approached the Pit. "Looks like a bed now," he said uncertainly.

"Could be a bed. Try it out."

He stepped out of his sandals, got inside, and stood considering. Then he lay down. The Pit was just long enough. He folded both arms behind his head and squirmed deeper into the pillows. "It fits," he said. "Can it be mine?"

"It's yours for now," Kate assured him. She knelt down beside him, reaching for the nearest book. "Should I read to you, like you're in your bed and it's nighttime?" There was just room for her to lie beside him, though her feet stuck out over the end. She thought longingly of Katherine's by now icy bedroom as the warm airstreams of the two revolving fans moved over her like crossing currents. She opened the book, a hardcover version of Noah's Ark. Katherine had been big on Bible stories. Kate thought she remembered this one; actual quotations from Genesis and richly detailed illustrations. The broad book opened up into two-page spreads of animal couples. As she leafed through, certain images began to seem sharply familiar memories. Loping giraffes mounted a ramp to barnlike doors and darkness; gazelles with doelike eyes stood waiting. Why did artists never render the inside of the ark, but always a barnlike visage with broad open doors flung wide and the creatures streaming in? Such an ordered choreography. Perhaps the end of the world bridged all boundaries.

Jonah moved closer, his head just at her shoulder.

"Don't you love the way the animals look?" Kate asked. "I remember the pictures. You know, these books were mine when I was little."

"Yeah." Jonah yawned. "They look old."

"Doesn't seem like it will ever rain again. If we read this, maybe it will." She began, turning the book toward him as she spoke. His lashes brushed her bare shoulder as he blinked sleepily. The words were sleepy too, and deep, older than any sleep explored by the living. *Come thou and all thy house into the ark . . . And they went in, two and two of all flesh, wherein is the breath of life, . . . as God had commanded.*

"We could get on," Jonah said drowsily. "Two of us, two of you, two dogs. But what about the mothers?"

"Which mothers?"

"Your mother and my mother. They're by themselves. And what about Alexander? He's by himself."

"Well—" Kate began.

"We'll let him on," Jonah raised his head to assure her. "No one will notice. You could carry him, like mothers do babies on airplanes."

"Right," Kate said. "He wouldn't need his own seat. And the mothers. They get on as well."

He lay back on her arm as she angled the book to better display a full-color spread of the closed ark assailed by waves. Gushes of spray burst about the bow and glanced off the stern. She was too tired to go on. They were both too tired, but the words went on without them. *The waters of the flood were upon the earth . . . the same day were all the fountains of the great deep broken up, and the windows of heaven were opened.* Jonah's head dropped against her. The intercom breathed its airy hum. The hum grew softer, more constant, moving under and around her. The sound was a presence, rhythmic and afloat. She could see the backpack sticking up on the empty beach, but she was too far away to see Alexander inside it. Still, there were no dogs near him, no lions or tigers or bears, and the pack was upright, just as she'd left it. Were there green flies? Were they biting him? She strained to hear a cry and heard the sea. Then it was Sam she saw, Sam who was scared, a small form just at the edge of the ocean. She could feel his fear across the water, blowing toward her like a storm. Once, back when Matt lived in the second-floor apartment of Kate's old house, Jonah had wandered off and Matt had gone to look for him, directing Sam to stay in the house with Kate. Oh! He'd stood just by the door, peering fixedly through its opaque square of glass and waiting with such agonized, private longing that any sympathy was mere affront. Now he walked back and forth on the white shore, all alone under the vaulted sky. She wanted to tell him Jonah was coming back, they would all come home, but she was putting her baby down and running into the sea.

10

Kate changed the flowers as soon as they began to wilt. Last week she'd found lilac branches in an expensive florist's at the mall. Big, bountiful, they breathed an essence of delicate blue and mauve into Katherine's room for nearly a week—false spring nurtured in some rarefied hothouse of sun and glass. Here in the real world, their surprising bounty abated day by day as tiny petals fell like papery knots. A remnant of fragrance stayed, a scented dust Kate wiped away with her palm as she took the branches carefully from the vase. The new irises, baby's breath, tulips, bright everyday pastels from the grocery store, might not be surprising or special, but they would last a good while, and flowers had to be fresh. Changing them was a project with visible effect, something she did that Katherine could see and notice. Implements lay arrayed for the ritual: newspaper spread for the old stems, fresh flowers in their tissue, scissors, the vase displayed on the hospital table. The table, a mobile bed tray, adjusted for height and rolled on silent wheels. Kate moved it to the foot of the bed when it wasn't in use and kept the flowers there, high enough that her mother could see them whenever she opened her eyes.

"A matching suite," she said now, touching Katrina's small circular form beside her.

"The flowers?" Kate asked.

"No, the furniture." The corners of her mouth moved in an approximation of her old smile. She hadn't wanted a hospital bed, or the table, or anything they'd rented, but the doctors had said it was time if they were going to keep her at home. She'd stayed in bed most of September and couldn't always sit up on her own. She groaned when they tried to lift her, hold her up long enough to hurriedly push pillows and blankets in place, prop her upright. Katrina had her own pillow, placed just at the curve of Katherine's waist. She lay sleeping now, content; in fact, the little dog moved about less and less. Kate took her outside at intervals. There was no need to attach the little chain to her collar now; Kate only stood watching, then took her back upstairs. Katherine was weaker now; Kate didn't want them separated.

Watching her mother's face, Kate fanned the irises wider, more room for the tulips as they opened. "The bed's an improvement though, isn't it, Mom? Better than being hauled up and down?"

"I suppose," Katherine murmured.

They kept the head of the bed elevated a bit to ease her breathing. Soft feather pillows were tucked at her shoulders and behind her head. She looked straight into the room, unmoving except for her eyes. Her eyes were so deep now that Kate couldn't always find her inside them. All her mother had been, the form she'd assumed and animated and adorned, used for childbearing, child-rearing, teaching, now seemed the powerful surface of a commingling depth more and more apparent as she grew weaker. She'd worked hard. She'd made things happen. Now she was drowning in her own eyes.

No, Kate told herself. Katherine was here, crowded, pushed into a smaller place. She put the wrapped lilacs aside, went to her, picked up a comb on the dresser, began to smooth Katherine's hair. "I'm sorry about the bed, Mom."

"The bed?"

"The hospital bed. I know you don't like it."

"Easier for you," Katherine said softly, echoing her own words. The dog stirred beside her, breathing with a tiny whistle. Katherine moved her hand and Katrina nestled her bony head closer.

A week ago, when the bed arrived, brought upstairs by deliverymen from the rental company, Kate had remarked on its graceless utility: easier. Easier for *you,* her mother had retorted quickly, then closed her mouth in a thin line. It was the most alert she'd seemed in days. Sometimes, as the medication took effect, she couldn't say she was uncomfortable, but moved in her drugged sleep and seemed to struggle. Agitated,

Kate wrote in the journal. The doctors counseled this meant she was in pain; Kate should increase the dosage. But suppose she were trying to move, speak, demand, her requests met only with more numbing, stifling sleep? Float of morphine, pain knocking behind it like heat in a complex of pipes. Tapping a message.

"I could sit up a bit, not too much," Katherine said.

She sometimes assented to the chrome bed rail that snapped in place; the controls were tied there by rubberized cord, buttons to push forward or back. She never touched them herself. I can't quite tell where they are, she'd told Kate. Now, as always, Kate took her mother's hand and moved it to enclose the palm-sized box, then pushed the buttons gently with Katherine's fingers. As though Kate could teach her, as though she might learn.

"There. Is that high enough? Shall we brush your teeth?" The bed hummed. Kate hated its engine sound and calibrated efficiency even as she was grateful for the mechanisms that raised head or foot by smooth degrees.

"I did this morning. Is today Friday?"

"No, Saturday. So that would have been last night. I'll get your toothbrush, and the basin."

"That's right," Katherine said. "It's Saturday, and Matt is home today. Is he out with the boys?" She accepted the cup Kate offered, moistened her mouth, and took the toothbrush carefully in her hand.

"No, the boys are away. Matt's out doing a few things."

"Does he have his pager?"

"Yes, he always does on weekends. Why? Do you need something?"

Slowly brushing her teeth, Katherine shook her head no.

"You're not worried about that storm they're forecasting, are you? It won't hit until late tonight, and they're pretty sure it's going to miss us altogether."

Katherine finished. "No," she said, "I'm not worried about any storm. I suppose we'll be ready." She felt for a towel.

"Ready for anything," Kate agreed, fighting the impulse to help her. Surely it would be easier if she were more upright. "If you need to sit up more, Mom, just push the button forward." She stroked her mother's arm as though to interest or coax her. This was Katherine's bed; she should control it. It wasn't really her bed, of course. Her bed, the inherited antique she'd stripped of its dark finish when Kate was a child and "brought back" with steel wool and oiled rags, hand-rubbing the wood until it shone, was in her room at home, in her locked house.

"I wish you didn't have to be so far from home, Mom. I wish I could have taken care of you there."

"Well, you couldn't. Everyone understands that," her mother said. She finished and handed the rinsed toothbrush to Kate. She lay back on her pillow, feeling for Katrina's sleeping form. "There, there," she said to the dog, petting her lightly. "Just rest."

Kate searched for a tube of Chap Stick on the cluttered bedside table. Katherine's mouth stayed chapped and dry: the belabored effort of breathing openmouthed, sleeping, waking, floating, marooned in bed.

"Remember the drive we took, Mom?" Kate coated her mother's lips lightly with the clear pomade. "To look at the leaves, and the old Victorian homes by the reservoir?"

" 'Course I remember. That pink house. You always wanted a pink house."

"I did?" Kate couldn't remember any pink house by the reservoir, but she remembered how intent Katherine had looked as they drove, how shade and sun had dappled the interior of the car. The shade they entered was cold, and the leaves had begun to turn, nodding on their branches like bright little flags. Alexander fell asleep in his car seat, and Kate parked the car just by the front door. The air was so clean and warm that she unbuckled the seat and moved it onto the grass in the back garden to sit out with him as he slept. Katherine had walked into the house alone. She went to bed and didn't get up again.

"Your pitcher is nearly empty. I'll go fill it, and I'll bring you some lunch."

"Later, not now. And not that Ensure stuff."

"Tomato soup. Applesauce. Vanilla pudding. Okay? You need your strength. It's the weekend. You'll be getting your phone calls." Kate turned at the door and came back to gather up the discarded lilacs in their newspaper bunting. "Amy is coming by today. Soon, actually. We talked about it yesterday."

"Amy. She was a sweet girl," Katherine said absently. "She's coming here? Didn't she move away?"

"Yes, but she's back, and she's coming to see us."

"Amy got married," Katherine said.

"Back in June."

"That's right." A look of concern flickered across Katherine's face. "Did Amy have her baby?"

"No." Kate sat down, the wrapped flowers in her lap. "She must be six months along, though."

"And her husband," Katherine said. "We never met him. Is he coming with her?"

"She and her husband separated a few weeks ago, remember? Amy's been up visiting her family, and now she's moved in with a girlfriend here in Boston."

"Oh, that's sad. I'm sorry. You must have told me." Her hand fluttered toward the table. Kate realized she was reaching for a Kleenex and moved to get one for her, but Katherine's hand had fallen back on the sheet. After a moment she touched its hem to her eyes. Katrina shifted on her pillow, nestling closer. "Brave, I suppose," Katherine said. "To go off on her own. But what about the baby?"

"They've only separated, not taken any legal steps. He's still in Basic, living on the base. I think she just didn't want to stay down there where she didn't know anyone, and he was never able to see her."

Katherine nodded. "That's right. And she's coming by. I have to remember all this."

"You will." Kate stroked her mother's thin forearm. The wrapped flowers in her lap rustled in their paper.

Katherine spoke as though to herself. "Don't mention it all unless she does."

"Mom, you can mention it. Amy would expect you to."

"But what if I don't remember, when she's sitting there as close as you are now?" She turned toward Kate, looking stricken. "Maybe I'd better not see her."

"She wants to see you. Amy understands. Either you'll remember or you won't, and she'll tell you, or neither of you will mention it. You'll talk about other things and she'll just sit by you. She'll take Katrina out for you and get you whatever you need. Maybe I'll do an errand or two while she's here."

"That's right. She'll help me, or maybe Camille will be over. You go out, spend the morning. Amy will stay, and help with lunch." Katherine nodded almost absently, lightly stroking the curve of Katrina's back. "That's right," she repeated. The words had become a mantra of sorts, a short-hand, perhaps a way of comforting herself, or responding in conversation when the struggle to understand or continue speaking was too much.

Kate stood to leave the room and paused at the table. She turned the vase just slightly, so that her mother saw the flowers from a better angle. "Do you like the tulips?"

"Pretty," her mother said, "but you don't need to keep replacing those flowers." She waved her hand in the air. "When they're gone, they're gone."

Amy's bangs had grown out and were held in place at her temples with barrettes. Despite the neat rounded mound of her pregnancy under her denim dress, her face looked thinner, or maybe it was the hair, less blond, straight, jaggedly layered. A smatter of formerly concealed freck-les across her forehead stood out as dark specks.

"It was just so lonely," she was telling Kate. "He couldn't even phone me from Basic. I took a three-month lease on a little apartment in Beaufort. There's a university extension in the town, but I was too late to register for classes. The transmission on the car had gone out and I had incredible morning sickness, so I took a temp job afternoons, just down the street from the apartment—'receptionist/assistant, no experi-ence required,' for an obstetrician. I thought it was the perfect job for a somewhat pregnant person, but I was the girl in the room during ultra-sounds, hearing this or that problem discussed every day. All of it, the job, the town, being alone—things started appearing to me in their true faces."

"True faces?"

"Well—" She bit her lower lip with even white teeth, looking sud-denly very young. "I started thinking about my first life, alongside the life I sort of inherited after my mom died. Coming from a big family, helping with the younger kids, I always assumed I was the type who'd marry my high school boyfriend and have children, four or five of them. Everyone who knew me thought so too, but that was just confusion. My own mother had only two children, and one of them was Hannah, whose birth was very difficult. They almost lost Hannah. Why should pregnancy come easily to me, and why hadn't I ever dated anyone but my first boyfriend?" Her faceted eyes widened, as though she were asking Kate in earnest, but she went on. "Then too, I thought about you and Matt, all you've both done and what you're managing, how much things can change, your new lives, my dad's new life. I realized I'd never changed, or I was just beginning to. Yet there I was, pregnant, married." She touched her abdomen with her palm, a tentative comforting touch that ached in Kate like a memory. "The baby feels like part of it all, more real than anything I've ever done, like he's demanding I change as fast as he is, but I'm not sure I want the marriage, or any baby but this one."

"Well," Kate said cautiously, "it's a turbulent time. You've known your boyfriend forever, but in a sense you haven't really married yet. I mean, you haven't really lived together. Isn't it difficult to judge? What does he think of all this?"

Amy frowned worriedly. "He thinks it's hormonal, and the fact we can't be together, which sounds very logical, like him—but one reason I settled on him so early is that he will always be exactly who he is." She looked up at Kate almost wonderingly. "I won't. I know that now."

"When is Basic over?"

"Another week. Then he'll come here for a weekend leave before he goes to Camp Lejeune, six weeks of rifle training. He'll finish before the baby's born, but he's likely to be reassigned somewhere in the South. They'll give him a week for the birth."

Kate nodded. "You can't know yet how you'll feel after the baby is born. When his training is finished, you'd be able to live together, wouldn't you?"

"That's right," Amy said.

The phrase resonated with a particular power, intense and small. To cover her disquiet Kate half stood, about to get some ice for them from the freezer, pour glasses of water, but Amy reached to stop her. "I know you said Alexander's sleeping, but can we look in on him before I see Katherine? I think of him so often. I know it's crazy, but sometimes, down there, I used to worry about him."

Kate fixed a tray so that Amy could help Katherine with lunch easily. Everything was ready; bouillon in a microwave bowl, covered with wax paper, cold items set aside in the fridge, napkin, silverware. Just as she was pulling on her jacket, thinking she'd pick up extra milk, eggs, batteries, in case the storm really hit, the phone rang.

Camille sounded less ebullient than usual. "I've missed you, hon. Can you come over?"

"Amy is visiting. I was just going out to do some errands. Why don't you come over here? We haven't seen you for days, and I know Mom—"

"No, Kate, you come over here."

"Are you all right?" There was no reply, and Kate said, "I'll come over." She left the tray on the kitchen table. Upstairs, too soon, she heard Alexander waking up. She couldn't leave Amy for long with both of them; she would do the errands later. Now she walked quickly down the driveway, across the walk to Camille's. Camille's kids were both home; maybe something had happened. Olivia, her daughter, cooked in a tapas restaurant in the Bay Area; she was twenty-three, tall and thin like Camille. She opened the door when Kate rang, and reached out to exchange a quick hug.

Kate saw that she'd cut her dark hair very short. "You okay, Olivia?"

"I'm fine, but she's not." Olivia nodded toward Camille, who sat in the darkened stairwell. "Landon smacked her around."

Camille stood up. One eye was blackened and swollen. "I know I look awful," she said. "I didn't want Katherine to see me."

"He's never hit you before, has he? When did this happen?"

"We finally, really split up, well, last week, and I wanted all my letters back, letters and photographs and anything I've ever left in his apartment, and he wouldn't give me some pictures we'd taken in Mexico, pictures of *me*, very private ones. He has no right any longer to those pictures."

"That *fuck*—" said Olivia.

"We were in his car, by the harbor, yesterday. I tried to grab the pictures, and we were struggling. He hit me and ordered me out of the car, then he opened the door and shoved me out, and just left me there on the sidewalk."

"How did you get home?"

"A doorman at a restaurant called her a cab and gave her some ice," Olivia answered.

"Here he is, making partner, and he beats me up. It just galls me. I think they should know who they're promoting, what he's really like. I'd love to sue him for battery, and my doctor said he would back me, but I wouldn't win—I was too ashamed to call the police. And Landon has so many friends to rise up and defend him, so many glad-hand pals. I'm at least going to write a letter to the other partners, they should know . . ." Miserably, her voice trailed off.

"You have friends too, Camille, but don't decide now what you're going to do. Just let me try to get the pictures back."

"Why should he go on in his life without a ripple, smack someone and it doesn't matter?"

"It does matter, regardless of how he phrases it to himself. He'll never feel right about what he did. I'll talk to him about the pictures."

"Then you'll have to phone him at work," Camille said. "It's the only place he'll take calls, where his secretary can screen them. He won't speak to me. No apology, nothing."

" 'Course not, Mom. Now that he's screwed up, he's thinking like a guy who's talked to his lawyer." Olivia nodded toward the kitchen. "Kate could try him at home. He'll answer, as long as it's not you. Let her try."

Kate stood in the kitchen dialing, out of earshot of Camille and Olivia, who waited by the stairs. Odd to think of Landon behind a polished desk, making partner. His answering machine picked up. "Landon? It's Kate." She vaguely remembered the chrome, sleek look of the apartment; he'd lent it to her brothers the weekend of the wedding. Richard's annoyance at Landon's flirtation with Lynette came back to her: "He came by to pick up the keys as we were leaving. They were talking about their kids, and he kissed her good-bye on the mouth. Then he was gone, you know, quick." The line seemed to engage, but no one spoke. She heard him breathe. "Landon?"

"Hello, Kate." He paused. "How are you?"

"Landon, I think it's time we had that lunch. Are you free?"

"Right now?"

"It's about the pictures," Kate said. "It's hard for me to get away. I have things covered here briefly, and I could meet you in half an hour."

"I see."

"Please, bring the pictures. We should talk about this."

No change of tone. "You want to talk? All right, we'll have lunch." He named a restaurant in the North End. Camille could tell her how to get there, he said, and where to park.

Kate walked back through Camille's narrow hallway to the stairs. "I can't guarantee he'll give me the pictures, but he agreed to meet," she told Camille. "I can't go, though, unless you come over to sit with Mom. She's so much weaker, and I heard Alexander waking up as I left the house. I don't want to leave Amy alone with both of them." She sat down on the step beside Camille. "I'm not sure she'll notice your eye. I don't think she sees well at all now. When I help her with meals, she sort of responds by touch, as though she doesn't see the spoon. She focuses differently; her eyes seem almost reflective when you look into them."

"Of course I'll come over with you. I just didn't want her to worry."

"She doesn't need to."

"What do I say if Amy asks?"

"What does everyone say? You walked into a door."

Kate checked on her mother just before she left to go downtown. Amy had taken Alexander out in the stroller. Camille sat beside Katherine's bed, tears in her eyes. "Still hurts?" Kate whispered, but Camille shrugged dismissively and got up, gesturing for them to leave the room. In the hallway, she took Kate's arm. "No, it's just that I haven't seen her for over a week, all this with Lannie, and I didn't realize—how fast it's all going now. I see a difference." Camille's voice broke. "I'm sorry you're having to do this now, of all times—"

"Never mind. You won't have any more to do with him, you said so. Should I ask for the negatives?"

"I have the negatives. In this situation, I seem to have all the negatives."

"Don't be so sure," Kate said.

"You were right, she didn't seem to notice my face. She's just holding that dog and talking about the garden, which perennials are really established, what should be planted in the spring, what we'll put in later—"

"Has she complained of pain?"

"No. She talked about her lilacs. Did you have very tall, President Grevy lilacs? I thought at first she was talking about a person, then I realized it was the name of the lilac."

"They were taller than the house, the ranch house my father built. They grew all along her bedroom windows so thickly you couldn't see through them, but she would never let him cut them back. I never knew the name."

"Well, darling, that's what they're called, and I'm going to plant some for you."

He stood as Kate crossed the room. The tables were small, round, intimate, rather formal, with their white tablecloths and freesias. The decor was shadowy, an Italian grotto look, rough stone walls partially whitewashed, and light filtering down from above through street-level windows. The patio, visible through open doors, was empty of diners, and the air was eerily still. Maybe there really would be a hurricane; what was that phrase Katherine used? *The calm before the storm.* Landon had chosen to sit inside, and they were nearly alone in the room. Kate was already regretting her ploy; she should have met him on a street corner or in the Public Garden, and simply made the exchange: three minutes of persuasive understanding for his pictures. She realized she might well fail in her mission, despite this quasi date: it would be just like him to smooth-talk and no-comment his way through lunch, then force her to leave empty-handed.

He stood as she approached the table, and sat when she did. "I took the liberty of ordering wine before I remembered that you don't imbibe. At least, I assume that's still the case—I haven't seen you for a few weeks. You're still nursing?" His eyes flickered over her as she nodded. "But we have bread and water. I asked the waiter to give us a minute; I wasn't sure if you were actually here for lunch." He paused a beat, then smiled the old Landon, share-a-complication smile. He was just the sort of man Kate would have taken on temporarily in another life, a handsome wounded charmer who would have left her or forced her to leave him. Not now. Recently married, ensconced with her child, she mostly saw Landon as a species she'd once moved among. Yet it was so easy to be vulnerable when some sadness caught up with you; like Matt's ex, like Matt, like Landon himself. There was a long past, sincere uncertainty in his mouth, in his look, Kate thought; that was why it worked. The smile faltered rather professionally as he looked directly at her. "Thanks for doing this. I know things are bad now, with your mom."

"What about your mother, Lannie? I've never heard you mention her."

"Died when I was fifteen. Camille never told you? Car wreck. She was just gone, suddenly. And no, I haven't been searching for her ever since—not in women, anyway. Camille is the first older woman I've ever looked at twice." He shook his head, holding up both hands in a trucelike gesture. "I regret what happened. It was horrible and I feel horrible. I should have refused to meet with her, but she insisted. I've never hit a woman before, and I didn't mean to hit Camille."

"Camille is talking about suing you," Kate said quietly. "That would be a shame. It would make it harder for either of you to move on."

"She wanted everything back, and there was one demand I didn't meet," he said levelly. "I didn't mean to hit her. We were struggling, and she was hitting me."

"You don't seem to have sustained injury, however."

"Does solidarity require you share *all* of Camille's perceptions, her versions of—"

"A black eye is not a *version* of anything."

"I'm not so sure. What else could she hold over me? Thank God I never made any promises she could accuse me of breaching."

Kate looked at him deadpan. "So Camille was planning and scheming throughout, thinking of ways—"

"Camille wasn't thinking, and I certainly wasn't. But I'm sorry. I'm sorry about all of it and for all of it. I'm sorry about your mother and I'm sorry about Easter. Not a great time to hit on you"—he sighed ironically—"speaking of hitting."

"Wasn't exactly a hit, Landon. You mentioned lunch. I'd call it a gentle tap. But it wouldn't have mattered, where or how."

"Because of Camille. I mean, surely it's not because of *me.*"

"Because of my closeness to Camille."

"That doesn't stop some people."

"Are you referring to yourself?"

"No. I'm referring to certain other friends of hers who've been chatting me up and rubbing against me since day one. You were her loyal friend, nearly my age. I'm very observant of boundaries—I usually like them intact, one of Camille's key complaints. I just was . . . I hate holidays, holiday dinners. And Camille has so many of them, family for a day, happy groups, everyone's problems on hold. The only thing more horrible than a happy holiday group is fleeing one alone." He paused. "You were always so beautiful with the baby. Maybe you reminded me of my wife, when my kids were little and I was married, and everything looked the way it was supposed to. You're too inexperienced at divorce to know what I'm saying."

"Matt is divorced."

"Of course he is. But I mean *your* divorce; you haven't had to leave your kids, or share them with a detached person, or be far away."

"I couldn't do that."

"I couldn't do that," he repeated, mocking her. "No, you can't do it, but sometimes you have to." His jaw tightened and he looked at her, eyes moist with anger or contempt. "You know, you might have given me an inch, just as acknowledgment. That was really all I wanted. It's not always life or death."

"It's not?" Kate looked at him across the table. His mother, she thought. The holidays after she died, then the ones without his kids. But the appearance of agreement was surely called for. "All right," she told him. "I didn't know you weren't serious, and for Camille, I didn't like it. You seemed to be testing me—"

"I don't mean that I wasn't serious," he interrupted in a steely voice. "It wasn't a test."

"What were you going to do? Whisk my baby and me off somewhere?"

"Men don't think that way, Kate, it's not our job. I was thinking about you." He spoke pointedly, overenunciating as though to a dim, exasperating listener. "Your face, your foot, *you,* for God's sake."

"If you were approaching me, I supposed you habitually—"

"Not true."

"You would say that," she retorted, suddenly thinking of Lynette, and her brother's words, *he was gone* and *they were talking about their kids.*

"Suppose I would," Landon said, "if I'm who you think I am."

"I don't know who you are, Landon. How would I?"

He cupped the globe of his wineglass, and kept his eyes on her. There was an awful quiet in his hands. "You always think there's someone who can change things, make them better, make them *good,* despite whatever odds. Even the merest suggestion of that possibility—"

Kate waited.

He laughed. "—is surely the basis of all human endeavor."

"If you want rid of Camille," Kate said evenly, "why keep the pictures?"

"Because they mean something to me," he said rapidly, his voice low and tense. "Because the physical part was the one thing she didn't control or summon or direct. And I want her to remember that."

"You think she'll forget it?"

He leaned forward. "Drink your wine."

Kate was angry. They were fighting. He'd gotten to her.

"Just . . . *drink* it," he repeated. "Drop the pleasure of self-sacrifice. You're *out of the house.*"

She sat back from the table, her face burning. She took a breath. The gold-rimmed wine goblet sat before her. Prismed glass, etched and scrolled like an antique. She straightened deliberately, then crossed her hands behind her neck, let her head fall into them and stretched, flexing her arms, her shoulders, arching her back enough to breathe and get away from him. She closed her eyes to shut him out, reached for the glass, brought it to her mouth. One long slow swallow, then another, and one more. When she opened her eyes, he was watching her. He hadn't moved.

"That's it," he said quietly, "that's all we get."

He opened the briefcase beside him and gave her a manila envelope. Kate slipped it into her purse and stood. "Yes, you'd better get home now," he said quietly, "before the hurricane." At his mention of the word she must have betrayed obvious anxiety; he dropped the sarcasm. His gaze softened and warmed; he seemed to look at her completely openly. "Not to worry, Kate. The storm's blown out to sea. Just a lot of wind and rain, and a few broken things."

She turned and left the table. Outside, as she walked up the stairs to the street, she saw him through the window. He was looking directly at her, as though to move toward her despite the distance expanding between them. She gained the street and walked quickly through spitting rain along the narrow brick sidewalk. The sky was a glowering gray tinged with green. Small trees along the walk, their trunks encircled with iron railings, swayed and moved, limbs lifted up as though in exaltation or fear. The storm would menace the coast and be over, but summer was ended. Now the cold would come after them all.

. . .

She pulled into the driveway just as Matt was getting out of his van. He turned to face her, waiting, unmoving. Kate wondered if the weather advisory had changed; perhaps the storm had shifted course.

"What is it?" Kate asked, reaching him. "Has the storm turned?"

"No, no." He reached out to embrace her.

"But you look— Where have you been?" Then, over his shoulder, she glimpsed Katrina's carrier through the window of the van. The little airline carrier she'd ridden in on the plane from home had sat in Katherine's closet all these months.

"Right after you left, your mother asked Camille to page me. The carrier was on the bed, and the dog was asleep on her lap. Camille left the room, and your mother said it was time to do this. Camille had helped her make the arrangements, and she wanted me to do it while you were out. She wasn't emotional; she was very resolved, calm."

Kate stepped back from him as the wind whipped her hair around their faces, remembering her mother's fingers on the sleeping dog, the constancy of her touch. "But—"

"I thought about trying to dissuade her. I sat down and she took my hand. I didn't say anything more, and she didn't, but it was as though some energy passed from her to me."

Kate looked up at him, surprised. "What do you mean? A warmth?"

"It really wasn't physical. But it was very apparent, very definite." He turned from her and opened the door of the van. Kate took the carrier, but it was light, empty. Just behind it lay a small form no larger than a loaf of bread, wrapped in a white towel. Matt cradled it in one arm and they moved toward the house. The tall thin cedars at the front door were tossing in the wind, spraying them with rain, but the rain had stopped. The bruised green of the sky had gone darker, tinged with rose.

They stood in the foyer as Kate shut the door behind them. She heard Amy's voice in her mother's room, and Camille's, and Alexander's incongruous laughter. Yes, they should stay near Katherine, with Alexander. He was beautiful and new, he made noise, she loved him. Katherine wouldn't hear them at all. And please, Amy wouldn't look down into the yard, she wouldn't see. Quietly, Kate followed Matt into the kitchen, where he placed the swaddled form on the kitchen counter. Kate stood near it.

Matt took a small shovel from the kitchen entry and stepped into the yard. He began to dig near the dogwood tree, by the back door, so close the house he couldn't be seen from upstairs. The volume of the wind was constant and powerful, like a slowly accelerating motor. Kate could see him through the window, digging in gusts of rain. Katrina's narrow chain lay stretched out in the grass behind him as though someone had pulled it straight, each silver link glistening and wet. Kate stepped closer and placed her hand lightly on the towel. The small heart was stilled but the dog was warm, as though she lived now in some fearless state. Kate stood touching her, waiting, then she took the small covered form in her arms and went outside to Matt.

The air is beautifully still. Ten miles from town, the mountains seem steeper, the cerulean sky visible only as slants of sun poured down across the glinting asphalt of the narrow road. They sit in her mother's big car, looking up the skewed slash that serves as Rip's driveway. "He can't possibly go on living up there as a really older man," Katherine is saying. "All winter he leaves his car down by the paved road and walks up."

"Shouldn't we do the same?" Kate asks, then realizes the steep road is too strenuous for her mother. She puts the car in drive and steers toward the sharply ascending bank as the tires spin and catch. The drop-off on the other side is aflame with brilliant coreopsis.

"I would never leave my car along this road," her mother goes on. "Some yahoo is likely to take the turn too fast and ram right into it, summer as well as winter. We'll be fine unless there's a cloudburst."

Kate guns the motor as the Chrysler climbs. "In that case, we'll slide down."

The whole of the verdant landscape seems at a height of bloom, a dense zenith of bower and heat and bounty. Rip's domain is perched on a mountainside; meadow turned garden, barns, a white frame house whose narrow porch hangs unseen above the highway and the cliff. Danger, Soft Shoulder read signs along the twisting roads, and public schools close a week each fall for deer season. The two-lanes blasted out of ledges have been left to pock and warp; now they are landscape itself, overgrown linkage between far-flung hamlets, nearly impassable in winter.

The new interstate is for travel, across and away from here. Kate parks on the level ground of Rip's yard and turns off the ignition; the hum of air-conditioning ceases. She glimpses an uneven back patio of native stone, flowering hillsides, a broad weathered barn up to the right. Towering sunflowers and tangled marigolds mark the boundary of the big garden, keep squirrels and rabbits from the lettuce and pea vines.

"Look at that garden," Katherine says. "He brings me asparagus and corn. It takes years to bring on an asparagus bed, you know. There's Rip now."

Kate sees him coming out onto the back porch, a cigarette in his mouth, carrying three tall glasses filled with ice. The screen door slams as he waves them forward rakishly. Kate waves back. "He's incredibly thin," she tells her mother. "Is he really all right?"

"He's fine for long periods. I think he does have a sense of borrowed time."

Katherine gets out of the car without further comment; Kate waits a moment longer before following. One day, her mother will be too ill to live alone. When the call comes, Kate realizes, it will come from Rip. Understated, matter-of-fact. Rip will tell her. That's why they were meeting. Her mother stands by the rough-hewn table. "Don't bother locking the car. Believe me, our purses are safe." She's laughing as Kate approaches. "He's made sun tea. Remember it, Kate?"

"Huge glass jar, fresh mint, sugar, all day in the sun?"

"Exactly. Here's the very jar." Rip lifts a widemouthed jar from the stones at his feet onto the table. "High noon. Time for something cold."

Kate touches the drip of moisture down one of the iced tumblers. "The glasses are weeping. It's summer."

"Let's take our tea and walk up to have a look in Rip's barn," Katherine says.

"Right now?" Kate asks.

"I believe your mother is anxious for you to see something up there. But let's leave the tea here, the better not to stumble over our feet." He exchanges a look with Katherine.

"I'm sure there's plenty to see," Kate replies, but the other two have turned to walk the gentle slope. It seems obvious there's nothing romantic between them, yet they've known each other since long before Kate was born, shared a first death, gone separate ways over a parenthesis of

forty years. Her mother's male friend. Kate catches up as they reach the barn. The boards are silver in the sun, weathered to a silken sheen. "Do you actually sell antiques?" she asks Rip.

"I trade, mostly, and fiddle." He reaches for the massive barn door, grasps a thick rope loop fixed there in lieu of a handle. The door pulls open, creaking mightily, a dark mouth revealing fulsome shade, yet the interior opens up into deepening space crosshatched with bronze light, twenty degrees cooler, nearly dark in patches. Rip leads them past piles of horse harnesses, stacked chairs with split bottoms, cupboards missing doors or glass. Armoires and chiffoniers stand open, rockers are turned up, an old sledge stands empty, still fitted with sleigh bells.

Kate's eyes adjust; daylight streams in through the haymow window. No hay, just the smell of hay, and no haymow, just the space of the barn, open to the beams of the roof. Motes of dust swim in gold shafts. Rip stops. Kate comes up behind him and sees the bassinette, a white wicker basket with a high curved hood and handles, set in its own wicker stand. Bright in surrounding dusk, set off to itself, it seems sudden as an apparition. Open, diamond-weave wicker; Kate sees into it with the certainty that she will look through it one day to see her baby's face. Rip has placed the basket just so in this filtered light, or the sun has picked it out at the perfect moment.

"You've seen it before, but you don't remember," her mother says softly.

"In some way, I do remember." Not scrolled dark wood, Kate is thinking, but these bare bones, a place among the rushes. The light shifts. Kate looks up at the haymow window to see a clutch of crows alight on the sill, broad wings outspread. Then, with an airy rattling, the black birds fly, lifting straight into the sky and disappearing. A patch of azure remains, gleaming and jewellike.

"It was broken along one side," Katherine says. "I'd always intended to give it to you someday, so I asked Rip to refurbish it. He'd finished, and then here you come, with your news." She reaches to touch Kate's hair, then runs her hand along the curled edge of the basket. "It's old wicker, very strong. All my babies slept in it the first weeks, and Mother's too. You want them beside your bed, where you hear every breath."

"I can't take credit for the transformation," Rip says. "There's a basket maker I know up the road, I keep him in vegetables. He fixed it and I painted it, because I knew I'd be seeing your mother. Then I forgot it yes-

terday. Too bad—I might have seemed psychic. But Katherine called this morning and we hatched a small plot."

"So you know. She told you."

"She did, very happily."

"I'll buy it an airplane seat," Kate says.

"No, you won't," her mother admonishes her. "I have to make a long eyelet ruffle that comes down over the basket, get some foam for a mattress, sew sheets and knit an afghan. You and Matt will drive down and get them all when he has time for a real visit."

"Let's move it out of this barn. It's far too pristine for such company." Rip lifts the stand and Katherine takes the basket as they carry it through the shade into bright sun. "I intended to make this presentation later, with good champagne," Rip calls back to Kate, "and I'm still going to. We'll celebrate before lunch. I have bread and cold soup and some other things."

Kate follows her mother. Outside, she leans against the barn door to push it shut, conscious of warmth at her back as she watches Katherine bear the shining bassinette down the path.

11

The jack-o'-lanterns on the stoop had grown soft, soggy, their insides runneled with a blue jam of rot. The outer surfaces of all three were snowy with a fuzz of white mold, a webbing wispy as gossamer. Kate wanted to remove them immediately, find a shovel, lift them carefully into dark green garbage bags and put them on the sidewalk to be picked up at dawn, but she forced herself to leave them. It was four a.m. She would do it later, she really would. After Elmira arrived. In three hours.

Elmira would say, "She bad today. A big drop from yesterday."

Standing on the front stoop, looking into the dark, Kate could hear the exact, particular tone of Elmira's low, almost drawling voice. She couldn't seem to call up images anymore of her mother healthy, laughing, making a wry comment or ironing a dress. She couldn't remember the faces of the women her mother had worked with and supervised. She couldn't even see her mother's garden, the baby's breath and marguerites. Hundreds of miles away, the garden bloomed around her mother's empty house. Mums now, and late roses. She couldn't hear her mother say the names of the flowers.

But she could hear Elmira. Elmira spoke slowly, unhurried, as though her thoughts moved stolidly, the way her big body moved. The others always walked from the subway station, but Elmira came in a cab the six blocks up the hill. "My knees," she would say, "this damp weather. I ain't no hero."

Kate was no hero either. This was abundantly clear. The image of

Elmira reaching across the backseat to pay the cabbie had begun to fill her with relief, as though a burden shifted the moment Elmira emerged and the chassis of the cab, perceptibly lightened, rocked just slightly. There she stood, her shoes white, the seams of her support stockings straight, her uniform spotless. Elmira would straighten her shoulders before bending to pick up her "carryall," an open black valise containing purse, lunch, vast white cotton sweater, magazines, spiral notebook for "keeping track." Her familiar gait as she lumbered up Kate's half circle of driveway was heavy and deliberate, as though she shifted and squared her dense weight with each footfall. Elmira "managed cases"; she'd done terminal care for fifteen years. "The others might come and go," she told Kate, "but Elmira is here. I be here right through."

Katherine had stopped chemo; she was seldom out of bed. The health plan sent a VNA nurse who recommended a health care agency. Start working with people now, she counseled Kate, while Katherine was well enough to establish relationships. And so Elmira came four mornings. Mornings were worst; Alexander was eleven months old but still nursed twice during the night. At seven a.m., when Katherine needed help, breakfast, medication, Alexander needed changed, nursed, fed cereal and fruit, bathed, dressed. Elmira said that baby needed the crying cure, Kate might as well have an infant. Kate read the books dutifully but admitted in her pediatrician's office that she couldn't face "curing" Alexander now; she wasn't sure she ever could. He'd nursed on demand all his life. Timed verbal reassurances and repeated abandonment in the glow of a night-light would seem deliberate cruelty. Was that what mothers should teach babies? She asked her mother's counsel. In her day, Katherine said, they had to do everything on schedule from the beginning. Babies got used to it before they knew any better. Now women did what felt right and bore the brunt. But you're bearing it too, Kate said. Did she mind Elmira helping her? Elmira was a busybody, Katherine said, but very dependable.

She liked Colleen most. Colleen, an Irish girl in her twenties, came two afternoons. Her cheerful Irish brogue, her light touch and breezy pampering, seemed to comfort Katherine as Kate could not. *And how are we today, dearie? There now, shall I wash your hair for you? Not feeling up to it? Well then, I'll read to you a bit.* Even if Katherine didn't want to move, she cooperated with Colleen. *I can change your linens and hardly disturb a'tall. Move you a bit this way, a bit that, and finished before you know it.* Colleen had perfect pitch for dealing with a sick person, a pitch she maintained by not being too close, too identified. "Leaves me to my schedule," she said of terminal care, "I can work it in." Lots of Irish girls did this work, she'd told Kate, sometimes to augment other employment. Colleen didn't do mornings, "not a'tall"; she needed her sleep. She arrived at two and left promptly after dinner. Dark-eyed, brunette Colleen frequented the Kells or Malone's most evenings with friends; she had another life, other jobs. Though she was full of small talk, she said little about herself and left only the agency's number should Kate need to reach her. A few others had helped occasionally if Kate had a pediatrician's appointment, or a rare dinner out with Matt, but as Katherine grew more ill Kate stopped using them. She changed her appointments, ordered Thai or Chinese takeout once a week. Matt and she ate by modest candlelight when Camille could sit with Katherine. Kate was afraid her mother would awaken and not know who was with her.

Elmira was the only one who wore a uniform. She fastened the buttons to her throat, smoothed the white rayon fabric against her dark skin. "I'm old-fashioned," Elmira said. "I supposed to nurse, I want to look like a nurse. They can call me Hospice, VNA, whatever, but I nurse." Kate thought of her as someone who lived here, in the trenches. "How was your night?" Elmira always asked, and Kate gave the report, went over her notations in the clothbound book kept beside her mother's bed.

Matt said it was good for all of them to have people coming in. Insurance paid for limited personal care because people were expected to use it. Someone had to be there during the day, when Kate was with Alexander. It was true Katherine needed things done, more and more, but Kate knew it was her own need that dictated hiring strangers. Kate could do trays, feeding, bedpans, attention and sitting by. Afternoons, if they were alone and Alexander was awake, she took him to Katherine's room to play, shutting the door and keeping him in as long as she could entertain him. Plastic toys with hard indestructible edges were his passion now: bright Playmobil cars with limbless plug people, the bead tube, the shape box with its twenty holes and specific cubes, circles, spheres. She gave Katherine medication while Alexander held on to her knees, calling for his own spoon until she gave him one, inscribed with his name in bright blue marker. He played with plastic mixing cups and animal-shape cookie cutters as she wrote down Katherine's dosages, careful requirements that waxed and waned. Kate could do nearly all of it, but she could not bathe her mother.

She was ashamed. There were times when the baby slept, or when Amy came by to play with him, when Kate could have bathed Katherine and did not. She wanted a bath every day, in the tub if she was well enough, or in bed with cloths and sponges. These were measured recitals Kate could not perform.

She could help her mother to the bathroom, balance her carefully in the portable toilet chair, pad the steel arms with blankets, help her off with her gown and wrap her in her robe. She could arrange towels, pour Vitabath in the foaming water, test the temp. Katherine weighed eighty pounds. Kate could have lifted her into the deep, warm bath, held her fast like a damaged child, but Kate did not. She didn't think she was afraid of dropping her, hurting her. Truly, she was afraid of seeing her, of holding her, revealed with nothing between them, of moving her poor body, shivering and small, forsaken, through the air into the water, through the water into the air, to towels and bed, received, exhausted, spent with effort, covered, warmed. Kate could oppose the illness, fight it constantly, but she could not hold in her arms the open declaration of its dominion, anoint what it was doing and had done. She could not pull Katherine free of it, or even receive her in this shattered state to nurse forever. She could not make the torture stop in exchange for one pain-free night, one morning in which Katherine awakened unoppressed in look or expression, for the duration of a conversation.

She knew her mother's body. Katherine had dressed and undressed in front of her children until they were adolescents; she didn't want them, particularly Kate's brothers, to be unfamiliar with women's bodies. As an adult, visiting home, Kate often sat and talked with her mother while she bathed. She lathered her mother's back, so similar in shape and complexion to her own; if Kate was more elongated, angular in the face, with her father's fine, fair hair, she knew she'd inherited her mother's form: the narrow wrists and forearms, compact breasts and generous hips, knobby knees. It was not their physical similarity that paralyzed Kate, or the continuation of intimacy, but the momentum of hopelessness, the fact that they were beaten. What they'd endured was preamble. Her mother was instructing her now in the depths of sorrow just as she'd once taught her the sounds of her letters. Stutters and sighs combined to make words that existed apart, opened and became miraculous, while death, common as rain, deepened and deepened and was bottomless. You forget, her mother had said of childbirth, you know, but you forget. For Katherine, death had preceded childbirth; she'd married and lost her mother in the same few months, enduring descent and forgetfulness before there was ever a child. All her life, she'd wept when she remembered. Hold your head high, she'd told her little daughter, never explaining why such fortitude would be required. Kate held Alexander to her chest as he forced his downy head higher, up into the curve of her throat; she breathed him in like oxygen.

Elmira did the baths, and Colleen. They knew to keep the door ajar, in case they needed help. Elmira grumbled. What was the sense. What help would Elmira need with that little slip of a thing. You just letting in the cold air. But Kate could hear water sounds, murmurs. Listening, she went to Alexander's room and watched him sleep, or read him books. She stroked his velvet skin. Nursing was a double verb, a figure eight they turned inside, traversing decades. Feeding Alexander, rocking him, she heard the sluice of water as the tub drained and willed herself years in which to raise him, years to watch him change, to hold his children. When she must leave him she willed that her heart stop or her car explode, fast and certain and no mistakes; never this awful progression, this slow winnowing in which the soul crouched smaller and smaller in its shell, surrendering itself in agonized increments as though to repay a terrible debt.

She remembered Katherine's instructions when her children were small: *Don't whine about it, just do it.* For years she'd taught first grade. One little boy whined famously. Finally Katherine asked him in exasperation, "Johnny, why don't you *talk?*" "Me can't talk because me whine," Johnny replied, and Katherine was apt to repeat this phrase when people complained or didn't measure up. Katherine did not whine. She'd always said she could take care of herself perfectly well. Maybe a little too well, Kate would point out; she'd spent so many years alone. I'm not alone, she'd say, I have you. I suppose that's something, Kate would answer. More than you know, Katherine always replied.

Summer, when Kate had walked with her father and Alexander by the river, seemed long ago, but she thought frequently of Waylon's big hands on the handle of the stroller between them, of his heavy familiar stride close to her. She heard him repeat, in sparkling sunlight: You can't do all your mother will need.

Alone in Aunt Raine's house, Waylon phoned on weekends. He knew Katherine was failing. He never asked to speak to her but passed on hometown news that Kate might relay. Their conversations were short and the phrases he spoke remarkably the same. "How is she?" he would ask. It would be Sunday evening. In late fall he would have the window open and Kate could hear traffic pass on Main Street. No rain all week, he might say, dusty as hell. After they hung up he'd call Kate's brothers, as though Kate hadn't spoken to them herself days before. She'd told them to come soon, separately, while Katherine could still talk to them. They were both short of money; Richard was struggling to establish himself in his new job and Doug had been laid off. Kate paid for airline tickets out of Katherine's dwindling account and mailed them to her brothers.

Snow dusted the cold grass and withdrew. The afternoon darkened. Cold, fine, soundless rain began. Kate sat at the kitchen table, feeding Alexander a late lunch. Luna crouched at her feet, tail thumping occasionally in guilty compensation. Alexander made Luna nervous. He threw crackers she soundlessly devoured off the floor; he also threw jar lids, wooden blocks, plastic keys that clattered. When Elmira came downstairs at the end of her shift, she called a cab and sat at the table to wait. Today Luna slunk to her side and leaned heavily against her.

"I don't like me any dogs," she sighed, "but this one desperate." She went so far as to stroke Luna's ears. "No escape from that baby today," she went on, "cold rain like this."

"Is Mom all right while I finish here?" Kate asked.

"Oh yes, fast asleep." Elmira looked at her watch. "You gave her medication—when? Ten past?"

Kate nodded. "I wish the rain would stop. All of us from southern, kinder climates feel these long winters. Don't you feel far from home?"

"What you saying, now?" Elmira shook a finger at Kate, mock scolding. "I'm far from Detroit, is all I'm far from. My people from Georgia, I *sound* South. But I ain't been South and not about to go." She leaned down to take a baby bed sheet from a basket of unfolded laundry on the floor, furling it out over her ample lap before creasing the fabric into neat squares. "No sweet air there for me or mine. No sir."

"You have children, Elmira? A husband?"

"Ain't no husband. I raised four boys, five counting my nephew, but no girls. No one ever going to do for me what you're doing." She raised her brows at Kate. "Boys, oh, they take off. Be about they business." She shook her head. "I had kids at home, I couldn't be doing this work. It gets near someone's time, I got to be there all hours."

"Alexander and I went to a hospice support group this morning," Kate told her. "They were saying people hold on if they don't feel permission to go. They worry the ones they're leaving aren't safe."

"Lord," Elmira said dismissively, "all this about *holding on.*" She cast her eyes toward the ceiling as though considering the woman in the bed upstairs. "She not holding on. It just ain't her time to go. When it's their time, they *can't* hold on—they just have to go. My case before this, he was a nice man. I used to get him up to sit in a chair and watch TV. He liked me to sit beside him. He wouldn't really watch, would doze off, but we would sit down in our chairs. One day we were sitting there and I was holding his hand and he died." She continued folding the rectangular sheets, pressing them flat with her slow, efficient hands. "Just that fast. Never said nothing. I felt for his pulse and he was gone."

Kate nodded.

"Mama!" Alexander shouted. He banged his tray but turned his face when Kate tried to feed him another spoonful.

"He's tired," Kate said, her eyes on Elmira.

"Now, some," Elmira allowed, "they have to work harder. They work awful hard to die because they got some kind of strength from somewhere, no matter how sick they are. They talk about leaving, they talk about going. They know they going to go." She put the pile of sheets in the basket. "You follow me?"

"Yes." Kate put the spoon aside.

"All this is, I'm working up to tell you your mother, while you were gone to that meeting this morning? She was up out of her bed. I went down to get the water and the ice and when I came back with the tray she was up standing, leaning back against the mattress. I told her real calm, now we had to get back in bed, but she was fixing to walk somewhere. Restless, weak as she is." Elmira clasped her hands before her for emphasis. "I got the bed rail up now. You need to keep it up except when you're in the room near her, near enough to reach."

"How could she have the strength to get out of bed?" Kate asked.

"Sometimes they have this agitation before they go into the sleep. If they end that way—if they have a sleep." A horn sounded in the driveway. Elmira got heavily to her feet. "I hope the weekend will be all right. Things get bad, you call me. I'll come."

"Thank you, Elmira." Kate took Alexander from his chair and walked her to the door, held it open as she stepped onto the front stoop. "Don't you want your umbrella?"

"I won't melt." She turned to Kate, the rain a fine mist behind her. "Getting near, my girl. She is not too far." Shouldering the carryall, she pulled her coat closer. The cabbie revved his motor but Elmira paid him no mind. "You keep that rail up," she told Kate in her usual measured phrases. "Call them at the agency and ask about a night shift. You're going to need it soon."

She stood at the open door of her mother's room with Alexander. He threw out his hand and pointed, but Kate didn't move to go in. The room looked dark, there was so little light outside, and the tiered rail of the hospital bed obscured Katherine's face. Kate heard the drumming of the rain and saw her mother's dark hair against the pillow, her brow. It seemed to Kate the bed should be elevated a bit more. She started into the room and the sound of the rain grew heavier, as though drawing closer. She caught herself; she'd begun wondering how much Alexander should see, what he might remember, what she'd want him to remember. The commonsense assumption was that he'd remember nothing. If that was so, why the debate about crying cures and trauma? There were quiet traumas too, slow ones, sadnesses, years of long confusions. She kept Katherine's door shut now when Sam and Jonah were here. She couldn't look normal anymore, or wave hello to them, and Kate was afraid she'd seem frightening, or worse, a curiosity divorced from herself, drawn inward and still. After all, how well had they known her? They didn't ask about her, only ran past the closed door, dragging this, bouncing that, noisier than usual, or so it seemed to Kate. What had

Elmira said about boys? *Take off, be about they business.* Alexander held on to the railing of his crib and inclined his head to catch sight of them, urging them on with delighted squeals. He seemed to sense they were outside Kate's realm of influence, a loud, fast team, intensely exciting. Their wrestling provoked him to belly laughs. She wondered what Matt had told them but didn't ask; she couldn't blame him for saying nothing. They knew about Katrina; they knew where she was buried, near the dogwood tree by the back door. The little iron stake where her chain had attached stood near the spot. No one had moved it.

Kate put Alexander in his bed with a stack of board books. He was so tired; he might fall asleep on his own. "You read for a while," she told him. "I'll be back when you finish all these books." He looked doubtful. "You can do it, Mr. Tate," she said, smiling. "Mr. Monkey." He sidled back against the wall and threw her a grin, hiding in plain sight.

Katherine's bedside lamp had a three-way bulb. Kate turned the switch once to make a glow, a first station of light. Instantly the room looked warmer, and the railing of the bed lost its cold steel sheen. Katherine hated the bed rail. I feel like I'm in a cage, she'd said, every time that thing comes at me. Kate put it down, holding it so that it slid quietly, but Katherine grimaced in her sleep and turned her head, wakeful, as though the morphine syrup hadn't properly taken effect. She moved her head back and forth quickly, frowning. Was she in pain? Kate leaned near and said softly, "Mom, do you need more medicine?"

Nothing usually wakened her in the hour after her dosage, but she opened her eyes and said clearly, "No more."

"All right," Kate said, "that's fine."

"Stay here," she said. "Don't let the other one in."

"What other one?"

She looked at Kate intently, angry or frustrated.

"I'll stay, Mom. Shall I read to you?"

She didn't answer, but the force of her gaze changed, became softer, almost beseeching.

Kate took her hand. She should explain why they needed to use the bed rail now, why they had to take more care. "Elmira said you were up by yourself today, Mom. If you want to get out of bed, can you remember to ask one of us to help you? You gave Elmira a scare."

Katherine made an agitated, disapproving sound. Disapproving of

Kate? It was difficult to know when she was alert, or how much she understood. She might think Kate's tone patronizing. Or maybe she thought Elmira talked down to her. Katherine was so physically frail now. Elmira might seem overwhelming, too big, too strong.

"What is it, Mom? Are you uncomfortable with Elmira? I know she likes you. She's been so helpful—"

"I know how she likes me," Katherine said bitterly. "She likes me too much."

"Too much?"

"Dancing me around, holding on to me."

"Mom, what do you mean?"

But Katherine only turned her head, tightened her lips as though biting her own words. She wouldn't say more, or she'd drifted too far away to speak.

Alexander was crying. Kate put the bed rail up and went to get him. Not pausing to change or nurse him, she walked up and down the hallway, holding him while he fussed, too disturbed to stop pacing. It was unbelievable, but what if it were true? No, it wasn't true, but it was true in Katherine's mind. If she was afraid of Elmira, the fear would only worsen as she got sicker. Elmira couldn't be here again, not once more, not at all. Kate would have to call the agency and let Elmira go, let them give her another case and try to find Kate someone else. What would Kate tell them? She would tell the truth, but not all the truth. And she would have to call Elmira. She didn't want to explain on the phone, but it wasn't right to tell her Monday morning and then ask her to leave. Something had happened. Whatever it was, Katherine was afraid. Had she felt this way before, and Kate hadn't known? It wasn't possible; Kate couldn't think about it.

She got Alexander to sleep and went to her bedroom to make the call. Elmira must have just gotten home. "I knew it was you," she said. "Has she taken a turn?"

"Yes. She's responding differently to the morphine. And she's scared, Elmira. She seems afraid of you."

"Afraid of Elmira, is she."

"I think she got scared when you helped her back into bed today. And I can't really talk to her about it, she's too sick. Oh, Elmira, I'm sorry, but I think I'm going to have to get someone else to help us." Kate waited, not breathing, listening for some indication or awareness in Elmira's voice, some reassurance or corroboration in a silence or a pause.

"Oh, well," Elmira said evenly. "She that upset, that's what you got to do."

"I'll explain to the agency that temperaments just didn't work, and I'll tell them what a great help you've been to me."

"That's all right now," Elmira said. "They got plenty of cases. My knees are taking on so, I'll be happy for Monday off, and they'll have me somewhere else by Tuesday morning."

"I'm sorry, Elmira."

"That's fine. I wish you well, and I hope her way won't be too hard." She paused, and then said philosophically, "Oh, they do take on sometimes. She might be getting afraid of you. You need to know that and not take it personal."

The agency sent Olga to replace Elmira. She came five mornings. The first day, she stood at the door knocking almost soundlessly for a quarter hour before Kate realized she was there; she didn't like to ring the bell, she said, with a sick person in the home. She wore her heavy hair twisted into a chignon, fastened with clear wire hairpins that seemed of a different era. Standing in the foyer with Kate, she took her shoes off, producing from each pocket of her coat one soft-soled, ballet-type slipper rolled into a close circle. She spoke with a mild accent; was she Russian? Yes, but she'd left the Ukraine at five, and didn't remember it at all except for the wheat fields; her father spoke enough English to drive a cab, but her mother never learned; she'd shopped in the Russian stores in Brighton and depended on her children for everything else: messages from teachers, doctor's visits. Did they still live in Brighton, then? Olga turned her broad, naked face to Kate. Her brows were thick and perfectly, naturally shaped, darker than her hair, arched like fine-drawn wings over her mild blue eyes. Yes, with her father, her mother had passed away, oh, three years ago, at home. After that Olga began nursing studies, but it was slow; next year she'd have her R.N. She folded her colorless wool coat and laid it over the banister so deliberately that Kate didn't move to hang it up. Could Olga meet the patient now, and was there anything special for today?

"Yes," Kate told her. "While my baby's asleep, I was wondering if you could help me bathe my mother."

The tub was too great an ordeal now. Each day, together, they bathed her in bed. If Alexander was awake Kate brought the Play-yard into the room and gave him cloth toys, rubber blocks, soundless plastic bath books; often he sat watching them, seemingly diverted by their mirror-image movements, one on each side of the bed, each with her basin of warm water, cloths, towels. They worked as teacher and apprentice, silence and presence, trading forgetfulness and memory while the wind whispered in two languages through faraway fields they couldn't see. Like girls at taps folding the flag of their mournful nation, they turned down sheets together, smoothed blankets. Kate lifted her arms in tandem with Olga's long white limbs, imagining Olga's impassive, slightly inquiring countenance on her own face. Something untouched in Olga, maidenly and reserved, silently diligent, made her equal to the task at hand yet open to any instruction. There seemed an open question in her every aspect, an attitude of alert waiting, a studied quiet that made her seem more physically substantial than she was. She wore dark stockings or knee socks and knee-length, oddly shapeless straight skirts, and the same type of simple button-down white blouse Kate remembered teachers wearing when she was in elementary school; Katherine had worn such blouses, with circle pins on the collars, but Olga wore no adornment at all. Their eyes met over the bed as they sponged Katherine's sunken ribs, her swollen abdomen, her skeletal feet that had begun to turn in. They uncovered her in quadrants so that she didn't get cold, and protected the sheets with the same blue gauze-lined cloths Kate had used after childbirth.

Kate didn't forget Elmira, but she let herself stop questioning. When she told her mother Elmira had been reassigned, Katherine only nodded, but the first time Olga came and stood looking down at her, she took her hand and said, with immense peacefulness, "Olga. What a lovely name."

They entered a narrowing tunnel; Kate would not emerge until her mother did. She wrote only in the cloth book, completing the record of illness Katherine had begun. Olga came each morning. Colleen dropped another job and stayed every day from four to eight; "Katherine needs me now," she said. "She knows me." Afternoons, alone, timed to Alexander's nap, Kate sat by the bed. After he woke, Camille or Amy took him out nearly daily, to the park, to the river to feed the ducks, anywhere outside; Kate wanted him gone, into the world where the cold sun shone and the air was sharp, and then she wanted him back in exactly one hour, where she could see him and know he was safe, hear his oblivious jabbering and hold him.

When Katherine spoke, she was increasingly confused, indefinite. Kate always responded, talked to her, tried to explain or acknowledge. If she slept, Kate read, waiting for her to awaken. Today was quiet and cold. Snow light held white and still at the windows. By dark the first blanketing snow would blow in from the sea. The agency had promised night help in a few days. Her mother's old bed, the double mattress and box spring on its frame, made up just as she'd used it, was pushed to the side of the room. I could sleep there, Kate thought. She glanced out the window at the garden below. Brown leaves caught in the dried stalks of the flowers blew and moved like ruffled paper. Matt had said oncologists at the health plan sometimes visited terminal patients at home. If Dr. Jansson came to see Katherine, it might calm her, reassure her.

Kate turned back to the bed to see that her mother was awake. She lay on her side, looking at Kate intently, as though she'd been watching her, willing her to shift her attention. Katherine's gaze was steady, her eyes completely alert. Kate shut her book to lean near her. "Yes, Mom?"

Katherine moved her lips in a signal to come closer, as though trying hard to speak, or searching for words.

"What is it?" Kate touched her hand lightly to the side of her mother's face and leaned closer still. "What do you want to tell me?" She turned her head, put her ear to her mother's lips.

There was a pause. Then in the silence, with hushed, effortful clarity, Katherine whispered, "You're doing something . . . terrible to me."

"No!" Kate answered with a soft cry, as though she'd been slapped. "No, that's not true. I'm just trying to take care of you."

"Oh," Katherine said quickly, painfully, as though making amends, "I know you don't *mean* to."

Kate spoke over the thud of her heart. "It's the illness that's hurting you, Mom."

"I'd better go to the hospital."

"But you never wanted that. You wanted to be at home."

She nodded as though Kate finally understood. "I need to go home now."

"You mean home to your house?"

"Yes, I want to go home."

Kate sat back in her chair. It was true, she should be at home. Kate should have faced down her own fears and taken her home when the doctors first stopped treatment. Maybe it wasn't too late. Desperately ill people flew across the world. She would rent a hospital plane, fly into the little airport closest their hometown, have an ambulance meet them. Matt would be against it, but he would come with them on the trip. Amy would want to come, to see it through. Amy would help with Alexander, and Katherine's friends would be there. They would all help, and Katherine would be home. Kate leaned forward and took her mother's hands. "If you want to go home, Mom. I'll take you home. I'll find a way."

"Which home?"

"Your home."

"My home? Will Mother be there?"

Exhausted, Kate lay her face on the pillow beside Katherine's, and touched her chest. Under her gown, she felt the hard little circle of the port-o-cath, an inch-wide disk inserted under her skin when she'd first begun chemo. The device made IV's and lines unnecessary; now its opening was capped with a tiny inverted stopper.

Katherine blinked slowly, looking into Kate's eyes. "Mother's windows are above the tree by the road."

"What road is that, Mom?"

Katherine didn't answer.

Katherine woke. "I think I'd better see the doctor."

"Dr. Jansson?"

"Yes, that's his name."

"He's here now, Mom. Remember? I called him yesterday. He's come to see you."

"Be sure to wake me up."

"You're awake. You can sit in the chair while he's here, sit up for a while. Would you like to?"

"Oh, he's used to us."

"How do you mean?"

"He knows about us."

What did he know? Kate looked at him, his blond brows behind his glasses, his thick shoulders in the tweed coat, his light, patient eyes. "Yes, he does," Kate said.

"The sledge is by the porch," Katherine said. "They brought it through the snow."

Dr. Jansson stepped closer and bent down to her. "Are you with us, Mrs. Tateman?"

"Of course I'm with you. Good to see you."

Softly, on top of the covers, he put his hand on her distended abdomen. "Since you can't get to the office, I've come to see you at home. See if there's anything we can do."

"Yes," Katherine said, "something's got to be done."

"What would you like done?"

"Why, something's got to be done about my health."

"We can't do any more to help you," he said gently. "We've done all we can."

Don't tell her that, Kate wanted to cry out. She squeezed her hands together painfully, not to interrupt him. Wringing her hands. Lie to her! Kate wanted to command him. Later she'll only be frightened. At least comfort her now! That's why I let you in here.

But he went on in his softly modulated voice. "We can't do any more for you now. We're only trying to keep you comfortable. We don't want you to be in pain. Are you in pain now, Mrs. Tateman?"

Kate backed out of the room. She was waiting by the front door for Jansson when he came down a few minutes later. She thanked him for stopping; she gave him his overcoat and hat, his gray scarf that was printed with snowflakes. "Could she grasp what you were saying?" Kate asked.

"Yes, I think so."

"But isn't it better to comfort her now? She's so scared."

He pulled the heavy coat on and stood holding his hat, looking out through the storm door. "She was always so forthright," he said carefully, "and it was very important to her that I be honest. I'm trying to speak as gently as I can to who she really is, underneath the medication and the illness." He bent down to get his bag and straightened to look at Kate. "You're doing a good job," he said clearly, slowly, as though willing the words into her. "I wish everyone could have the kind of care you're giving her."

Kate couldn't bring herself to answer. He touched her shoulder, and then he was gone, into the dark. Cold emanated from the opaque glass of the door; across it Kate's reflection stared back at her. Care? There was no care.

She checked on her mother at midnight, again at two or three, when she nursed the baby, and again at five. It wasn't enough. They needed one more person. Katherine shouldn't be alone anymore, not for half an hour, not at all. She was not *with herself;* she was not there. She was like a babe adrift on the ocean in a basin the size of a bedpan, or a beating heart exposed in the palm of a hand. Someone must stay by her.

That person was Kate. Even in sleep, she drifted like an obtuse consciousness to the chair beside her mother's bed. She could not truly sleep and her mother could not truly wake. It was all reversed and surreal.

Sometimes Katherine roused, drifting in time, back and forth and across, oppressed by pain so monstrous Kate fought it like an evil force, trying to utilize just enough morphine. Enough to lessen the pain, stifle it, bind it, yet allow a slant of light, so that some dream occurred in the dark. It was hard to know or measure, and Kate feared being wrong. At night the house slept and there was no one to ask.

The agency phoned to say they had a night person available, and Vilma came to interview Kate. She did night work only, in private homes. She chose her positions carefully and committed through closure, however long or short that time might be. Closure? The passing of the patient, she said in her distinct patois. Her close-shaved hair showed the ebony shape of her head and her small, tight ears; in dramatic earrings she would look tribal, exotic. Kate wondered if the small gold studs in her ears were a nod to professional decorum; she did seem formal, decorous.

She might be thirty or forty, and she sat and moved like a dancer. The casual man's shirt she wore, long, buttoned, didn't conceal her broad shoulders and defined muscles; her Lycra trousers fit her strong legs like gloves. How long had she done this work, Kate asked, why did she do it? Five years ago, she'd gone back to Port of Spain to help her sister pass. In the islands, anyone who had family passed at home, but here people often hadn't kin to help them. She realized she could work nights, when it was hardest for people to manage, and in this way raise her children and her sister's children, whom she'd brought to this country. Her musical, sliding tone of voice accented stops exactly, but lingered on some words, nearly transforming them; the word "help," rolled on her pink tongue, sounded patient and bell-like. This schedule was a help to her as well, she went on; she could eat breakfast with her husband and the children before he took them to school, sleep in the mornings, meet the children to bring them home, cook their dinner, see them to bed. How many children, Kate asked, and had she far to travel? From Field's Corner in Dorchester, St. Mary's Diocese. All five children attended parochial school there; her sister's three, Vilma's two. The station, where she changed from Kate's Riverside line to her own, was just near the school, and so this job seemed a possibility. Kate said she was thankful; she hoped Vilma would agree to help them. Yes, Vilma said, this would suit her. The simple gold chain at her neck moved in the light. Two slivers of gold, identical crosses, rested on her breastbone, which seemed to rise in the V of her shirt collar like a hard, dark shield. On each wrist, beneath the cuffs of her shirt, she wore plain ivory bands, wide bangles that didn't move. She stood to follow Kate upstairs, her upright carriage concentrated in her shoulders. When they stood by the bed she reached to take Katherine's pulse in a careful, efficient gesture almost indistinguishable from touch.

An hour later, after Vilma left, Kate drew a chair close to her mother. Vilma had said, *You've come a long way, but I can help you now.* Kate wished she could say those words to Katherine and make good on them. It was nearly time for her medication; Kate must wake her, hold her upright, coax her to swallow before the pain began. "We found someone to help us at night, Mom. You were asleep when she was here, but her name is Vilma, and she has the most beautiful voice."

Katherine didn't acknowledge Kate's words, but roused when she felt the spoon at her mouth; she swallowed with difficulty and moved her hand across her belly. "There's a knife cutting me here." She made a fist and turned it to and fro against herself with surprising intensity. "Digging in me."

Kate called Dr. Jansson. "We have to do something else," she told him. "What we have is not enough."

Kate was in charge of the morphine pump. The pump, a metal gauge, held vials of liquid morphine dispensed continually through a line into her mother's port-o-cath. Dr. Jansson showed Kate how to change the vials, flush the line, control the dosage. "You can turn it up," he told her. "If she's conscious now, anytime she's conscious, she'll be in pain." Kate looked at him straight on. They stood beside her mother's bed, an arm's length from one another. Holding her gaze, he told her again, "You can turn it up."

"How far up?" she asked.

He didn't answer, and Kate nodded.

Once, when Kate and Vilma were wiping her arms and face with cool cloths, Katherine said, "I can't tell if I'm sitting up or lying down." The words haunted Kate. She lay awake in her own bed, imagining a sensory deprivation so acute as awareness burned on inside, flickering. Her mother wouldn't want her to simply turn up the morphine. Even now, Katherine was struggling with a pure tenacity. She'd want Kate to give her just enough.

Kate always explained what she was doing, prepared Katherine for any movement near her. "I'm changing the vial now, Mom," she explained one late night, "giving you medicine."

"You're giving me pain," Katherine said.

"Are you in pain? Do you need more?" But Katherine turned her head and didn't speak.

Kate thought of a horse led out of a barn, blindfolded, sensing fire near. She turned up the dials on the pump.

Dr. Jansson had meant it was up to Kate. What would she do if it were her child suffering there, with no hope of surcease, and not her mother? Her child, in simple need of deliverance, unable to cry out? Suppose it were Alexander who had gradually deserted his body, and she was left with only the thread of her voice to bind him to her until he should return. But Katherine could not return, not to this. And Katherine was her child now, was she not? More than once in the past weeks, she'd said weakly, aware of a sound in the room, of Kate near her, "Mother?" At first Kate had taken her hand and said, "It's Kate, Mom. It's Kate," but later she said simply, "Hello, darling. Do you need anything?" Katherine would grow vague immediately, as though eased.

It wasn't simple. Kate knew her wishes, even if she could no longer express them.

"I may need to sleep in there," she told Matt.

"Don't do that. She's just down the hall, and Vilma is with her."

"But people drown in inches of water. That's what's going to happen, isn't it? She's going to drown."

"Vilma is with her; she knows to call you. You can't be up all night and all day. Alexander needs you, and I might like an audience with you too."

"I can't think why."

"I can barely remember myself." He pulled away from her. Arms behind his head, he looked into the dark. "It changed the minute she moved in, nearly a year ago. We changed."

"I was almost eight months pregnant," Kate said to him. "We would have changed anyway."

"Sometimes I wonder what we'll have left when this is over," he said.

Kate nuzzled close to him, fit the curve of her pelvis to his hip. "Me and thee," she whispered. Later she remembered her mother had referred to herself and Kate in those words, when Kate was very little and Katherine was explaining a treat or chore set aside just for the two of them.

The final weeks, she was never alone. Olga, Kate, Colleen, Vilma. Katherine's insurance paid for some of it; Kate did the paperwork, filling out the forms, writing the checks. They read to Katherine, bathed her, played music for her, attempted to spoon-feed her. Chicken broth, water, tea. No solid nourishment, only liquids. Kate was in and out all day, checking the pump, talking to the nurses. She thought of them as nurses, though they were not; they were only women, young women, now that Elmira was gone, women with supposedly slight marketable skills or education, women who might instead have worked as waitresses or barmaids, housecleaners or baby-sitters, illegals perhaps, who had signed on to care for the dying, for those who suffered so intensely they could not communicate. They were Kate's atmosphere, her comrades. Coming and going in shifts, shoulder to shoulder, they were her sustenance, capable of all that mattered, thin-limbed bulwarks to whom nothing needed explained. What moved among them was understood. No weeping, no panic; arriving and departing, they negotiated between them the encroaching dark. They could not intervene or direct; they watched and tended; listening, touching, waiting, doing. Kate needed their distance, their calm, the fact this work was their present vocation, a voluntary and paid assignment for which any monetary remuneration remained symbolic. This passage no one controlled was a terrible pushing, a labor into which they delivered themselves.

Katherine was unconscious. She tried to breathe. The rasping agonal power of her breath was heard in every room. All else hushed, and Kate found she was not afraid. These women knew; they had listened before, all of them, in their own countries; they had crossed oceans to meet beside this bed. The qualities they possessed were surely innate rather than taught, and so they were paid less than those who did word processing, for instance, who'd completed a two-year course in punching buttons. Hospice workers were paid standard wages, though not all were equally skilled; those who supposed the work required little but time were quickly disabused of the assumption. These women were strong enough to care for the dying, and Kate endeavored to be one of them.

Occasionally Amy sat by the bed while Kate took Alexander outside, into the yard, bundled up against the increasing chill. Sometimes she needed to be outside with him, on the cold grass, where the leaves rattled along the fence; he raised his arms and walked to her outstretched hands, lurching forward and chortling, exhilarated. But they stayed in the yard, within the boundaries of the fence; Amy could open the window and call to Kate if need be.

Kate asked them to talk to her mother, though Katherine no longer spoke. Speak to her as you would if she were conscious, she told each of them. Not constantly, but often enough that if she can hear, she'll know she isn't alone, and who is touching her. Speak to her no matter how deeply unconscious she seems—describe what you're doing for her, mention the weather, Alexander, anything. She would want to know we're here as long as she can. I don't know where she is, Kate wanted to say. Where has she gone?

Each in her own way, they seemed instinctually aware of how much or what to say to her. As Kate went in and out of the room, about the house, passed in the hallway with the baby, with laundry, she heard their low, intermittent voices, musical and private in their varying accents. Other times they just sat near in the chair, "letting her rest," as though she were napping, keeping a constant record in the clothbound journal Katherine herself had begun. Notations in her hand were simple lists of medications, when and what she'd taken, never a mention of any thought, wish, fear. The nurses' entries referred to her as "Patient": *"Patient personal care performed, 7:30 a.m. . . . Mouth care, 8:10. Skin clammy . . . 11:40, Patient agitated, daughter called. Medication increased."* Kate referred to her mother as "K." *"K. turned to right side, mouth care, 3:20 p.m. Hands and arms moistened with lotion. Read to her."* The journal was bound in an ordinary calico print, small daisylike flowers on a purple ground. It reminded Kate of the cloth her mother had used to make her a centennial dress the year the town had staged a pageant marking one hundred years of statehood. The dresses should be of patterns common to the time, Katherine had said; sprigged calico was what they'd used. She'd made a bonnet to match, starched with sizing, and found Kate an authentic pair of antique button-top boots in brown leather. They'd owned a Polaroid Land camera at the time, a bulky, miraculous thing that developed its own pictures in square black envelopes. Kate had found one of the prints among photos in her mother's drawer when she was looking for the insurance papers—a faded, silvery image three inches square. There Kate stood, ten years old, completely swathed in sprigged fabric. Faceless in the deep bonnet, holding up her long skirt to show the shoes. What had happened to those shoes, and the pearl-handled buttonhook they'd used to fasten them?

The last time she was out of bed, Matt and Kate lifted her into the chair, the same upholstered chair where she'd held Alexander as a newborn. Now she could not see; she could not feel her limbs, and so they held her carefully upright. "The baby walked seven steps to me across the grass," Kate told her. "Alexander is walking."

"And so proud of himself," Katherine said. "Bless his heart."

She didn't know him the last time she touched him. Kate took him to her, and she thought he was Richard's son, a baby again, one of the children for whom she'd grieved after Richard's divorce. Kate, startled and dismayed, drew back, but Alexander reached down for Katherine with a loud welcoming cry. Kate held him just close, near Katherine's face and throat, and her hand stirred on the bed. Kate took her hand and moved it to the back of the baby's head, just to the nape of his neck. Her fingers moved in a vague caress.

Vilma arrived and departed in darkness, for she was strongest. She wrapped her close-cropped head in a kerchief or head cloth before entering the room, as though to be tightened and ready. Sleeping fitfully, Kate knew Vilma was awake and alert, a honed calm negotiating their course by the light of the dim lamp and the silent clock. She moved with fluid equanimity and seemed to arrive each night from a ceremony of preparation in a field or by a hearth. When she was alone with Katherine her patois became more musical, less exact; often she hummed a tune that was low and constant and never the same.

Each night, Kate spent the first hour of Vilma's shift in Katherine's room. It took that long for them to look and wait, to assess, for Kate to prepare to leave. They knew it would happen at night and so they drew together. They spoke to Katherine. They told her Vilma had arrived, the baby was asleep, the night was cold and clear. They had washed her hands, her face. Vilma would read to her. Kate would see her soon.

Tonight they stood side by side, touching the fluttery pulse in Katherine's throat.

"I don't think I'd better go," Kate whispered.

Vilma raised her dark eyes to Kate's. "You must have a bit of sleep. Just an hour, yes? I will wake you. If she draws near, I will come to your room."

Kate fell into oiled, brilliant darkness. She was going with her mother. She waited in the kitchen of her mother's house as Katherine made preparations. Tonal birdsong in the flowering trees by the windows was a delicate ricochet, an intricate filigree of signal and response that continued as she and Katherine stood together in the elaborate country house where her mother had been a child. Katherine was explaining to the funeral director who ran his business now in its grand rooms that she was born upstairs on the sleeping porch—an August so warm crickets were silenced, and the fields surrounding the house so rife with lightning bugs that the ground appeared to glitter all night. The paved road that led to town was a dirt lane then, said Katherine's voice, a cloud of dust in dry weather, and she took Kate's hand as the ocher dust came up around them, moistened, drifting like mist. Bats rose in the wet dusk like smoke that dipped and turned, and Kate recognized the oval lake that lay like a reflecting mirror beside the Temple of the Tooth. How surprising her mother had brought her here, to the Sri Lankan hills above Kandy, but then she realized this was the birth road. The same narrow looping track ringed the lake with blond dust, and the vast beech tree whose shade had been her mother's bower hung its sheltering limbs over the broad marble steps of the temple. Yet the doors were closed; the pilgrims had withdrawn. A doll's chair and table, placed just so beneath the tree, sat empty. Never mind, Katherine said. Arm in arm, they turned their backs and proceeded higher still, into the mountains of a strange country. Together in a saddle basket, the rough hide of elephant against their bare legs, they heard rhino thrashing below them, cutting furious widening circles through high grasses ringed with ditches. Now she understood that hoarse ravaged breathing, the crashing and slamming of all their pounding hearts. Her mother's hands on her shoulders turned her this way and that, knowing and certain at every turn as the field grew darker, blacker, obsidian black, until it was Katherine's rasping breath calling her, and Vilma's hand on her shoulder. By the glow of the clock Kate saw the delicate pinkened lines of Vilma's mahogany knuckles, and the shell-like, almost iridescent coral of her plain unpolished nails. No words were spoken. It was midnight, and Kate rose to step through the darkened hallway toward the door of her mother's room.

The empty basket, arrayed on flat green lawn, looks as though it might hold highly charged, protected air, or some invisible gift.

"The bassinette looks beautiful on the grass like that," Kate says.

"Rip's place is beautiful," Katherine answers.

"Wait till you see Paris," Kate reminds her.

"I don't need to see Paris," her mother tells her thoughtfully, "not now. It would take such energy, and I conserve mine, being in a place I know. That way, I have more time. And I want, so much, to be here. Familiar things are so intensely themselves. It's almost magical."

They gaze past the bassinette into Rip's garden. Beans climb on taut strings. Silver foil and jingle bells strung over the corn on transparent fishing line hover in midair, and bits of bright paper turn and flash. Occasionally there comes a dreamy twinkling of sound, but the air is nearly still. Rip serves soup made of cool, blended fruit, herb bread, a salad of greens and dill. Kate wants to ask him about her mother and that boy, the one who died. Were they chaste, were they lovers? Another pilgrimage interrupted. Because his parents were dead, Katherine, at seventeen, planned his funeral. Did she see a sparkle of light, ever, across his hands, his face? He was just a boy.

Rip is opening champagne. "A moment," he says, disappearing into the house for fluted glasses. Returning, he brandishes three in one hand like playing cards.

Katherine reaches for them and sets one before Kate.

"Not for me," Kate tells her. "I'll drink with you spiritually."

Rip pours the champagne. "She clings to her convictions. Speaking of spirits, I'm wondering, how does the dad feel about this?"

"Very pleased, as he scrambles to cope."

"Fabulous." He fills his glass. "A love child. I'm absolutely in favor."

"I'm afraid you'll have to keep that under your hat. Mom has me married."

"Ah, yes," Rip says. "The neighbors and the ladies, bridge club and church. Only here." He takes rolling papers and pouch tobacco from his pocket. "And Waylon. He's in favor of this plan?"

Kate looks at her mother. "He doesn't know about it."

"Oh. Lumped in with the ladies."

"Waylon would certainly tell his Aunt Raine," Katherine says, "and she would tell her children, Waylon's cousins."

"This is probably true," Rip agrees.

Kate addresses her mother. "Might we consider striking out as pioneers? People might be more accepting than you think."

"Doubtful," Rip says.

"I really don't feel like pioneering," Katherine says.

"I know," Kate says quietly.

"Regardless," Rip says, "it's wonderful. I'm happy for you, both of you."

Katherine clasps her hands before her, as though, like a child, she holds a wish inside them. "I want to hold this baby."

"You will," Rip tells her. "Champagne." He fills Katherine's flute to the brim.

Kate raises her cup of water to join the toast, but Katherine shakes her head. She wets her finger in the bubbling fizz of her glass, then leans forward to touch Kate's lips with a moistened fingertip. "For luck," she whispers.

ALSO BY JAYNE ANNE PHILLIPS

*"[Phillips] writes beautifully, capturing elusive moods
with startling images and scenes."*
—The New York Times

FAST LANES

Jayne Anne Phillips has always been a master of portraiture. The stories in *Fast Lanes* demonstrate the breadth of her talent in a tour de force of voices, offering elegantly rendered views into the lives of characters torn between the liberation of detachment and the desire to connect. Three stories are collected in this edition for the first time: in "Alma," an adolescent daughter is made the confidante of her lonely mother; "Counting" traces the history of a doomed love affair; and "Callie" evokes memories of the haunting death of a child in 1920s West Virginia. Along with the original seven stories in the collection, these incandescent portraits offer windows into the lives of an entire generation of Americans.

Fiction/Short Stories/0-375-70284-9

MACHINE DREAMS

Widely regarded as one of the finest novels of our day, *Machine Dreams* is the story of the Hampsons, an ordinary American family living in extraordinary times. Having lived through World War II, Mitch and Jean struggle to keep their marriage intact in the decades of change that follow. Their son, Billy, dreams of airplanes and goes to Vietnam. Their daughter, Danner, becomes the sole bond linking their family, whose dissolution mirrors the fractured state of America in the 1960s.

Fiction/Literature/0-375-70525-2